THOSE WE DROWN

THOSE
WE
DROWN

AMY GOLDSMITH

DELACORTE PRESS

Text copyright © 2023 by Amy Goldsmith
Jacket art copyright © 2023 by Fabian de Lange
Interior art used under license by Shutterstock.com

Visit us on the Web! GetUnderlined.com

Educators and librarians, for a variety of teaching tools, visit us at
RHTeachersLibrarians.com

Library of Congress Cataloging-in-Publication Data
Names: Goldsmith, Amy, author.
Title: Those we drown / Amy Goldsmith.
Description: First edition. | New York : Delacorte Press, [2023] | Audience: Ages 14+. | Summary: When seventeen-year-old friends Liv and Will are accepted in a semester-at-sea program, they are excited to spend six weeks aboard the luxury cruise ship The Eos, but after Will disappears the first night, Liv grows suspicious that something sinister is lurking below deck.
Identifiers: LCCN 2022019325 (print) | LCCN 2022019326 (ebook) | ISBN 978-0-593-57009-8 (hardcover) | ISBN 978-0-593-57010-4 (library binding) | ISBN 978-0-593-57011-1 (ebook)
Subjects: CYAC: Foreign study—Fiction. | Cruise ships—Fiction. | Sirens (Mythology)—Fiction. | Horror stories. | LCGFT: Horror fiction. | Thrillers (Fiction) | Novels.
Classification: LCC PZ7.1.G6515 Th 2023 (print) | LCC PZ7.1.G6515 (ebook) | DDC [Fic]—dc23

The text of this book is set in 11.3-point Adobe Caslon Pro.
Interior design by Cathy Bobak

Printed in the United States of America
10 9 8 7 6 5 4 3 2 1
First Edition

Random House Children's Books supports the First Amendment
and celebrates the right to read.

For NJC

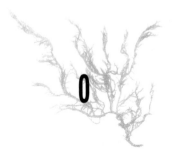

0

THE CRUISE LINER HAD DOCKED HOURS AGO; MOST OF ITS passengers, satiated by the late-summer sun, had long since poured onto waiting buses and into taxis.

Silence slunk down the now-deserted corridors under the impassive gaze of buzzing wall lamps. Blandly uniform doors yawned into empty rooms, raggedly stripped to their bare bones.

The soberly dressed staff methodically swept up crumbs, sprayed down surfaces, and emptied bins of discarded memories. Orphaned suitcases were tossed into dumpsters, the pricier sunglasses, watches, and handbags distributed among the tight-lipped crew.

The decks were industriously polished so that not a single stain remained.

And beneath sea level, on the shadow-steeped lower decks, prayers were whispered; hushed and fervent.

The sea provides.

Then the singing started.

Deep within the belly of the ship, salt-stained and brittle with barnacles, voices rose, as clear and golden as the dawn. Voices that called to mind the teasing chase of sunlight on turquoise waters. The weightlessness of warm foreign seas. The tropical scent of sunscreen and sea salt carried on a gentle breeze. That familiar call to *forget* that seeped into sun-warmed skin.

It was an old song; ancient, in fact. A song passed down through centuries. A song that unsettled the hardiest of sailors, that could lull and lure even the most reluctant traveler. That called insistently to some dark center, that agitated the blood.

For long moments, the staff stilled; all heads turned in the direction of the sound, bewitched and beguiled by the terrible beauty of the melody.

Finally the singing stopped, and hidden deep within the rusting hull, harrowed and hungry, they waited.

1

THE *EOS* HAD SIX DECKS, TWO SWIMMING POOLS, FIVE themed restaurants (one with an à la carte menu—whatever *that* meant), and a fully equipped gym.

The *jewel* of the Atlantic.

At that point, I could pretty much have worked as a rep for the damn ship, I'd spent so long obsessively rereading the single sheet of information SeaMester had provided, which Dad had wonkily printed at work. I'd folded and unfolded it, tracing the well-worn creases that obscured the ink in places, while barren fields and nameless gray towns flew by the window. Constantly checking that it was actually *my* name there, typed at the top, and not some mistake.

From ccs on the email confirming my place, I'd figured out there were six of us—including my friend Will and me—embarking on this *grand opportunity across the Atlantic.* The seventh name listed, the sender, was the group leader of this year's SeaMester (*Experience education—at sea!*), one Mr. Justin Ashburnham, who, judging by the thumbnail on the SeaMester website, was almost as young as us.

An entire term at sea, calling at ports I'd only ever dreamed of visiting, all in the name of cultural enrichment—my eyes grew wider every time they scanned the list of destinations: New York, Miami, Buenos Aires, Barcelona.

Both Will and I had applied for the opportunity on a whim after a suggestion from Mr. Simmons, our form tutor, but neither of us had thought any more about it after we'd clicked the submit button. Winning some fancy enrichment trip aboard a cruise ship wasn't supposed to happen to invisible kids like me. So months later, when the email from SeaMester pinged into my inbox, I almost deleted it, thinking that sending the application had only led to me being added to yet another mailing list.

But as I took in the subject line, my entire body began to shake, my finger still poised over Delete.

Congratulations, Ms. Olivia Larkin! Your application has been successful!

I read the email within a second, gobbling it down greedily with my eyes, then read it again and then once more, sure I'd missed some small detail that would bar me from the trip. But eventually I allowed it to sink in. It was all there. Clearly typed in black-and-white, size 12, Times New Roman. My application had been successful. I'd won a scholarship aboard a luxury world cruise—all expenses paid.

Mum immediately called every living member of family we had in the world, then held an open conference with our neighbors, ardently gabbling on about things she'd never once mentioned to me: my immense literary talent; how she had known, the moment I picked up a crayon at two years old, that I was destined for greatness and so on.

And since then, I'd spent every single minute daydreaming. Imagining myself as one of those stylish travel influencers who constantly filled my social feeds, my vintage suitcase beautifully packed, ready to vlog my every experience. Picturing myself on the bus down to Southampton, sitting next to some cute Brazilian student who I'd start a passionate (though ultimately doomed) love affair with halfway across the Atlantic.

It hadn't quite worked out like that so far.

For a start, instead of my sitting with a hot Brazilian, the familiar bulk of Will was wedged beside me on the bus, furiously tapping away at WhatsApp as hip-hop pounded tinnily out of his AirPods. Every now and then he would nudge me to share some ghoulish fact about our trip.

"Hey, did you know most cruise ships have an actual *morgue* on board?"

I rolled my eyes.

"Why do I get the feeling this trip's going to feel more like six years than six weeks?" I groaned.

Dad's car had taken ages to start (dead battery again), so we'd had a rushed peck on the cheek. A *Get on the bloody bus— quick! Before it goes, Liv!* type of goodbye. During which Mum sniffed away her tears while basically ordering me to have fun. I mean, honestly, the absolute *pressure* of those words immediately led me to worry about how I'd need to fake it if I wasn't bouncing off the walls with giddiness during our three phone calls a day.

Will's dad's sleek gray Mercedes drew up alongside moments later to drop him off. Neither Will nor his dad looked particularly happy, and Will leaped out several seconds before the car actually stopped without a backward glance. I knew things had been difficult for him lately. At least the trip would take his mind off all *that* for a while.

I'd spoken to Mr. Ashburnham—*Hey, call me Justin*—on the phone the week before, and he'd casually dropped in how I was the only one on the ship who had won a full scholarship. Reading between the lines, I interpreted this as meaning everyone else in the group was filthy rich. Not pretty damn rich (like Will, whose dad worked as a hedge-fund manager—a job I'd been disappointed to hear involved no actual hedges—and who had memorably invited the entire class to a go-kart-racing party when Will was eight), but properly minted, private school, three-skiing-holidays-and-the-South-of-France-twice-a-year rich. This was corroborated by the impossibly grand email addresses cc'd alongside mine: @StClarysCollege and @OurLadyoftheFields.

Not exactly a natural extrovert, I found it all a little intimidating: there'd be no hiding in my cabin. The info from SeaMester explained that our first week—the duration of our trip to New York, our initial destination—would be spent getting to know the rest of the group.

So I'd gotten up an entire hour earlier than I needed to that morning, perfecting the "effortless" outfit I'd planned for weeks, one I hoped wouldn't immediately mark me as Scholarship Girl. I'd settled on my favorite distressed jeans paired with a silky camisole (sadly polyester mix—not actual silk) beneath a kimono (Mum's—so *technically* vintage), and my well-worn Stan Smiths.

"Seriously, Liv . . . check this shit *out!*"

Will reached past me and pointed out the window. My stomach complained noisily as the bus began to slow and pull into Southampton harbor. I hadn't been able to manage any breakfast other than the enormous can of energy drink Will had fished out of his backpack, and that was in danger of resurfacing. Steeling myself, I took my first glance at the *Eos.*

It wasn't an exaggeration to say it *loomed* above us. A daunting sleek white monolith, almost too bright to look at in the late-September sun.

"God, I am so hyped for this trip," Will continued, pushing his unruly dark hair away from his face. "Since Dad got with the banshee, the only place they ever want to go is Puerto Banús. It's proper embarrassing."

"The banshee" was Will's dad's new girlfriend. On the few occasions I'd met her, she'd actually seemed pretty sweet, but I don't think the fact that she was only a couple years older than us exactly helped matters.

Whatever I'd been expecting, I still couldn't process the enormity of the ship. Soon, all we would be able to see of it was a sheer wall of metal.

Despite our having gotten the earliest bus available and leaving practically in the dead of night, we just made our boarding slot and were two of the last in the queue. Ahead of us was an endless wavy line of smart-looking older couples, the women in vertiginous heels, carrying expensive leather handbags; the men in a uniform of belted shorts and checkered shirts. Dad had prepared me for this. Apparently only the seriously well-off and retired had the luxury of time for a lengthy cruise.

"Hey—look," said Will, giving me a conspiratorial nudge. "Do you reckon they're part of our group? They're the only people under fifty I've seen so far."

I followed his gaze to the check-in desk ahead of us, where three literal goddesses, effortlessly casual in floaty chiffon and flat leather sandals, were tossing back their golden heads and laughing the tinkling laugh of the insincere.

"Oh God, please, no," I murmured. "Did I miss the memo?"

Will smirked. "What?"

"To bring glam. All I've brought is jeans and hoodies."

Since it *was* a ship, I'd imagined us boarding via a steep and wobbly wooden gangplank, but instead we all trundled down a swanky carpeted tunnel, which emerged directly onto one of the decks. As we walked out onto the polished wooden flooring, I swung around to get my bearings and immediately wished I hadn't. On the other side of the railing, the world dropped away sharply, and a rank breeze stinking of oil and seaweed drifted upward. Swallowing, I staggered away.

Will gave me a playful nudge. "Seriously, Liv. Remind me again why you're scared of the sea?"

I brushed away his arm.

"Sure, where do you want me to start? The whole drowning thing? *Jaws*? Portuguese man-of-wars, the bends, the Mariana Trench, *actual* pirates—"

He flashed his familiar crooked grin.

"Fair enough, but we're about to step onto a ship the size of a small country. No one's asking you to swim across the Atlantic."

It wasn't only the sea, though. It was everything that came with it. The acrid, briny reek of it. The noxious viridian slime that clung to the rotting wood of the docks. The raptor-like screech of gulls. The way everything was eventually eaten up by salt water—turning rusty and corroded and brittle. My parents were as surprised as I was when I made the decision to go—but after I read all the info, it was clear that I would be comfortably ensconced within a massive floating hotel the entire time. I didn't even need to go out on deck if I didn't want to.

Suppressing a shudder, I followed Will through a set of shiny double doors into the ship's main atrium and sucked in a breath.

The cavernous room we stood in reminded me of childhood visits to the Sealife Center: dim and slightly dank smelling but lit with a delicate aquatic light that rippled across the space like cerulean silk. The walls were enormous tanks filled with gracefully gliding exotic fish. Beneath my feet was a thick carpet of navy flecked with gold. There was a churchlike sense of reverence within, punctuated by the occasional flash of someone's camera. Roped brass posts guided us through the gloom to where several staff members stood wearing starched blue uniforms and holding glittering trays of drinks to welcome us.

Will approached the nearest attendant: *Orlaigh*, according to her name badge. She flashed us a chilly smile.

"Greetings, you two. Welcome aboard the *Eos*. Have you traveled with us before?"

I thought it was fairly evident that the likes of us had *not*.

Will confidently reached out for the sparkling wine, but Orlaigh whisked it away like a magician's trick, replacing it with a tray of much-less-glamorous orange juice in plastic cups.

"We're *seventeen*," he protested.

"Exactly." Orlaigh smiled. "So you'll be needing to take it easy."

Despite the soft Irish lilt of her voice, she had the kind of face that made me reluctant to argue with her. Perfect features but hard, no-nonsense eyes, her lips accentuated with a slash of cold red. Blond hair scraped back into a chic chignon, not a single hair out of place.

"And what are your names, please?"

I cleared my throat. "Olivia Larkin and Will Rexham."

A flash of recognition entered her eyes. "Ah, you're part of the SeaMester group. Isn't that just fabulous for you both? We hope you enjoy your trip." She handed us each a key card and a folded piece of paper that, given the size of the place, I sincerely hoped was a map. "You'll find your cabins on Deck Four. The rest of your group are already here, actually. They're waiting for you over in the Neptune Lounge. Just follow the signs, all right?"

She gestured in the direction of one of the well-lit passages leading out of the room.

Ignoring the proffered orange juice, we made our way down to the lounge, tinny steel drum music trailing us out of the atrium.

The ship was undeniably impressive. Everywhere I turned, I was confronted by acres of politely pale wood, almost plastic-looking in its perfection. Everything that could be had been polished to within an inch of its life, from the vast swathes of glass to the multitude of brass fittings.

The Neptune Lounge was halfway down a corridor lined on one side with enormous full-length windows that looked out over a drab expanse of gray ocean. Above the entrance to the lounge was a cheesy plaster depiction of Neptune himself, dashing across the ocean with his chariot of sea horses, definitely more Disney than authentic Greek mythology.

Will grabbed my hand, squeezed it briefly, then dropped it before pushing open the double doors. I stared after him, my skin flushed with unwelcome heat.

Okay—that was weird.

Particularly from someone who had been studiously leaving me on read for the last couple of weeks.

He's just being friendly, Liv, I chastised myself. The drive down had been so normal, almost like things used to be, and I was keen to keep it like that. I'd learned my lesson about reading too much into things the hard way.

Inside was a vast room busily studded with circular tables and blue velvet tub chairs. The mirrored ceiling above us amplified the slate gray of the swelling ocean on the far side, where most people were congregated, and a glittering bar took up the entirety of one wall.

We stood stiffly in the doorway for a moment, drinking it all in.

"Better find our group, then," I muttered, a little wrong-footed, stiffly dragging my suitcase behind me. It was Dad's and had a ropy wheel, which caused it to bang repeatedly into my calves.

Laminated signs were affixed to some of the tables, marking them reserved for different groups. At one of the tables sat two of the girls we'd seen checking in ahead of us. They had to be on their way to film a movie or to take part in a modeling shoot. One of them was glued to her phone, while the other tossed back a glossy mane as she perfected a selfie of herself sipping an expensive-looking cocktail—guess their attendant had given them less trouble about that than Orlaigh had given us. The sign affixed to their table simply read *Sirens*.

Turned out we'd wandered past the SeaMester table several times before realizing it was the one we were meant to be sitting at. I don't know about Will, but I'd been on the lookout for a group of students like ourselves: clad in battered hoodies or jeans, various colors of Fjällräven backpacks discarded about the table. But everyone seated at this table was the picture of sophistication. Stacked beside the table was a neat pile of expensive-looking luggage. I recognized the familiar brown-gold Louis Vuitton print and a red-and-green Gucci luggage strap.

There were two empty seats. I double-checked the printout stuck to the table.

SeaMester.

Yep, this was us. In black-and-white. My inherent awkwardness reared up within me like a braying donkey.

Then I felt Will's reassuring hand on my back.

"Right, then, here we go."

For the first time since we'd boarded the bus, Will's voice had lost its permanently amused edge. He was nervous too, I realized. After staring at the table for longer than was appropriate, I bunched my hands into tight fists and followed him over to the group.

"Hey there, guys!"

I winced at the unexpectedly strangled sound of my voice. Everyone at the table immediately stopped talking to turn and stare at us.

Mr. Ashburnham—Justin—stood and extended his hand, directing an easy smile at me. My shoulders relaxed a little. I recognized him from his photo. Like all tutors, he looked decidedly less glamorous than his moody black-and-white college website headshot with his tortoiseshell glasses and untidy stubble. He was shorter than I'd imagined and dressed head to toe in North Face, as if he were about to go out for a hike.

"Aha!" he called out, delighted. "And here they are! The final two members of our SeaMester crew. Guys, meet Olivia and Will."

2

THE SEATED GROUP MURMURED A SERIES OF HALF-hearted greetings, four pairs of eyes slipped over us: the judgment commencing. Will slid smoothly in beside a ridiculously beautiful girl with a pool of dark red hair, so I took the remaining empty seat, opposite Justin. He grinned at me; a warm smile that crinkled the corners of his eyes.

"Good to meet you both! So, what are your first impressions of the *Eos*?"

What level of honesty was sensible at this point?

I mean, obviously it was ridiculously, *obscenely* impressive, with its enormous sci-fi atrium full of floating exotic species, not to mention the expansive rainforest that had been sacrificed for all the wood. But I didn't want to appear too small-town. So I gave a casual shrug, as if I was used to all this grandeur and found it tedious.

"Yeah, it's, uh . . . big, isn't it?"

A blond guy sitting to my left snorted, immediately making me wish the tub chair would swallow me whole.

"*Big . . . ?*" he drawled. "I do hope you're not here on the basis of your creative writing."

His voice was rich and laconic, as if he could barely be bothered to speak. Risking a quick look in his direction, I shrank under the wintry glare of his gaze. From across the table, Will looked wary. I forced myself into a weak laugh.

"Well, uh, now that you mention it . . . ," I joked feebly.

No one so much as cracked a smile in return. A sly, sweeping glance around the table confirmed my suspicion that everyone was in a different bracket of wealth from myself.

It was all in the small details.

Tiny diamonds twinkling in delicate double-C studs. The polo player stitched onto a crisp white shirt. The glint of perfectly straight, white teeth. Tans fresh from lazy summers in Barbados, not direct from a spray bottle. Settling back in my chair, I ordered myself to relax. No one, other than Will, knew who I was. I could be anyone right now, anyone I wanted.

Except who was I kidding, with my thrifted bracelets and off-white sneakers. My wonky-wheeled suitcase and cheap watch.

Justin tipped a half-empty bottle of wine in my direction.

"Drink, guys?"

Wine?

Only five minutes in and this trip had already confounded my every expectation.

"Uh, sure," I replied coolly, pretending it was completely normal for me to be drinking actual wine in the middle of the day on a cruise ship. With my chaperone, of all people. "Why not? I guess we're celebrating, right?"

"That's the spirit!" agreed Justin, filling my glass to the top with warm, sticky chardonnay, then pouring one for Will. He raised his.

"Let's raise a toast, y'all. To adventure! And to SeaMester, to the *Eos,* and to all who sail on her."

The guy beside me sighed as he raised his own. "This shit is appalling. Tastes like vinegar."

I shot him another look, and this time he met my eye with cool appraisal. He was pale and pointed, like a statue escaped from an Italian museum.

"Shall we begin the intros now that we're finally all here?" asked the red-haired girl in the manner of a no-nonsense teacher, her wide green eyes examining both myself and my tattered backpack with unabashed interest. I winced as I caught sight of the threadbare gorilla key chain Will had given me in primary school, still affixed to its front pocket.

"Great idea," agreed Justin. "Let's go around the table and say a little bit about ourselves, shall we?"

I'd been dreading *this* particular moment since the minute I'd received the acceptance email.

He nodded at me. "Olivia. Why don't you kick us off?"
Great.

I cleared my throat and sat up straighter. First impressions were bound to count.

"So, uh, hi, everyone. I'm Olivia Larkin—I prefer Liv, actually. I'm hoping to major in English at university next year. And honestly, while my grades have been fine, I, uh, need that extra something in order to apply to Oxbridge, so this totally fits the bill."

I gave another little nervous laugh, then grimaced. Across the table, Will raised an eyebrow.

"And . . . honestly, I've never been on a cruise before, so this is all totally new! I'm um, pretty nervous."

"Never would have guessed," murmured the red-haired girl in a bored tone, as if she already knew everything about me.

A built guy opposite spoke up next, his accent similar to Justin's—American or Canadian—and booming with brash confidence. Like everyone else at the table, he was improbably attractive, with huge doe eyes, impeccably neat black hair, and a physique I'd only ever seen before in movies.

"Name's Raj, great to meet you guys. I'm an artist. And yes, my folks *are* predictably mad that I'm not planning a career in medicine, so that's fun. . . ." He gave a knowing wink in the direction of the table of supermodels or whatever they were. "And I'm hoping to make some new *friends* on this trip."

Several members of the table snorted at this. Justin peered at him over his glasses. "Hey, let's keep it family-friendly, guys?" He nodded at the red-haired girl, who rolled her eyes as if we should already know who she was.

"Adora Rillington—Dor to my friends—and I'm a writer. You guys have probably read some of my stuff already, and not realized. I'm an Insta-poet—I get shared a lot. I mean, a quarter of a million followers can't be wrong, right?"

"Ah, right. An *Insta*-poet," said Raj with a smirk, as if it suddenly all made sense.

"My turn now?" said the girl beside him, also American, her voice a silken drawl. She was dressed in expensive-looking loungewear that appeared to be cashmere, draped artfully off one shoulder, her black curls scraped tightly into a bun. Somehow, she was managing to outshine everyone in the room without wearing a scrap of makeup. Delicate gold-framed glasses sat daintily upon her nose. "Hey, all, I'm Cintia and I'm not sure what I want from this trip yet. . . . Some kind of life experience, I guess."

"Hoping to be inspired by all the cultural delights in store, no doubt," Justin chimed in.

He really was *very* earnest.

We were interrupted briefly by the waiting staff laying our places with shining cutlery. I thanked them, then immediately regretted it since no one else did.

"Ugh, God, I hope it's not a buffet," groaned Adora, flipping her red waves over her shoulder and nearly whipping me in the eye. "I can't abide them. Shriveled offerings; wilting sacrifices under the impassive gaze of heat lamps."

She gave a wide smile revealing teeth so perfect they must have been professionally whitened, brushing her hair back once more with a melodic jangle of the gold on her wrists. "Must write that one down."

"So, what about you, then?" I asked, turning to the guy beside me.

He was an intimidating presence. For starters, he didn't only look expensive, he *smelled* it, contained within a cloud of soft, citrusy fragrance worlds away from the musky reek of Lynx Africa all the guys at our school smelled of. He had sharp, strong features and a tangle of short, untidy curls the pale yellow of primroses.

"Constantine—I prefer Con. I'm planning to become a biochemist."

"Really?" I said without thinking.

He gave me a wry glance.

"Should that come as a shock?"

Before I could embarrass myself further, Will introduced himself with annoying smoothness, as if he was already best friends with everyone. Then a rallying cheer went up as the captain announced our departure over the speakers. Beneath our feet, the ship began to sway, finally inching away from the dock. My stomach rolled hard. I cleared my throat, trying to disguise its loud gurgle.

This was it. There was no turning back. The next time I'd set foot on solid earth would be in seven days' time, when we reached our first destination—New York. I wobbled for a moment but was soon distracted by the return of the steward with a tray of celebratory champagne. I waited for Justin to wave her away, but instead he began doling out the glasses, an action that seemed to surprise no one—except me. I thought back to the teen dramas I binged at home, full of rich kids for whom ID checks didn't seem to exist. For my new companions, it looked like the drinking age was just another minor complication you could buy your way out of.

I examined my glass warily. I didn't want to get drunk and say something I'd spend the entire trip regretting.

"So, I don't know if you guys were aware, but Olivia's here on a scholarship," said Justin. "So an extra congrats to her—cheers!"

As *if* they hadn't worked that out already.

"Oh—clever little you," said Adora with a patronizing smile as we clinked glasses.

I kept sneaking glances at Constantine. I couldn't help it. He was probably on par with Raj in terms of God-tier looks, but Raj had an entirely obvious appeal, with his jock accent, broad arms, and pearly grin. Constantine, on the other hand, possessed a detached otherness that made me want to ask him endless questions, coupled with an imperious beauty that made me shy to.

"And do you two come as a pair?" asked Justin with a grin, looking at me but nodding toward Will.

I looked across at Will, mildly panic-stricken for a moment. His face was a smooth mask of amusement as he immediately answered for me.

"Nah, no chance. We're just friends—since we were kids, actually."

It was mostly true. We'd grown up close, with the same kind of antagonistic relationship as a brother and sister, our mums having been friends since forever. And when Will's mum had sadly passed away several years ago, we'd grown even closer, my parents stepping up for him when Will's dad couldn't. But lately, after an eventful summer, we'd drifted apart. I'd been secretly thrilled when I found out he would be on the trip too. It was the perfect chance to re-cement our friendship.

Still, his casual brush-off was a little harsher than I'd liked.

Cintia nodded over to the table of blondes.

"So, we got some Victoria's Secret Angels on board or something?"

Adora gave her a knowing smirk. "Close enough. They're the *Sirens*. Influencers, y'know? Kind of a big deal on social media. I mean, we're talking followers in the seven figures. I saw on their Insta that they recently made some deal with the cruise company—like, a promotional residency type of thing. Trying to attract younger guests instead of all the usual ancients, I think."

"Bet that was worth a cent or two," muttered Cintia.

Will laughed. "Makes sense. Don't think they've looked up from their phones since they got here."

"Been staring, have you?" I teased. He didn't laugh.

"And what exactly *is* an influencer?" asked Justin, evidently amused.

"Oh, come on, boomer," said Raj. "Don't act like you've been living under a rock for the past few years. You know the type, always snapping themselves in front of infinity pools and trying to get into places for free. No *way* have they paid for this trip."

"Speaking of which," said Adora, aiming a cruel smile in my

direction, her green eyes twinkling with amusement. "*You* must be the replacement."

I stared at her, confused.

Replacement?

No one had mentioned anything about me replacing anyone on the acceptance letter.

"Hey, what do you mean, replacement?" I asked lightly. "Replacement for who?"

Adora lowered her voice conspiratorially.

"Well, I have it on good authority that Tavi Liddle was meant to be our number six—but then she disappeared. It's all anyone's been able to talk about in the group chat lately. We have mutual friends, you know." She looked at Con. "You knew Tavi, too, didn't you, Con?"

Knew?

Constantine looked distinctly unimpressed by the question, glaring furiously into the middle distance.

"A little," he replied, fiddling with his napkin. "Tavi's an heiress—her family travels in similar circles to mine. She went missing about a month ago, but I'm not sure why Adora felt the need to share that with everyone."

I looked over at Justin, who also appeared to be annoyed.

"I have no idea how you found that out, Adora," he murmured. "And I should point out that Miss Liddle hasn't been *officially* declared missing—not yet, lest any of you take it upon yourselves to start spreading that rumor. But yes, the whole matter's tragic. That poor girl."

"It's not tragic for Olivia," bulldozed Adora. "One girl's tragedy is another's girl's opportunity, right?"

"*Lord,* Adora," chided Cintia.

Adora only shrugged. "I speak my mind. It's how I keep my energy clean."

There was a long-drawn-out silence, during which I felt my facial temperature rise several degrees.

"So, um, anyone know where the ship's name comes from? The *Eos*?" I asked in a desperate bid to change the subject.

Constantine blinked at me. "Are you sure you want to apply to Oxbridge? It's from Greek mythology, obviously. She's the goddess of the dawn."

Will spoke up from across the table, his tone short and sharp. "Look, we're both from St. Leonard's Comp, mate, not *Eton.* The classics aren't on offer there."

I winced. I knew I should be proud of my background, like Will was, but I wasn't. It didn't even matter to Will; his dad was loaded, so he could act however he wanted.

Constantine said nothing, only knocked back his drink.

"Replacement or not, Liv's probably the most talented out of all of us," continued Will. "You should read some of her stuff. . . . It's . . . it's bloody amazing."

News to me that Will had ever read anything I'd written, but I smiled at him anyway, grateful for the gesture.

"Is that right?" said Adora icily. "Perhaps you and I could do a little collaboration together later, Liv?"

I genuinely couldn't think of anything worse.

"I'm, um, going to find the ladies," I said, ignoring her suggestion, desperate to get away from the table for a minute and digest what I'd just heard. If I'd known I'd be a last-minute replacement for a missing girl, would I still have come?

Standing abruptly, I somehow managed to get tangled in the legs of Constantine's chair. Windmilling my arms to try to keep my balance, I staggered a few steps backward and collided heavily with whoever had been walking behind our table.

There was a sharp gasp and I turned, watching with mounting horror as the large glass of red wine they'd been carrying sloshed violently over their pristine white dress. And, looking up with dread, I found myself staring into the perfectly made-up eyes of one of the Sirens.

"What in the actual—" she seethed, her dark eyes wild. "You *moron*. This is *vintage* D&G!"

The dress was absolutely ruined. She looked as if she had been shot, the red stain spattered violently over the white bodice, expensively stitched with trailing blue roses.

I stood there for a few moments, my mouth wide open, speechless as I hovered dangerously between groveling and hysterical laughter. Then, behind me, I heard Will.

"Hey, watch your mouth. It was as much your fault as it was hers. You were too busy staring down at your phone to look where you were going."

Finally, I located my voice.

"Yeah—crap, I'm so sorry about your dress—I really am— it's gorgeous—*was* gorgeous. But it was an accident. I tripped. I . . . I didn't mean it."

The girl's eyes blazed with cold fury. She was no longer

beautiful but somehow terrifying, her arms crossed, perfect brows low and knitted. I mean, vintage or not, it *was* only a dress. Surely it wouldn't be too hard for her to wangle another freebie or arrange for some thorough dry cleaning.

Behind her loomed another of them. "*Shit,* Thalia. Your dress is trashed. What happened?"

"This—" She paused, gesturing at me while searching for an insult to describe me. She gave up, which impressively managed to be even more insulting. "*This* barged into me."

"What the—? I *said* I'm sorry."

Will appeared beside me. While I was grateful for his sudden attack of chivalry, I definitely didn't need him fighting my battles in front of the others.

"Look, let's just let it go, hey?" he said a bit more firmly.

The girl turned to Will and immediately deflated. It wasn't unusual. I'd seen him have that effect on people before. Despite his height and stocky build, he had a sort of nice-guy authority about him. Like a hot dad defusing a fight at a football match, inoffensively attractive with his mop of dark curls and arresting blue eyes.

"Yeah, well . . . This dress is expensive. If she apologizes—"

"I *did* apologize," I muttered. "I'm not doing it again."

She took one more appraising glance at Will, utterly ignoring me.

"Well, fine—whatever. I didn't like it much anyway."

With a final basilisk-eyed glare at me, the girl stalked away.

Back at the table, everyone politely ignored my run-in, and, after an hour of stilted conversation and average soup, lunch was finally over. Once we'd agreed to meet that evening in the Aphrodite Lounge for "orientation drinks," we were free to settle into our cabins.

Outside in the corridor, the difficult part over and the entire ship now ours to explore, a feeling of overwhelming freedom crashed over me like a cooling wave.

"So," I said to Will, beaming. "What do you think? What do you *think*?"

"I think," said Will slowly, pausing for effect, "I think that our suspicions were correct. That they are, in fact, a bunch of posh wankers."

I hooted with laughter, scaring an elderly couple as they walked past, the tension that had seemed to sully the table for the past hour sluiced clean away.

"But," he continued as we began wheeling our suitcases down the corridor in the direction of the elevators, "some of them seem like *nice* posh wankers."

"Yeah, I already love Cintia—and Raj seems like a laugh."

"Glad Justin is chill too—especially about the occasional drink and all. But the other two . . ." He snorted. "Adora is off the bloody planet and Constantine appears to be . . ."

I remembered his Greek jibe and cringed all over again.

"A massive *dick*? Agreed. And I *knew* about Eos—the goddess. I've looked up everything there is to know about this damn ship in the past week. I was . . . trying to make conversation, y'know?" I attempted a laugh. "And what about those influencers . . . Jesus."

Will flashed me a crooked smile.

"That one you walked into was literal fire, though," he said. "Let's hope you haven't already alienated the only other people under fifty on this ship."

I rolled my eyes.

"Don't worry, her opinion of *you* didn't seem affected."

Our cabins were next to each other in a dimly lit corridor full of identical-looking doors. Will turned to me with a grin as he inserted the key card that opened the door.

"This is going to be amazing, Liv. Really amazing."

I grinned back as I rummaged for my own card, wondering whether to invite him in for a bit, but when I looked up, he'd already disappeared into his cabin. He'd probably had as little sleep as I'd had last night.

Opening the door to my own cabin, I stepped into a cool, dim oasis. The room was tiny, but I'd expected that, though I was disappointed to see it had no window. Mind you, did I really want to stare out onto a stormy sea? Given the circumstances, it was probably a blessing. The furniture was sparse and purposeful: a narrow bed, a desk/dresser combo with a small flat-screen TV hung above it, and a compact wardrobe. Another door led into a small but immaculate bathroom. Cozy—and better yet, all mine. Ditching my suitcase in the corner, I collapsed onto the bed and shut my eyes for a few blissful minutes, allowing the tension to slowly drain from me.

Being with Will so far had seemed like old times. Truth was, we'd hardly spoken at all in the past few weeks. My messages to him had been left on read but unanswered or, worse, replied to with a single bland emoji. But now that we were stuck here together, we could use the trip to get back to how things used to be.

But it wasn't all about Will, though.

I was on a swanky-ass cruise ship, headed around the world with a wealth of stops along the way—a whole host of places I'd never imagined I'd see. And there was no doubt this experience would stand out on my university application, meaning I had a real shot at getting into Oxbridge, a pipe dream for kids from nondescript suburban schools like me.

Things were looking up.

After a short nap, I took a long shower and once sufficiently zen, sat at the dresser to put on a little makeup. The glam stakes on this trip seemed high. Then, with a twinge of apprehension, I headed out to become better acquainted with the rest of SeaMester.

3

MINUTES AFTER I ENTERED THE APHRODITE LOUNGE THAT
evening, my mind was made up. I loved it here. I *belonged* here
and wanted nothing more than to live permanently aboard the
Eos, forever drifting about the Atlantic in a shimmering evening gown.

Around me, the room glittered and twinkled like a mirror
ball of plush crimson and gilded bronze. A vast bar of polished
white marble segued into gloriously gaudy gold seashells at either end. And beyond the bar, the ocean glimmered, onyx dark,
outside the windows.

Will was already comfortably ensconced beside Raj, wearing
an unusually smart striped shirt that brought out the disarming
blue of his eyes. Adora and Con were perched like exotic birds
at the bar, dressed to the nines in that way that appeared annoyingly effortless. Adora in a long paisley dress that swamped

her tiny frame, the kind that would make me look like a frumpy chintz sofa rather than the delicate bohemian goddess she resembled; Con in expensive-looking knitwear over a checkered shirt. Beside them stood two of the glittering Sirens chatting animatedly to a broad, grizzled walnut of a man dressed all in white. The ship's captain, I reckoned. The girls wore wispy silken slips held up by barely-there straps, their cascading golden hair silky and sleek. Feeling distinctly underdressed, I stared down at my battered Jordans and leggings, agonizing over whether or not to change. But into *what*?

"Liv!" Will grinned, making space for me beside him. "Got you a drink."

"Thanks." I sank into the plush booth. His hand brushed my knee as he slid over a glass of sparkling wine, the glass frosted with condensation. I blinked, looking at him in surprise, but he didn't seem to have noticed the touch. A flush of warmth shivered through me, light dancing over water. I hoped there'd be an opportunity to talk later. *Properly* talk.

Cintia sloped into the booth next, wearing exactly the same casual wear as before. She raised an eyebrow at my full glass.

"You know, where I'm from, you gotta be twenty-one to drink. I'll have a soda."

"International waters. Eighteen's legal here, and Justin's cool," replied Will with a shrug.

A little *too* cool in my opinion. Will was already looking tipsy.

"Hey, I get it, though—I'm no good with all this either," she muttered to me, stifling a yawn.

"With what? Socializing?"

It struck me as strange that a girl who looked like an off-duty model could be at all socially anxious. Also, was it *so* obvious I was the fish out of water?

Cintia nodded. "It's pure torture. This *and* the whole glam thing. It's not for me. To be honest, I'd rather be in my cabin eating Doritos and watching Bravo."

"Least you fit in here," I commiserated. "Everyone thinks Will and I are charity cases."

Cintia gave me a mischievous smirk. "Nope, not Will—I see him sitting there in his Ralph Lauren shirt. Just you."

I winced. "So, it's that obvious?"

"No. I mean, *yeah*, but no one cares. If you've actually got money, you don't spend all your time thinking about it, y'know?"

Adora drifted back to our table in a cloud of sickly perfume. I was surprised and mildly alarmed when Con squeezed into the space beside me.

"You guys are getting along well," remarked Raj, giving Con an unsubtle wink.

Adora gave a dismissive wave of her hand. "Please—I attended the same school as his sister."

"Yes, vague acquaintances," muttered Con.

"So, who's going to introduce us to those guys, then?" Will said with a smirk, nodding over to the table of Sirens. He'd clearly forgotten our earlier run-in.

"Smart move of the ship, employing them," said Raj, casting a glance around the room. "Most people here look ready for assisted living."

"So ageist," I murmured, annoyed with them both.

"Con knows them, don't you? Or one of them at least," Adora said with a sly grin upon her perfectly painted mouth. "Rather well, or so I've heard."

Huh. Who *didn't* Con know?

He said nothing, only gave the slightest shake of his head as he stared down into his drink, completely ignoring her.

Adora blithely carried on. "And, Liv, you're already acquainted with another. I doubt they'd be anywhere near this place if they weren't being paid. From what I've seen, they're generally lounging on some billionaire's yacht in Portofino." She grinned charitably at Will, then lowered her voice. "Let me fill you in since Con's gone shy. The uber-tall one is Thalia—she's an heiress. Her father's the Marquis of Stanton or Stauton—something like that. If you recognize her, it's because she was a finalist on one of those dreadful talent shows last year—singing, of course. The curvier one with the dark roots is Leda—she's a model. Well, her dad owns the agency—make of that what you will. And the tiny one is Lexie. Some kind of fitness guru, I think."

"*Influencers.* Load of superficial bullshit," said Cintia darkly. "The kinda crap they peddle doesn't influence me."

"Now, now," said Raj chidingly. "Do I detect a little jealousy?"

"You're not wrong," she replied with a ready grin. "The

day some guy decides to pay someone like me to hang on his yacht posing with nothing but a quart of diet tea is the day hell freezes over."

"Speaking of money," said Adora, pouncing from nowhere. "Olivia, you're the only one of us here for free, right?" She trapped me across the table with vivid green eyes.

I shifted in my seat, my hand gripping the stem of my wine-glass tightly. What exactly *was* her problem?

"Yep," I said breezily, trying to act entirely unruffled. "I guess the guys at SeaMester were so impressed with my talent, I was allowed on here gratis. Lucky me, huh?"

Adora looked down at the table with a thin, unpleasant smile.

"Ha. Yeah, but nothing's *really* free, though, is it?" she countered. "I mean, *we're* all probably paying for you, one way or another."

"Adora," warned Justin, blessedly appearing behind her like a guardian angel. "Olivia is here on account of her academic prowess, exactly like the rest of you. No one here's any more or any less deserving than the other, so let's shut that conversation down right now."

"It's *Liv*," I muttered, wishing, not for the first time, I was witty enough to come up with a snarky retort faster than four hours later when I was back in my cabin alone.

"I'm going to the bar," announced Constantine, who to my mortification had been carefully watching this exchange. "Liv, help me carry some drinks?"

As much as his delivery sounded like a direct order to the staff, I still got up, grateful to slip away from the spotlight of Adora's disdainful stare.

"Don't mind her," he said once we reached the sanctity of the bar. As Con confidently ordered another round of drinks, I waited for the bartender to ask for his ID, but he only nodded at Con, his manner almost deferential. I looked up and self-consciously smoothed my dark hair in the mirrors above us. Constantine's eyes boldly met mine, the corner of his mouth turning up in a smirk.

"Who?" I said innocently, then pulled a face. "She's a complete *cow*. Where does she get off asking me stuff like that?"

He chuckled.

"Dor exists in a bubble. She's not even sure what day of the week it is most of the time. Her mum's a Reiki instructor who spends every waking hour traveling the globe visiting retreats, and her dad believes in harnessing the energy of the moon to cure all known diseases. Both of them treat her like some kind of inconvenience."

That didn't muster the sympathy in me he seemed to expect.

"So you know her *and* the infamous Sirens too? Popular guy, huh?"

He looked in their direction and gave a vague shake of his head. "I only know *them* through my dad's business connections. They're . . . they're not for me."

I gave a surprised laugh.

"No? I mean, *damn.* If they're not for you, who *is*?" Now

dimly aware I might have accidentally entered the realm of drunken flirting with that remark, I looked at the wineglass in my hand that had been refilled for me all evening and decided this would most *definitely* be my last.

"Are you genuinely interested or are you making conversation in order to ward off the inevitable awkward silence?" he replied. His words were clipped and cold, but his eyes were amused.

"Interested? In you, or your answer? And *is* the silence inevitable? I thought we were doing quite well." I sipped the dregs of my drink, silently thanking it for my wine-induced wit.

He paused, smirking. "The latter, and yes, I suppose we are."

Then, precisely as the awkward silence was manifesting itself, Will appeared behind us, his glittering eyes seeking mine in the mirror.

"Ah, there you are. So, Liv, are we going to talk or what?"

I looked back at him in surprise. As much as I wanted *the* talk, I wasn't sure if I wanted it when either of us was tipsy.

"Right now?" I hissed, sneaking a glance over at Con, who was pretending to scroll through his phone. What was Will playing at?

He lowered his voice, then ran a distracted hand through his dark hair. "Yeah, why, is it not a good time?"

I must have been unconsciously avoiding eye contact with him the entire way here because when his blue gaze locked on mine, everything in the room seemed to whine away to nothing.

"No, it's just—talk about . . . about what exactly?"

Truthfully, I knew *exactly* what. But I wasn't ready for this, not yet and not here. We had the whole trip ahead of us. It was definitely something we should avoid right now, with strangers and alcohol in the mix. All of a sudden, the vast room seemed too hot, my clothing constrictive, my body sweaty and clumsy, the ground no longer steady beneath my feet.

His eyes flickered over to Con again, his gaze darkening.

"Right. I get it, I get it. Never mind." He swiped his drink from the bar.

I watched him swagger away, a pathetic part of me wanting to run after him and apologize.

"Friends, hmm?" remarked Con with a raised eyebrow, not even bothering to look up from his phone.

"Whatever," I muttered, heading back to the group.

The next few hours passed in a blur of increasingly drunken conversation. The kind that seems like amazingly smooth and witty repartee at the time, but that you recall the next day with ever-growing levels of cringe. On my return to the table, people had switched seats again, so I was wedged on the cold side of Raj and Justin's endless hockey banter for what felt like hours.

I was debating whether or not to have one more drink, if only to prevent myself from dying of boredom, when a ringing voice sliced through the hazy hubbub of the room like a golden beam of light.

> *A sailor's life is a merry life,*
> *They rob young girls of their heart's delight,*

It was a sweet voice, lilting and delicate. Beautiful in its sheer effortlessness yet full of half-guessed-at emotion. The sound of someone well versed in heartbreak.

I peered over the crowds, searching for its source.

Leaving them behind for to weep and mourn,
And never knowing when they will return.

By the end of the very first line, every other voice in the room had stilled too, as if embarrassed into silence by its comparative ugliness. Beside me, even Raj and Justin had finally stopped talking about hockey. But the singing stopped as soon as it had started. I wanted to groan aloud with disappointment. Around me, applause swelled. I looked over to where it was directed.

It was the feted influencer table. I should have guessed. Thalia was modestly waving away the applause and pleas for an encore.

And beside her sat Will.

"What's he doing over there?" I muttered, nudging Justin.

Justin turned to look at me in surprise, as if only just realizing I was there. He grinned. "Looks like Will got himself a private performance."

"Lucky guy," murmured Raj.

Will was sitting between Adora, no doubt his ticket in, and Thalia. He looked lost to her.

Even I had to admit they looked well matched. He was indecently attractive tonight in his fancy shirt, his black curls gleaming and combed neatly to the side. He'd always been so inoffensively good-looking that most of the time I didn't even notice it until other people pointed it out.

I *wanted* to be happy for him. And I'd accepted we'd make our own friends on the trip. I'd always been more introverted than him and was already conscious of not being a social burden or anything, piggybacking on his naturally gregarious nature. Besides that, whatever first impressions I'd gained of them, the fact that Thalia was an influencer didn't automatically make her shallow or unintelligent or any of the other unpleasant things people seemed to assume. Let's face it, jealousy was never a good look.

"That life isn't as great as you think, you know," said Cintia across from me, noticing the direction of my stare. "They only ever show you what they want you to see. There's a darker side to it all. I mean, for every fan, they probably block about a hundred trolls. And I'd hate to think of the delights that wind up in *their* DMs."

I gave a vague nod and looked back over to Thalia. She looked as if she'd bounced off the cover of a high-fashion magazine. Her flawless face was angular, her features strong, framed by silky bangs of dark blond. It would be easy to cruelly dismiss her, say it was all freebie Botox and sponsored extensions, but even from here I could tell how genetics and bone structure had played their part.

But the more I stared, the more I realized something was off about how she was interacting with Will. There was something sly about her furtive smirks to her friends. The way she reared back away from Will every time he leaned closer, reminding me of a bored cat toying with its prey.

Wine or not, after a few minutes of watching this, I slowly filled with a cool and righteous anger for him.

"I'm going to go and say goodnight," I said to Cintia, getting up. She said something in warning that I didn't catch.

When I reached Will, I knew immediately that he was drunk.

I'd seen him drunk countless times before, at a million friends' parties, but tonight he was properly wasted. Beside him, Thalia sat sedately, her chic black slip accentuated with a bright silk scarf, her posture upright and perfect. Long, pale fingers that ended in pointed black talons played with the golden chain of her handbag. Chanel, of course. She raised her eyes to coolly meet mine, and my mouth dried up. I'd never seen eyes so blank and so dark—a deep black—as cold as the ocean beneath us.

"Oh. It's you. So *now* you wanna talk?" slurred Will, noticing me.

He said it in a dull way that I knew meant he wanted me to disappear. I'd annoyed him earlier, that much was clear. But I was his friend, and I'd like to think he'd do the same for me if I were sloppy drunk and Constantine (just for example) were leaning away from me as if I were something unpleasant he'd stepped in. Besides that, drunk people fell overboard on cruise ships all the time—or so Mum had been endlessly warning me. What kind of friend would I be to leave him in this state with a stranger?

"Hey, I'm off to bed in a bit," I announced with a bland,

cheery smile. The awkwardness rating for this encounter was already violently ticking off the scale. Thalia stared at me, then gave a theatrical snort.

"Wow. Was that an *invitation?*"

Her voice was deeper than I remembered, husky and confident. I glared at her.

"*No.* This is my friend. I'm reminding him we have an early start tomorrow morning, that's all."

The second bit was a total lie, but there was no way Will would have known that in his current state. Thalia shifted farther away from him. "Sure, well, if you've got to go . . ."

"What the hell are you talking about?" he murmured. He could barely focus on me, his cheeks flushed pink. I blinked at the harshness of his words.

"Will. You're like crazy drunk."

"And?"

"*And* I think you need to go and sleep it off."

Thalia stood with a bored sigh. "I'll be at the bar if you want to continue our conversation," she said, looking at Will, deliberately ignoring me.

Will put his head in his hands and groaned, distinctly pissed off. I stood before him like a limp noodle.

I had no idea what to say now.

"God, I knew this would happen," he said, trying hard to focus on my face. I swallowed. I had an inkling of where this was going, and I definitely didn't want to hear it. Not now. Not yet.

"Will—Will, hold up a sec—" I started, but he barreled on.

"I've said it . . . You've said it . . . We've *both* said it. It was a mistake. And I know you've got the wrong impression, but—"

"The wrong *what*? Will, are you on drugs?" I interrupted, trying to claw back ground. "Look, I don't care if you want to hook up with hashtag try-hard over there, but tonight is not the night, my friend. It's our first night. You're trashed and you're going to make an idiot of yourself if you don't go to bed. And I'm not just going to leave you here like this. . . ."

His brow furrowed. "Like what? Having fun? And it's not *our* first night. It's *my* first night. We do not need to spend every minute of this trip together."

"And we're not? Or hadn't you noticed. I'm just trying to watch out for you—I mean, what if your drunken ass topples off the side of the boat?"

"The side of the *boat*? Liv, sounds like I'm not the drunk one here."

He managed to look up at me then, catching my eyes with his intense blue gaze, lowering his voice, suddenly sympathetic.

"Come on. Let's talk about what this is really about, huh?"

A picture fell into my head then, neatly slotting into place like an old-fashioned slide, projecting unwelcome images upon the wall.

A balmy summer's night, the two of us parked up in Will's dad's old Mercedes, the sea spread out like silk before us, lit with a luminous aqua glow by the moon, and a sky full of stars. Whispered laughter and a freeing confidence, that belief you can do anything, the type that comes with drinking too much cheap vodka from the corner shop. The smell of the new pine car freshener so clinically strong we'd had to wind all the car windows fully down, letting in a sultry ocean breeze. I was tipsy. I was *emotional*. A bad party. The culmination of a bad *month*. And then—

"Fact is, I can do whatever I like, and I don't need you breathing down my neck this entire trip," Will went on. "God's *sake*. You know, I knew this would happen. I mean, let's face it, would you even have come if I hadn't been here too?"

I was wrenched back into the present. *Now* he'd gone too far.

"Afraid *what* would happen? That you'd get wrecked the first night and embarrass yourself? Yeah, I was afraid of that," I fired back. "And yes, of course I would have come without you! This is a massive opportunity for me. Not everything is about *you*, Will!"

He narrowed his eyes, exhaling noisily.

"Isn't it? Might want to tell yourself that. Why are you *like* this lately? Why can't you be . . . fun Liv anymore? Look at where we are! But of course you manage to find a way to ruin it. Jesus, just . . . just *piss off*, will you?"

Will was raising his voice now, and people around us had stopped their own conversations to watch the show.

I didn't know whether to keep trying—at least try to calm him down again—or to give up, gather what was left of my dignity and run. I couldn't look in Thalia's direction, but I could practically *feel* her staring at us from the bar, a sly smirk on her face as she listened.

Hot tears blurred the sight of him, his familiar face soured in a sneer as he continued full-on yelling. A wave of unpleasant heat enveloped my body as his words washed over me. I could feel the eyes on us. All these people—these strangers—*staring*. The length of this trip, the endless drinks, the impossible opulence of the surroundings, felt sickening suddenly, like too much rich cake.

Liv. Get. A. Grip. Tell him he's talking crap, for a start.

And I wanted to, I *needed* to, because he *was* wrong—so wrong—but as it happened, I couldn't say anything. Not once I'd seen how Will was looking at me. Angrily—like I was nothing more than an inconvenience. I knew that when I spoke, my voice would crack and the tears would start to fall, and I'd look even more pathetic. So instead, I turned and stomped unsteadily toward the double doors that led out to the hall, a smothered shriek of cold laughter clearly audible behind me.

Tears rolled from my eyes so thickly, I could barely see as I stumbled down corridors in the vague direction of my cabin.

It wasn't only because of Will.

I'd been painfully, breathtakingly anxious all day and had drunk far too much to compensate. I was exhausted, and as much as I hated to admit it, I was already homesick. I groaned aloud. How pathetic to miss home and worse—my parents—so soon. It was probably a legitimate maritime crime.

My phone hung uselessly in my hand. If I were back home, this would be about the time that I called my mum. But while the introductory texts Cintia and I had swapped earlier had gone through fine, the Wi-Fi I'd reassured my parents about seemed to have trouble managing long-distance messages.

I'd already taken several wrong turns and ignored the murmurs from concerned passengers, kindly asking if I was all right, before I finally chanced upon the corridor where my cabin was. It stretched out far ahead of me, silent and unwelcoming, the lights now low. Leaning against the wall, and trying to collect myself, I wondered how late it was. Since I'd boarded the ship I'd lost all concept of time. Clumsily, I rummaged in my tattered backpack (Chanel handbags were as far out of my league as Mars) for my key card.

"Hey—Olivia?"

The voice drifted down the silent passage, wrapping itself around my wrist like a spectral hand, rooting me to the spot.

I froze, mortified. Fully aware of how my mascara had slid down the blotchy mess of my face, leaving me looking like a deranged panda.

"Yeah? What?"

It came out more harshly than I'd intended.

Footsteps padded down the hallway as he drew nearer, but I remained frozen, my gaze fixed on my door. Even after just one day, I recognized that voice, and in my current state I wanted to avoid facing him for as long as possible.

"Are you all right?" Constantine asked, stepping closer. "I, uh, said I'd come check on you. Your *friend* is quite . . . quite the character, isn't he? Is he *always* like that?"

Great, so everyone in the group had heard us too. This trip

was getting off to an amazing start. And why hadn't they sent Justin? Or someone nice, like Cintia?

I wiped a finger under both eyes and took a deep, shuddering breath. Reminded myself that I *needed* this trip to go well.

"Yeah, yeah. Sorry about all that back there." I forced a laugh; one of the most pathetic sounds I'd ever made. "Will's a bit wasted. Should have known better than to tell a drunk they're drunk, right?"

Well, look at us. Already exposing ourselves as the drunken lower-class louts everyone expected us to be. Downing as much free booze as we could get our hands on, then starting a screaming match in a bar while everyone around us daintily sipped champagne and exchanged *I told you so* glances. I swallowed down another sob, disguising it as a cough.

"Quite," Constantine answered. "Justin's dealing with him. Whatever was said, he shouldn't have shouted at you like that."

Reluctantly, I turned to face him. Even in the semidarkness of the corridor, he looked exquisite. His short blond curls now slightly awry, cheeks flushed pink with drink, his sea-gray eyes glittering in the low light. Truthfully, I wanted several things from Constantine at that moment, but his pity was definitely not one of them. I was about to tell him this—well, the last part anyway, but apparently, he wasn't done yet.

"Look, I also wanted to say . . . Don't be intimidated. . . . By us, I mean."

He continued to watch me, half lounging against the wall. He'd removed his sweater, his checkered shirt unbuttoned at the neck, the sleeves messily rolled up, strands of his golden hair glowing white in the light of the wall lamps.

I stood straighter, clearing my throat noisily.

"*Us?*" I asked warily. "What do you mean by *us?*" I didn't realize we were . . . divided in some way."

He stepped closer. His eyes glinted silver in the low lights of the corridor.

"We're not. Not exactly. You know what I mean, though."

And I did.

What he *meant* was don't be intimidated by our wealth. By our expensive educations, the finest money can buy; by our fine ethical clothing and designer luggage. By the trust-fund safety net that allowed them to sashay easily through life while girls like me wobbled on a tightrope, terrified to make a single mistake and fall.

"What makes you think I'm intimidated?"

He gave me the barest ghost of a smile. "Are you always this difficult? I was *trying* to be nice. All I said was *don't be.*"

"Well, I'm not. Least of all, by you," I blatantly lied. "You know, the nineties emo movement called and want their world-weary act back."

He gave a soft breath of a laugh.

"Is that right? Well, since you're evidently fine, I'll leave you be, then."

"Thank you *so* much," I said with aggressive cheerfulness, already busy fumbling with the door to my cabin. I followed it up with a hissed *"dick"* as he walked away, hoping he heard.

4

I LAY AWAKE FOR HOURS ON THE HARD FOREIGN BED, THE unholy triptych of my drunken fight, new surroundings, and soured wine circling my mind endlessly, like dirty suds down a drain.

An insistent part of my brain assured me that Will would knock gently at the door at some late hour, spilling soft apologies over the threshold. That we'd make up, that he'd climb onto the bed (on *top* of the sheets, of course) and together we'd watch some lame documentary about serial killers until the dawn came, and everything would be sunny and exciting and new again.

Even the gentle, restless seesawing of the ship didn't lull me as everyone told me it would. It only made me more aware than ever that I was stuck on what was essentially a giant piece of iron in the middle of an enormous ocean hundreds of miles from anywhere, and I'd just had a blazing argument with my only friend in this entire place.

When I did eventually fall asleep, my dreams were full of the intent faces of the group. Staring. Judging.

Don't be intimidated by us.

Their expressions now questioning, confused. A grim Greek chorus.

Why is she here?

Charity case.

She's just a replacement—

If only that girl hadn't gone missing . . .

Why does she have to be here?

She doesn't belong here.

She isn't one of us.

A slow, sustained dripping gradually woke me, as insistent as a soft shaking.

At first, I ignored it and screwed my eyes tightly shut, desperate to return to sleep, the place where my head and stomach hurt decidedly less.

A leaky tap, I told myself. No big deal.

But the sound nagged at me, refusing to allow me to tumble back down to my hangover-free oblivion.

The bathroom door was shut, I remembered that much. Reason being, the cabin was so small, if the door was open, it made access to the rest of the room tricky. But the bathroom door being shut didn't match up with that loud, incessant dripping. It sounded as if it was only a few feet away.

Did ships spring *leaks*?

Was that slow, steady dripping about to turn into a cavalcade of drenching water, leaving me drowning, floating only a centimeter from the ceiling in this small cube of a room?

I cracked open an eyelid.

When I'd got into bed earlier, the room had been pitch-black. I remembered that, even in the state I'd been in, but now the edges of the sparse furniture glowed with a warm golden sheen.

A light was on somewhere.

I struggled up, confused, my throat parched and sore. Immediately I noticed the source of the light. It spilled brightly from under the closed bathroom door. Well, I was right about that at least. The door had been shut. But I was 99 percent sure I hadn't left the light on. All right . . . more like 75 percent. But that was beside the point. If the bathroom door was closed, then where was the dripping coming from?

Reluctantly, I moved my head in the direction of the sound.

My lungs seemed to immediately empty of air. My scream a panicked wheeze that lodged in my throat.

Sitting in the armchair beside the desk was Will.

He was wearing the same clothes as earlier, but they were shiny and dark now, absolutely drenched. Water dripped from the ends of his hair, vanquishing his curls and enhancing their glossy shade of black. His face was the unhealthy white of mushroom flesh, lips tinged with gray. Large, fat drops plopped from his pale, spongy fingers, to be instantly absorbed by the carpet below.

I scrabbled back.

"Will! *Shit.* What happened? Why are you *wet*? Are—are you okay?"

Part of me wanted to go to him. To climb out of bed and offer him a towel.

But it was impossible. I couldn't move. I couldn't even blink, let alone leave the sanctity of my bed and go over to him. And I knew why.

I was afraid.

Slowly, he raised his head to look at me. His eyes, normally the bold, arresting blue of summer skies, shone like cold silver coins in the half-light.

"Will . . . I . . . I—"

My voice froze on my lips as I shivered violently. The room was ice-cold.

Will didn't move. Didn't say anything. Just sat in that chair, his hands rigid on the armrests, staring at me with those cold silver eyes. Beneath him, the carpet was dark with damp.

Something here was very wrong.

And then he spoke.

"The sea *provides,* Olivia."

His words seemed as if they had been dredged up from the bottom of the ocean: rusty and serrated and *ancient.* It sounded nothing at all like Will.

"I'll get someone," I breathed. "You—you don't look well."

But we both knew I was lying. I couldn't escape. I wasn't about to get anyone. I couldn't leave the bed. I couldn't even *move*. All I knew was that I couldn't go anywhere near the Will-thing that was sitting in that chair.

"The sea provides," he repeated in that awful, grating voice. "But only if you *feed* it."

He was so pale—an unhealthy, glistening milk-white—the same color, same texture as raw squid.

"You're not real," I murmured. "When I shut my eyes, when I go back to sleep, you won't be there anymore. You're next door, Will. You're passed out on your bed, snoring."

He chuckled then, more of a gurgling sound than anything resembling humor, water streaming down his face like desperate tears, and drummed his fingers on the arms of the chair. His nails were dirty, the ends ragged and yellow with what looked like bits of green seaweed or algae trailing beneath them. I shuddered violently; my body wracked with fear.

"They don't want us, you know," he said, his voice lower and gleeful now, as if he were divulging a secret. His smile was unpleasant, his teeth larger and much more yellow than I remembered them. "They're greedy. They took what was offered and damned us all. Maybe they didn't think it was real, didn't believe it, but soon they'll have no choice."

He began to stand, a sluice of water falling from his lap and crashing to the carpet as he did so. My breath came in short, harsh bursts.

"No," I said, my voice hoarse and shaky, as he took a lurching step toward me, wobbling unsteadily like a drunk. Whatever he was, he was no longer Will. His hands were outstretched, flabby, the fingers too thick—bloated now. Whatever he was, I knew he couldn't get near me. I couldn't stand the thought of those cold, moist fingers touching me. I shrank back against the headboard, desperately looking for an escape from the tiny space.

From somewhere close by—outside the room, down the corridor, I couldn't be sure—I heard a faint disturbance. Dim shouting, a loud banging followed by panicked screaming.

"No. No, no no no no. *No!*"

Was it me? Was I the one screaming?

I took a final, breathless glance at Will, closer now, too close. Leaning over me. His smile wider, revealing a mouth crammed with too many teeth, brackish-looking seawater streaming from it in dirty rivulets. Layers and layers of teeth. His mouth an enormous dark circle of death.

Then the darkness rushed in like a night tide and, uttering a strangled cry, I let it carry me away.

5

I WOKE THE NEXT MORNING, DISORIENTED AND CONFUSED, wondering where in the hell I was. Then, with a rush of disappointment, I remembered.

Stuck on a ship with a bunch of snobs and one single supposed friend who now apparently hated me.

On top of all that, I felt *truly* disgusting.

My skin was clammy and greasy—of course my drunken ass hadn't bothered to remove my makeup—my hair a snarled mess. My mouth tasted like bile and sour wine. After chugging the entire bottle of lukewarm water the ship had thoughtfully provided on the dresser, I headed into the bathroom to drench myself under the shower, where I slowly returned to my human form.

As the warm water cascaded over me like a blessing, I shut

my eyes. Any peace I felt was rudely cut short as unwelcome fragments of the night before started to resurface.

Will.

Last night's nightmare came back in violent Technicolor. I shuddered. Only a cheese dream, my mum would say. I knew I should have exercised more restraint around the snacks. But still, only a dream. Will might have acted like a proper tool last night, but at least he wasn't really a bloated aquatic zombie.

They damned us all—

Stopping the water, I cocooned myself in fluffy towels and left the bathroom to crash back onto the bed. From there, I cast a suspicious glance at the armchair where zombie Will—or whatever he'd been—had sat last night in my dream. Feeling like an absolute idiot and glad there was no one around to see, I climbed off the bed, got down on my knees, and patted both the seat of the chair and the carpet beneath it. Both were bone-dry, of course.

What had I expected?

Still, our argument had been nightmarish enough and that had definitely been real.

Hurriedly, I got dressed in sweats, trying valiantly to disguise my gray skin with some tinted moisturizer before giving up and sticking on some sunglasses. My head throbbed—I was no drinker—and I desperately needed some form of stodgy carb to silence the acidic swill in my stomach. To add to my general sense of confusion, I had no idea what time it was anymore, my iPhone still stuck in UK time for whatever reason.

Picking up my phone, I felt a wave of cool relief when I saw I had three missed WhatsApp calls from Will. Unlike calling my parents, contacting anyone on board through the ship's (admittedly slow) Wi-Fi was proving to be easy. Investigating further, I saw that the calls had all been around four a.m. While he hadn't left a message—who did these days—no doubt he'd been calling to apologize. And even if he wasn't, at least he'd wanted to talk. Buoyed by this, I made my bed and straightened up the rest of the room. As I moved the chair out of the way of the desk, in order to unplug my phone charger, I frowned. Something stringy and slimy to the touch was attached to the foot of the chair. Grimacing, I pulled it away and held it closer to the light. It looked like a piece of dry electrical tape, but I'd lived by the coast my entire life and knew exactly what it was.

Seaweed.

I flicked it into the trash can. Looked like the cleaners weren't as thorough as they might be. That was all. It was hardly unusual for a literal ship to contain remnants of the sea, was it, now? With a shake of my head, I grabbed my bag and headed down to breakfast.

The daylight that shone into the corridors was gray but bright, and unpleasantly amplified the thumping in my brain.

I paused outside Will's room, debating whether or not to knock, but something made me reluctant to. Instead, I put my ear to the door, hoping to catch the low burble of the TV. Perhaps we could walk to breakfast together and talk it out before we met the others. But the room beyond was silent.

As I approached the bland corporate expanse of the Neptune Lounge, I relaxed a little, already imagining Will sitting at the table shoveling a greasy fry-up into his mouth and offering me an apologetic grin.

"Aha, and here's another of us!" called Justin as he saw me approach, his voice far too loud and jolly, making me wince. I swept a glance across the table. All of SeaMester was there, present and accounted for.

Except for Will.

Beside Justin, Raj, annoyingly fresh-faced and perfectly groomed, grinned. "Livster! Rough night, huh? Bet you regret giving me shit for drinking water yesterday."

I couldn't summon a smile. Instead, I swallowed and nodded at the empty seat.

"Is—is, um, Will not up yet?"

My stomach clenched as I watched a series of complicated looks cross the table. It was a few seconds before Justin moved, pressing his lips together as if preparing to speak. I noticed that beneath all his cheery leader bluster he was pale, his eyes filmy and red-rimmed. Looked as if I wasn't the only one who hadn't slept well last night.

"What's up?" I asked, nervous now. "Has something happened?"

Cintia caught my eye, flawless as ever in ribbed champagne-colored loungewear, and gave me a reassuring smile.

"Will's gotten sick," she said in a soft, low voice.

"Yes, he's sick," echoed Justin resolutely, hands patting the air in a gesture of calm. "He got sick during the night, Liv. Real sick. The ship's doctor is with him now."

A bright, cold note of alarm pounded through my head. I saw him in that chair in my nightmare again. Cold and dripping wet. I swallowed down a mouthful of bile.

"Really sick?" My voice came out strangled. "Hey—what do you mean, *sick*? Like because of all the alcohol?"

Had he gotten alcohol poisoning or something? Was it serious? I imagined him lying on a hospital bed, surrounded by tubes and beeping machines. What had Justin been *thinking* last night? We were on an educational trip, not some kind of bacchanal. I imagined Will's dad unleashing a torrent of threats upon our chaperone. I mean, he could legitimately afford the best lawyers the UK had to offer. Although, whether he would care enough to hire them or not was an entirely different matter.

But Justin shook his head.

"No, we thought it was that at first. I mean, he'd definitely overindulged last night, shall we say. But when he started raving . . . about the strangest things . . . I knew it wasn't only alcohol. So, I fetched the doctor, who confirmed he had a dangerously high fever. I mean, he was delirious—"

"Raving? Shit. Is he in his room?" I stood immediately. "I need to see him. I'll be back in—"

Justin shook his head again, more firmly. "No, Liv . . . You can't see him. He's been quarantined."

"Quarantined?"

The word was something I'd only ever heard in movies about plague outbreaks or zombie apocalypses.

"But why? What's wrong with him?"

And—is it infectious?

I reddened, ashamed at how quickly the thought flitted into my mind.

Justin's coffee cup rattled alarmingly as he placed it in its saucer.

"The doctor's not entirely sure yet. They're running a bunch of tests, but if it is something contagious—well, you understand how quickly it might spread through the ship. Because of that, there's to be minimal contact with him until he's fully recovered or until we're sure that whatever he's got is no longer infectious."

It sounded as if he were reading from some bland script. There was no genuine concern in his voice at all. I floundered, a recount of my nightmare poised dangerously on my lips. Justin squinted his eyes at me.

"And how are *you* feeling this morning, Liv? You look a little pale."

How was I feeling?

  a) Awkward and embarrassed after all the drama of
     last night, not to mention hungover as hell
  b) Now seriously concerned I'd contracted some
     contagious zombie disease, or
  c) The most honest answer . . . feeling massively
     alone with the prospect of no Will.

I fixed my face, remembering how much Mum and Dad wanted me to enjoy this trip. This was a stumbling block, nothing more. We were on an expensive cruise ship filled with passengers used to nothing but the best. Will was in safe hands and anyway, some time apart would give us both the chance to cool off after last night.

"All right, I suppose. I mean, I don't feel sick or feverish or anything, if that's what you're asking. How long will it be before we can see him?"

Justin shrugged. "I don't know, to be honest. The doctor said he'd contact me as soon as there was any change. I was saying to the group before you came that you guys need to keep an eye on your temperature too. Let me know if you're not feeling right and I can grab someone to get you checked out."

I sank into one of the seats.

"I mean . . . but how sick is seriously sick? How soon after I left last night did all this happen?"

"Your *friend* was the last one standing. We'd all gone to bed," said Constantine dryly.

Justin nodded in confirmation. "Yeah, I was called to his room by the staff. He'd been creating a bit of a disturbance. Not entirely his fault, of course."

A *disturbance*?

"Wait, what? I didn't hear anything?"

My room was next to his and I'd been half-awake, tossing and turning, for most of the night. Although come to think of it, I'd not even heard Will come back—I'd been lying there for a while, half listening for him to return. Vaguely, I recalled some banging and shouting at the end of my nightmare. Could that have been reality intruding?

Justin looked shamefaced. "I can't help feeling responsible . . . I shoulda kept tighter reins on you guys."

At this, Adora looked indignant. "Now, hang on a minute, Justin—you can't blame yourself. I mean, most of us are eighteen—legally adults—or *almost*, anyway."

I looked at Justin curiously, now feeling slightly aggrieved toward him for my hangover. There was no denying alcohol was definitely a large part of why things had gotten so heated last night. Why hadn't he put a stop to it?

Raj gave a smug shake of his head. "You Brits and your drinking . . ."

I frowned. Besides, Justin, our supposedly responsible leader, was Canadian, not British (and definitely not American, as I'd discovered last night).

"International waters," replied Con.

Before Justin could respond, a raucous laugh from somewhere behind me sliced through the conversation. Turning, I saw the Sirens seated at the next table, perfectly made up in cropped pastel loungewear despite the ship's freezer-like air-conditioning. The girl Will had been sitting with last night—Thalia—caught my eye and gave me an unpleasant little smirk.

"Hey, was he—was Will—with her when you guys left?" I asked, lowering my voice, and casting a nod in their general direction.

Adora gave me a pitying look. "Maybe, although I doubt they left together. I mean, a girl like Thalia just *wouldn't*—"

"I don't *care* about that," I muttered, despite everyone blatantly thinking I did.

"Yes, speaking of which, has anyone told her that the person who had their tongue down her throat for most of the evening is now in quarantine with an infectious disease?" added Constantine. "If not, they probably should."

In the chilly morning light, his face was impassive, like it had been carved from marble. I looked at him, shocked, while Adora gave him a half-hearted slap on the thigh.

"Immodestly put, but good point," said Justin. "Actually, maybe you could field that one for me, Liv? I've got a lot on my plate this morning. I need to call Will's parents, for one."

I nodded a reluctant assent, to Justin's obvious relief. I'd intended to speak to Thalia anyway. To clear things up between us, if only for Will's sake.

"Well, the morning's yours, guys," he continued, all his infectious Canadian zeal apparently dimmed after only one night. "But remember—you're all expected to follow the SeaMester orientation schedule for the first week—before we arrive at our first destination."

I hid my grin as I clocked the enormous eye roll Adora directed toward Con.

"There's an official welcome from the captain at noon—you're all expected—and then we'll meet back here in the Neptune Lounge for dinner tonight. Spend some time getting acquainted with the ship today. There's plenty of activities running during the day, so you won't be bored. This week is all about getting to know each other—and the ship—before we reach New York. Sure, it's sad about Will, but remember, he's in good hands. Try not to worry, and make the most of every minute."

I wanted to tell Justin to wait, to tell me about Will again, to tell me everything from the start, but there was no point.

He was sick, that was all, and all I could do was wait for him to get better.

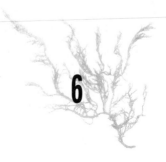

6

ONCE THE OTHERS HAD GONE, MOST OF THEM MUTTERING about returning to bed, I hastily tapped out a message to Will.

Hey you 😬—heard you're sick

I paused a moment after I hit Send, wondering whether I owed him an apology. All I'd been doing last night was trying to look out for him. Being ill didn't excuse you for being a dick. Nope, it was up to him to say sorry. But I wasn't about to ghost a sick friend, however angry with him I was.

Glancing over at the Sirens' table, I reluctantly got up. Better to get it over with.

As I approached, one of them—Leda, I think—rolled her eyes and whispered something to Thalia, who gave that same thin smile as before, not even bothering to look up from her phone.

"Hey, guys." I gave an uneasy smile, already resenting Justin for palming this off on me. "Could we talk for a minute? It's Thalia, isn't it?"

Three pairs of eyes looked at me, coldly appraising my baggy "Class of 23" hoodie and leggings from top to bottom. I had hoped we could do this in private, but clearly that was not going to be the case. Still, I soldiered on.

"I wondered if you knew that Will . . . Will got sick last night. He's in quarantine at the moment."

Leda gave a short, bitter laugh.

"Oh yeah—with what? The world's most insane hangover? Or did his sloppy self take a tumble over the deck?"

I gave a fake laugh, instantly hating myself for it.

"No—*no*. Actually, he's genuinely sick. He has a fever and stuff, apparently. . . . The doctor's keeping a close eye on him. I was—I mean—we were—just wondering how you were feeling. . . . Did he seem sick at all to you last night?"

Because last time I saw him, he was drunk, but definitely not sick.

"Look, I'm sorry to hear about your ex or whatever," Thalia said, then turned away from me again to address her friends. "This is the one who was pissed I was chatting to that drunk guy last night. Funnily enough, the same girl who ruined my dress." She turned to me again, her eyes flat. "You need to get over it because he's definitely over you."

"He's not my *ex*," I replied, dimly aware my voice was rising. "Like I told you, Will is my friend." I took a steadying breath. "I'm letting you know that he's sick in case you need to get checked out too."

She glared at me. Once again, I was struck by how dark her eyes were. Almost black and entirely inscrutable—like a shark's.

"What exactly are you implying? We were *talking*, that's all." She sighed, lowering her voice and casting me a pitying look. "Look, I don't *know* you, but I know you need better friends. I mean, after that reaction of his last night, has it crossed your mind that he isn't really in quarantine, that maybe he's just trying to get away from *you*?"

I blinked, staring at her. Had I misheard her?

"Sorry—sorry, *what?*"

"Anyway," she continued, turning away again, her interest lost, "I'm feeling fantastic. Thanks so much for your *concern*."

I stalked back up the corridor to where our rooms were.

On top of Thalia's rudeness, Will still hadn't replied to my message, but to my annoyance, he *had* read it. The blue ticks never lied. High on righteous indignation, I hammered hard on his door.

"Will!" I shouted. "Will, I know you're in there. . . . You don't need to get out of bed or anything, but you do need to talk to me—through the door or whatever. Or, you know, you could try *replying* to my message for once!"

We'd always promised never to leave each other on read. One of the three friendship vows we'd created last year after we both failed our mock science exam in spectacular style and spent the afternoon in his childhood treehouse, drinking an entire bottle of my mum's peach schnapps in recompense.

There was no response. The silence down this corridor felt weirdly heavy.

I pushed my ear up against the door to see if I could make out anything . . . the insistent murmur of his music, the shower running, anything at all—but there was nothing.

A much-less-welcome thought struck me. What if he had *died* in there and no one knew? Choked on his vomit or worse. If he was really sick, shouldn't he be on a medical deck or something? I hammered even more loudly on the door.

"*Will!* Look, I need to know you're okay. I'm sorry we fought last night. I don't even know what it was about. If we could just talk, then—"

"Is everything all right, miss?"

I whirled around, almost screaming in surprise.

Directly behind me stood an incredibly tall, incredibly thin man dressed entirely in crisp whites, similar to how the captain had been dressed the other night. His badge read "Eduardo, Hotel Manager." He was immensely tan with a set of overly large, white teeth and a wispy, dark comb-over. He must have walked like a cat; I hadn't the faintest idea anyone had been coming up the corridor. I put a hand to my chest and gathered myself.

"Hey—sorry, you startled me. Look, my friend is ill . . . and . . . he's not answering me. I need to know if he's okay. If you could open the door for me, then . . ."

The hotel manager gave a series of curt nods as if he already understood everything. His voice was high and fluting, carrying a trace of an unidentifiable accent.

"I understand, miss. The boy in this room is a Mr. William Rexham, is he not?"

All right. So he knew what was going on. Clearly the staff on this ship were *on* it. Well informed and efficient. I relaxed a little.

"Yes. *Yes*—that's right. So, *can* you open the door? To see if he's okay?"

The hotel manager's face was still fixed in a humorless rictus grin. It was a little disconcerting.

"There is little point since he is not there. We would not leave him here alone in his cabin. Did you expect us to do nothing but paint a red cross upon his door?" He gave an eerie little laugh at his own joke. "He has been taken to the infirmary. The doctor is currently running some tests. All being well, he shall be returned to his room by tomorrow morning at the latest."

Well, that at least explained why Will hadn't answered. Marginally reassured, I thanked Eduardo, who nodded again with that same chilly smile and remained where he was, hands behind his back, clearly waiting for me to leave. As I wandered aimlessly back up toward the main decks, I felt my phone buzz in my pocket.

> **Will:** Yeah, not feeling the best. With dr at mo. Message properly later x

The sight of those words caused every muscle in my body to relax, the tension oozing out of me.

So he was okay, then. Thank *God*.

"Funny old card, that one."

I turned. An elderly woman who must have been around seventy, dripping with jewelry, her silvery white hair set in chic chin-length waves, shook her head in the direction of Eduardo. "It's the smile, isn't it? Doesn't quite reach the eyes."

I laughed politely. "Yeah. Yeah, I know what you mean."

"You're here studying, aren't you?" she continued in her slightly husky voice. A pair of tortoiseshell-rimmed glasses swung from a gold chain around her neck. She looked expensive in a pleated ankle-length skirt and a fluffy leopard-print sweater.

"Yep, part of SeaMester," I confirmed, peering behind her for an escape route or an excuse. I never knew what to say to old people. It was always awkward.

"Must be pretty rotten for you, hanging out with us oldies all day?"

"Oh no," I lied. "It's been great so far."

"You might want to tell that to your face, love." She chuckled. "Tell you what. If you're at a loose end, I could use a bingo partner? Give us a nudge if you're bored."

I highly doubted I would ever be that bored, even on this ship, but in a bid to get away, I nodded furiously. This place was huge—there was no way I would run into her again.

"Yep, great, definitely. Nice to meet you, uh—"

"Hilary, dear. And yes, I will see you later."

Not if I could help it, I thought, hurrying down the corridor.

7

"SO, WILL'S GOOD, THEN, RIGHT?"

Cintia regarded me levelly with warm brown eyes over her steaming coffee cup.

"Yeah. I mean, he messaged me, so things can't be that bad. Says he's feeling crappy but hasn't got the plague or anything."

The day stretched out with alarming emptiness now that Will was gone. On the bus journey down, we'd made an entire list of cheesy things we'd wanted to do once aboard. Act out various scenes from *Titanic* (*obviously*), play bingo non-ironically, enter an air guitar competition—and not a single one of them seemed remotely appealing to do without him.

Now Cintia and I were sitting in the Athene Coffee Lounge.

With its cheerfully mismatched sofas and thrift store furnishings, it was much warmer than the cold glitter of the

Aphrodite Lounge and more my scene than the bland vibe of the Neptune Lounge. Around us were pockets of cruise-goers, dosing themselves up with coffee and flaky pastries, speaking in muted tones. Overhead, large screens comfortingly murmured the UK and US news, intermittently displaying the map that detailed our progress over the Atlantic. At the moment, the East Coast of the US wasn't even visible.

"You know, the inconsistency with the names annoys me," I mused, taking another sip of my drink and staring at the sign above the counter, where waistcoat-clad baristas toiled away. "Eos, Athene, and Aphrodite are all Greek, right? But Neptune is Roman. I mean, was Poseidon too much?"

Cintia rolled her eyes at me.

"You were so hilarious last night!" she said, clearly trying to steer the conversation away from mythology. "Seriously, Liv, I was dead. I swear you were trying to get it on with our exalted leader at one point."

I felt my face heat as that particularly ill-advised fragment of last night drifted back to me.

"Did you know he's Canadian?" I said, holding my head in my hands. "I must have asked him what America was like about a hundred times last night."

Cintia burst out laughing.

"No, but I *do* know he's gay. I tried taking your drink off you, but every time I turned around, you had a fresh one."

Sheepishly, I sipped my coffee. "Yeah . . . Not my finest hour. My parents would literally kill me if they knew."

Cintia chuckled again, a warm sound. I felt her eyes linger on me as I took another sip of my drink, a hint of worry creeping into her tone when she spoke again.

"Is Will always like that? I caught most of it and I'm not gonna lie, he was so rude to you. If he tried speaking to me that way . . ."

She gave a sharp shake of her head. I looked down, already tired of making excuses for Will.

"Don't sweat it," she said, her tone softer now. "No one was bothered. Justin's cool. Hey, I noticed Con running straight after you when you left. . . . Did he make a move or what? Spill."

The thought drew unnecessary heat to my face. I mean, Lord, if *only*.

Don't be intimidated by us.

"I mean—what do you think of him?" Cintia prodded. "Would you be down for it?"

"Honestly . . . ? I don't think I've met anyone so hideously arrogant and entitled in my life," I said decisively, trying to convince myself. "Y'know I saw him literally snap his fingers at the bartenders last night? And *no*, he did not make a move. He acts like me going to a regular school is contagious or something."

Cintia cackled.

"I get it, I do, but it's problematic in that he is *fire*, right?"

I groaned.

"Yeah, but he so *knows* it, though. That definitely loses him points."

"But he immediately gets 'em back due to the fact he is *filthy* rich. Y'know his father's some bazillionaire shipping magnate?

How else do you think Con, of all people, got a place in this program? Apparently, his dad has ties to the cruise line that owns the *Eos*. Dor told me he even bought a title and everything—earl, or count. Something like that."

"Shipping *magnet*? What even is that?"

Cintia chuckled. "Look—trust me. Whoever eventually snags him is set for life."

She kept her words deliberately light, staring down at her coffee, but there was a weight to them nonetheless—a meaning I couldn't quite detect. Was she trying to set me up, or was she into him herself? As ridiculously hot as Con was, it felt wrong to be thirsting over him while Will was so ill. I decided a change of subject was needed.

"So what *did* happen after I left? I mean, did Will seem sick to you?"

Cintia looked at me. I could tell she was weighing up how honest to be.

"We *are* only friends, y'know," I insisted. "I mean, I know he was with . . . whatsherface—the Siren girl. And I don't care. I mean, yeah, sure, I wish he had better taste, but—"

Cintia exhaled and nodded.

"Yeah . . . They made out a little after you'd gone. Then they left. . . . They left together, if you know what I mean."

I looked at Cintia in disbelief.

"What? You mean together, *together*?"

She nodded sagely.

A jolt of shock zipped through me. Even for a drunk Will, this was out of character.

We'd been to loads of parties together over the past couple of years, always vowing to prevent the other from making decisions they'd regret in the morning. And he'd never been into casual hookups. He'd be the one holding court all night with the Spotify playlist or running down to the corner shop for a bag of late-night snacks. He had the polished, hard-earned rep of a decent guy. One who only dated steadily and had lots of female friends.

Or, the thought snuck into my mind, had he hidden an entire side of himself from me under this bizarre but apparent belief of his that I was in love *with him?*

No.

No one outside of the cheesy thrillers my mum bought in the supermarket had the time for a double life. Will was *Will*. And the Will I knew spent vast swathes of his life livestreaming Overwatch from his bedroom in a bid to avoid unwanted encounters with his dad's new girlfriend.

I flopped back dramatically on the sofa, ignoring Cintia's concerned look. Either way, it was none of my business and honestly, I didn't want to think too long about it. Will was a big boy. He could do what he wanted. And maybe he was right, maybe I *did* have a problem. Only it wasn't my unrequited love for him or whatever the hell he had gotten into his head last night—it was more a case of me needing to realize we weren't nine anymore. We weren't the same kids that could huddle up together all day under a blanket watching crappy eighties horror movies or playing JRPGs without there being anything in it, or more accurately, *other people* insisting there was.

I finished my coffee and checked my watch.

"Hey—we better head to the captain's cabin," I said to Cintia. "It's almost time."

I'd checked the daily activity timetable on one of the screens after breakfast. There *was* a lot going on. Bingo. Aqua Zumba (despite the steadily falling rain). Dance classes. Language classes. Organized talks on timeshares and pyramid schemes. The list was both impressively endless and utterly uninspiring.

Cintia peered at me over her glasses. "You're serious? Nobody's *actually* gonna go to that. Sitting through the lifeboat drill was painful enough."

But I'd always been a pathetic stickler for the rules. Besides, I was already realizing no one else seemed to be remotely grateful to be part of this trip, except me.

I pulled a face, then reluctantly stood. "Well, *I'm* going to go—I'd feel bad if no one showed—plus, it would make Justin look bad too. Please don't make me go alone? It will be proper weird if it's just me and the captain."

Cintia raised an eyebrow. "You're going for real? What—you leave your underwear in there last night or something?"

I snorted. "*No!* Jesus, Cintia."

With an exaggerated sigh she got up and looped her arm through mine.

"All right, then. Let's get this over with."

Orlaigh, the steward who'd welcomed us onto the boat, was manning the passenger information desk in the main atrium.

I had to admit, the space made me oddly uneasy. It was at least the height of three entire decks. Still and dark and almost cathedral-like; the kind of place where only hushed tones were acceptable.

As we approached, she looked up at us, her wide blue eyes stern.

"Ah, good morning," she chirped. "And how are you both today?"

She affixed the same slightly eerie grin to her face as Eduardo had earlier.

"Fine—fine, thanks. We're part of SeaMester. We were told to come here to, uh . . ." I cleared my throat. "Meet the captain?"

A dark look crossed Orlaigh's face like a fleeting shadow. Were we too early? I glanced again at my watch. If anything, we were a few minutes late. Then I remembered. There were meant to be six of us. Still, she didn't say anything, only nodded in her businesslike way.

"That's fabulous. Captain Elytis is expecting you."

Cintia and I followed Orlaigh through a labyrinth of corridors and elevators until we reached a quiet lower deck that needed a key card placed in a slot in the elevator to access it. The lights were dimmer here, the ceiling lower and the doors between the cabins much farther apart than the ones in our corridor. Dark wood paneling lined the hall, while golden light spilled from delicate glass globes set into the wall. Orlaigh led on, her smart black heels sinking silently into the deep pile of the crimson carpet, eventually stopping to rap on a pair of grand double doors at the very end of the corridor.

They opened with a startling immediacy, as if the captain had been standing directly behind them, waiting. The man was an impressive presence, so tall he was hunched over in the dimly lit cabin. Broad-shouldered and black-eyed with a slick of glossy curls and a grin so white I reckoned you could see it in the dark, I imagined he was a massive hit with the older crowd.

"Ah, Captain Elytis," Orlaigh said, apparently unbothered by his abrupt appearance. "Here we have the young ladies who are part of the SeaMester education program. I believe you're expecting them?"

He nodded, waving us into the cramped quarters of his cabin. "Welcome, ladies." His accent was thick and transatlantic. Stuck halfway between America and the Mediterranean. I unavoidably inhaled his aftershave as I passed, an obtrusive woody scent that shouted authority.

"It is wonderful to meet such ambitious young people. The *Eos* and her staff welcome you gladly," he said effusively. "Tell me, what are you both studying?"

The moment I opened my mouth to reply, my stomach gave a painful lurch and a wave of dizzying heat washed over me. Had my nerves finally picked a time to act up or was my body seeking revenge for the excesses of last night? I brushed a hand over my clammy forehead and gave him a brief, distracted rundown of my studies, gritting my teeth against the pain.

The captain gave me a twinkly nod and turned to Cintia. "And you, my dear, where do your interests lie?"

As Cintia grinned and began to talk confidently about her passion for photography, I took a subtle deep breath, exhaling slowly as another wave of sickness roiled through me. Yep, either last night was still wreaking its vengeance or I was more prone to seasickness than I thought. I glanced over at the small porthole window, remembering it was supposed to help to stare at the horizon. But at the sight of the vivid green ocean seesawing up and down outside, I groaned.

Cintia immediately stopped talking.

"Whoa. Are you okay, Liv? You're looking kinda green."

I clutched a shaky hand to my mouth.

"God. No. No, I'm not. Ohh, I need a bathroom . . . quick—sorry."

I made an apologetic noise as the captain's eyes widened in alarm. He gestured with a hairy arm to a door at the back of the cabin.

"Through there—the first door on the left—quickly, please, quickly."

Clamping my other hand over my mouth, I nodded and stumbled in that direction while Cintia continued talking.

Through the door was the captain's bedroom.

The bed was pristinely made, and every walnut surface shone as brightly as the rest of the ship. I wrinkled my nose. It might have looked clean, but it smelled oddly dank, like a dirty fish tank. Still, it was much cooler in here, and almost immediately I felt my nausea begin to subside. I paused, drawing in a long breath of relief as I looked around the room.

The place was spartan. The only hint of disorder was a crumpled printout of a map lying on the dresser. Instantly, I recognized it from the screens dotted everywhere about the ship as the route the *Eos* was taking over the Atlantic. Equally spaced along the way, someone—the captain, I presumed—had scribbled seven large *X*s. I looked closer, suddenly curious, but no explanation accompanied the markings; no key, or description of what they might mean. Perhaps they were meant to represent our progress by day?

Regardless, I hoped that wasn't the only map he was using to steer the ship.

A large TV was affixed to the wall directly opposite the bed, and on the adjacent wall was an enormous custom-built aquarium—maybe the source of the smell. Something unpleasantly blobby and many-tentacled floated within like a moist aquatic spider. I shuddered, glad that particular design feature was absent from my own cabin.

Moving slowly in case my stomach acted up again, I braced one hand against a series of built-in wardrobes that lined the wall leading to a small door I hoped was the bathroom. One was half-open, leaking its contents: neat lines of identical, bland black trousers and starched white shirts. As I moved to close it, something shiny caught my eye, stuffed right into the back of the wardrobe, hidden behind all the uniforms. Impulsively, I reached forward and grasped whatever it was, rubbing the material between my fingers. The color reminded me of an oil slick, a shimmering purple-black. The material itself was thin but rubbery—like PVC. The feel of it made me recoil. Was it a costume of some kind? I gave a small smile. Well, the captain was allowed his secrets.

I ducked into the small bathroom—immaculately clean and

reeking of bleach—shutting the door quietly behind me. Sitting on the toilet lid, I closed my eyes and took a deep breath, waiting for the nausea to pass.

A soft thumping sound made me look up. My heart jolted. Had the captain come looking for me?

Instead, a bag swung lazily from a hook on the back of the door. A woman's handbag and, from the looks of it, an expensive one. The captain—or his date—had good taste. Already past the point of snooping, I stood and, ignoring the warm flush of guilt—I was just *looking,* after all—peered inside. There were only a few items within: an undoubtedly pricey, gold-cased lipstick, an open pack of gum, and the familiar cover of a UK passport. Without thinking, I fished the passport out and flipped it open, curious to see its owner. A pretty girl close to my own age, with glossy brown hair and a tan freckled face stared out at me, obediently unsmiling; her eyes the blue-black of deep oceans.

Oddly, the girl's name had been violently scratched out with black marker, leaving it completely illegible. I raised an eyebrow. Weird. How did she get *that* through passport control? And why would the captain have some random passenger's bag in his bathroom?

The answer to my second question, at least, presented itself in the form of a small plastic tag affixed to the purse's handle, bearing the words "RETURN TO PASSENGER." Did that mean this girl, whoever she was, was aboard the ship? I made a mental note to keep an eye out for her. She'd be easy enough to spot among all the pensioners, and God knew I could use a few more friends around here.

Realizing I'd been in here a while and there was absolutely no reason for me to be snooping about in someone's lost property or whatever, I dropped the passport back into the bag and flushed the toilet.

As I emerged, I nearly jumped out of my skin. The captain was standing directly outside the bathroom door, his back to the fish tank, as if hiding it from view. He wasn't smiling, and the atmosphere in the room seemed to have chilled several notches compared to before. He continued to stare at me, his eyes hard and glaring. He didn't even blink. I felt a hot and dirty flush wash over me, the type that left you feeling in immediate need of a shower. I looked over his shoulder to where Cintia stood in the doorway, obliviously flicking through her phone.

"Sorry about that," I said with an apologetic smile, my voice wobbling a little. "I, uh, think I better go and lie down for a bit."

He nodded briskly but didn't reply, his gleaming smile suddenly returning like the sun emerging from behind a cloud.

I blinked at him. Had I imagined his annoyance?

"Well, thanks for the welcome . . . ," I started, then trailed off.

I needed to fill the awkward silence. Hidden behind him, whatever was in the tank seemed agitated. Was I imagining it or could I hear a dull thwacking sound as it threw itself at the glass?

"Of course," the captain finally answered. "And there is nothing else you wish to see?"

Strangely, he barely seemed to even open his mouth as he spoke.

I looked over his shoulder once more. Whether he intended it or not, his large bulk was barring my way out of the room.

"Your accent," I said. "Where's it from?"

"Everywhere." His voice was singsong now. Deep, almost hypnotic. "You wouldn't *believe* the places I've been. The things I've seen."

"Uh, really?"

It's the smile, isn't it? Doesn't quite reach the eyes.

Hilary had been dead right earlier—and the captain's smile was the same. *That* was what was off about it. His eyes were flat and dark and bored unblinkingly into mine.

Was he angry? Had he seen me poking through his wardrobe?

"Well, we better be going," I said, louder now, stepping toward him in a direct effort to get him to move. At the last moment, he stepped aside, still blocking the view of the tank where the thumping sound was coming from. Rhythmic now, gaining in speed and volume. I half wished I'd taken a proper look at what was in there when I'd had the chance.

"Of course, it was a pleasure to meet you ladies. And if you need anything in the future . . . please, just ask."

We waited until we got onto the deck before I gave an indelicate snort of laughter. It was entirely born of nerves, but I was relieved when Cintia joined me.

"Pleasure to see you, *laydeeeees.* See—told you we should have skipped it."

"You were *not* wrong. What was *up* with that place?"

Cintia grinned. "Smelled like my grandma's nursing home. But hey, he was pretty hot for an older guy, right?"

I looked at her incredulously. Had I imagined the atmosphere in that room? Catching sight of my expression, she laughed again. "All right, maybe I have questionable taste. It's cool. I really do need a nap, though. I'll catch you at dinner, all right?"

8

I COULDN'T RELAX IN THE SILENT CONFINES OF MY WIN-
dowless cabin for too long, so, reminding myself I should be
making the most of this opportunity, I headed back to the
Athene Lounge to chill with a little reading.

But I'd barely even gotten out my book, a dog-eared copy of
The Turn of the Screw, before Raj and Con walked by. Raj did a
double take and headed over, Con trailing reluctantly behind.

"Hey—it's the Livster!" Raj called by way of greeting. "We're
off to check out the bar. You coming? You look like you could
use the hair of the dog, you party animal."

I raised an eyebrow.

"The bar? I thought you said something last night about
your body being a temple?"

Raj laughed. "Certainly is. One you'd like to visit, right?
Which is why I'll be drinking Perrier's finest with a slice of lime."

"He means the *pub*. And also, his sobriety is why *you* need to come," added Constantine dryly. "It's no fun drinking alone."

My last conversation with Constantine had left me thinking he was an arrogant twat who believed he was better than me. But maybe this was his chance to prove me wrong. I got up, shoving my book into my backpack. I was a great believer in second chances when they came packaged like him.

The Groggy Parrot, located on the deck below, was an oddly charming approximation of an English pub. It reminded me of something you might find at an American theme park. *Ye Olde Englishe Taverne.* The walls were crammed with random black-and-white photos of farmers and cottages apparently entirely unrelated to each other—no doubt a bulk buy off eBay—and the tables were ringed with glass stains and accompanied by rickety stools.

"Well, this is cute," I said, grinning, once we'd taken up residence in a booth. It was certainly better than the wide, soulless expanses of the upstairs lounges.

"This is all there is to do on a cruise," lamented Constantine. "Drink and eat and go to bingo. It's basically a taste of what retirement will look like."

"Are all you Brits so ungrateful?" said Raj good-naturedly. "Criticize all you want, but plenty of people would kill to be in our place. Y'know, my sister tried to reserve a cabin on this ship to visit once we hit New York. Apparently, it's solidly booked out for the next few years."

I blinked in surprise. I mean, the ship was nice and all, but it wasn't *that* nice.

"Well, *I'm* grateful to be here," I pointed out quickly. "And Con is not exactly what you'd call a typical Brit."

"Why do I get the feeling that wasn't a compliment?" remarked Con. "Anyway, Raj, shouldn't you be training in that dreary, windowless dungeon they call a gym? You certainly know how to live."

Raj postured, exposing a thickly muscled arm in my direction. "Ah, but the payoff is worth it. Right, Liv?"

Truthfully, I tended to avoid people who were obsessed with fitness. Not only did they make me feel bad for the pure bliss that doughnuts and kettle chips brought me, but I found conversation with them hard.

"Not everyone is into tire-armed 'roid heads, Raj," Con interjected. "*Some* girls prefer elegance and refinement."

"Speaking of which," said Raj, smiling, "how's Will?"

"I don't know," I replied honestly. "He said the docs are doing some tests at the moment. I mean, the fact he messaged me at all shows he's not, like, dying or anything."

Raj downed the rest of his water and slammed the glass on the table.

"Cool, well, I'm off to do some laps in the pool. Catch you both at dinner."

As soon as Raj bounded off like a golden retriever, an awkward silence descended between Con and me that seemed to last approximately twenty-eight wintry months, during which he fiddled inventively with a placemat while I sat and chugged my way through an entire pint of Diet Coke.

"How can he swim? It's lashing a gale outside," I muttered,

fumbling to fill the silence. We'd clearly not escaped the dark reaches of the UK weather just yet.

"Listen, I didn't intend to offend you last night," said Constantine, still not looking at me.

"No worries, I wasn't offended . . . ," I began diplomatically. Since I'd heard from Will, the world was pressing less heavily on my shoulders. Had it been the "x" at the end of his message? Will didn't usually end his texts that way, so I hoped it was a sign he regretted all he'd said.

"But," I continued, "I don't want you to feel sorry for me either. I mean, you don't intimidate me. None of you do."

And he didn't right now. He was only some posh kid—with admittedly beautiful hair.

"Your heroic consumption of alcohol last night tells a different story." He gave a slight breath of a laugh. "Ah, here I go again. Attempting to be nice—and failing."

I allowed him a small smile.

"Well, yeah, the drinking was a mistake. I was nervous—but that's not the same as being intimidated."

He nodded, running a hand over his mouth. Clearly a man of few words.

"So, what are you planning to do for the rest of the day?" I asked, refusing to let our limping conversation die altogether. "Join Raj for a dip in the pool?"

He stared at me, his eyes wide. They were pale gray, like beach shale, and framed by thick lashes, the type my nan always twittered were "wasted on a boy."

"No chance of that. I can't swim, for starters."

I was surprised. I'd thought posh people could do anything. That they were all tutored in chess, Olympic-level swimming, and Mandarin from the age of two.

"Nor can I," I admitted readily, clinging to the slippery bank of our common ground.

Not only did I hate the sea, but I also hated being submerged in water in general. When I was seven, my family had rented a caravan in Devon. I'd been playing in the shallows on the beach one afternoon—chasing my dad, who'd had a few beers at the time—when I'd slipped off a hidden shelf into much deeper water, slip-sliding straight under. Not that deep, but deep enough that I couldn't stand.

I'd been a slow swimmer anyway, still in need of the armbands I had been too embarrassed to put on that day. Dad had dived in, beery buzz immediately forgotten, and hauled me out in seconds, but those seconds were all it took for a lifelong hatred to grasp me. The invasion of the water up my nose, clogging my mouth as I tried impossibly to breathe. Thick and salty, choking and wrenching the air from my lungs.

"Never learned or never wanted to?" Con asked, pulling me back to the present.

"Both. How about you?"

He shrugged. "I'm not afraid of water, per se. I mean, you might find me on one of those unicorn-shaped floats accompanied by a smaller, thematically matching unicorn-shaped drink holder. In Miami. In June."

"That's oddly specific."

"I find it's important to be specific, don't you?"

I relented and smiled at him. Was it even possible he was nervous too?

"Ironic how we're both currently crossing the world's largest ocean and neither of us likes water. Wait, isn't your dad some shipping zillionaire?"

Constantine shrugged as if it were of no consequence. "Yeah. Or at least, that's what his employees tell me. Who knows anymore, I barely see him. I didn't even know he'd signed me up for this trip. His assistant came over one morning, told me to pack for six weeks, and lo and behold, here I am."

I stared at him in disbelief.

"Wait. You didn't *want* to come, then?"

He looked back at me in surprise, gray eyes widening. "*No*. Of course I didn't. I don't think anyone really did. I mean, did you, really? Six weeks stuck in the middle of the damn ocean? It's like being on a giant floating . . . *hospice*."

Blood roared in my ears. I cleared my throat.

"Actually, *yes*. I did. I know I might be . . . anxious about it all, but this trip is a massive opportunity for me. Not everyone is lucky enough to have a billionaire for a dad, y'know. . . ."

He scoffed, undeterred. "Liv, you can *fly* to wherever you want to. Far more efficient way of traveling, and you don't need to spend weeks on a boat with half of the world's elderly population. You spend longer lining up to get on and off the ship than you do at any port. The food is terrible. The drinks are overpriced and also terrible." He gave a dramatic sigh and tossed the now-destroyed placemat on the table, flopping back against the cushioned seat. "Anyway, my dad's in town at the moment—so that means *I* need to be gone. He thinks I'm a miserable failure and you know, I do hate to disappoint. You see, I have the perfect older brother—runs his own law firm. I have a sister who's never received a grade less than an 'A'—Then here I am, failing chem, failing everything really, and then there was that business in Greece—"

Business in Greece?

But he stopped dead, collecting himself, as if he'd been about to divulge something he shouldn't. "Well, *anyway*," he started again, in a deliberately lighter voice. "No doubt it all seems horrendously ungrateful to you, but truth is, I'd rather be anywhere else but here."

No lie there—it *did* seem ungrateful. I remembered my excitement, my parents' excitement. A luxury cruise was something we'd only ever dreamed about.

"I'm sure your dad doesn't really feel like that," I replied half-heartedly. "So, uh, what happened in Greece?"

Constantine threw a troubled look in the direction of the bar and then picked up the placemat again. I was surprised when he began to answer.

"Oh, you know, the usual recipe for disaster—"

"Aha, *there* he is!"

I groaned inwardly as a familiar plummy voice cut through his story. "We've been looking everywhere for you."

It was Adora, somehow managing to look sickeningly chic in a high-necked, ankle-length, black lace dress and tattered gray sneakers, accompanied by one of the Sirens. Leda—the curvy one with the strong cat-eye in a low-cut embroidered peasant top and leather pants. They sat down opposite us, plonking their designer clutches on the cheap table. I felt somehow shrunken in their presence, their glamour and confidence making me feel childlike. To my surprise—and instant terror—Constantine immediately shot up.

"Have you now? Shame I missed you, but I've got to go meet Justin."

"But, *Con*," wheedled Adora, "I've been dying for a catch-up."

"Yes, well, I'm sure we'll have ample opportunity for that later. We *are* stuck together on this boat for weeks, after all."

And with that, he sauntered off, leaving me in the most awkward situation I'd found myself in yet. I expected them to both get up and leave me without another word. Like the unpopular kid at the lunch table, the one with stinky egg sandwiches.

"You know," said Adora coolly, "his last girlfriend was the daughter of a viscount and even that lasted less than a month. But I can offer you a few pointers, if you want."

I rolled my eyes.

"Olivia," she continued. "Meet Leda. Leda, Liv and her friend Cintia seemed very interested in you guys last night."

Leda raised her eyebrows in place of a smile. She was blond, like the other two, but her hair was thicker and more obviously dyed. An expensive silvery platinum that must have cost a small fortune to maintain.

"Oh?"

I gave Adora an irritated glance. She smiled back widely, no doubt pleased she had cleansed her energy again.

"We were just saying how we'd love to travel the world like you guys. Head out on private yachts and things, but I don't see it happening." I gave a little laugh.

Leda smiled icily. "Yes, I don't see it happening either. So, Adora tells me it was a stroke of luck you are here?"

I frowned. Apparently, it was my turn to fiddle with a place-mat.

"*Luck?* No. I'm here on a scholarship, actually. In some ways, you could say Adora is the lucky one."

I couldn't look either of them in the eye while I said it, and my voice was low and stilted. But still, I *did* say it.

Adora gave a cold little gasp. "I meant lucky because there's no way you could afford to be here otherwise."

I forced myself to look at her.

"Oh? And how do you know that? I didn't realize you were so intimately acquainted with my personal finances?"

Leda chuckled, clearly enjoying the drama, while Adora looked awkwardly around the room. They hadn't even ordered a drink. Why were they still here?

"Thalia was a little harsh on you this morning. You must forgive her—she's not always great with new people." Leda smiled at me before continuing. "I hear you replaced the missing girl."

"*Leda!*"

Even Adora looked shocked at Leda's statement, uttered in the same emotionless tone as she'd said everything else, the smile still present on her generous features. Her lips a perfect cupid's bow, the bottom lip insolently pouty.

"Yeah, I know *nothing* about that," I replied coldly. "And honestly, I'm not sure I want to."

Leda pressed on. Lowering her voice to a throaty rumble. "Well, *I* do. You see, my friends and I work these cruises, and whenever Con's father shipped him off to one, he couldn't keep his eyes off me. But then *she* came along—*Octavia.* They were on vacation together, cruising around Greece, when she quote-unquote disappeared. Did he mention that during your cozy little chat, I wonder? Knowing Con, I *doubt* it. He keeps his secrets close."

The shock must have been clear on my face. When Adora had mentioned it yesterday, I thought Con had been vaguely aware of the missing girl's existence—mutual friends, like Adora was. But not only did he know her well, he'd apparently been in a relationship with her when she disappeared? No wonder he had immediately clammed up yesterday. Leda and Adora continued to stare at me across the table, thirstily drinking in my reaction with sardonic little smirks.

Hurriedly, I got up, pushing my chair back with a screech.

"Well, I'm sorry to hear that, Leda—and nice to meet you—but I . . . uh, I need to be somewhere."

I could feel their amused stares all the way down the corridor. Snatches of yesterday's first conversation returned to me, so much of it drowned out by the low hum of my ever-present anxiety.

So, there'd been a girl before me—Octavia, or Tavi—who'd

paid for her place on this trip and hadn't been able to take it, hence here *I* was. Clearly scholarships were *not* the priority at SeaMester. And somehow she'd disappeared while Con had known her. *And* he knew Leda and Adora too? A small world, as my mum liked to say. However, if he was filthy rich and moved in wealthy circles, I suppose he had a certain amount of celebrity. Occasionally, I'd stalked minor members of the aristocracy on Insta just to see how the other half lived. And on the whole, it seemed *spectacularly*.

Curious now, I pulled out my phone and typed Constantine's name into Insta. Nothing popped up, even when I tried a combination of shortened versions. I should have guessed he was *above* social media. Interestingly, though, he did show up frequently on Adora's Instagram. There were several photos of him with her on sun-soaked vacations among large groups of similarly glamorous friends up until as early as a month ago, his arm frequently flung about a variety of bronzed shoulders.

One girl caught my eye.

Annoyingly, Adora hadn't bothered tagging anyone in her pics, but the girl was in a couple of Adora's photos and usually stood next to Con. Slim and bronzed, with a sleek curtain of silky black hair and arresting dark eyes, she seemed somehow familiar. Since she looked, predictably, like a supermodel, maybe I'd seen her in a magazine before or something—

A flash of recognition jolted through me. No, I *had* seen her before—today, actually—her picture in a battered passport, her name scratched out. Was this the mysterious Octavia? And if she *was* the same girl who had disappeared, what the hell was her passport doing swinging about in a bag in the captain's room?

I shook my head. I was reading way too much into this. There were loads of beautiful, dark-haired girls in the world and particularly in the orbit of guys like Con. So she looked a little similar to the girl from the passport—big deal.

Feeling guilty for snooping, I swiped out of the app, deciding the anxiety of accidentally liking a photo of him from years back wasn't worth it. I gave Will another call. Just hearing his voice would be good enough, even if it was nothing more than a sickly groan. I'd seen him with a mild cold before, and it was not a pretty sight.

After a few rings, I nearly dropped my phone in surprise as the call connected.

"Will?"

The line sounded bad—crackly and faint. Should I hang up and try again? But what if he didn't answer?

"Will—you okay? It's . . . it's Liv. How are you feeling?"

I could hear water falling, a vast amount of it by the sound of things, crashing noisily in the background. Weird. It certainly didn't sound like the quiet hospital surroundings I'd imagined him in. Was it just some kind of static?

"Liv—"

A harsh voice erupted in my ear, breathless and murmuring that single word, immediately followed by the staccato beeping of the call cutting off.

Adrenaline coursed through me at the sound of his voice.

"Will? *Will?*" I breathed, fumbling for the redial button. I paced the corridor in short circles, anxious now, needing to know everything was okay, as the phone began to ring again.

But this time, he didn't pick up.

9

UNSETTLED, I MADE MY WAY TO DINNER. MAYBE WILL'S
service had just dropped. If he was feverish, like the doctors
said, then sure, he *would* sound a little breathless, disoriented
even. Everything was fine. God, why was I making it so difficult
to enjoy this trip?

For dinner, we were meeting at the ship's buffet, no doubt
much to Adora's distaste. I was a little late—arriving a few minutes after seven—and already an enormous line snaked out of
the Neptune Lounge. I joined the end of it behind a stony-
faced older couple and their kid, all rocking socks and Velcro-
strap sandals, and debated the possibility of room service.

The kid turned around to consider me carefully with solemn brown eyes. She was a little spooky-looking, with two long
black braids that fell down her back, accessorized with colorful
rainbow ribbons.

"Did you know every single sucker on the tentacles of the Humboldt squid is lined with razor-sharp teeth?"

I stared at her for a few seconds, then looked around, unsure if she was talking to me.

Apparently, she was. I recalled that odd black thing in the tank in the captain's room and pulled my cardigan tighter around me.

"H-huh?" I stammered. "That's, uh, interesting. Also . . . *disturbing.* Are you interested in fish? Must be cool, being on a cruise at your age?"

The girl, who I reckoned was between seven and nine, wrinkled her nose. "Actually, squid are cephalopods, not fish. And no, it's not cool being on this cruise. This one's *weird.*"

I gave her an indulgent laugh. In front of us, her parents seemed oblivious to our conversation. Holding hands and staring dead ahead.

"Weird how?" I lowered my voice and gave her a grin. "A lot of old people, right?"

The girl nodded, lowering her voice too. "Part of it's that they don't want to be old. That's why they're here."

Quite the imagination, it seemed.

"Still, if they're having fun, good for them, right?" I reasoned. We crept forward in line.

"That's not what I meant," she corrected me quietly. "And— I think . . . some of what *they* call fun . . . isn't fun at *all.*"

I stared at her for a few moments, deciding something was definitely being lost in translation. Not sure what else to say, I gave her an appeasing smile as we shuffled along, and I shifted my focus to the buffet.

Truthfully, I didn't much blame Adora for her food snobbery. I'd never been keen on buffets either. It was the weird mix of smells as much as anything. Staring at your pie and mash while the strong aroma of five-spiced pork washed around you. And that was before we even got to all the coughing and sneezing over the trays.

Instinctively, I moved aside as a group of people jostled past me, ignoring the queue and loudly hailing one of the chefs.

The Sirens, of course. I made a mental note to check out their content on Insta later. No doubt it would be *riveting*.

"If you want my advice, stay away from those ladies," said the girl in front of me, with a knowing nod in their direction.

I laughed. "Oh, don't you worry. I have no intention of hanging out with that bunch of bitches."

Instantly, I clamped my hand over my mouth.

"Oh God, sorry." I glanced nervously up at her parents. Thankfully, they were still staring resolutely ahead.

The girl grinned back, revealing shiny silver braces. "Don't worry. I've heard way worse since I've been here. I'm Laila, by the way."

I frowned a little at her comment, once more glancing up at her oblivious parents.

"Well, I'm Liv. Good to meet you, Laila."

We made idle chatter about the scariest type of sea creature (according to Laila, something called the "sarcastic frill head," which, if nothing else, sounded like a good nickname for Constantine) until finally we reached the food. By now, my appetite had almost completely disappeared, so I lightly filled my plate with wontons, bone-dry Singapore noodles, and a vat of sweet chili sauce. Only criminals mixed cuisines.

I wandered desolately around the packed lounge with my plate, looking for the group, until I caught sight of Justin waving enthusiastically at me. Cintia and Raj were already there, tucking into plates piled high with what looked like a bit of everything on offer.

"Where are the other two?" I asked, pushing my food around my plate.

Cintia rolled her eyes. "Buffet food isn't good enough for Lady Adora. Think she's probably gone to the à la carte place with Con."

I was surprised by the thin needle of jealousy I felt. I mean, if nothing else, I had been deprived of the opportunity to look at him.

"Heard from Will yet?" asked Justin casually.

My face fell. Part of the reason I'd been looking forward to dinner was the hope that Justin, our auspicious leader, might have had some news to share himself. The empty seat beside me a clear reminder of Will's absence.

"Not exactly. I mean, he messaged me this morning, but since then, nada. I tried to call him, but something was up with the line when he answered."

I looked down at my phone for what must have been the fiftieth time in the past hour. Still nothing. He was probably dosed with painkillers when he answered earlier. Hopefully he was getting some sleep now.

"Did you manage to get a hold of his dad?"

Justin nodded, shuffling through his rice with his fork. "Uh-huh. Understandably, he's extremely worried but appreciates Will's in good hands. I mean, it doesn't sound like there's too much to be concerned about at the moment, does it? He's conscious, not in any real pain other than aches and a fever."

I frowned down at my plate of noodles.

Had Will's dad been "extremely" worried, or had he only sounded it? He'd never been particularly worried about Will before. It was no secret that Will hated his dad for replacing his mum with a younger model at the same speed he replaced his cars. I put down my fork, shoving my concerns to the side.

"So, he's getting better?" I asked, forcing cheerfulness into my voice. "That's great! Does this mean I can go see him?"

I'd expected Justin to immediately agree, but instead he appeared vaguely irritated. He wouldn't look at me, only attacked his food with increased violence.

"Sure, Liv. Like I said before, as soon as the doctors give us the okay."

It took effort to resist rolling my eyes, my teeth clenched as I spoke. Why was this so hard?

"Sure, but I only want to *see* him—wave at him from a safe distance or whatever," I pushed back. "Y'know, just to reassure him. It's not like I'm going to catch whatever he has through a *door*."

Justin's voice was dangerously tight. "I get that, Liv, but since neither of us are doctors, I'm sure you'll understand my wanting to stick to their advice."

I stared down at my plate, silenced by his acerbic tone. Hot tears pricked at the edges of my vision, in immediate danger of plopping onto my plate. He was probably stressed about the whole situation—worried about insurance or whatever. I needed to get a grip. Sobbing at the table was not going to endear me to anyone.

From across the table, Raj cleared his throat, cutting through the thick atmosphere.

"Right, so I'm, um, gonna grab some more food."

Despite Cintia's best efforts, conversation dried up further, and I picked at my noodles. Gradually an odd feeling began to wash over me. The feeling of being watched. An inexplicable, highly unpleasant sensation that was almost physical, unable to be denied. It was suffocating, almost making me afraid to look up in case I caught the stares of everyone in the lounge. Every pair of eyes trained on me. But I knew it wasn't everyone—it was the table directly behind me.

The Sirens.

Eventually I *had* to turn. I did it quickly, pretending to be looking through my bag, slung across the back of my chair.

None of them were looking at me.

Why would they be? All eyes were on the head chef, standing over their table in his immaculate whites, delivering something in a silver dish covered with a cloche.

Cintia followed my gaze and gave me a knowing smirk.

"Do they ever actually eat the food or just take pictures of it? Hashtag blessed!"

I grinned too, hurriedly turning away once I caught sight of Thalia glancing my way, a frown rumpling her perfect features.

"We're probably being harsh, aren't we?" I conceded. "Jealous we don't get to travel the world for free and stay in fancy places."

As I continued to chew on my limp noodles, dry and tasteless from sitting for God knows how long under heat lamps, I felt that odd, almost burning sensation in the back of my neck again.

On pure impulse, I turned around once more, only for the briefest of seconds, aware I'd already been clocked by Thalia as a weird starer.

Immediately, I twisted back and stared down at the table, trying not to choke on my mouthful of wonton.

What in the ever-living . . . ?

No. There was no way I'd just seen what I'd thought I'd seen. Because, what I *thought* I'd seen was Lexie, sitting at the table, busily *devouring*—there was no other word for it—what looked like an entire eel, its silvery flesh writhing as she swallowed it down whole, her throat rhythmically pulsing as it went down. It was obscene. And from the large silver dish placed on the table had come movement, a revolting, silvery mindless writhing— like a pile of thick, blind worms. Was that what the chef had brought out? A platter of live eels? Was that some kind of new social media trend I didn't know about?

"Cintia—*Cintia*," I hissed in a low voice, kicking her under the table. "Hey, turn around and tell me I'm not mad. What are they *eating* over there? It looks like . . . live fish—whole eels—something . . . weird."

Cintia crinkled her forehead, then turned for a few long seconds.

"Liv, seriously. Do they not even have sushi where you're from? It's not *alive*—it's just raw."

My face flushed red. I'd had my fair share of California rolls, and they looked nothing like that. Had I been mistaken? I gave an uneasy laugh, not able to stomach turning back again. "Oh yeah. Sushi."

I forced myself to look a final time, if only to set my mind at ease. The dish was covered again and Lexie, the smallest of the Sirens, doll-like and fragile, had turned to stare directly at me. I opened my mouth to challenge her, to ask her what she was looking at, but the look on her face stopped me dead. It was dull and blank and hungry. Her mouth hanging open in a small O.

Swallowing hard, I turned away.

Unnerved after the events at dinner and with Will still on my mind, I declined Cintia and Raj's invite to chill in the Aphrodite Lounge and headed back to my room. A cheesy rom-com and the chance to open the sharing bag of Maltesers I'd stashed in my suitcase was the key to improving my mood. Not to mention the opportunity to stare obstinately at my phone for as long as I wanted without being judged.

As I sloped down the familiar champagne-colored corridor,

my feet sinking into the plush carpet, I noticed the maid's trolley parked in our hall. These decks were like labyrinths, their passageways stretching the entire length of the ship. As I got closer, I realized the trolley was directly outside Will's room. Were they getting the room ready for his return? Was he back already? I sped up, my heart beating hard and hopeful.

Inside, two maids were busy stripping the sheets from his bed. The room itself was completely empty.

"Hey. Hey, *wait*!"

Both maids turned to look at me with large dark eyes. I faltered for a second.

"Wait—you can't do this. Where's all the stuff that was in this room? There's someone still in here—my friend—Will. Who told you to strip it?"

One of them shook her head and rattled off something to the other in what might have been Greek.

Ignoring them, I stepped into the room and looked around. *Everything of Will's was gone.*

It was indisputable. I'd spent hours in his bedroom back home, and he was *not* a tidy person. But there wasn't a single trace of him left here.

I thrust open the wardrobe. Empty; the hangers rattling together like bones.

I scanned the room once more, catching sight of a flash of brilliant fuchsia under the bed. Bending down, I grabbed at whatever it was. A delicate silk scarf adorned with white skulls. The same scarf Thalia had been wearing that first night in the Neptune Lounge.

"No one in here anymore," announced the other maid in careful English. "You speak to manager and he will tell you so."

"Yeah, I *will* speak to the manager. I mean, you shouldn't be moving his stuff without his permission. This is still his *room.* We're here for weeks."

The maid stared at me blankly, giving a slight shake of her head. "No. There is no one here anymore. Speak to manager. He will tell you."

Not knowing what else to do—it was hardly their fault—I gave up and stepped back into the hallway, then entered my own cabin and flopped down on the bed. Warily, I eyed the scarf in my hand. There was only one reason it would be in Will's room. The realization sent a sharp bolt of pain through my chest.

I raised it to my face and sniffed. It had an odd, musty smell to it. Like a stagnant pond. It reminded me of the smell in the captain's room. Was it just some general odor about the ship? But every time Thalia had wafted past me, I'd almost gagged on her perfume; something intense and floral.

On a whim, I logged back in to the ship's Wi-Fi and opened Instagram on my phone. After typing in @Sirens, I was immediately rewarded by a profile, the small circular picture showcasing the now familiar sight of all three of them decked out in carefully mismatched white swimwear, lounging on the deck of a yacht. By the looks of it, the account was a group effort—their personal brand.

I swiped through the rest of their photos.

It was exactly what I'd expected.

Endless shots of a lifestyle millions aspired to, but only one percent would ever live, all carefully passed through a filter of perfection. Here they were, laughing on beaches with powdered white sand. Shots of long, bronzed legs lying on loungers before indigo infinity pools. Action shots on Jet Skis. Shots of them on cobbled piazzas, dressed in broderie anglaise, weighed down by designer shopping bags. All accompanied by a thousand hashtags: #blessed #dreamlocation #wishyouwerehere #dreamlife. Thalia taking center stage in most of them.

So far, so predictable.

I scrolled back up to the more recent shots, taken aboard the *Eos*. There was a promo shot of them sipping champagne on the deck and fake laughing, all dressed in white. *The New Face of Nepenthe Cruises*—apparently. Were they here for free or had they been paid on top of their trip? Going by the *Eos*'s current clientele, it made sense why they were trying to give cruises a glow-up. Another of them, all wearing captain's hats, the captain himself in the middle of the trio, looking as if he couldn't believe his luck, and—*bingo*—some shots of them in the Neptune Lounge on that first night.

There was Thalia in her slinky black slip accessorized by the same bright pink scarf. Will was in the periphery of one of them, already looking worse for wear, his gaze unfocused. So was Con, standing beside Leda, an amusing annoyed expression on his face. The last couple of photos on their feed, oddly enough, were black squares, but captioned with the words #TheSeaProvides. Strange, but maybe they'd been tipsy and forgotten to turn on the flash. We'd all been there. I scrolled back, then zoomed in on Con again, spending a few guilty moments admiring how photogenic he was before tossing the phone aside.

Why *was* I so hung up on them?

So, Will had hooked up with Thalia, and she'd gone and left her scarf in his room. And okay, Will was sick—bad timing and generally crappy—but that was it.

As if to confirm this, my phone buzzed in my hand.

Will.

My fingers scrabbled to open the message.

> Sorry about earlier—phone's acting up. They've moved my stuff so I'm closer to the doctor. Want to keep an eye on me and all that. Feeling better, though! x

I exhaled slowly, leaning against the cabin wall in relief.

So, he *was* all right. I mean, obviously he was. People didn't just vanish on cruise ships. Well, not unless it was over the edge. Will had gotten sick, that was all. Con had mentioned earlier how mass outbreaks of diarrhea and vomiting were almost common on these kinds of ships, hence his dislike of buffets, so they were just taking extra precautions. Still, the tone was unusual—much more formal than Will's usual style of communication, with no abbreviations, full punctuation, and everything—and what was with the "x"?

Telling myself it must be a side effect of the medication he was on or something, I hunkered down into bed, put my phone on charge, and reached for the Maltesers.

10

THE ANNOYING JANGLE OF MY PHONE'S ALARM WOKE ME
sharply, pulling me from the drowning clutches of a nightmare
and beckoning me back into the warm nest of my bed. Already
the dream drifted away from me, vaporous and vague in the
gray dawn light that seeped under the door.

I sat up and yawned, the fierce growl of my stomach sternly
reminding me I needed breakfast. What was going on with
all these nightmares in the last couple of days? They were so
vivid—not to mention tiring. I self-diagnosed a combination
of stress and anxiety. Maybe I'd speak to Justin later—the ship's
doctor might be able to give me something for my newly discovered seasickness.

Opening my phone, I navigated to the orientation schedule
I'd saved earlier. SeaMester was due to meet for breakfast in
the Odysseus Room on Deck 6—a fancy expanse of wine-dark

carpet and expensive walnut tables that Justin assured us possessed a magnificent pancake station.

At the elevators, I paused to take a look at one of the many maps that were (necessarily) placed around the ship. My current location demarcated by the usual red stick figure.

YOU ARE HERE.

Was I, though?

So far, I'd felt only half here.

My worries for Will, the unpleasantness of the first evening, and my anxiety around making this trip work for me were beginning to crush any hope of actually having some fun on this ship.

I studied the map again. The Odysseus Room was two decks up from where I currently stood. Stifling a yawn. I summoned the elevator.

When it arrived, I was relieved to see it was empty, leaving me alone to enjoy the tinny steel-drum music echoing from hidden speakers. One of the challenges of the trip so far had been dealing with perkily inquisitive guests so early without the help of caffeine.

Moments later, I found myself in another anonymous corridor, this time carpeted in brash tiger stripes of red and blue. Its huge windows looked directly over the currently deserted swimming pool outside, sun beds stacked precariously around it like giant Jenga tiles. The sky overhead was vast and gray, a fierce wind whipping the closed umbrellas into mournful flight.

I padded down the silent corridor.

This deck appeared utterly devoid of passengers, which

struck me as strange, considering it was peak breakfast time. On my left were several of those brightly colored info boards that lined most of the main corridors—usually providing bland information on some aspect of cruising—how the ships were built, or a timeline showing how they evolved over the years. In this corridor, though, the boards were devoted to detailing marine life.

The first board caught my eye. It was a bright, garish graphic of Laila's beloved Humboldt squid. Also known as the "devil squid," as the board ghoulishly divulged. It was a revolting-looking thing, the same livid red as a raw burn, with a cruel-looking beak. A magnifying-glass icon depicted one of its tentacles in vivid detail—each and every sucker lined with tiny shark teeth, just as Laila had said. Not exactly the most visually appealing creature for a decorative board, but as I continued down the seemingly endless corridor, things got decidedly worse.

Next was a delightfully gruesome picture of a lamprey— a hideous, slimy eel-like creature—its monstrous maw ringed with countless rows of teeth. The boards continued in this vein for several yards; next was an unholy thing called a goblin shark—so ghoulish I half wondered if we had veered into the land of make-believe. It was a veritable hallway of horrors. I wondered if the designer of this corridor had won much subsequent work based on *this* charming portfolio.

Increasing my pace, I slipped through the door at the end. The space beyond was windowless and inevitably darker. It looked as if it was being used as a temporary hallway of some sort, although thankfully, it didn't appear to be dedicated to any more horror fish.

Blue-felt display boards stood in regimented zigzag lines, and on them were neatly pinned hundreds of pictures. They were all photos of passengers on the ship and available for purchase—no doubt some cynical marketing ploy for the older generation who didn't know how to work an iPhone.

Here was the glamorous coven of Sirens, all pulling practiced poses accessorized by blinding white smiles, designer sunnies obscuring their eyes. I grinned at a picture of a scowling Laila (giving perfect Wednesday Addams) and her parents—their heads unfortunately cut off by the photographer. And there—my heart gave a painful twinge—there were Will and I, both oblivious to the camera. Will grinning and pointing something out to me while I stood beside him, dozy and uncomfortable, caught in an unflattering half blink.

On the far wall of the mini gallery was a series of ornately framed photos of the other cruise ships owned by the same company as the *Eos*—Nepenthe, I recalled. A portrait of a handsome older man in a crisp white shirt took center stage, his sharp features and glittering eyes somehow familiar. *Christos Konstallis*. Maybe I'd seen him on TV or something. Beneath that were several pictures of past celebrations aboard the *Eos*, all under an ornate banner proclaiming *The Sea Provides*. Judging by the amount of champagne being sprayed in the photos and the way the guests were all dripping with diamonds, it certainly did.

I frowned and squinted a little harder at the left-most picture.

One of the guests at the forefront of the picture looked oddly familiar. Something in the gumminess of their smile, the distinctive wave to their silver hair.

Was that *Hilary,* the elderly lady who'd accosted me by the elevators the other day?

She looked much older, though, her face webbed with deep lines, a walker discarded by her chair.

Had she been ill at the time the picture was taken? Or could it be a relative—a sister or her mother? Even so, the resemblance was uncanny.

I glanced at the date on the photograph and snorted.

1997.

Okay, I was *definitely* reading too much into this.

The soft shuffle of footsteps on the carpet made me glance up.

Just someone passing by on the other side of the room, completely obscured by the felt display boards that divided it up, except for their feet—two people actually, judging by the brief glance I got between the gaps.

My stomach growled again, reminding me of the pancakes that awaited, so a minute or two later, I turned and followed the pair out of the gallery, exiting through the glass double doors into a long featureless corridor. This deck was a *warren.* The corridor was low lit and seemed rarely used, the wallpaper a dated textured gray. On one side, dark windows of smoky glass looked down into the inside of an empty auditorium, while the other was lined with anonymous numbered doors, all sensibly shut, except for one, which appeared to lead directly into a storage closet. Up ahead, an easel stood outside the auditorium entrance, displaying the details of the next conference.

#Goddess Vibes! Songs and stories from the Sirens—the new face of Nepenthe Cruises! 2 p.m. daily—featuring sea shanties from Thalia!

And, nearing the far end of the corridor, were the couple who'd passed by a minute ago.

I stopped dead.

There was something familiar about the taller of the pair, only their back visible at the end of the corridor. Something about the long, loping gait, the untidy tangle of short dark curls. They were wearing white—some kind of tunic by the looks of things.

Or—a hospital gown?

"W-Will . . . ?"

For a split second, both of them seemed to freeze. Then the taller of the two turned—only slightly and only for a moment—but I caught a familiar flash of vivid blue eyes set into a face much paler than I remembered.

"Will?"

And who was he with? Someone slight and dressed soberly in black, long dark hair trailing silkily down their back.

A name flashed before my eyes, a neon warning.

Octavia?

I rubbed my eyes. What the *hell.* If for some reason that *was*

Will, the person he was with could only be a nurse or member of the staff. Besides, whoever it was didn't turn around, but proceeded on, as if they hadn't heard me.

My heart thumping, I started after them. I'd only gotten a few steps when a loud bang behind me made me jump and whirl around.

The storage closet that had been open was now shut and, more than that, the corridor now seemed much brighter.

It took me a few seconds to realize that the sudden brightness was because the lights had been switched on in the neighboring auditorium. I whirled back around, looking for Will, but it was too late—both he and the woman with him had disappeared.

I glanced through the window, down into the lit theater again. Was that where the couple was headed? Okay, so, thinking about it, it was less and less likely to be Will—I mean, he was sick—infectious, even; why would he be headed to an empty theater? Still, if I got a proper look at whoever it was, then I could put the idea to bed.

Hurrying now, I raced to the end of the hall and slipped through the auditorium door.

I was standing at the very top of the theater, the velvet seats folded up in neat red crescents below me. The stage itself was brightly lit, illuminated by clam-shaped footlights, but the rest of the cavernous space was in deep shadow, only the pale green emergency lights, regularly interspersed along the walls, providing any light.

I skipped a few steps down. Two enormous columns of

gleaming black marble flanked the stage, fitting in nicely with the ship's Greek flavor. The scenery beyond had been painted to look like the sea. There was even a beach, and fishing boats bobbing in a bay. It was so quiet in here, the only sound the steady hum of the fluorescent lights below. I swallowed. *Why* exactly had I come in here again? No one was in here—let alone Will. Shaking my head, I turned back in the direction of the door.

And that was when all the lights went off.

Somehow, I resisted the urge to scream. My thoughts ticked along, reassuring me it was just whoever was backstage, finishing up whatever it was they'd come in here to do. I reminded myself that the lights had been off when I'd originally walked past. It was no big deal.

Then from somewhere close—too close—I heard an ungainly snort, as if someone had their hand crammed over their mouth, trying desperately not to laugh. Was someone hiding under the seats? Kids, maybe? Although other than Laila, I'd not seen many so far.

"W-Will . . . ? Is—is that you?"

With fumbling fingers, I reached for the flashlight on my phone, illuminating the central stairs ahead of me. For some reason, I had it in my head that it was highly important not to swing the light around, not to focus its bright white beam on the rows of empty seats. For some reason, I knew I shouldn't, *couldn't* do that.

Because what if they suddenly weren't empty anymore?

Helpfully my brain imagined row upon row of silent, white-masked figures, their eyes black and dispassionate, all staring at the stage.

Get a hold of yourself!

Forcing myself to take a deep breath and staring fixedly at the ground, I hurried back up toward the door I'd come in from. Grasping the smooth silver handle, I wrenched it back.

The door didn't budge.

Someone had locked it.

No.

Swallowing a moan, I wrenched the handle again and again, juddering the door violently in its frame, but it remained firmly shut. From somewhere far below, cutting clearly through the rattling I was making, came that same throaty laugh.

I whirled around, shining the flashlight in the direction of the stage. Of course, I couldn't make anything out—I was too far away. The stage was enveloped in perfect inky darkness. Forcing myself to breathe, to calm down, I tried to examine the situation logically. So, a member of the crew had walked past and locked the door—I supposed it shouldn't be open unless a show was on. There would be other doors, though, on the ground level of the auditorium, a busier deck than this one, so even if the doors *were* locked, someone would soon notice me—

A noise from the stage startled me. What sounded like a short, fast burst of footsteps. As if someone had run from one hiding place to another.

"Hey! Is someone there?" I said, my voice cracked and hopeful. "Hello?"

That same smothered laugh again. Was someone playing a crappy practical joke? Raj or Con, maybe?

"Hey—look—can you let me out of here? The door's locked."

More irritated than scared now, I walked down the stairs toward the stage, my flashlight bouncing off the velvet curtain, casting crazy patterns on the walls. That giggle again followed by something that made me freeze.

The singing was soft at first, just words whispered beneath the breath, the voice girlish and high.

> *The sea it sways, it sways and churns,*
> *The pact is made, they never learn,*
> *That once the ink dries upon the page,*
> *They're given to the ocean's rage.*

It *sounded* exactly like something Thalia would sing. Was it her? Part of me relaxed a little.

"Hello?" I called out, bolder now. "Thalia? Look, do you know where the light switch is? It's kind of dark in here."

The singing stopped immediately, as if a radio had abruptly switched stations, the air now filled with static uncertainty. I took a few steps closer to where I'd heard the singing.

"Thalia?"

This time, the words weren't sung but *hissed*. And much closer now, *dangerously* close; low and insistent and poisonous.

The ship it sways, it sways and lists,
A boy unloved, a girl unkissed,
Drawn like flame by darker songs,
They hit the rocks
And then are gone. . . .

I recalled the board outside the conference hall. *Sea shanties.* That was what they were. But this voice was different from Thalia's. Harsh and shrill, entirely lacking in her gentle fragility, almost mocking.

I forced myself to speak, my voice thin and wavering and so very *un*-brave.

"Look, you sound great and everything, but uh, can you help me find the lights or . . . ?"

The footsteps came swift and determined, striding across the stage and hurrying down the steps toward me. Before I could move away, two hands clad in black rubber-like gloves clamped hard about my wrists, causing my phone to tumble to the floor, its light illuminating something I did *not* want to see.

A masked face was pushed close against mine; moon-white and chalky; its eyes huge black holes, the mouth wide and downturned in a rictus of tragedy. I screamed in shock as whoever it was began to whisper raggedly in my ear, their breath cold and fetid. It carried the same disgusting stench as in the captain's room. Filthy water, long hidden from the light.

You sail upon a ship of fools, drifting blindly into
Charybdis.

The voice was ugly and abrasive, like something lying rusting on the ocean floor. The sound unwillingly drawing me back to my first night here. Will but somehow *not* Will. Sitting in that chair, frigid and dripping.

Heart pounding painfully, I tried to twist away, but their grip was impossibly strong.

"Get *off* of me!"

> *And there is no Orpheus to save you. The sea provides*
> *but only if you feed it. Seven is the bargain and seven*
> *have been promised. The ocean is dark and deep and*
> *keeps its secrets.*

A gurgled laugh followed before the grip loosened on my wrists and I was able to break away, my breathing harsh and hollow. My desperate hands found my phone, and I frantically swung my flashlight up and around—but whoever the masked figure was, they were gone now, vanished as quickly as they had come. Chest heaving, I stumbled along the bottom of the stage until I met the wall. Up ahead, I saw a faint glimmer of light beneath a door. I staggered toward it, my hand closing around the handle, and—heart hammering—opened it, terrified of what I might see beyond.

I was backstage.

The area was crammed with a multitude of random props and staging. There was a makeshift balcony painted with pink roses for a cruise-ship Juliet. A ratty-looking bear suit hung mournfully from a hook and a circus podium stood in the center, painted crimson and white.

A few feet away, a discarded porcelain mask lay on the floor on top of a black cloak, the exact mask that had been leering in my face minutes earlier, now cast aside, its wearer gone. I'd seen that kind of mask before, recognized it from history books and from the theater department back at school when Mr. Bennet staged his highly unpopular Greek tragedies. I forced myself to take several deep, grounding breaths.

Then a low voice spoke into the gloom, and I smothered my shriek with a shaking hand.

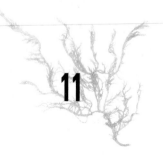

11

"HEY—YOU OKAY? YOU LOOK A LITTLE SHAKEN UP."

Standing in front of me was a guy. Not much older than me, athletic and tan with the bland good looks of a boy-band member. I stared at him.

Had it been him?

I nodded toward the mask and cloak, lying discarded on the floor like a flattened body, my breath shaky.

"Hey—did you see—was that . . . ?"

He followed my stare. "What happened? I heard footsteps a second ago—someone give you a scare out there?"

Thoughts collided in my mind like a demented kaleidoscope. *Had* I ever even seen Will? Had someone lured me in here? Was I seeing things? Was I sick too? Had I caught what he had? Was I feverish? Hallucinating?

I cleared my throat.

"Yeah, um, someone was out there. You didn't see anyone pass through just now? Someone wearing that—that mask or one like it."

The man gave a short shake of his head.

"Nope, not through here. Kinda glad I didn't, going by how spooked you look. Although, it's not exactly surprising given *this* ship, right?"

Fear trickled down my spine, and my stomach flopped heavily over. I narrowed my eyes.

"Wait—what do you mean? What's wrong with this ship?"

I took a closer look at him. He was dressed incongruously with the drab surroundings, in a smooth black velvet dinner jacket, and held a top hat in one hand, a wand in the other. A series of colored handkerchiefs trailed from the hat like wilted flowers.

A magician.

He shrugged and held out his hand. "I don't know, really— I mean, don't you think this place has a weird vibe? Apollo, by the way. I'm part of the entertainment."

I took it, giving it a weak shake. "Apollo, hey? How . . . on theme. Liv. Someone—someone threatened me out there. They—they were dressed all in black and had a mask—exactly like *that* mask."

The magician wrinkled his nose in distaste. "Stage name— and they were probably just some overeager actor. These places are full of theater school dropouts. Honestly, I try to avoid work on cruises when I can—they tend to be packed with crazies." He paused for a moment, a bleak look in his eyes. "Only took this gig at short notice because it seemed like some kind of divine intervention."

I debated whether to stay and listen, still unsure if he was my assailant or not, but he continued regardless.

"Yeah—the good ship *Eos*. It's the same ship Dahlia was on."

He glanced about, as if checking we were completely alone—then dug out his phone. Moments later, he held it up, revealing a picture of a cheerful-looking blond girl. The family resemblance was immediate and undeniable. The girl wore a short, shimmering turquoise dress and had a bronzed arm wrapped around Thalia, of all people. Behind them, the sea twinkled merrily.

"My sister—she works these cruises as a dancer. Only last month she went missing. Didn't disembark where we'd agreed to meet. I waited for a day or so before I contacted the ship and when I did, they said they had no record of her ever being on board. But she sent me this photo with one of those Siren girls—she's obsessed with influencers, you know. It's proof they're wrong, right? And it's the last thing I have of her. You—you haven't seen her here, by any chance?"

That churning feeling in my stomach tightened. I shook my head.

"No—sorry. Wait—so what happened? Do you think Thalia—the other girl in the photo—was involved somehow?"

He gave a surprised laugh. "What, *her*? No—of course not. But she clearly knew my sister, at least well enough to pose for a photo together. I've been trying for a while to get work on one of these Siren cruises—y'know, ask a few questions, see if anyone remembers her or what she was planning on doing next. It's been pretty tough—seems like the Nepenthe group has a pretty loyal staff—but luckily, I got this job last minute. I'm hoping that she, or someone around here, might be able to at least answer a few of my questions. Dahlia's always been kinda flighty. Y'know, only last year she moved to Dubai for six months with some guy she'd met on another ship and known for all of five minutes. . . ."

As Apollo went on, I debated whether or not to confide in him about Will. About how he was last seen talking to the very same girl before *he* disappeared.

A coincidence—or something more sinister?

I ran a hand over my face. Down here, it was uncomfortably sweaty and humid, as if the heat had been turned up way too high.

No, Liv. No, this is not similar at all—Will's sick. He hasn't disappeared.

Apollo turned away from me to fiddle with an enormous glass tank behind me. Part of his act, no doubt.

"Anyway, hon, I better get on. It's curtains for me if I don't get this act right. Literally. Maybe I'll catch you at the show tonight, huh?"

I muttered a vague assent in return and left. The door to the main corridor was directly behind me, unlocked and waiting.

* * *

The same guy's picture—with added megawatt smile—was on a large board directly outside the Odysseus Room, a golden cloak billowing out behind him.

THE AMAZING APOLLO! LIVE! TONIGHT AT 7:00 P.M.

I wandered through the doors in a daze, mumbling my cabin number to the staff member on duty. SeaMester had already finished eating by the time I sat down with nothing but a giant mug of coffee, my appetite entirely gone.

"Not hungry?" remarked Justin, easygoing demeanor locked firmly back in place this morning.

"No, actually," I began, the shock of what had happened sinking in and making me feel horribly breathless. A glance around at the serenity of the table forced me to downplay it. "Not to be dramatic, but someone dressed up in a creepy costume just chased me through a deserted auditorium." I gave a shaky laugh. "Not Halloween yet, right?"

Across from me, Adora nearly spat out her chai latte.

"I'm sorry, what?"

I ignored the amusement in her voice. Justin looked concerned. His brow furrowed, his mouth a firm line.

"Hey, wait—someone *chased* you? Seriously? Liv, what happened?"

So I explained, as comprehensively as I could, leaving out most of the weird stuff they'd spouted at me. I could barely remember it now anyway.

Justin gave a grim nod. "It's more than likely bored kids.

Some parents need to take a little more responsibility on trips like this."

Bored kids didn't whisper about Greek mythology, and the grip on my wrist had been firmer than any child's. But I ran a shaking hand through my hair and agreed, not wanting to discuss the matter any further in front of the group.

"Shit, Liv," said Cintia. "What a crappy morning. Was your evening any better? We missed you in the lounge last night."

Cintia's warm smile helped me come back to earth a little.

"I was still dead from the night before. Went to bed with a cup of tea and *Gilmore Girls* reruns."

She chuckled. "I swear you're my grandma, come here in disguise to keep an eye on me."

Justin gave me another wary look and then addressed the table.

"So, you'll be pleased to hear we have our next orientation activity this evening. I've gotten us all tickets to the main show in the theater tonight. Pretty awesome, huh? These things book up fast."

Constantine shot Justin an incredulous look from across the table.

"You do realize it's a magician? In common parlance, a children's entertainer."

Cintia shrugged, the only person in our group to be continually unmoved by Con's icy disdain. "So what? Maybe if you took that stick out of your ass, you might have some fun. Besides, what else is there to do—drink the bar dry yet again?"

After the others had sloped off, I awkwardly asked Justin if we could speak in his cabin. I didn't want him to get the impression I was flaky or prone to dramatics, but how else could I get across that niggling feeling that something was *wrong*?

And was it? Was I simply overtired? Or did I have some insidious sickness? Should I be quarantined too? I mean, at the very least I'd be with Will.

Deep in thought, I jumped slightly as Justin opened the door and ushered me in, gesturing for me to sit on the armchair, identical to the one in my own cabin.

The one I'd seen drowned Will sitting in only the other night.

I pushed my hair behind my ear, forcing those thoughts away, and gave Justin a tight smile. Nothing to see here. Everything was perfectly fine.

"So, Liv. How *are* you feeling?"

His voice was soft and sympathetic, his warm brown eyes concerned. Not a sign of the tetchy, on-edge Justin of the other night.

"Uh, fine. I mean, I guess it must have been bored kids messing about, like you said. Not that this ship is boring or anything, but . . ."

Justin leaned against the wall, arms folded, and tilted his head, the poster boy for caring counselors.

"You look exhausted. Are you sleeping properly? I was considering whether or not to call your parents."

I looked at him in alarm. The last thing I wanted was for

my parents to start worrying about me after only the second day of the trip, alone and unreachable in the middle of the Atlantic.

"What—why? About what? I said I'm fine."

Justin steepled his fingers, his overly sympathetic look starting to grate.

"You don't *look* fine, though. Forgive me for being blunt, but you look a little . . . strung out."

I stared at him, now unsure of my next move. But if I could trust anyone, surely it would be Justin.

"Look, it's Will," I confessed with a deep, gulping breath. "Him being sick has really . . . thrown me off . . . I mean, honestly, he's like a brother to me and all of a sudden he's just—just *gone*. I mean, one moment he was *there* and the next . . ."

Justin nodded as if he'd suspected this all along.

"It must be tough."

"So when will I be able to see him? If I could just *see* him, then—"

A shadow fell across Justin's face, immediately hardening it again.

"Liv, the doctors know best. We have to trust in them. Besides, nothing's stopping you guys from texting each other—or talking on the phone?"

But his messages don't sound *like him. I have a thousand messages from him on my phone containing every stupid emoji and gif under the sun, but nothing he has sent me since he got sick even remotely sounds like him.*

I grit my teeth. "He—uh—he won't pick up."

Justin nodded sagely, as if he suddenly understood everything.

"Ah. Some of the others mentioned you two had a fight the other night. So, maybe some space is exactly what you guys need, right?"

I exhaled slowly, glancing about the room, trying to rein in my mounting frustration. Above the desk, where the TV was in my room, was an ornately framed map just like the one I'd seen in the captain's cabin, detailing the ship's route across the Atlantic. At the memory, an image leaped into my mind: the creature thumping in the captain's fish tank; the dank, musty smell.

But what about my nightmares, Justin? What about all the weird shit that happened to me this morning that you've conveniently brushed off as "just kids"? What about what they said—about bargains made—

Where is *Will?*

I chewed the inside of my cheek. Justin was right. My anxiety around Will, coupled with the fact that I was alone, in a completely unknown environment, was just manifesting in strange ways.

Justin patted my shoulder awkwardly. Playing his pleasant-camp-counselor role again now that he was confident he had solved all my problems.

"Look, if you jot down the details of what happened this morning, I'll make an official complaint on behalf of Sea-Mester. Other than that, keep your chin up, Liv! I know this is a great opportunity, but it's also a lot—particularly for someone from your background. Once the first week's over and we get into the coursework and day trips, it'll be a whole different story, I promise you."

I could only stare at him. My *background*. Wow. Was I really so different from everyone else?

Justin continued babbling on, his expression sunny, as if glad to be done with me, directing me toward the door.

"When I get an update from the doctor today, I'll ask if he can have visitors yet—and as soon as I get the okay, you'll be the first to know."

Justin opened the door, once more placing a reassuring hand on my shoulder. "He's in the best possible hands, Liv. Try to understand that and take some time to relax—that's an order. And I'll see you at the show tonight."

12

WE COULD HEAR THE WHOOPING A DECK AWAY, AS
SeaMester—minus Will and also Con, who apparently couldn't
be bothered to come—all shuffled dutifully into the main theater minutes before the show began. As we clambered past
large groups of chattering women—all decked out in sequins
and expensive highlights—to our seats, I was surprised to see
the place was practically full. Dramatic music played in a loop
in the background while we all stared expectantly at the lowered velvet curtain before us, the logo of the *Eos*—an oceanic
horizon with a black sun rising from it—projected onto it.
After what seemed like hours, the sound of a drumroll rumbled
through the auditorium.

"Ladies and gentlemen," boomed a loud, disembodied voice.
"Prepare yourselves for a night of mystery and magic. From
beyond Atlantis, from the very heights of Mount Olympus, the

Eos is proud to present to you the Amazing Apollo, master of magic and mayhem."

The cringe was real. Constantine had been right. I shot a despairing look at Cintia, but she only laughed.

The first part of the act was mildly diverting. Apollo wandered around the aisles, charming his audience by pulling bunches of silk flowers out of various orifices and performing a few card tricks. I'd never seen the appeal of close-up magic myself. It was possibly one of the most boring things I could ever imagine watching. So, you found my card . . . *amazing*. I made sure to turn my eyes down every time I felt him scanning the audience like a prison searchlight, looking for his next victim. He was loud and bombastic, winning over the older generation with wince-inducing flirting and jokes even Raj would think twice about repeating.

After a while, he retreated back to the stage.

"My next trick is a classic—not to mention thematically in line with the ship."

Cintia nudged me excitedly, and I rallied a grin as the large tank I'd seen him fiddling with earlier was wheeled out onstage, now filled to the brim with briny, green water. A large hollow formed in my stomach. I'd never enjoyed watching these Houdini-like escape stunts, even on TV. All they did was ramp up my anxiety to unbearable levels. I cast a quick glance at the exit, wondering if there was a way I could politely leave without annoying the group.

"Didn't someone try this kind of thing on that dreadful talent show recently and actually *drown*?" Adora remarked airily.

Meanwhile, onstage, Apollo was still droning on about all the (failed) previous attempts by other magicians to do this horrendously difficult trick.

"Whoa, hold up," whispered Cintia. "Magician boy's about to strip for us."

Clearly, I had not been with a guy for far too long, as I discovered myself thinking that he did look aesthetically pleasing in his shiny gold trunks. Beside me, Cintia was doubled over, wheezing with laughter.

"Now, before I attempt my daring escape," boomed Apollo, "I have a special guest to introduce tonight. The wonderful Thalia de Staunton will be singing for your entertainment while I escape the tank."

There came an explosive round of applause as Thalia slunk onto the stage in an exquisite fishtail gown of sea-green sequins, luminous in the soft stage lights, that clung to her like a glove. For a guilty moment, I was glad Con hadn't come tonight.

Raising a microphone to her lips, Thalia steadied herself and began to sing. I'd been impressed by her voice the first time I heard it, but now, in the sublime acoustics of the theater, it was utterly unearthly, making me surer than ever it hadn't been her lurking about under the stage this morning. Smooth and lilting and true; bathing the room in its own deep light, rippling like waves across the walls. Like before, I didn't recognize the song; I didn't need to. Her voice floated around the dark space, every word mournful and steeped in longing.

While she sang, Apollo—now chained up and straitjacketed—was lowered into the pool. Though the first part of the evening had been decidedly pedestrian, *this* was something else. Beside me, Cintia shifted uncomfortably in her seat, drawn forward as if physically lured by Thalia's voice, while on the other side, tears streamed down Adora's face.

I felt a brief pang of sympathy for Apollo as he struggled away in the tank. It seemed as if the entire audience was now focused on Thalia rather than him. How had she lost whatever competition she had been in? However unlikable I found her, there was no denying her talent.

Listening to Thalia's fluting voice, the whole auditorium seemed under a spell. So much so that when a man in the front row stood and shouted, it was several long seconds before anyone, including myself, even reacted.

"Seriously—is he okay?" repeated the man urgently.

With a sick feeling of foreboding, I wrenched my attention away from Thalia and back to Apollo.

He'd managed to get out of the straitjacket (to not a single smatter of applause) but seemed to be having trouble unlocking the chains that were clasped around his ankles and preventing him from floating up to the top of the tank. Before, his movements had been smooth and practiced, but now he seemed frantic, his actions jerky and desperate.

Thalia, oblivious to the murmurings in the audience and the struggling beside her, sang on, as if determined to draw the song to its natural conclusion even as the shouting and commotion in the front rows grew louder and louder. I watched, dry mouthed, as Apollo banged fruitlessly on the wall of the tank, the sound not even registering above Thalia's amplified voice.

I stared, not wanting to see, but unable to tear my gaze away as several people in the front row jumped onto the stage and began attempting to shove the tank over.

One of them, a gray-haired man wearing a baseball cap, strode over to Thalia and wrenched away her microphone.

"Hey, are there any doctors in here? We've got a man drowning, can't you *see*?" I expected a look of shock or realization on Thalia's face but was unnerved to see she was *enraged*. Her face was chalk white, her dark eyes glaring fiercely at the man who'd taken the mic.

An enormous crash announced the tank finally tipping over, drenching Thalia's fancy dress with a torrent of water. She gasped, muttering something harsh under her breath, then stormed off the stage, not even bothering to look back at Apollo, lying stricken on the floor, a fallen hero smote by the gods.

I blinked, still unable to speak, as people around me began to get up, quickly ushered out of the auditorium by pale-faced staff.

"Is he okay?" Cintia murmured, her face a mask of shock, as we obediently traipsed out of the theater. I snuck another look at the stage. Several staff members were now crowded over Apollo, as if trying to block his body from view. Thalia had rejoined them, crouching over the fallen magician, her shimmering green dress giving her the appearance of a snake about to strike. A broad, tanned arm hung limply over the edge of the stage. I shuddered.

"God, I don't know," I replied. "But I hope so."

13

WE ALL FILED OUT OF THE AUDITORIUM IN A STUNNED daze, the horror of what had happened coursing through my veins and leaving me barely able to speak. Ahead of me, I watched Cintia rest her head on Raj's shoulder; saw him put an enormous, reassuring arm around her. I'd be pleased for her—if I hadn't just spent ten minutes watching a man potentially *drown*.

Unsettled and still consumed by thoughts of Will, I drifted to the Athene Lounge in a daze, hoping a hot chocolate might settle my nerves.

I couldn't lie—as I stood in the dwindling line, I was pleased to see Con sitting at a table in the corner, deeply absorbed in a book, and even more pleased to see that he was alone. I perched opposite him on the aesthetically beat-up leather sofa. Outside the window, the night was dark. The sea and the sky one immense black morass. My reflection was doll-like in the lights. Wide green eyes; pale freckled face framed with sleek dark hair. Con raised an eyebrow, glancing at my marshmallow-laden drink with vague disdain.

"You look even paler than usual. Is it Will?"

Shaking my head, I gave him the rundown of what had just happened in the show. Con smirked.

"Jesus—sounds like it actually might have been worth a watch."

"Seriously, Con? The guy might be dead!" I took a deep breath, adrenaline continuing to course through me like haywire electricity. "This *ship* . . . Fair enough, I'm not exactly familiar with cruises, but something seems off. I mean, take Will. Don't you think it's *weird* we can't see him at all—and—and why isn't he answering his phone?"

He shrugged. "Come on. This ship is safer than most. It was probably all an act—give the audience something to write home about, you know?"

I shot him a sideways look, annoyed at his endless minimizing. How much *could* I confide in him? There was every chance he would go directly back to Raj's room after this and spend the whole night laughing about crazy old Liv. But I was tired and on edge and needed to vent. Justin hadn't listened; maybe Con would.

"And there's something else," I continued. "This morning when I got chased through that auditorium, whoever it was started spouting all this crazy stuff about Orpheus—and—

and—bargains—and the sea providing if there were seven. It was *weird*."

At that last part, Con frowned. I glanced down at the book he'd been reading, now lying facedown on the coffee table. A fancy clothbound edition of Homer's *Odyssey*.

"Well, I can't exactly argue with you there," he said mildly. "That does sound weird."

But he wasn't looking at me with the concern I'd hoped; he was only half listening, picking up his book again. Usually, I'd avoid guys like him, but here, on this microcosm of a ship, I felt drawn to him. Where I would have felt intimidated by him in everyday life, here, marooned aboard the *Eos,* we were somehow the same. And now it was time for me to play my ace. I leaned forward.

"Look, you can keep brushing me off as much as you like, but from what *I* hear, you might know more than most about what's going on here? Your dad has some link to this company—the one that owns the *Eos,* right? I mean, imagine Will *is* actually in trouble—health-wise or not—imagine he *dies*—and this gets out? Hope this ship's ready for a PR disaster of epic proportions."

To his credit, he put his book back down and at least seemed to think about this.

"Fine, I'm listening, but you have to admit there's no evidence that Will is in any danger or that the staff has done anything but act in his—not to mention everyone else's—best interests. If he's infectious, then he needs to be kept away from others until he isn't."

I sipped my drink, the velvety sweetness instantly relaxing me. Of course he was right.

If Will was infectious—bleak thoughts of cholera and Ebola crossed my mind—then yes, he should be quarantined. The fact that he hadn't texted me much was neither here nor there. And I had no idea exactly how ill he was because—according to the ship—I wasn't family and it was none of my business.

But Justin knew.

There were probably certain rules around confidentiality to follow. So long as Will's dad had been informed, then surely it was all aboveboard.

I rubbed my hands over my eyes, suddenly exhausted.

"*Fine,* but I hope someone on this ship's currently checking out the small print on the insurance regarding the accidental deaths of entertainers." I shot him a resentful glare, which he studiously ignored. In the following silence, my thoughts circled back to the Amazing Apollo. When we'd talked, he'd said he'd been searching for his sister. His sister who had supposedly disappeared and was last seen with—

Enough with the endless conspiracy theories. Even I was fed up, and Constantine had made me feel small enough for one night. Seemingly picking up on this, he set down his book once more and turned to look at me properly, his moon-colored eyes soft.

"In all seriousness, you don't seem to be having the best time. It must be hard for you, being here without Will."

Here he went again with the condescension. The implication being that all the others had arrived on their own and weren't stage 4 clingers like me. But at the same time, wasn't he right? I *was* letting Will's situation completely ruin my own experience. Would Will be acting the same if the roles were reversed and *I* were the sick one? It was something I tried not to think too much about, because I wasn't sure of the answer.

"Yeah, well, like I said . . . it's not just about Will."

Con shrugged and stood, collecting his coat from the back of his chair.

"Look, if you still haven't heard from him in a day or so, I'll see if I can pull some strings if it'll help put your mind at rest. Until then, try to enjoy yourself, yeah?"

Pull some strings? Exactly how closely *was* he linked to this cruise? However, that wasn't important right now. I looked at him, hope blossoming brightly in my chest.

"Wait—you can really do that?"

He nodded, stifling a yawn and reaching down to collect his book. "You'd be surprised." He hesitated before leaving, casting a thoughtful look back at me. "Look, if you want to . . . let's get together in the morning and talk some more?" Despite him making it sound like he was arranging a business meeting, I didn't exactly have much else going on at the moment. So, I smiled.

"Yeah, I'd like that—thanks."

Even with the troubling events of the evening, I slept well that night out of pure exhaustion; a heavy, obliterating type of sleep, but refreshingly nightmare free. And as I luxuriated in bed the next morning, still in a blissful state of semiconsciousness, my phone chimed. I scrambled to pick it up, praying it was Will. It now felt like weeks since I'd last heard from him. It was as if he'd dropped off the face of the earth.

Or off the side of the ship . . .

I buried the thought, reminding myself he'd answered his phone yesterday—I'd heard his actual voice. No doubt he'd been delightfully high on a cocktail of fancy drugs and didn't need me constantly bugging him.

Disappointingly, the message was from Hilary, the old lady I'd met the other day, reminding me of my promise to play bingo with her. Our cabins were located down the same corridor, and I'd had to give up my number after she'd cornered me in an elevator yesterday. I gave a loud groan. I had a few hours to kill before I met Con later that morning. What else did I have to do?

Hilary was waiting for me in the bingo lounge, looking more glamorous than ever in a shimmering turquoise caftan, silver charms dangling from her wrists.

"Here, my love, I got you a dabber. What's wrong? You look a little pale, dear. Seasickness starting to play up again, is it?"

Where to *start*, I thought grimly, accepting the pen and pulling my card toward me.

"Yeah, the ship is a bit . . . roll-y today, isn't it?" I answered weakly.

In front of us, Bingo Bob, who was probably visible in the dark thanks to the alarming fluorescence of his fake tan, began rattling off numbers. The numbers on the card swam in front of my eyes.

"How much do I owe you?" I asked, remembering nothing on this bloody boat came for free. SeaMester provided us with a small monthly allowance, but I doubted it extended to bingo.

Hilary waved me away. "Don't be silly. I'm just grateful a glamorous youngster like yourself is keeping an old fuddy-duddy like me company. It's all bloody couples on this boat, isn't it? If I'd known it would be a love ship, I wouldn't have bothered coming. Just makes me miss my old Phil, you see. He was a good 'un. Dreadful complainer, though. You name it, he'd bloody whine about it. . . ."

She shook her head, her eyes closed in disdain. I smiled a little.

"Well, none of us are couples, so you're welcome to come and hang with SeaMester, if you want," I said, half listening.

I let her words wash over me like a warm tide, happy to let her chatter away as I dabbed off random numbers. Her soft East London accent sinking me into a bath of soothing normality. I'd decided cruise ships were just one of those places that were creepy by default. Like off-season hotels. All those dark endless hallways and cavernous empty ballrooms.

"And that was when we pushed him over the side."

I stopped, mid-dab, and stared directly up at Hilary.

I must have misheard.

"Sorry, you *what*?"

She was staring back at me with her round, rheumy blue

eyes that were empty of emotion. Almost challenging me to speak, her thin lips quirked in a gummy pink smile, her lipstick an aggressive slash of blood-red.

Behind us, Bingo Bob babbled on.

"Two little ducks—twenty-two!"

"So many go missing on cruises you know, dear. There's not much anyone can do about it either. Can't dredge the entire Atlantic now, can they?"

The ocean seemed to roar loudly in my head. I grabbed the underside of the velvet seating to anchor myself.

"Sorry, what . . . ? Say again—I—I missed the start of what you were saying?"

Her expression relaxed again as she gave a sympathetic nod of her head.

"I know—it's so loud in here, isn't it? I need to turn my blimmin' hearing aid down. I was talking about Phil. How he used to love bingo. You know, his favorite call was—"

"No—no, sorry. You said something about—about people going missing on cruises. That bit. What do you mean? What—what happened to Phil?"

Hilary patted my hand with hers.

"Don't be silly, my dear, I shouldn't bore you about my Phil. You don't want to hear all that. You look tired, my love. Are you getting enough sleep?"

No, as a matter of fact, I definitely was *not*.

Okay, fine, so I'd misheard. Not exactly difficult with good old Bob shouting increasingly random phrases in the background. But a stubborn part of my brain was insisting I *hadn't*.

Was she messing with me? Being old didn't make you devoid of a sense of humor—however bizarre it might be.

A cloud must have passed over the weak autumn sun because at that moment the whole lounge seemed to darken; shadows lengthening, stretching out from the corners of the vast space. Hilary continued staring intently down at her paper. Eerily silent now. Her dabber clutched so tightly in her hand, her knuckles were white.

I glanced around me at the rest of the lounge, so *dark* now, heads all bent, staring fixedly down at cards. How could they even see the numbers? Why were the lights so low? Hilary unexpectedly caught my eye, red lips bared over her yellowed teeth, a sneer rather than a smile.

And suddenly, I didn't want to be there any longer.

"Hey, sorry. I've just remembered I've got a—er—meeting with my tutor. Here—here you keep going, though. . . ."

I thrust my card in her direction and left the lounge, unable to sit in the semidarkness with her anymore.

I pictured Will listening to my wild flights of fancy. That patient but amused look upon his face, waiting until he'd heard everything before teasing me gently about the other occasions I'd let my imagination slip away unchecked.

There was that time in Year 7, when we'd drawn a Ouija board in chalk on the school playground in a moment of extreme boredom and I'd become convinced old cracks in the asphalt were the sign of some demon we'd inadvertently summoned, rising from the deep. Or that time we'd gone on a weekend trip with school to some spooky old house in the middle of the French countryside and I'd been convinced someone was creeping up the stairs from the basement every night. Even now, I maintain I *did* hear those stairs creaking, but Will had his ever-logical explanations about expanding pipes.

But now I'd been left alone with the horrors of my over-active imagination and no Will to explain things away.

Disquieted, I took the elevator up to Deck 4. As I walked into the Athene Lounge, Con called my name. He was sitting alone at one of the small tables facing the sea, an expensive MacBook before him. As I approached, I watched him hastily click out of his browser but not before I'd caught sight of the search results.

Disappearance on Ithaca.

My eyes narrowed. *Ithaca?* Was that another cruise ship? And why was Con researching disappearances on it?

Con smiled at me as I slumped into the seat opposite, far cheerier than normal. Definitely overcompensating for something.

"How's your morning been? Enjoy bingo? Any plans—things you want to do?"

I tossed my phone onto the table in frustration, the lock screen obstinately empty of messages.

"What do you think?" I asked bitterly. "And my *plan* is to try to see Will. It's been nearly two days since I heard from him now. If I can just *see* him—know for certain that he's all right—then—then maybe I can finally start to enjoy this trip."

"I *could* say something about why your happiness is so tied to his—but I won't," he mused, giving me a tight sideways smirk. "But I've been thinking about what you said last night, and while I don't totally agree with you, you're right. I do have a vested interest in what's going on aboard this ship. . . ."

My hopes rose. I debated whether to tell Con about my strange encounter with Hilary but decided against it. The room had been noisy and she was old—maybe she'd gotten a bit confused.

His grin widened. "Plus, I'm *insanely* bored and find your elaborate conspiracy theories vastly entertaining."

I flushed a little, my stomach doing a mini-flip at the prospect of spending more time with Con. While I tried in vain to think of a suitable snarky comeback, a steward strolled through the center of the lounge, slowly pushing a golden trolley piled high with luggage. Something bright and familiar caught my eye among the bags. Squinting, I realized it was one of the fluorescent gaming stickers that Will had plastered all over his battered gray suitcase. I half stood to get a better look.

In fact, I was 99.8 percent sure that *was* Will's suitcase.

Where were they taking it?

I clutched Con's arm across the table. "Hey—*hey*—look, that's Will's!"

Con followed my gaze in the direction of the trolley, clearly annoyed at having been cut off. "So? That's good, isn't it? They're probably just taking his stuff to him."

I nodded furiously, my eyes never leaving the steward's retreating figure. "*Exactly!* So if we follow them, we can find out where he is! Come on."

Con gave a drawn-out sigh. "But we already *know* where he is, Liv—the infirmary."

But I wasn't listening anymore. Grabbing my backpack, I hurriedly got up and followed the trolley down the corridor, Con tailing reluctantly behind me.

The steward stopped at the elevator foyer and I hung back. If my gut instinct was correct, if something shifty was happening on this ship, it wouldn't be wise to draw too much attention to myself. As the elevator doors shut, I watched the old-fashioned dial above it count down the floors.

Deck 12.

The lowest of the decks available to passengers. Jabbing the button of the adjacent elevator, I waited.

14

THE ELEVATOR ARRIVED MOMENTS LATER, AND CON BUN-dled in beside me.

"The infirmary's not on Deck Twelve," I remarked in a triumphant stage whisper, once the doors had firmly shut. "I looked for it on the maps earlier. It's on Deck Eight."

Con rolled his eyes.

"You know, when I asked you what your plans were, you never mentioned this Scooby-Doo shit."

I'd already worked out the algorithm; the lower the deck, the creepier. Darker and more cramped than the bright upper decks; the corridors narrower and less populated, closer to the incessant primal roar of the ship's engines.

Eventually, the elevator doors opened onto a silent, empty passage, much gloomier than the floors above sea level, the ceiling much lower. The carpet and walls were identical, the sickly pink of cocktail sauce, while the arrow-shaped signs on the wall demarcated nothing but cabin numbers.

"Let's split up," I murmured. "That way, we won't miss him. We can meet back here in a few minutes."

After a few false turns, I discovered the steward and the gold trolley disappearing behind a set of double doors bearing the warning *Staff Only* at the very end of the corridor.

Feeling increasingly stupid, I crept up to the doors and peered through a circular window.

The room beyond was vast and gray and windowless, a kind of industrial basement, lit brightly by utilitarian fluorescent lights. A sickly sweet smell drifted out from under the doors. Enormous multicolored bins stood in regimented lines, and at the end of one row, beside a pile of broken-up cardboard boxes, sat Will's case.

It was unmistakably his.

A battered gray shell plastered with bright stickers. Carefully, I pushed open the doors and crept in. The room appeared to be a giant waste disposal. My hands shook as I unzipped the case, already feeling sick and hopeless at the sheer weight of it.

Everything was in there.

All his clothes, a gray geometric wash bag full of toiletries—including toothpaste and his brush—the wax his hair always smelled of, a couple of well-thumbed graphic novels, a tangle of chargers. I choked back a sob at the sight of Sad Bear, a ragged old one-eyed thing that Will had carried around since he was a kid and apparently still did.

What the hell was his suitcase doing down here, discarded

beside the bins like trash? Surely he needed it, wherever he was. A surge of helplessness filled my heart. There must have been some kind of mistake. Was the suitcase supposed to have been delivered to the infirmary, and ended up down here by accident? Maybe I could have believed that, satisfied myself with that explanation and boldly taken it back to my room—if it hadn't been for his weird messages, that strange encounter—

What *was* going on, on this bloody ship? And more importantly, where was Will?

For the past day or so, I'd managed to convince myself I was overreacting. My usual paranoia brought on by anxiety. I'd lived with it long enough to recognize the signs. I'd read and reread Will's texts again and again, trying to eke out any hidden meaning in them, only to find nothing. But now this? How to explain away *this*?

Somewhere, beyond the bins, came the sound of a door opening followed by heavy, purposeful footsteps. I was never one for breaking the rules, and aware I was somewhere I definitely shouldn't be, I hurried back into the corridor.

Enough was *enough*.

I needed answers. And I needed to find Con.

Lost in thought, I turned the corner, then stopped, confused. This was where I had expected the elevator to be, but instead the corridor stretched on blankly into the distance, no exit in sight. All I could see were polite lines of sensibly shut doors. I unlocked my phone to look at the map I'd snapped earlier, completely disoriented now. Clearly, I'd made a wrong turn. It was easy to get confused down here with no windows and barely any points of reference.

I pressed on. Soon enough, I'd come to a staircase or an elevator and rejoin Con. Even though it was only late morning, these corridors were lit entirely by unflatteringly bright artificial light, making me wonder if this deck was below sea level.

This area of the ship was unusually silent, disconcertingly silent, leading me to half jog down the corridor. At the end, it took a ninety-degree swing to the right, and facing me was yet another identical passage. With a sigh, my pulse beginning to hasten with unease and frustration, I made my way down this too, hurrying past door after silent door. At the end, the corridor took yet another right-angle swing, revealing a further bland hallway—although this corridor somehow seemed more cramped—the ceiling even lower. It was as if I were buried deep in the bowels of the ship. Ariadne lost in the labyrinth without her ball of string. Were the rooms down here even occupied? The doors of the cabins on the main deck that I passed on the way to breakfast were forever opening and slamming—the maid trolleys usually parked outside at least a couple, cabin doors wedged open, allowing the weak Atlantic daylight to shine through.

The image of that strange dark figure assaulting me backstage came unwelcomely to mind. But, no. Aside from me and Con, wherever he was, there was *no one* down here. No one to hear my shouts. No one to notice if one of these endless doors swung silently open and an arm wrenched me inside.

Above me, the recessed lights buzzed loudly and dimmed,

momentarily whisking away the view of the pink, carpeted corridor before me and replacing it with utter darkness, the piped jazz music stuttering, becoming oddly distorted, mocking even. I gasped and steadied myself against the nearest wall, then increased my pace down the corridor, my feet sinking silently into the deep pile of the carpet, my footing forever unsure as the ship plowed on through the waves.

Halfway down I stopped.

Ahead, just out of sight around the corner, drifted voices.

I don't know why I stopped—I should have welcomed the sound of someone else down here—but it was something about the tone, the quality, of the voices. Throaty and guttural, the words seemingly spat out.

It was only going to be guests. Why was I so reluctant to keep walking?

Listening more closely, I tried to figure out what language the two of them—it sounded as if there were two of them—were speaking. Something fast-paced with elongated, stretched vowels and sharp consonants. One of them sounded more aggressive than the other. I assumed they were men; the voices were so deep.

I made myself keep on walking, more determined than ever to get back to the elevators and away from this stupid deck, but as I got closer, I was forced to a stop again.

Two shadows, cast by the hidden speakers, had been thrown large against the pale pink wall by the fluorescent lights. At first glance, they seemed normal enough. Everyone knew light could make shadows seem much larger than the objects that threw them. The figures appeared to be facing each other as they continued their hushed conversation. But when one of them waved a hand to gesticulate, cold fingers seemed to squeeze the nape of my neck.

Rather than a hand, the arm seemed to unravel into something long and . . . *writhing*. Like a tentacle. That was the only way I could explain it. It unfurled like a midnight fern, almost reaching the end of the corridor. I bit my tongue, my feet carrying me slowly backward, a low ringing starting up in my ears.

The sea provides, Liv, but only if you feed it—

No. No way. Shadows could play all kinds of tricks.

Forever a fan of puzzles and mysteries, I remembered reading about the Brocken spectre when I was a kid, some effect on a mountain that made people's shadows seem giant, thrown against the clouds. Or perhaps it was down to something the guy was holding or—

I cleared my throat, that claustrophobic, shut-in feeling stronger than ever. It was as if I were deep beneath the ocean, the weight of the water bearing down on me, squeezing me into unnatural, impossible shapes, the current roaring in my ears. I needed to get out of here—and these people, whoever they were, could likely point me toward the elevators. I had to be rational. As I took several halting steps closer, immediately both speakers silenced and I watched, dry mouthed, as that odd tentacle—or tool or whatever it *actually* was—swiftly retracted.

Clearing my throat again, even louder, I forced myself to walk around the corner. I had no other option. I'd announced myself now.

I'm not sure what I expected to see—two guests on the taller, older side, disappearing down the corridor, I suppose.

Instead, two almost identical-looking maids stood before me, both short and slender, their dark hair scraped neatly back into buns, wearing the somber black uniform of the *Eos*. They stood side by side in the corridor, no maid trolley to be seen, staring at me with round black eyes and those blank employee smiles that never reached the eyes.

"Miss?" said one. Her voice was wispy and high. Her English was perfect and without accent.

All words deserted me. I was desperate to turn and leg it down the corridor, back the way I had come, but I wasn't even sure of where I was going and they would *catch* me, so easily, and then they would—

Would what? Jesus, why was I *so* scared?

Obviously there *had* been two men there; they'd just disappeared back into their cabins as these maids came up the corridor. Mystery solved.

Except . . . except there had been no sounds to support this. No soft closing of cabin doors. No enforced greeting from the maids.

Wildly, I looked behind them, trying and failing to disguise my nerves. The other maid spoke, her voice similarly breathy, her intonation perfect.

"May we help? Guests don't usually stray *this* far down, miss."

I noticed then that both of them had their hands clasped behind their backs. Their pale faces stared into mine.

"I— Isn't . . . aren't these guest cabins?" I said, trying to force some normality onto the situation.

The other maid shook her head, a brisk, mechanical movement. "Not exactly. These cabins are for *private* charter guests. They are off-limits to regular guests."

Behind them the corridor seemed to stretch on forever, the ceiling lower still, the lights dimmed to the point where whatever did lie at the end of the corridor was shrouded in darkness.

The wrongness of the situation was growing. Neither of the maids had so much as even blinked yet; their faces immobile and emotionless, like fleshy masks.

"S-sorry," I stuttered, needing to go, to get away from these women, this dark corridor. Surely we were below sea level because I was drowning down here, the pressure heavy and unbearable, my ears starting to ache, my heart pounding so hard I could hear it. "I'll, um, I'll go back, then?"

"Best you do," whispered one of them, their voice dissolving into thick, sticky giggles. I forced myself to turn, but before I did, I noticed those towering shadows behind them, unchanged.

I stumbled around the corner, finally coming face to face with the elevator. Con wasn't there, but there was no way in hell I was waiting down here any longer. I jabbed at the buttons and hurried into the swiftly summoned elevator.

A minute or so later, I emerged back onto Deck 3 alone.

Brightly lit, noisy, and familiar, it was home to the atrium; the gaudy expanse of the Neptune Lounge; the little shop full of cheerful *Eos* memorabilia and upbeat marimba music. I stopped, allowing the blissful regularity of the deck to wash over me for a few minutes.

Around me, grinning couples in colorful slacks and chiffon dresses headed for lunch, hand in hand. Activity supervisors in baseball caps walked around high-fiving guests, encouraging them to sign up for indoor bowling or tai chi. The music was sunny, and the air smelled strongly of citrus, some kind of air freshener they must have pumped through all the ventilation shafts.

I took several deep breaths. No wonder I'd been freaked out back there. The lower decks *were* creepy. That was a fact. And with my helpfully overactive imagination, I was bound to get spooked.

Overreaction or not, though, it didn't change the fact that it had definitely been Will's suitcase discarded like trash beside the bins.

And where was Con? Was he still down there? I took a wary glance back at the elevator. There was no way I was going back to look for him.

Walking past the Neptune Lounge, I noticed its doors were closed, a sign stationed outside: *The Amazing Apollo.*

A wide strip of red tape had been placed across the sign, entirely obscuring the magician's face.

CANCELED.

I stopped by one of the huge windows and forced myself to stare out to sea for a while, fixing my gaze upon the distant gray horizon and working on my breathing until I began to feel calmer. Anxiety, I reminded myself—that's all it was. And how could I not be anxious? I was in the middle of the Atlantic aboard a ship full of strangers, and the only person I *did* know might be seriously sick.

I hovered outside the atrium, my mind running over the possibilities as I pulled out my phone. I needed to check; had to be 100 percent sure, before I opened up the Pandora's Box of Getting-Off-This-Ship.

> Will RU really OK? Do you even have your stuff with you? Thing is, I found your suitcase by the trash and am v worried.

My finger hovered over Send as I reread the very *un*-Will-like messages above.

Was it even Will I'd been messaging with?

I rubbed my hand over my face. Of *course* it was Will.

And it would be *madness* not to ask him first. I mean, who knew, maybe Will might actually shed some light on what the actual fuck was going on. And why hadn't I taken a picture of the suitcase? Already I could imagine Justin's condescending patience as he told me it was probably just a similar-looking case.

I pressed Send.

There had been so much I'd wanted to talk to him about on this trip, so much we needed to fix after that stupid, *stupid* night. And once we'd done that, there'd be so much to experience together. As a friend, or as . . . well, as whatever it was we figured out.

I received a reply in under a minute, which was very unlike Will. The message was business-like and bland, also very unlike Will.

Yes, I'm doing OK. Hope to see you soon x

I stared at the message, reading it over and over, the cheer of my surroundings draining away.

No.

No. It *wasn't* Will. It just couldn't be. Just the "Yes" was enough to convince me—let alone the use of a comma. Besides, why had he completely ignored my question?

For the tenth time that day, I called him, but as ever, it went to voicemail. My frustration bled out through my fingers as I furiously began typing.

Will. Can u answer pls? I NEED to talk to you. It's important. Please.

I watched as the words *Will is typing* appeared. I waited, minute after minute ticking endlessly by as I stared avidly at the screen.

But nothing arrived.

Closing my eyes briefly, I swallowed down a sob.

Will, what are the three unmitigable rules of our friendship?

Nothing.

Then.

> And which one did we break in August?

Still nothing. A sob escaped me.

> And do u regret it? Because I just can't bring myself to
> but I think you do

Tears plopped messily onto my hoodie, onto my phone. And finally.

> U have no idea how much I miss u. Please Will. I have to know ur OK. I have to hear ur voice. Please.

His response chimed through only a few minutes later, as I sobbed quietly, slumped into a seat facing the sea, hoodie pulled down over my head, praying no one from SeaMester would find me here but also unable to get up. Sniffing loudly, I wiped my eyes, surprised and suddenly desperately embarrassed, wishing I could somehow redact what I'd sent. With shaking fingers, I opened his message, my heart pounding, anticipating the awkward response, the quick dismissal, outright denial, or even derision. But instead, there were only three words in harsh, strident capitals that caused everything around me, the people, the ship, the ocean, the entire *world,* to still and shrink and whirl away.

> HELP ME LIV

My hand shook as I hurriedly pressed the call button beneath his photo—only seconds after the text came through.

But his phone was switched off.

15

I DON'T KNOW HOW LONG I SAT THERE, FROZEN, ALMOST
catatonic, reading and rereading those three words, stopping
only to repeatedly call his number again and again, only to
listen to the same bland message, as I worked myself up into
more and more of a frenzy. All my thoughts hitting walls. And
strangest of all was the slick sliver of relief I felt.

There *was* something wrong.

I wasn't anxious or tired or crazy.

No. I was *right*.

I hit redial yet again. This time, a woman's chirpy tone
sounded from my tinny speakers. *The number you have dialed is
unavailable. Please try later.*

I pulled the phone away from my ear. Had his cell simply
run out of battery? Or had he lost a signal?

HELP ME LIV

The words swam in front of my vision. But how? What was I supposed to do?

Did I shout at the staff, brandishing my phone—my *evidence*—demanding I see him now? Or run to the infirmary, screaming his name? And what if he was there, drugged up, semi-sedated, happily typing inane nonsense to everyone in his phone book? What would my outburst look like then? I was positive Justin would take a dim view of it.

"Ah, there you are," Constantine said, making me jump as he slumped down in the seat opposite me with a crooked grin. "As someone with a mild level of claustrophobia, I must say, I'm not a fan of the decks below sea level. Did you find Will? I did a quick lap but didn't see anything of note. I was waiting for you down there."

He must have noticed my expression or, more likely, my hideously tear-swollen face. Immediately, he leaned forward, his hand soft on my shoulder.

"Shit—Liv. What happened?"

The concern in his voice made me dissolve into tears again.

"*God*, Con." I sniffed. "Don't be *nice*—I can't take it right now. Tell me to sort myself out or call me a whiny little peasant or something."

He looked at me levelly with those still, slate eyes, his usually imperious features soft.

"It'll help to talk about it, whatever it is—I promise."

I snuck a glance around us. The corridor we sat in was completely empty. The clink of cutlery from a nearby lounge suggested most people were now at lunch. I took a deep breath, then thrust my phone in his face.

"He just asked me for *help*, Con. What does that *mean*? I don't know what to do . . . Who to tell or who to talk to or—"

Remembering my last desperate bout of messaging, I snatched back the phone before Con could read back further. "And it's not only that. I mean, *why* can't I see him? Where exactly has he gone? Y'know they've emptied his room—completely stripped it. And has anyone *really* told his dad? I mean, what have these people done with him? Now his phone's off—completely switched off the moment after he sent that. It was almost like someone had *seen*—and—and . . ."

My voice was louder now. I was dimly aware I was causing a scene. But the dam had been broken and all my darkest worries were flooding out.

And why is his suitcase, full of all his stuff, sitting by the trash?

Why does he need help*?*

Con steepled his fingers, the picture of calm, irritating me immensely. Needing to see some kind of reaction from him, I pressed on.

"There's something else, Con—something you should know. Tavi—that girl you knew—the one who went missing . . . Well, I—I think I found her passport in the captain's cabin the other day."

Con's gaze hardened into immediate disbelief. "*What?* What are you talking about? You've never even met her."

"*No*, but I saw her picture on Adora's Instagram—or at least,

I think it was her. You two looked . . . together." I blushed, my words sounding less convincing by the moment. "Anyways, she looked just like the girl in the passport. I think . . ."

I hoped he didn't put two and two together and realize I'd indulged in a little light social-media stalking. He narrowed his gaze. Honestly, I was a little shocked at the 180 in his demeanor. From calm rationality to spiky defensiveness.

"You *think* or you *know*?"

I looked away.

"Well—her name was scratched out, but she looked identical . . ."

With a soft sigh, Con settled back in the chair. "Liv, I don't know whose passport you saw, but it wasn't hers. There's just no way. And look, I totally get it. I get your frustration, your need to make this make sense, but you're venting to the wrong person. It's simple. We'll find the hotel manager and ask him to take us to Will—and if he can't—then, then we'll escalate this. Get Justin involved, for starters."

I eyed him warily. "What makes you think they'll do what we say? What makes you think they'll listen?"

I already knew the answer. They wouldn't. Not to *me*, anyway. They *hadn't* listened to me. But they would listen to Constantine, heir to shipping millions.

Still, I could have kissed him for his calm, reasonable response. Why was I running around having panic attacks in dark corridors when all I needed to do was speak to the management? They would clear things up. They *were* here to help, after all.

Weren't they?

Regardless, Con handled it.

In that arrogant, entitled way of his that normally would have made me want to retch, but which right now I couldn't have appreciated more. Everything about him screamed lazy confidence, from the way he strolled down the corridor into the atrium, leaning casually over the customer service desk, to his low, efficient tone.

"Look," he drawled, "my friend hasn't been seen since his first night on the ship and we need to see him. We don't need to come into contact with him—I mean, we understand the quarantine situation, but we need to *see* him. And I'm not asking you—I'm telling you." His voice was steady but stern. "We need to see him *now* or I fully intend to escalate this. There's an issue with his phone, and it's causing my friend here all manner of anxiety. Surely you want your passengers to enjoy their experience aboard the *Eos*, not spend every waking moment sobbing?"

Across the desk, Eduardo looked distinctly annoyed but took one glance at my sweaty, swollen face, then answered Con with a deference he definitely hadn't afforded me the last time we'd spoken.

"I appreciate that, sir, but you understand we have very strict rules that apply when someone is in quarantine—"

"Yes, I appreciate that completely—as I already said," Con replied crisply. "But we're not looking to swap saliva with the guy; we only want to *see* him. Otherwise, I *am* going to have to take this further. My friend here is beside herself with worry."

He stopped short of saying *Do you know who I am,* but it was implied, and I got the distinct feeling the hotel manager did.

Eduardo flicked his dark eyes over to me again and then back to Con.

"All right. Very well. Follow me, if you please."

A cautious bubble of joy floated up in my chest, my heart lighter than it had been in days. Then I remembered the most recent messages I'd sent Will and flushed with hot embarrassment, but I would rather deal with that head-on than continue this miserable uncertainty.

We followed the manager to the elevator and took it several decks down, to Deck 8—the *right* deck, I noted with relief. In addition to the infirmary, the deck appeared to be where the kitchens were, and staff busily bustled past us pushing silver trolleys laden with cloches and cutlery. At the end of the corridor was a plain door with a frosted window set into it, a bell and card reader on the wall beside it. Eduardo opened it with a swift swipe of a card. Beyond was a smaller passage, brightly lit and clinically white, that led into a small waiting area manned by a single nurse. The air smelled acridly of bleach. Several rooms led off from the smaller passage with windows that looked out into the corridor.

"The infirmary—the medical area of the ship, you see," explained Eduardo as if he were giving us a tour. He gestured through the round window of one of the rooms. Inside was a single bed and on it, a sleeping shape curled on its side, completely covered by a sheet.

"Here is your friend, safe and sound. I cannot open the door, you do understand?"

Beside me, Constantine gave a gentle sigh.

"It's just a lump under a sheet. It could be anyone," I announced dully. Slowly the rage that had been simmering for days began to leak from me in dark floods. I faced Eduardo. "You *said* you would take us to Will. You said we could *see* him. How do we know that's him? You could have just gotten a member of the staff to dive under the sheets before we got here. He messaged me asking for *help* not even an hour ago. Why would he do that? What is going *on* here?" The words burst from me in a rush, my voice breaking as I continued, "Where's *Will?*"

The hotel manager gave me an exasperated look, his hands thrown up in denial. "*What?* Why on earth would we deceive you? We are a *professional* staff aboard the *Eos*. We have only one person in quarantine currently on this entire ship and that is a Mr. William Rexham, who is currently asleep in that bed. His *name* is on that clipboard." He gestured furiously to a holder on the door. "That will be why he is not answering his phone. He is evidently sick and possibly sedated."

"But he *did* answer his phone. And he asked for help! Wake him up somehow. I need to *see* him. *Jesus*—" I stepped toward the door and began determinedly hammering on it. "Will! Will! Hey, wake up. It's me, it's Liv! I'm here!"

The shape beneath the covers didn't move. I rattled the handle, but of course the door was locked. I whirled around to face Eduardo.

"*Why* have you locked him in? What the hell do you think he *has*? Bubonic *plague*?"

Con shifted awkwardly beside me. "Liv—"

Eduardo's face was hard, his eyes flashing with warning. The nurse from the reception area approached us, placing a firm gloved hand on my arm. Her voice stern but weary.

"I need to ask you to step away from the door, miss, and lower your voice—"

I *hadn't* imagined that message.

Will was in trouble.

Sucking a deep breath into my lungs, I yelled with all my might. "Will! Will, I'm *HERE*! Wake up! Tell me you're all right!"

Constantine placed a firm hand on my shoulder. I shrugged it off.

"*Liv* . . . Come on now—"

"What in the *world* is all this commotion?"

An older man with neat white stubble and small round glasses emerged from a room farther up the corridor, frowning, his voice sharp with authority and disapproval. I stopped my hammering. His badge announced him as *Dr. Daggett.*

"You're keeping my friend hostage in a locked room," I accused breathlessly. "Have you drugged him? Why isn't he ever properly awake? You should know, he just messaged me, asking for help. That's—that's evidence . . ."

Dr. Daggett ignored me entirely and looked at Eduardo.

"*Evidence?* A friend of the patient, you say?" He hummed. "So this is the reason for the commotion?"

Eduardo gave a noncommittal shrug.

The doctor peered over his glasses at me, his mouth set in an irritated line.

"And perhaps your friend did send that message, perhaps he did. It's perfectly likely. People do funny things while delirious. He is currently under heavy sedation. I'm surprised he managed it, to be honest. You see, his fever was abnormally high overnight. We are concerned for him—it could be meningitis, which, besides being potentially *deadly,* is also highly communicable, especially among people of your age group. Now, since I have answered your questions, might I ask why you are accusing my medical team, who have looked after him with the utmost courtesy and care, of keeping him *hostage?*"

He spoke so sternly and patronizingly in his cut-glass accent, I felt immediately belittled . . . *stupid,* in fact. I swallowed, my words choked, stuck in my throat. Con spoke up.

"She hasn't seen him since the first evening she got here. He's her best friend. You can't blame her for being concerned—"

"Not at all, but I *can* blame her for being abusive to my staff."

"I wasn't *abusive*—"

"Now, provided all is well and he responds to treatment, I will alert you tomorrow as soon as he is fully conscious and you may indeed see him. *If* you promise to stop kicking up such a fuss. You must believe we have your friend's best interests at heart. Do no harm. Hippocratic Oath and all that."

I gave a dismissive shake of my head.

"So why did he ask me for *help?*"

The doctor stared at me, disbelief edged with annoyance evident in his sharp blue eyes, but Will's message was still burned into my retinas.

"Why are we continuing to discuss this?" he snapped. "I've told you; you will need to wait until tomorrow. I can't promise more than a wave from the corridor, but you'll get your wish."

Even I could see there was no point in arguing any longer. It would only result in me being refused access to the infirmary again, or worse.

"Fine," I conceded. "I'm sorry. But you promise you'll let me know as soon as he wakes?"

"I will. Leave your cabin number with Georgia at the desk, and we'll call you. All being well, you can visit him tomorrow."

"Visit him? As in . . . actually talk to him?"

He nodded dismissively. "It's possible. Now, if you'll excuse me."

The doctor bustled off back to his office.

Eduardo, clearly unimpressed with my outburst, led us silently out of the infirmary, the atmosphere as thick and oppressive as the gray clouds outside.

"Hey—thanks," I said to Con once we were alone. "Thanks so much for helping back there."

He angled his gaze awkwardly to the window. "No worries. I know you're missing him."

Part of me wanted to tell him that it wasn't like that. But honestly, I wasn't sure it wasn't. I buried my face in my hands and groaned loudly.

"Is it me?" I muttered between my fingers. "I mean, did that really all seem legit and aboveboard to you?"

Con hesitated for a long time before answering.

"It does seem a little . . . odd that we can't even see him," he began with a considered diplomacy that world leaders would admire. "But, on the other hand, there's no actual reason for them to lie, is there?"

"I'm—I'm worried he's not on the ship anymore," I said, my voice breaking as I formed the words. "And I'm worried . . . I'm worried we're not safe."

And I'm worried that my sanity is slowly slipping away.

Con frowned. "What do you mean, not on the ship anymore?"

What else *could* I mean? But I couldn't elaborate. It was as if speaking it into the universe would make it real. That somehow I would be in even greater danger if I fully verbalized my worst imagining.

"Never mind. . . . Hey, if you aren't doing anything, do you want to come back to my cabin and chill for a bit?" I asked impulsively, not wanting to be alone. "I swiped a tube of Pringles from the buffet yesterday, and there's always some terrible reality show on the ship channels. I'm a couple of episodes into a vintage season of *The Bachelor*."

Con paused. He was going to decline. I couldn't exactly blame him—I mean, who'd willingly spend time locked in a cabin with someone who appeared to be rapidly losing their mind?

"Ah, I'd love to—but I said I'd give Leda a hand with something."

I narrowed my eyes.

Leda? As in, the girl who said you couldn't keep your eyes off her, before?

But I thought those girls weren't for you. . . .

The words were on my lips, but there was no way I could say them. Besides, Leda was for anyone with eyeballs. She was gorgeous—*beautiful.* So instead, I gave what I hoped was a breezy, unbothered smile. "Cool, no worries. I'll see you later, then—probably down another dark corridor."

I unlocked my cabin. Even Con's rejection wasn't enough of a distraction to prevent my thoughts from trickling down to darker places.

I knew the doctor was lying, knew it in my bones. But why?
HELP ME LIV

My head was throbbing. Part of me wished I could do what everyone was telling me to. Just accept that Will was sick and try to enjoy myself. Except there was no way I could do that—not now, not after that message.

As I was failing to nap, a knock at my door announced Cintia, with an invitation to chill by the poolside, which I gratefully accepted, eager for the distraction of her company.

And, for the first time since we'd started this trip, the sun decided to show its face, peeking wistfully through the thick swell of cloud. Out on deck, it felt almost balmy. I'd risked shorts and a strappy top—no way was I breaking out a bikini—particularly with Con potentially skulking about in the shadows like some kind of sexy shark. Cintia headed over to the deck bar, confident she could mooch us a couple of beers, while I got comfortable on my sun lounger and dug my book out of my bag.

Minutes later, Cintia returned, handing me an ice-cold bottle of Corona. Taking a swig, I shut my eyes and enjoyed the warm sun on my face, feeling myself begin to relax a little for the first time since I'd stepped aboard this damn ship.

If I could see Will tomorrow, I could let myself believe everything was all right—

—HELP ME—

"You okay, Liv? You're looking a little off. Still a bit shook after yesterday morning's auditorium fun?"

I debated whether to confide in her, but to be honest, I'd had enough of Con's smug glances, and I couldn't deal with Cintia's too.

"No—just—just missing Will, I guess."

She grinned. "Ugh, you've got it *bad*. He's only been gone for, like, a few days."

It felt like so much longer.

Was I overreacting? If the doctor was right, then Will was fine and I'd see him tomorrow. But that word *gone* sounded so final.

A cold spray of water across my face made me gasp and shoot up. I cursed as a grinning Raj flipped me off, water dripping off his taut abs as he strode off farther up the deck. He was closely followed by Lexie of the Sirens, wearing a tiny, crocheted two-piece.

"The body is *insane*," whistled Cintia, sinking down beside me and blatantly staring. "I mean, I consider myself body confident, but that is a whole different level."

"Which *one*?"

To be fair, she could have been talking about either of them. We continued staring as they stood together at the bar, sunglasses on, looking like an ad for *Love Island*. I pulled my chunky cardi back on. Despite the sun, it wasn't exactly bikini weather—they must have been freezing.

"Way too much effort for me," Cintia said. "I'd rather eat a few Oreos once in a while, you know?"

I laughed. "I hear you. So, has Raj gotten lucky with a Siren?"

Cintia wrinkled her nose.

"Looks that way. Perfect match, if you ask me. Both on a similar intellectual level, anyway."

"Get out. Isn't Raj some artistic genius?"

Cintia turned to me and raised her sunglasses with one finger. The look she gave me was distinctly cynical.

"*Raj?* Really? Only you and Will are here on account of academics." She rubbed her thumb and forefinger together. "Everyone else has different reasons."

With that, she dropped the glasses back over her eyes and flopped down onto the sun lounger, leaving me to examine her comment. Con had already admitted he was only here because his parents frequently shipped him off when they felt he was in the way. But what about the others? I remembered Con saying something about Adora's parents never being around either. Was it the same for Cintia?

I looked back over to where Raj stood, my sunglasses giving me the perfect excuse to stare. He was now leaning casually against the chrome railing of the deck, gesticulating as he chatted away to Lexie, who was nodding along to everything he said.

With a sigh, I picked up my book again, wishing I'd brought something a little cheerier to read than a ghost story about a governess possibly losing her mind. Beside me, Cintia was glued to her phone, laughing softly to herself every time she came across a particularly amusing meme.

I don't know what it was that made me look up a few minutes later, but it felt like something more than the need for distraction. Some disturbance in the atmosphere, the sudden unshakable feeling that something horribly wrong was about to take place.

It all happened in less than two seconds.

Raj was still there, leaning back, muscular arms braced against the deck railing. That implacable white grin on his face, no doubt mansplaining to Lexie how to swim or something similar, when Lexie seemed to lurch forward toward him with insane, impossible speed and then back again. It was a split-second attack, like a snake striking. I saw the flash of something that glinted painfully bright in the sun, blinding me for a moment. Teeth, nails, even a blade. I couldn't be sure. I didn't see an outstretched hand, saw none of her connect with any of him—it was all a blur.

But what I *did* see was Raj lose his balance. Both arms slipping off the rail and into the void beyond, scrabbling desperately for purchase but finding nothing, faltering in midair for a single moment, his smile now gone. And, at that precise moment, an elderly couple ambled past my sun lounger, arm-in-arm, momentarily obscuring my view.

I scrambled forward, desperately looking around them, but by then, Raj was gone.

16

THE WORLD WHINED AWAY, AND FOR A FEW SHAKY MO-
ments everything went dark.

I collapsed hard against my sun lounger, my mouth filled
with bile, my hands clammy and trembling uncontrollably.
Then, as soon as I had the strength, I struggled up into a sitting position, staring at where Raj had stood, his back to the
hard blue sea, only moments ago. Lexie was now lying on a
sun lounger a few feet away from the railing, casually flicking
through her phone.

Nobody around them had batted an eyelid.

What the fuck?

I stood, staggering, the world lurching crazily around me
as if it hadn't caught up with me yet. Beside me, I could hear
Cintia still chuckling away at her phone, her laugh lowering,
elongating, stretching out elastically just like the time. I walked

the few steps toward the railing on unsteady feet. Bracing myself, I peered down.

Anyone that fell here would avoid the sea's shocking embrace and instead bounce off the deck directly below, which was a good three or four stories down, currently obscured with broad blue sunshades.

I'd braced myself for the sight of Raj's broken body, limbs splayed at impossible angles, blood slowly leaking from it, oozing between the gaps in the polished wooden floorboards. But all I could make out was an elderly couple strolling, in and out of vision beneath the shades, sun visors on and wearing matching fluorescent shorts.

Squinting my eyes, I leaned over farther.

One of the shades appeared broken. An inner arm awry, its canopy slightly sagging.

Was I going *insane*? Was it even possible that only *I* had witnessed Raj fall?

Why had no one else noticed? Why was no one calling for help or running to alert the crew? The deck around me was busy. A glamorous older couple sat directly opposite where Raj had fallen, both engrossed in papers. A group of women wearing colorful caftans sat beside Lexie, all chattering away as they sipped cocktails. One of them caught my eye and gave me a sly smile.

Had Raj somehow sprinted inside when those people had walked in front of me? Or was he just hidden behind someone? Had he taken off his top again and merged with the half-naked crowd in the pool?

But all in a split second? Literally the time it took me to *blink*?

And I *saw* him.

I saw him lose his balance; I saw—

"Hey—hey? You look terrible. Everything all right?"

Cintia had come up beside me, frowning at me. She shook her head and looked skyward.

"You didn't hear a word I just said, did you?"

"I'm sorry," I said, exhaling, "It was the weirdest thing. I thought—I—"

"What? Oh God, don't tell me you caught your boyfriend's disease? I just drank from your beer. . . ."

"*No.* It's Raj. I thought he fell off the side just now. I mean, literally, over the side of the ship—off the deck. I think . . . I think he might be gone . . . Cintia."

She snorted loudly. "Shit, Liv, if Raj fell onto the deck below, the whole damn ship would rock. The *size* of him. Wishful thinking, my friend."

I knew she was right.

There was no way he could just topple off the deck in broad daylight with no one aware, with no sound, and yet . . . that was what I saw.

Wasn't it?

Whatever Cintia might have said, and despite the complete lack of reaction from anyone else on deck, there was no way I could just lie back on my sun lounger and return to my book.

My pounding heart wouldn't let me. Muttering excuses, I immediately headed inside and took the elevator several floors down to the deck directly below to investigate.

The elevator doors closed with an efficient swoosh behind me and I hurried down the corridor, on the hunt for one of the sliding glass doors that would allow me access to the deck. It was gloomy down here, the sun now hidden, the silence weighty.

Up ahead, where the corridor opened out, becoming floor-to-ceiling windows that looked out over the deck, stood a yellow plastic freestanding sign that read *Closed*. A sudden feverish heat washed over me, slowing my pace. Coincidence? There was no sign of any staff around, so I kept going, hesitantly now, edging past the sign to where the glass doors led directly outside.

From where I stood, all I could see were several neat plastic tables, their huge blue sunshades mushrooming out above them and rippling in the wind. Grasping the handles, I made to yank open the doors and take a further look. As the seconds passed I was becoming more and more convinced I'd been mistaken. If someone had tumbled three stories below, there was bound to be *some* kind of disturbance. Some screaming at least, or some doom-laden announcement over the intercoms.

Maybe it was just another of his stupid jokes?

"For someone here on a scholarship, I'm surprised you are not a better reader." A familiar and decidedly *unwelcome* voice. The towering, false-grinning form of Mr. Eduardo stood behind me, eyes sparkling with menace. "The deck is closed—as the sign says—for promotional work."

Promoting *what*?

Raj's splattered remains?

I forced the hysterical thought from my head.

"I—uh—need to get my bag," I said, looking at him carefully. I'd read some article in psych class about tells that gave away when a person was lying. General lack of eye contact, the need to fiddle with something. But Eduardo stared me dead in the face with his huge bulbous eyes. "It's—it's got medication in it. I need it. Besides, it's not very high-class to close off an entire deck during the day, is it?"

"It doesn't seem very *high-class* to accommodate a bunch of demanding, drunken students," he replied, his voice a low hiss, "but yet again, I find myself doing it. Now, *miss,* if you wouldn't mind heading back the way you came."

I couldn't just leave. Not yet.

"Look—I—I thought I saw someone fall overboard—from the deck above."

Even to my own ears it sounded crazy. Eduardo looked back at me, incredulous.

"Are you making some kind of joke? The deck above is very busy—you do not think anyone other than yourself would have noticed?"

I stared at him, floundering. He was right, of course, but that didn't mean I didn't see it. Did it? For a second, I swayed on my feet in time with the ship, its hazy listing adding to the current air of unreality. I had no idea what to say.

So I acted instead.

Muttering a pointless apology, I slipped past him through the half-open door onto the deck, hands fluttering by my eyes, bracing myself for a scene from a nightmare.

This part of the deck had been recently cleared, some kind of black silken cloth covering the ground in front of me, and standing in the center of it were the Sirens.

I stumbled a little as they stared at me. I'd never noticed how similar they looked before—as if they were sisters. Different builds, different hair, but the eyes—dark and unknowable—they were the same. They wore long identical black shifts, seeming to almost blend in with the cloth on the floor, reminding me of Macbeth's weird sisters. It looked as if I'd interrupted some bizarre ritual. For one insane second, they all stared at me blankly, as if barely registering who I was. I turned to Lexie, who minutes ago had been in the pool. How had she gotten here before me, not to mention had time for a costume change? What were they doing down here? Dressed like this, *exactly* where Raj had fallen?

Lexie spoke, her voice cold and haughty.

"Can we *help* you? We're in the middle of a brochure shoot."

My jaw dropped open. Then I took in the large white screen directly behind them, blocking the view of the rest of the deck, the photography equipment scattered on a nearby table.

"I'm sorry—I tried to stop her, but she just barged in—"

I turned, surprised at the obsequiousness in Eduardo's voice. His eyes bored into mine. He was furious.

In combination with the screen, the Sirens were acting as some kind of human barrier, preventing me from getting a good look behind them. And something about the way they were looking at me made me falter. I didn't *want* to move closer; I didn't want to go *near* them. It was as if the ancient reptilian part of my brain were screaming silently in warning. And in that moment, I realized—

I was afraid of them.

Gathering myself, the fierceness of Eduardo's expression unsettling me further, I turned to leave, murmuring vague apologies.

Undeterred, I hurried on to my next destination, rapping hard on the door of Justin's cabin. He answered seconds later, looking unusually disheveled, bleary-eyed and unshaven. The sight of him was jarring. A familiar, revolting smell slunk from his cabin—that same thin, mildewy stench the captain's room had reeked of, like long-rotted seaweed.

"Liv? Is everything okay?"

"No, Justin. It's *really* not. Can we talk?"

17

LESS THAN TEN MINUTES LATER, JUSTIN AND I WERE EN-sconced in the Athene Lounge, the smell of coffee and cake comfortingly soothing my nervous system, my usual hot chocolate topped with marshmallows—that looked delicious but which I hadn't the stomach to touch—steaming away before me.

"Look, I know you had a bit of a fright the other morning," Justin began, his warm brown eyes full of concern. "And are probably feeling a bit unsettled. I'm glad you've come to check in with me. It's not unusual to feel"—he gave a self-indulgent little chuckle—"all at sea, when you embark on an opportunity like this. New surroundings, new people. The feeling of being far away from home. It affects people in different ways. On top of that, there's Will getting sick. I get that it's been hard for you to deal with. So . . ." He patted his knees in anticipation. "What can I do to support you?"

I nodded, grateful for his calm and easy presence. I could trust him. He was one of the good guys, sitting there in his fleece and beige slacks like a cuddly dad from a sitcom. I lowered my voice.

"Justin, something is very *wrong* on this ship."

He gave me a hesitant smile, as if prodding me to go on. But was it my imagination, or did his eyes harden a little? "Wrong?" he repeated. "What do you mean, *wrong*?"

I couldn't keep carrying it alone. If I wasn't crazy already, I soon would be. And so I told him—everything.

About how Will hadn't messaged me once in a way that truly felt like Will. About the staff's refusal to even let me *see* him even when I'd visited the infirmary.

About his suitcase discarded by the bins like trash.

About the Sirens and how uneasy they made me feel, how Thalia had been the last person to see Will before he disappeared, and about the strange things I'd seen that night at dinner.

About how Apollo had been searching for his sister—missing on another cruise—before his apparent drowning in the theater, and what I thought had just happened to Raj.

I lowered my voice.

"Should we speak to the captain? I mean, can we ask him to dock the ship early somewhere? Justin, there's something going on. We all need to get off this ship before one of us is next. We need to find out *exactly* what has happened to Will—*and* Raj—before it's too late. I think—"

I swallowed, my voice merely a whisper. "I think we might *all* be in danger. All of SeaMester, I mean."

Justin was quiet for a long while.

Too long.

He wouldn't look at me, only fiddled about with the tiny, plastic-wrapped biscuit that accompanied his coffee. And the longer the seconds ticked away, the more obvious it was that I'd made a terrible mistake.

Finally, he cleared his throat.

"Before it's too *late*? Sorry—just to clarify—you're telling me you saw *what*? Raj being pushed off the side of the ship in broad daylight by a girl half his size? Liv . . ."

Something twitched in my jaw. I picked up my cup, squeezing it so tightly it was in danger of smashing. I'd been so desperate to offload it all to someone, someone who could help, I hadn't thought about how it would all *sound*.

"I mean, I literally walked past Raj two minutes before you knocked on my door. He's—he's absolutely fine." Justin shook his head in amazement.

My skin felt hot, my palms clammy.

What?

I stared at Justin.

Was I sick? Feverish? Maybe this was why my thoughts were shimmering and overvivid; like pictures with the saturation turned way too high. Did I have what Will had?

I ran a clammy hand over my face.

"I mean—I said I *thought* I saw that. Obviously, I *didn't*. But even so—"

"Liv, I have to ask—are you on any medication for these delusions you've been experiencing? You're supposed to declare any prescription drugs on the form, and I don't recall you . . ."

He carried on. All stern and businesslike now and still unable to make eye contact. *Why* had I mentioned those things? Things I wasn't even sure I'd seen myself because they were impossible. But if they *were* impossible, then how had I seen them?

Was *I* the one who needed help?

And I almost believed it—almost believed that the fault lay with me—except for one thing. Black text on a white screen. Undeniable.

HELP ME LIV

I balled my hands hard into my eyes and tried to focus.

"—*very* serious implications. I mean, if you can't be relied upon to act in a coherent manner in a closed environment, how can we trust you in the wider—"

I took a deep breath. "Justin, I am *not* taking any medication. And everything I've said is true. I can show you the message he sent me."

"Liv . . ." He exhaled deeply. "To clarify, you're telling me you want to get off the cruise?"

I perked up at this. I hadn't been sure it was possible. But if it was—and, even better, if I could get Will off the ship, too, before—

But Justin was shaking his head. There was a cold, impersonal anger in his eyes now that scared me. What had happened to calm, supportive Justin?

"You should know I've already had a discussion with the captain about your previous behavior, *and* I've received a complaint from the hotel manager concerning your outburst in the infirmary earlier. The fact is, offboarding you would mean the ship would need to make a detour to the nearest port—which would be Bermuda, of all places—as we're too far away from shore for coast guards or airlifts. It would mean every damn passenger on this cruise would lose three days of their hard-earned vacation because of your actions, and for what reason? Because you're letting your anxiety get the better of you?"

I stared at him dully.

"Not to mention the fact that you'd need to pay for your own flight back to the UK, and if any offering universities asked us about your experience on this trip, well . . ." Justin shook his head and flopped back against the couch, hands behind his head and staring at the ceiling. "I just don't *understand* it. Will being quarantined with a non-life-threatening disease—no, it's not ideal—but he'll be fine in a couple of days, yet you're prepared to let this ruin *your* whole experience? This could be life-changing for you—yet you're telling me you want the ship to change its course, affecting all three thousand passengers on board, because you're having *nightmares*?"

Oh *God.*

I dug my nails into my palms, trying to stop myself from screaming. Why had I thought coming clean to Justin would solve *anything*? All I'd managed to do was deepen the level of shit I was in. I looked at him desperately.

"So there's no way of getting off this ship?"

"You'll need to wait until we hit the first port in three days. Then yes, I'd start seriously thinking if you want to remain on this ship—or even if you *should*."

Justin gave a lengthy sigh, the anger in his eyes now totally extinguished.

"Honestly, I'm sorry you're feeling this way, Liv. I know you want to leave, but if you do, I wish I could tell you how much you'll regret missing this opportunity in the future." He patted my hand. "Try to enjoy tonight. I've booked you guys into the ship's club this evening. Let your hair down and do your best to relax—it might go some way toward helping. I mean, you've been *told* you're going to see Will as soon as he's awake. . . . Focus on the positives until we dock, then we can reassess, okay?"

I nodded at him mutely. There was nothing else to say. What I had hoped was a lifeline was just a dead end. Giving me a wary glance, Justin drained his coffee and got up to leave. "I'll see you at dinner tonight, okay?"

Now he knew it all and thought I was utterly unstable. Great. And *was* I? There was a cold rationality to his words. I *hadn't* been sleeping and I *was* seeing Will soon—if the doctor was to be believed. So why couldn't I relax—at least until tomorrow?

Once I'd gotten back to my cabin, I collapsed under the

covers with an agonized groan, my mind spinning. I was both angry and terrified at Justin's reaction. *Was* he right? Was I just overreacting?

But what if I wasn't? If I wasn't—if Will and Raj had disappeared, or been taken—who would be next? And if Justin had something to do with this, then I may as well have just Sharpie'd a massive "next victim" on my forehead.

If I *was* right, if people were vanishing from this ship, then I couldn't just sit around moping. I needed to do something.

But what could I do when no one was taking me seriously?

My heart sank when I ambled into the Neptune Lounge a few hours later and saw only Justin and Cintia at our usual table.

Still no sign of Raj.

"Hey, Liv," greeted Justin with a bland smile, buttering a roll in his fastidious manner. "All good?"

"Mmm, fantastic," I muttered. It looked as if we were pretending our earlier conversation hadn't happened, which, I supposed, was currently for the best. But I wasn't about to say nothing. "Although, doesn't it seem like our group is growing ever smaller?"

Justin only shrugged. "Not exactly a surprise on trips like these. Take it from a veteran. As students get more familiar with the ship and with each other, we encourage them to be independent. I mean, no one really wants to hang with the teacher, do they? Although, I certainly don't mind if they do." He gave me the tepid, reassuring grin again. "You wait, we'll all be thoroughly sick of each other by the end of the week, believe me."

"Missing anyone in particular?" smirked Cintia. "Maybe a certain shipping heir with a superior attitude?"

"Not at all," I said too quickly. "So where *are* the others? New dinner spot open up? I'm getting major FOMO."

I didn't want to press too hard, but it seemed odd to me that there were only three of us here. Raj had never missed a meal with the group yet.

"Raj pulled a muscle in his back in the gym earlier," explained Cintia. "I headed down to check on him an hour ago. I guess I hadn't seen him in a few hours, and . . . well, I felt a bit weird after what you said. He reckons the machines weren't calibrated properly or something. He thinks he'll still make it to the club tonight, though. You in?"

I stared at Cintia.

"Uh, yeah, of course. So, you've *seen* him, then?"

She looked at me with warm, twinkling eyes. "Yeah. Don't worry, I've already told him you thought he took a backflip off the deck."

"Funny in retrospect, huh?" said Justin, although there was no warmth in his words. Was it my imagination or was something off with him this evening? He seemed distracted and nervy. Stroking his roll across the surface of his soup rather than eating it, jogging his knee up and down beneath the table.

"Yeah." I forced a laugh. "I guess I had a touch of sunstroke. Weather was nice for once, huh?"

Justin nodded, apparently satisfied. Turning to my plate, I began to pick at my salmon. Like all the food on this ship, it was bland and covered with a glut of creamy, unpleasantly sweet sauce.

"So let me guess, Lady Adora and Lord Con are fine dining?" said Justin.

Cintia shrugged. "Who the hell knows? Maybe Daddy paid for them to take a helicopter off the damn ship to dine on their own private island. They'll be around later, though."

I smiled despite myself.

"Yeah, Raj was telling me earlier that Con's father owns this ship and several others," said Justin, admirably holding the torch of conversation aloft. "All part of the Nepenthe Group. Makes you wonder why he's slumming it with us when he has connections like that."

A bright bolt of fear shivered across my skin.

"Wait—what?" I said. "Con's dad actually *owns* the *Eos*? I thought he was just . . . vaguely involved in the business?"

No wonder he'd started listening to me.

"Apparently so," said Justin, nodding.

"Guy's full of secrets," said Cintia, making a disapproving face. "Isn't he the one with the missing girlfriend?"

"Yeah," I agreed, glad it was Cintia who had brought it up. "What is the story behind that girl who was supposed to be here? The one I apparently replaced?"

"You don't know? I thought you would have gotten that out of Con by now, seeing as you two have been spending so much *time* together?" teased Cintia.

I shook my head. There was a look that came over Con's

face whenever I'd breezed across the topic. A dark distance that made me reluctant to push it.

Justin looked uncomfortable. "Look, I can't really go into much detail," he said. "Privacy regulations and all that. I'm sure you understand. Besides, there's not much to know other than she went missing on vacation a few weeks after she was selected for SeaMester. Her parents never filed a missing person's report of any kind, so a case was never opened—in fact, it's far more likely that she just ran off." He offered up a forced half laugh. "I spoke to her father after he withdrew her enrollment, and he confided in me that his daughter was a bit of a wild child. Apparently, she's pulled stunts like this before." He frowned. "Sorry to disappoint, girls, but the whole situation is much less dramatic than it appears."

He made it sound so simple—a girl there one moment, gone the next. But if this trip had taught me anything, it was that people *didn't* disappear.

Things happened to them. Usually bad things.

The conversation shifted after that and as soon as I could, I made my excuses and left. There was an hour or so before we were due to meet at the ship's club, somewhat amusingly named Hades.

If Raj was resting in his cabin like Justin and Cintia insisted, there'd be no harm in my popping in to check on him, would there? In fact, it would only be polite. I remembered him saying he had the cabin next to Con's, and I knew exactly where that was—for *reasons*.

I made my way to Raj's floor. From far up ahead of me, I

heard a cabin door clunk shut and watched in surprise as Cintia emerged into the corridor. She'd still been at the table when I'd left, teasing Justin about his dance moves. How had she made it here so quickly?

I stopped and watched, far enough away that she didn't see me, as she put her phone in her pocket. Then on turning, she immediately clocked me and walked over with a wide, easy smile.

"Brought him a plate. He's a growing kid, y'know."

So she had seen Raj. He *was* all right. A soft wave of relief gently washed over me.

"Oh right. I was gonna see if he was okay too," I breathed.

A teasing smirk played on Cintia's lips. "I see you, Liv. Not happy with snaring our resident millionaire, you've now set your sights on the himbo, is that right?"

"No," I insisted, a little too quickly. "And anyway, I haven't snared anyone."

Cintia shrugged. "I'd come back in a bit, to be honest. Pain meds are wearing off, so he's not in the best state. Besides, don't we have a night out to get ready for?"

18

I COULD HEAR THE MUSIC FROM HADES AN ENTIRE DECK away. The familiar hard pounding beat of a club. Pretty different from the line-dancing music I'd been expecting. I mean, it *was* a cruise, after all. Strobe lights made the darkened corridor, lined with couples in glamorous evening wear, seem alive.

Inside, the club was much fancier than I'd expected, decadently done up in plush crimson and gold, kind of fitting for a place that was basically named after hell. The music was throbbing house stuff I'd never heard of and that you'd need to scream over to have any kind of conversation. I hovered awkwardly outside, debating whether or not to go back to my cabin—after the events of today, I wasn't exactly in the mood for partying—when one of the staff, dressed in a shiny sequined blazer, approached me with a beaming smile. He placed a whistle over my head and pushed a drink voucher into my hand.

"More young people!" he shouted in glee, turning me around and shoving me over the threshold. "Your mates are already inside!"

Wandering in, I wondered how I was ever going to find anyone in here. The dance floor was a sweaty mass of writhing bodies of all ages. The young, the middle-aged, and the elderly.

I politely pushed my way to the bar. A drink would *definitely* help.

Exchanging my voucher for a garish rainbow-hued cocktail, I turned to scout the crowd for a familiar face. The music pounded on and on, the beat repetitive, some woman warbling shrilly over the top.

At first, I thought the strong, familiar scent of vanilla was coming from my drink. But it was Adora, smelling as ever like an expensive cake. Her delicate hand, jangling with expensive bangles, snatched away my drink and placed it back on the bar, sloshing its contents everywhere.

"Seriously, don't drink that shit! I swear they make it from like all the dregs of the night before to save cash. Con's just ordered a bottle of Grey Goose."

She looked amazing in a minidress of rainbow sequins, accessorized with an expensive-looking pair of Jordans, her red hair swishing silkily around her face. She took my hand in hers and, dancing, led me over to a roped section of the club where a bored-looking Con and Justin were sprawled, both engrossed in their phones.

"This place is everything I expected it to be—and more," deadpanned Con, looking incongruously casual in sweatpants and a hoodie. He filled a chilled glass with an alarming amount of neat vodka and handed it to me. I cast a curious glance at Justin, apparently still turning a blind eye to all the drinking despite the drama of our first night. Maybe Con had paid him off.

I took a tiny sip and winced, my eyes watering.

"Shit, Con, I know your dad sent you here as punishment, but you don't need to take it literally," shouted Adora. She turned to me. "Knock that back, then come dance with me and Cintia."

My initial reaction was no, hell *no,* but after I finished my first drink, my view on the matter swiftly changed.

"Coming?" I asked Con hopefully. I liked him dressed down; it somehow made him seem more attainable. He raised an unamused eyebrow, then turned back to his phone. *"No."*

I followed Adora into the mass of seething bodies, where Cintia was dancing with one of the Sirens, Lexie. I hesitated a moment, but Cintia immediately wrenched me into a bear hug, screaming greetings in my ear, and I forced myself to relax.

Thirty minutes later I was sweaty and euphoric. Buoyed by the vague hope of seeing Will tomorrow; screaming and leaping up and down every time a vaguely familiar track came on; taking time to hug the random passengers that occasionally joined our circle. Justin had been right. This *was* what I needed. To let loose and relax. I cringed as I recalled our earlier conversation. Why had I said anything at all? I should have just kept quiet and waited until tomorrow—

But Raj—

Thoughts began to crowd back into my head like angry

wasps, combining with the music to give me a pounding headache. I needed a break.

"I'll be back in a sec, guys," I yelled over the noise.

I made my way through the sea of people toward the neon sign of the restroom, the vodka warming its way through my veins, tinting the night with gold.

When I emerged from the stall, Leda was standing in front of the mirrors, expertly applying a glossy red lipstick. I hovered in the doorway for a moment, wondering whether to silently shut the door again until she was gone. Drunkenly, I snorted. This wasn't *school*. Still, I didn't make eye contact as I began to wash my hands, not wanting an unpleasant run-in to spoil my night, but to my surprise, Leda locked eyes with me in the mirror and smiled.

I hesitated, looking behind me, in case another of her coven was lurking there but no, it was only me. Not knowing what else to do, I grinned back.

"Olivia, isn't it?"

She looked more intimidating than ever in a simple black bodycon dress, her lush silver waves raked back into a tight, shiny bun.

"Liv, actually."

I mean, I wasn't actively trying to be unfriendly, but we hadn't exactly gotten off to a great start. Besides, girls like Leda, beautiful, wealthy, and well connected, did not hang out with average girls from St. Leonard's who had a total of sixty-six followers on Insta, forty of whom she was directly related to.

Leda finished applying her lipstick.

"*Liv*, then. How's your friend?"

I blinked at her, unsure if I'd imagined the mocking tone to her voice.

"I don't know," I replied, the resentment in my voice unavoidable. "I haven't been able to see him since he got sick."

"Unfortunate for him—though, perhaps not for you, hmm? It seems we have similar tastes, you and I."

"Wait—what do you mean?" I asked in surprise, alcohol making me bold. I shook my head, my tone growing sharper. "By the way, I've been meaning to ask, actually—why *did* Thalia lie about going back to Will's room on the first night? Was he not good enough for her or something?"

More confrontational than my usual style, but it was Will we were talking about here. He deserved defending.

Leda chuckled. A deep, husky sound. "Not good enough for either of you, if you ask me. Men like *that* should be culled at birth."

"*Jesus*, Leda—"

Shrugging, she smoothed her hair with her hand and looked at me again with those dark, flat eyes. Like a doll's. Of all the girls, I found her style the most covetable. She didn't favor blatant labels the way Lexie did and didn't try to pull off the fashion-forward androgyny of Thalia. Instead, Leda's generous curves were always delicately accentuated in jewel-colored silk wrap dresses or vintage crushed velvet.

"Just my opinion. I mean, you think he treated you well?"

Had he? I stared back at my reflection in the mirror, feeling somewhat diminished beside Leda; a flickering flame before a blaze. There was no denying he hadn't the last night I'd seen him—and even before that—

The *last* night? I blinked. What was I thinking? Will *was* coming back.

"And I don't see your other friend tonight either." She smirked. "Raj—wasn't it? Your leader seems a little careless, doesn't he? Losing so many of you. Here . . ." Leda held out her tube of expensive-looking lipstick. "The color will suit you."

Staring at my reflection, I accepted it, slowly drawing the rich red over my mouth while Leda looked on approvingly. I had to admit, it did suit me—a bold contrast against the black of my hair.

"Beautiful," she said, her voice low. "Watch out for Con. He wants what he wants until he inevitably gets it. Then he doesn't want it anymore. Just ask his last girlfriend." She held her hand to her mouth in mock surprise. "Oh wait—you can't."

I opened my mouth, desperate to know more—but she had already left, the door swinging behind her. Taking one more glance in the mirror, I followed her out into the throbbing cacophony of the club.

Con and Justin had now joined our circle on the dance floor, both looking a little glassy-eyed, their dancing consisting of little more than jumping around and whooping.

"You look different," Con yelled in my ear once he caught sight of me.

It was pointless trying to have a conversation over the music, so I smiled in a way I hoped was seductive.

The night rushed past, the music and the alcohol turning time into quicksilver. Everyone smiling, the lights in the club as deep a red as the fixtures. In the moments framed by the club's large gold mirrors, it looked as though we were dancing at the bottom of a volcano, in the midst of a raging inferno, in the fiery depths of hell itself. I don't know if it was the drink or how tired I was, but it was all too much.

The music began to change from an up-tempo throb to a hellish, discordant whine, becoming deafening one minute and then shrinking back to an unpleasant rhythmic chant. It became harder to make out anyone's face, too, smiles turning into too-wide leers, teeth much too big and white, eyes too large, too red. People's limbs seemed to elongate as they moved their hands, turning into vast shadowy tentacles that flicked and flipped about the room.

From the corner of my eye, I thought I saw a lovelorn Raj, trailing behind Lexie. My heart jolted. I turned, ready to call out, but just as quickly, he—or the person I'd thought was him—had melted back into the crowd.

Your leader seems a little careless—losing so many of you—

I blinked, rubbed my eyes. Then I saw *her.* That face—so striking—impossible to forget. It was the girl in the passport I'd found in the captain's room, I knew it—the girl I thought I'd seen with Will yesterday. Beautiful but remote. Far away at first, so far, I had to push through the crowds to see her, stumbling and tripping. Then, without warning, she was beside me, dancing. Her sleek dark hair trailing down her back, her eyes a deep fathomless black. She whirled around to face me, flashing even white teeth, her finger upon her lips, mouth quirked in a secret smile.

Octavia.

"Shh," she hissed. "Don't *tell*."

No, it was impossible—she wasn't here; no one knew where she was—she was missing. It was just the booze in combination with my overactive imagination. My mouth was dry and tacky—I needed some *water*.

Dark figures, clad in sleek, shiny rubber, seemed to flit in and out of our circle, too quick to properly see, their too-smooth hands in mine one second, then stroking my face. I turned, desperate to find them, knocking violently into someone and staggering back, almost to the floor.

"Shit—Liv, are you okay?"

Con was a million miles away. A distant ship, far out to sea, a speck on the horizon. I wanted to ask where Will was. Couldn't they see I *needed* him? He'd always been there. His room a sanctuary. His familiar voice always at the end of the phone. I was alone without him and we had so much to sort out—

"Hey, hey—she needs some water. Dor, give me a hand?"

Hands clasped at me, small and sharp-nailed, nipping me. Their faces now devils. Their mouths hellish maws ringed with teeth. I fought them off. The sounds around me ebbed and flowed like the waves on the ocean.

The sea provides, Liv.

Feed it—

It was funny to think I was actually on the ocean. A black ocean. A midnight ocean. A black sun . . .

Water splashed over me and I gasped. Had I toppled in? Had I been thrown over the edge of the ship? Like Will? Like Raj? Was I next? I coughed violently, the world returning.

"Liv?"

I blinked.

I was sitting on the carpet outside the club, a concerned Con leaning over me. He thrust a bottle of water toward me. "Think you overheated a bit. Here—drink some more of this."

Gratefully, I chugged the water. What had I been thinking—knocking back neat vodka? Another thing on this ship that didn't seem exactly normal. I'd pay for *that* in the morning. I rubbed my hands over my face.

"God, sorry. I just felt a bit faint there."

Con nodded, reaching down to give me a hand up. "It happens—it was hot in there. You okay now?"

Was I?

I stood shakily, appreciatively clasping his hand, as Leda swished past us, a secretive smile upon her red lips, directed solely at me.

Your leader seems a little careless . . . losing so many of you—

Had she been deliberately hinting at something? Or even taunting me?

"Yep—I—er—think so—thanks."

Distracted, I watched her slink away down the corridor. And

what had she meant earlier about Raj? Did she know something? Had she seen something on that deck earlier? Delirious or not, there was only one way for me to find out.

"Liv—what— Where are you *going*? You need to get some rest—*Liv*—hey!"

I ignored Con.

Leda moved ahead of us, dreamlike, her silver hair shining like a star, leading us through the maze of darkened corridors, down stairs carpeted with gold, deeper and deeper into the bowels of the ship.

"Liv—hold on—*wait!*"

I shook my head, dismissing him, and glugged another mouthful of water. One flight of stairs below us, I saw Leda disappearing through a door.

This part of the ship was much fancier than the decks above, despite its lack of windows. The walls were paneled with dark wood, the doors accented with gold. It was all a little odd to me. I'd have thought the posher parts of the ship would be on the higher decks, where it was brighter and they'd have access to balconies and the like.

"Hey—hey—*Liv.*"

Con pulled me back, his cool hand gently encircling my wrist.

"Look—" he started, but I motioned for him to hush, gesturing up ahead.

Leda had stopped at the end of the corridor, which led to

a pair of ornate double doors. We watched as she used a glimmering key card to open them and slip inside. The glimpse I caught of the space beyond revealed a room that was entirely dark. As soon as the door clunked shut, I crept down the corridor.

"Seriously—what are you *doing*?" hissed Con from behind me.

"What do you think?" I whispered back. "She mentioned something about Raj earlier—I think she knows something—I want to find out what's going on."

He fell back against the wood-paneled wall, crossing his arms. "Stalking girls down dark hallways is really *not* a good look for me."

I hushed him, quietly placing my ear to the door.

Con caught my eye, his own eyes bright—hovering somewhere between unease and amusement.

Behind the door I could hear low voices—Leda and someone else. Another girl, no doubt Thalia or Lexie. Were they all sharing a cabin? Annoyingly, the heavy wood of the door was too thick for me to make out exactly what they were saying. I gestured for Con to join me and, with a roll of his eyes, he did.

Pressing even further against it, I began to make out the occasional word.

"*—has no idea.*" A sharp laugh, Leda's. "*—nearly caught us earlier, but it's nothing I can't handle.*"

Caught us? Doing *what*? And were they talking about *me*? Did they mean out there on the deck?

The other person began speaking, their voice too low for me

to make out any words, and I watched Con visibly pale before me. The color leeching from his cheeks.

"What?" I hissed. "What is it—what did you hear?"

And then *I* heard it. Unmistakably. Clear as a bell. The rest of the sentence was unintelligible, but there was no mistaking that word.

Will.

My hand immediately gripped the door handle. Was he *in* there? I was driving myself mad second-guessing everything. Now was the time to start acting—

Con's hand closed over mine.

"No," he said very quietly and very firmly.

I looked up at him. He must have heard it too. To my surprise, he looked—*afraid.*

"Con?"

"We—we need to go—and now. I'll explain—I'll explain in a minute."

Part of me wanted to struggle, to resist, but another part of me, a deeper, more instinctual part, knew he was right. There was something about this silent, dark corridor. Something about the hushed intimacy of the conversation behind the door that screamed danger.

Safely back in the SeaMester corridor, we paused outside his cabin.

"Okay, so what was wrong back there?"

Con shook his head, looking confused now, almost embarrassed. "It's uh, nothing—it was just awkward, that's all. I mean, how am I meant to explain lurking outside Leda's door at one a.m.? I had images of us falling through the door into their cabin."

I exhaled with annoyance. "Why would you need to explain—I was right there with you. You *heard* it—I know you did. I saw your face. She said 'Will.' Why would she say that unless she was involved in some way?"

Con gave me an exasperated look. "Maybe she knows another Will? It's a fairly common name. Or maybe she was just using the word in a sentence?" He paused, looking at the ground for a moment as if debating whether to say something else. His gaze snagged mine, dark with concern. "Look, it's been a . . . a long night. I'm going to get some sleep. And I suggest you do the same—you're obviously in need of it."

I stared after him, watching in disbelief as his cabin door slammed shut. I hadn't imagined that fearful look on his face.

And I *hadn't* imagined them saying Will's name.

19

I DON'T KNOW WHAT IT WAS THAT WOKE ME, HOURS LATER. I had a vague recollection of some kind of noise, a hushed whispering or laughing. But when I woke, the room was silent. Silent, but not fully dark.

I half opened a wary eye.

The door to the bathroom was open—only a crack—and the light was on; the bright fluorescence creating a yellow wedge on the floor.

I *knew* I hadn't left it on tonight.

The cabin had been completely dark once I'd settled down to sleep. I might have been afraid of the sea and numerous other slightly irrational things Will had always scoffed at (clowns, spiders, storms, electrical lines), but I wasn't afraid of the dark.

What I *did* know was that I wouldn't be able to sleep a wink until I got out of bed, confronted the fact that a switched-on light was far from the worst thing in the world, and turned the damn thing off.

Muttering curses, I padded the short distance to the bathroom, opening the door and letting the sharp light pour into the main room.

The room was damp—that was the first thing I noticed. The same as it was after I showered, that wet humidity thick in the air. The mirror was fogged up, as was the shower stall, its glass door tightly shut.

Now, I might have been persuaded that I'd left the light on, but I knew I hadn't left the shower on. I would have *heard* it, for starters. So then why was the glass all steamed up?

Unsettled now, I peered more closely at the bottom of the shower. Through the hazy condensation on the glass door, I could see a pool of black on the floor.

The hell was *that*? Had I left some clothes in there? Was there an issue with the drains?

With shaking hands, half wondering if this was a dream, I wrenched back the door, sending it slamming against the sink, then gave a shrill, shocked scream.

Spread in the bottom of the shower, pulsating darkly, was a large black octopus-type creature, its tentacles splayed out, spider-like over the entire floor. I toppled out of the bathroom, immediately shutting the door with a panicked crash, shuddering violently; another shaky half scream escaping from my lips.

What in the absolute *fuck*? Had something somehow escaped from the atrium? But how? It was a *sea* creature. The image of an octopus, lurching its way drunkenly down the corridor, using its tentacles as legs, came to mind, and I rubbed my hands fiercely over my face, gasping at the onset of hysteria.

Resolutely, I pulled on my robe over my pajamas and headed into the corridor, only just remembering to pick up my key card before the door thunked shut.

I stood in the corridor, trembling, wondering what the hell to do. I needed to go somewhere. I certainly couldn't go back in my room again, not with that *thing* in there . . . like some kind of giant aquatic arachnid. I imagined it scuttling out of the shower cubicle and running up the walls or a whole host of them skittering down the corridor after me.

My first thought was the atrium and the help desk. Maybe Orlaigh would be there with her no-nonsense, get-things-done nod. But what if Eduardo were there instead? He wasn't so far removed from a spider himself; angular and long-limbed, dark hairs bristling out of his face at odd angles.

Besides, it must have been the middle of the night. Would there even be anyone on duty at this time?

Yet again, I found myself wishing Will was here. He'd know what to do. And even if he didn't, he'd have let me crash in his cabin, no questions asked.

The corridors were shadowy and silent, the lights dimmed low. I couldn't go to Justin, not after our earlier conversation. He clearly thought I was unhinged, and this would be the final straw. I might find myself locked up somewhere for my own safety. Steeling myself, I padded a few doors down, to where I knew Constantine's room was. While we hadn't exactly parted on good terms earlier, this might be the evidence I needed to finally convince him something was up.

I tapped lightly at his door, still not entirely sure what I was doing.

After a good few minutes of harder tapping, with no response, I began to doubt he was even in there. But the thought of going back to my own sullied cabin alone increased the force of my knocking. Moments later, I heard definite sounds of movement alongside several mumbled expletives.

The door opened a crack and Constantine peered out, wearing sports shorts and a tee, his curls an endearing tangle. He did a double take when he saw me.

"Hello, again. This is somewhat unexpected?"

I gave him a tight smile.

"Can I come in for a sec? I mean, you don't have company or anything?"

He gave me his now-familiar amused grin. "Alas, no." He opened the door wider. "To the company part, I mean. Of course you can come in."

As I stepped into his room, I wished I had thought to bring some more grown-up nightwear with me rather than my faded unicorn-print pajamas. No doubt Thalia and her crew all wafted around in translucent silk kimonos.

"Come for a sleepover?"

I noticed his room was fastidiously tidy. His suitcase neatly parked in a corner; the counters clean apart from a tidy stack of paperbacks.

"Rein it in. There's something . . . something . . . *weird* in my bathroom."

He raised a teasing eyebrow. "*Oh?* Surely that's a job for the maids—or maybe a plumber?"

"*No.* Not like *that.* It's . . . it's some kind of creature. An octopus, I think. In my shower."

"A *what?*" He ran a hand over his face and snorted. "Look, Liv, I realize we're on a ship, but they don't come up through the drains like spiders."

"I swear it's there." I wished I'd had the forethought to snap a photo now that I'd realized what a giant lunatic I sounded like. "Come and see if you don't believe me."

He gave an exaggerated sigh and collapsed into the chair beside the bed, long limbs sprawled out before him. Feeling distinctly awkward—I didn't know where to look—I perched uneasily on the edge of his mattress. He gestured to the sleep-rumpled sheets.

"I mean, if you want to stay, you don't need an excuse. I'm hardly going to say no, am I?"

I raised an eyebrow, looking back at the door to disguise my heated face. Well, there was some information I had no idea what to do with. Still, now was hardly the time. I feigned annoyance.

"Will you come and look, please? If only to confirm I'm not insane. I would have knocked on Justin's door, but I couldn't remember his room number," I lied. "Besides, you're awake now anyway."

"I don't need to go to your cabin to confirm that you're insane," he said, grabbing a pair of sweatpants and heading to the small bathroom. "One sec."

I stood quickly, managing to hit my thigh on the half-open nightstand beside Constantine's bed. Cursing softly, I went to close it, my eyes sweeping over the contents within: a box of condoms (open, I drolly noted), a neatly coiled charging cable, and several brown bottles of medication.

Curious, I picked up one of the bottles at random. The medication label was long-winded and impossible to pronounce. Some kind of prescription medication I'd never heard of. The name *Constantine Konstallis* was printed neatly on the side.

Konstallis?

Why did that name ring a bell?

The warning printed on the bottle swam before my eyes.

Caution: May cause hallucinations.

I recalled what Justin said earlier.

Are you on any medication?

At the sound of the bathroom door opening, I dropped the bottle back into the drawer as if it had stung me. I had no business snooping.

As we hurried in the direction of my cabin, I found myself bizarrely praying the octopus—or whatever the hell it was—would still be there when we returned. Otherwise, this would look like some deliberate and ridiculous ploy to get him into my cabin. Ushering him into the room before me, I dramatically thrust open the bathroom door. But of course, when Con emerged shaking his head, a slight smile on his lips, I saw the bottom of the shower was now empty.

"What the—?" I said, shaking my head too. "Where could it have gone?"

Con might have been joking about the drains, but he was right. There was no way something that size could have slivered back down it.

I pushed past him into the main room and began cautiously lifting cushions and checking under the bed.

"I mean, as excuses to seduce me go . . . *There's an octopus in my shower* is one of the better ones."

I stood, the room upturned around me, and stared at him, standing confused and sleep-disheveled in the doorway. Despite everything, I burst into laughter. Moments later, he laughed too. Then we stopped laughing and looked at each other. I sank down on the bed.

"What was it earlier?" I asked, unable to let it go. "Outside Leda's cabin. You looked—"

Scared wasn't exactly the right word. *Apprehensive? Shocked?*

He knew what I meant, though.

"That voice on the other side of the door—not Leda's—the other one. I thought . . . I thought I recognized it." He looked away for a second. "But there's no way—it's impossible. I was mistaken."

Now was my chance—finally a chink in Con's armor of casual denial.

"Who? Who did you think it was?"

Octavia?

That name flashed in my mind again, paused on my lips, a neon warning, but Con said nothing, continuing to stare steadfastly at the ground. Something prevented me from asking. Con's absolute iron-cast denial the last time I'd brought her up.

"Con, I know you don't want to believe it—but something weird is going on and Will needs help. And—and maybe he's not the only one. Maybe all of us are in some kind of . . . danger. I can't keep acting like nothing's happening. I need to do . . . *something*. I just don't know what. . . ."

He softened. "Look, I'll admit that message from him was odd, but you're forgetting, the doctor said you can more than likely see him tomorrow. Which I guess is today, technically, looking at the time."

And then maybe you'll stop all this insanity. He left it unsaid, but it was there, unspoken, all the same.

And okay, he wasn't wrong. Once I did see Will, once I could confirm he was okay, then maybe my brain would stop creating these insane conspiracy theories and—

"Hey, what's this?"

Con was peering down at something on the dresser—the paperwork relating to my scholarship. Flushing with embarrassment at the idea of him knowing the gory details of my financial situation, I gathered it up and hastily shoved it in a drawer.

"Nothing—just boring info about my scholarship." I noticed he was frowning. "Why?"

He shrugged, still looking disconcerted. "Thought I recognized the name of the company, that's all."

I gave him a wan smile, fervently wishing once again I wasn't wearing my drab pajamas. Why was he still standing there in silence? For some reason, I got it into my sleep-deprived head that he was waiting for me to open the door for him so he could leave. I was taking a few steps closer to him, intending to do exactly that, when he spoke.

"I mean, if you're truly worried that an octopus might be lurking under the bed, I could be persuaded to stay."

His voice was lower than before, softer, and meeting his gaze, I realized he was now looking at me in an intense kind of way that could have powered twenty thousand cruise ships. I swallowed. What was I supposed to say to *that*? Obviously, allowing him to stay would be a monumentally bad decision, and a thoughtless one too—what with Will still missing and—

Wanting Will to care doesn't mean he does.

I pushed the thought away. Con was still looking at me, clearly waiting for a response. *Why* was I so bad at this? I knew something flirty was required, something clever about the odds of an octopus being in my bed increasing if he stayed, but as I was thinking it over, he stepped closer, meeting me halfway, and every rational thought flew out of my head like sea spray. Even at this time of night, he smelled utterly glorious—like admittedly slightly sweaty citrus and salt.

"You know, honestly, it's been a little frustrating trying to get to know you better, Liv. . . ."

That soft voice that I instinctively recognized as dangerous. I sucked in a sharp breath as he placed sure hands on my waist. A million electric impulses shuddered through me at his touch. I had never felt anything *like* this before. A terrible yearning and with it a need that was almost making me want to avoid him, I was so embarrassed by it.

Forcing myself to stop staring at the floor, I belligerently looked up at him. God, his eyes were beautiful, the same color as the moon. I wanted to unapologetically stare into them for twenty-four hours. I wanted to paint them, a massive mural on my bedroom wall. I wanted *so* badly to touch him, feel the lived-in soft cotton of his T-shirt. I wanted to—

"Sorry, what?" I said, realizing he had been saying something else.

"Never mind," he murmured, not breaking his stare.

I bit my lip. His hands were burning conflagrations at my waist. Logistically, he was at least a head taller than me, but if I stood on my tiptoes—

But how could I even *think* about this when Will was missing? Would he behave the same? Flirting with some girl while I malingered in a sick bay. And Constantine was clearly some kind of fuck boy. I mean . . . Leda, Adora—probably—even some missing girl.

And now her replacement.

"I can practically hear you thinking," he said dryly.

I opened my mouth, ready to babble something in my defense, but with admirable grace, he lowered his head and kissed me. It was chaste and soft, his lips barely brushing my own. Despite that—or maybe because of it—blood roared through every part of my body like a tsunami, drowning out all my thoughts, swallowing the world. I reached up with shaky hands, desperate to run my fingers through his hair, to grab handfuls of it, ready to be done with this gentleness. As I did, I felt the heat of his tongue flick my lips, his mouth meeting mine once more.

But then he pulled away, stepping back and bumping into the door. His eyes flickered to the bed behind me.

"I should go," he muttered, already pulling the door open. "I should *really* go. Good night, Liv. Hope your night remains octopus free."

20

FOR THE REMAINDER OF THE NIGHT, I BARELY SLEPT, AND IN the snatches of sleep I did get, thoughts of rogue octopi and Constantine's offer to stay in my cabin managed to combine themselves into some pretty surreal dreams.

As gray light began to filter under my cabin door, I clicked on the TV and found an old sitcom, needing some downtime to order all the circling thoughts in my head to the gentle soundtrack of canned laughter.

A sudden bleep from my phone made me sit up straight. Scrabbling for it, I saw a message was from Con. The fact that I wasn't immediately disappointed for once made me feel momentarily guilty.

Meet me on Deck 4.

Thoughts of last night flashed through my head, filling me with a delirious, delicious heat. Yes, I'd been kissed before, but somehow it had all felt so different with Con. I'd never met someone so at ease with himself, so confident, his kiss controlled and precise. None of the usual nerves or awkwardness, only the easy presumption that I'd wanted it too. Still, did his message have to sound so much like an order?

I sat up straighter.

Wait—how could I have forgotten? Today was *the* day.

The day the doctor had told me there was a chance I'd see Will or at the very least hear from him. After all that had happened, I still had hope.

On the off chance, I picked up my phone and dialed Will's number again. Still that same irritating robotic voice.

The number you have dialed is unavailable—

Getting dressed, I put more thought into my outfit than usual, even putting in the time to carry out a perfect cat-eye for myriad reasons. I was too anxious for breakfast, but at least meeting Con would prevent me from sitting outside the infirmary, waiting, from the moment it opened.

As I went to leave, I saw a leaflet had been pushed under the door of my cabin, advertising an upcoming Murder Mystery night—*Official invitation to come,* apparently. I screwed up my nose in distaste. Hopefully that particular delight wasn't on the orientation schedule.

Con was waiting for me up on the windward side of the deck, perched upon a sun lounger and wrapped in an expensive-looking wool coat. He didn't look at me as I approached but continued staring out to sea, which this morning was the flat, uninviting gray of steel.

"You know, it's impossible to find somewhere quiet on this ship."

While I'd not expected him to swoon into my arms, I'd hoped for a bit more of a greeting after last night. Self-consciously, I wrapped my jacket tightly around myself.

"And you're surprised by this? You're on a boat of three thousand passengers, not in the middle of your dad's country estate. Why did you want to meet out here again? It's bloody freezing today."

He chuckled. I liked the sound of it.

"It's a *ship*, not a boat. Why do you think I wanted to meet out here?" He gestured to the joint he held in one hand. "So I can smoke without Justin alerting maritime law."

I balanced gingerly in the middle of an adjacent sun bed.

"Ship, boat. What's the difference?"

He passed me the joint wordlessly. Not wanting to look un-sophisticated, I took it and inhaled deeply. My eyes immediately watered, and my throat burned in protest.

"My dad always said a ship can carry a boat, but a boat can't carry a ship."

I brushed the tears from my eyes and handed it back. "Nope, none the wiser, but I guess he'd know. Hey, does he really own the *Eos*?"

Con only shrugged, as if your parent owning a luxury cruise liner was no big deal. "He owns the company that owns the *Eos*."

"*Jesus*, Con—"

Con gazed over my head, out to sea again, and sighed, one arm wrapped tightly around his flapping coat.

"See, this is why I don't tell people. It makes them . . . weird."

Already my mind was racing with possibilities. Surely Con could just order the infirmary staff to let me see Will or—

"I've not really got any proper sway on the ship, if that's what you're thinking," he said, dryly, apparently reading my mind. "Dad and I aren't exactly on the best terms. The other morning was probably the limit."

Not entirely convinced, I decided to change the subject for now. I didn't want Con to think I was only here for his connections.

"Hey, was Raj at breakfast? I'm worried about him."

"Nope, I didn't see him. But let's face it, Liv, when are you *not* worried?"

I decided to ignore that.

"It was the weirdest thing. Yesterday, Cintia and I were on the swim deck. Raj was there—with Lexie—and I swear, I *swear* I saw him fall, right over the railing, onto the deck below. I thought—I thought I saw her push him."

Constantine did turn to look at me now, regarding me with amused gray eyes.

"You *saw* him fall over the railing? Only you. Not one other person on deck noticed?"

"I *know*. I know it sounds ridiculous, but Con, no one's seen him since."

He laughed. "Yes, they *have*! Cintia's with him now, bravely nursing him through the pain of a pulled muscle. Liv, I mean,

I like a good old conspiracy theory as much as the next person, but you elevate that shit to new levels."

I tried to relax. Could it just be the strain of the trip getting to me? I read in psych class about a DJ who hadn't slept for two hundred hours and started hallucinating flames coming out of drawers and mysterious dark figures coming to take him away. Seemed I wasn't far from that stage.

I would see Will today. Time to dial back the crazy.

"Anyway, about last night—" I stumbled on. He gazed back out to sea again as if already bored. "I wanted to make sure you didn't get the wrong impression."

"Oh?" He quirked an eyebrow. "And what impression would that be?"

I'd guessed he wouldn't make this easy.

I sighed, determined to solider on. "What I mean is, I don't want to cause any drama between you and Leda or—"

He cast me a dark look.

"I don't care what Leda thinks about anything. And neither should you."

Did he treat all his exes so delightfully?

"Wow, Con."

He grimaced at my expression. "You don't understand. Whatever she might infer, we were never together. Sure, we'd flirt or whatever when we ran into each other on one of my dad's cruises, but even that ended when I overheard a conversation between her and my dad and, yeah . . . I didn't like it. It's part of why we aren't friendly anymore."

My eyes widened to saucer size and Con chuckled.

"Wait—wait—not like *that*. Yeah, my dad's an arse, but he's not *that* bad. Or at least, I don't think so. All my dad's ever been interested in is money."

"Okay, so what *do* you mean?"

He paused, pushing a hand through his hair distractedly. "Something along the lines of me not being her first choice—it all sounded quite hissed and angry between them. Anyway, believe me, there's nothing between Leda and me anymore. Not after overhearing that little exchange."

"Well, good, because when you offered to stay, I thought you—I thought—"

I stopped, feeling woozy. What *was* I trying to say?

"Are you wondering if I wanted to fuck you?" he said, still not looking at me. "Save you wondering, the answer's yes—despite the terrible pajamas."

He turned and grinned at me. Heat rushed to my face and I had to look away. "What is it between you and Will, though? Only friendship? Or is it . . . *complicated*? Because honestly, the last thing I need is complicated."

I smiled back. I couldn't stop myself, hope still bubbling away in my chest.

"Seriously, *just* friendship."

There. I'd pinned my colors to the mast. Hopefully, he'd take the hint.

But he said nothing and we sat in vaguely uncomfortable silence for a while, both staring out at the wide expanse of sea. The distant hum of the ship's engines seemed to grow gradually to a steady roar, and the inky sea before me reared up alarmingly. The waves swelled, crashing over the railing, an impenetrable wall of salty oblivion, and then Constantine's face swam before mine. His eyes were huge, gray as storms. Blond tendrils of hair drifting over his face like seaweed. He looked like Poseidon, god of the sea.

"You look like a god," I breathed.

He shifted away, out of my eyeline again.

"Are you sure you're all right, Liv?"

Shit. I should *not* smoke. I scurried up from my prone position on the sun lounger, clutching my arms around my chest against the cold.

"I said . . . Oh God. I think I need to lie down. How strong *is* that stuff?"

I got up, the deck swinging back alarmingly beneath my feet, and staggered a few steps, the swell of the waves beneath me not helping.

Snorting, Con attempted to get up too, immediately collapsing back on the lounger.

Thankfully, after I took a few deep breaths of sea air, the ship stopped swaying so dramatically. I composed myself and reached down to give Con a hand up. He accepted, rising with an elegance that made me think his imbalance was an act.

Then, stepping forward, he took my other hand, neatly closing the distance between us.

"Oh no," I muttered as his hands slipped leisurely within my jacket, resting on my waist, urging me gently backward until I met the smooth wall of the ship. He crowded closer, his body warm against mine, against the biting wind, tilting my chin up to meet his gaze, his lashes casting shadows against his pale cheeks.

"No?"

His voice was soft, barely audible over the insane hammering of my heart.

"No—yes—*yes*. I mean, didn't you want to be alone?"

"No, I wanted *us* to be alone," he murmured between soft, tilting kisses. I sighed, melting into him.

At that exact moment, my brain helpfully reminded me I was here as a replacement for his now-missing ex.

What happened to her?

Were you really the last person to see her alive?

But his kisses grew demanding, almost furious, and then I couldn't even think, easily keeping up with his fervor. It was like a growing fever between us, grasping and desperate, our hands wandering everywhere beneath the secret sanctuary of coats.

Then, without warning, he took a brisk step back, looking surprised, wiping a hand over his mouth, a hand through his hair.

"You know, we probably shouldn't do this here," he said with an embarrassed laugh, glancing around. "Might give someone a heart attack."

"Nobody's looking," I said, disappointed he'd stopped. But following his eyes, I saw I was wrong. An elderly couple a few feet away, standing at the railing, were already looking over at us with clear disgust.

I waited, hoping he would suggest we meet somewhere quieter after I'd been to see Will. But instead, he gave me an apologetic kiss on the cheek. "I'm sorry. I don't want to hold you up. We'd better go, hadn't we?" He paused, giving me a meaningful glance. "Time to see Will."

21

AS I HURRIED INTO THE ATRIUM, CON HUNG BACK IN THE corridor, saying he had to make a call. The reception desk seemed more crowded than usual; no doubt people were busy booking day trips as we got ever closer to the first port of call. As I waited in line, I caught sight of Laila, standing before the tanks, staring at the fish.

"Hey!"

She turned, her expression as somber as ever.

"You love looking at these fish, huh? Too old for the kids' club?" I joked weakly.

Laila gave me a pitying look and nodded toward the tank.

"You know, there's the usual fish you expect to see—clownfish, zebrafish, angelfish. But some, though . . . some I don't recognize at *all*." She frowned, her forehead scrunching. "It's weird—like everything else on this ship."

I considered telling her it was unlikely she had encyclopedic knowledge of every fish in the damn ocean, but I wasn't used to young kids and didn't want to make her cry or anything.

"And sometimes," she went on, her voice low, "*sometimes*— there's someone in there . . . just watching."

I blinked at her, incredulous.

"Some*one*? What, a person, you mean?"

"Yeah, they're wearing scuba gear and they just stand in the tank, half-hidden at the back—in the shadows behind the weeds—and all they do is watch. It's weird."

Damn right that was weird. Not to mention hugely unlikely.

"They're probably just cleaning the tank. Ha—this will make you laugh. There was one of those black squid things in my shower last night."

Instead of laughing, she stared at me, totally horrified.

"What—really? Did it . . . get on you? Touch you?"

I chuckled, trying to show her I was fine, that it hadn't been her terrifying toothy octopus from the depths of the Mariana Trench, just someone's idea of a bad joke. Raj probably.

"No. It was flopping miserably about on the floor. Some kind of practical joke, I think. . . . It was gone when I went back in again."

She gave me a dark look. "You should be careful, Liv. You don't know what they are, and therefore you don't know what they're capable of."

"Laila, it's just a—a fish."

I was trying to be jovial, but it came out sounding how I felt.

Unsettled. I changed the subject. "What are you up to today? Tried any bingo? I had a go at that the other day—would *not* recommend it."

Laila gave an owlish nod. "There are a lot of games going on, on this ship, and some very competitive people. You should watch some of the older ones," she continued, her brown eyes huge behind her glasses. "They've been in on it the longest. You know, they've been on the ship so long, I'm not sure they're even human anymore."

A cloud passed over the sun, darkening the atrium and thickening the shadows. For some reason I thought of Hilary then and those words I thought I'd heard back in the bingo lounge.

And that was when we pushed him over the side—

Laila stared back into the tanks at a smoke-colored black squid, similar to the thing I'd found in my shower, as it glided in and out of the weeds.

"You should watch them dance—it's really difficult to look away," Laila said, her eyes on the squid. "I can't find any mention of them online. I've image searched and everything. None of the staff knows what they are either. Or at least, they *say* they don't. I know they *do*. They just won't tell me."

I thought again of that twisting, black creature in the tank in the captain's room. The way that octopus last night had been sprawled out like a gigantic arachnid on the floor of my shower—

It is a FISH, Liv, I told myself sternly. *There are things you are allowed to be afraid of on this ship:*

- *Will being sick*
- *Contracting whatever weird disease he might have*
- *People appearing to topple off decks*
- *Drowned magicians*
- *Bitchy influencers*

But you CANNOT be afraid of a bloody fish in a tank.

"Well," I said, my nerves making me jittery, "I better be going, but I'll see you around, hmm?"

She gave a distant nod, barely even listening, transfixed by the tank.

I was glad Orlaigh was on duty today. It was good to see a friendly face at the desk. She gave me her usual distracted smile, but something about her was different this morning. Her eyes deeply circled with shadows. She looked . . . tired, *anxious* even.

"Ah, good morning, Olivia. How may I help you today?"

I gave her a polite smile.

"Hey, I don't know if you remember, but I'm here on the SeaMester trip with my friend Will. He was the one who got sick the first night."

She nodded along with my words, adjusting her head to the side in sympathy.

"Anyway—yesterday the doctor said I should be able to visit him today. He did take my cabin number down and said he'd call, but I thought I'd be proactive and see if there's been any improvement."

"He did, did he?" She looked at me uncertainly. "All right, I can check, that's no problem. Let me give the infirmary a quick call and find out what's going on for you."

She returned with suspicious haste.

"The doctor says there's been no change at the moment—your friend is still unable to have visitors—but she'll let you know as soon as there is."

I stared back at her, so disappointed I nearly burst into tears. Then I picked up on what she'd said.

"Wait, *she*? No, you must have spoken to the wrong doctor. It was a man with a white beard that I spoke to yesterday. . . ." I shut my eyes for a second, desperately remembering. "*Daggett,* his badge read. Dr. Daggett. Can you try to get a hold of him for me? He'll know what you mean."

Orlaigh gave me a look so sympathetic I felt an immediate cold hand claw at the base of my spine.

"*What?*" My words were sharp. Almost as if I knew what was coming. "Are you able to call him or not?"

"Olivia, we only have one doctor on board. Her name is Dr. Hammond. I don't know of anyone on the staff named Daggett."

I stared at her.

"No, you're wrong. I spoke to him yesterday! My friend was there too—he can vouch for me—and Eduardo. I mean, Mr. Eduardo—the hotel manager."

She continued to stare at me with that pitying, blank look, giving me a sorry shake of her head. Somehow her pity was worse than any simple dismissal.

"I'm so sorry, Olivia. I don't know what else to tell you. Perhaps if I find Mr. Eduardo, he can clear up the confusion that's clearly occurred here? I'm not sure if he's on duty yet, but I could send him to your cabin once he is?"

I stared at her. The thought of Eduardo sneaking silently up to my room was not a pleasant one. She gave me a watery smile of apology. "Or maybe not."

Not knowing what else to say, I turned away, hot tears of disappointment welling behind my eyes.

But at least now I knew what I had to do.

It didn't take me long to reach the infirmary. I hammered impatiently on the door and rattled the handle. To my surprise, it was unlocked, opening easily.

"Have you been directed here by a member of staff?" asked the nurse manning the front desk before I'd even stepped through the door, the same no-nonsense blond woman in her fifties. "If not, I'm going to have to ask you to leave. This is currently a restricted area."

Not being confrontational by nature, I hesitated, unsure of my next move—until I saw the familiar figure of Eduardo slinking down the corridor up ahead.

"Hey!" I called out angrily, ignoring her. "Hey, excuse me, Mr. Eduardo. Wait a second!"

The nurse exhaled loudly with annoyance as I took a few steps into the waiting area. Up ahead, Eduardo paused and then slowly turned around. He seemed unnaturally tall in the dim corridor, almost stooping against the ceiling.

"Ye-es?"

"I need to talk to you," I said, aware my voice was rising, but desperate for answers. "Where's that doctor? I need to speak to him—the one we spoke to yesterday. I *need* to see my friend. You were there—it was all agreed I'd see him today."

Eduardo's blank smile immediately switched on like a light-bulb, his teeth whiter than ever.

"Dr. Hammond is currently on her break. I will inform her of your wishes when she returns."

What was he even doing, lurking down here in the infirmary again?

"Okay—but what about Dr. Daggett? You know—the bearded guy we spoke to yesterday. Where's he today?"

A pantomime-ish look of confusion flitted across Eduardo's face, and I felt my blood heat to dangerous levels.

"Dr. *who*? You must be mistaken? We have only a Dr. Hammond on board—"

"You liar!" I blurted out fiercely. Behind me, the nurse muttered something darkly under her breath and began getting up. "You absolute *liar*! You were right here yesterday when I spoke to him! He was old with a white beard and—and a badge and—"

"Right, I think you'd better go, my love," said the nurse, attempting to take hold of my arm. I wrenched out of her grip and whirled to face her, knocking over a flimsy wire rack of leaflets as I did, sending them scattering over the floor.

"I need to see my friend—that's *all* I want! The doctor said I could. *Please.* I just want to *see* him."

I need you to prove he's still on this damn ship.

"Miss—" The nurse's grip tightened uncomfortably and I scrabbled at her fingers. Instantly, she let go.

"Miss *nothing*! Don't you touch me again. You need to take me to Will right now. *Now.* I'm serious. Or—or—I'll call the police. I will call the police right now—or, or Interpol—the FBI—and I will report you all for child neglect."

The hotel manager stared at me with cold, hard eyes. "I kindly request that you stop destroying the ship's property and leave right away."

"Hey! Hey, Liv—what—*what* are you doing?"

I felt a cool hand encircle my wrist.

Con. Irritated, I shook him off.

"Why are *you* here?" I snapped at him. "And what does it look like I'm doing? I've had enough of this. They're all fucking *lying* to me!"

"Lying to you?" He looked at Eduardo. "Sorry about this. I'll have a chat with Liv here, and I'm sure she'll be back later to apologize and—"

I spun around to face him, incredulous.

"Are you for real? I'm not apologizing for anything! They *are* lying to me! I was told I could see Will yesterday and now they're acting like I'm crazy, like I made it all up! You were *here*! You *know* I'm not lying—"

Con lowered his voice to my ear, his breath politely mint-scented. "If you carry on like this, you'll be on the first flight home from the nearest port and your parents will be billed for the trouble—we're talking at least several grand. Adios to your good references. You know, the ones you so badly need. So, please, calm the hell down and come with me."

Glaring at Eduardo, I allowed Con to lead me away from the infirmary door and into the corridor.

I tore myself away from him. Even now, in my angered state, his closeness was distracting.

"You know, I was right about you," I spat, wanting him to hate me, wanting to hate *him* so I could stop wanting him. "From the first moment I met you, I knew instantly you were an arrogant, entitled, overprivileged, posh *twat*!"

"Is that so?" he said dryly. "Well, since we're talking home truths, then maybe you need to think about how you're coming across. You can't just pick fights with random members of staff because you're upset. Yes, your friend is sick and I'm sorry you didn't get to see him exactly when you wanted, but it doesn't give you the right to run about the ship acting like a spoiled child."

"His name's *Will*! And he's *gone*! His phone's been switched off since yesterday, and they've practically thrown all his belongings in the *trash*," I screamed. "And any one of us could be next! Your dad *owns* the *Eos*—you can do anything you want! So if you're not prepared to help me, then just—just fuck off."

"Don't tell me to fuck off. Look, someone needed to stop you—"

"I don't need *you* to do anything for me, Constantine. *Jesus*."

I made to push past him. There wasn't time for this. I needed someone who would actually listen to me. Cintia—or failing that, the damn captain. Someone needed to redirect this boat and investigate what in the hell was happening—

"Olivia, what is really going on with you?"

Something in his tone made me pause. I glared up at him, not liking the pity I saw in his eyes.

"Whatever, Con. You know what I think? I think you're probably involved in all this weirdness!" I shouted, on an un-stoppable roll now. "Seeing as your dad is in charge of all these creepy ships. So maybe you can explain what's going on, hey? Why people are disappearing. Will. The magician. *Raj.* I don't care about my bloody references anymore, Con. I care about getting off this ship! I mean, can't you do *something*? Call Daddy and get us a helicopter out of here?"

I was pleased to see his perpetually marble-carved face tinge with pink at this. His features hardened and he lowered his voice.

"Look, are you taking something? You look like you haven't slept in months, and some of the stuff you've been saying— Raj falling off the deck in broad daylight . . . and last night— passing out in the club—"

I gave a bitter laugh, already walking away from him. Ironic coming from the walking pharmacy of the seas. Images from last night flashed before my eyes. The weird turn I'd taken in the club. Con's drawer full of meds.

"Okay, okay. I see how it is. Leave me *alone*, Con."

22

OUTSIDE THE NEPTUNE LOUNGE, I STARED DOWN AT MY phone as if expecting it to give me answers, already regretting blowing up at Con.

Where ARE you, Will?

I had to know. Because I was becoming more and more concerned that he wasn't on this ship anymore and no one had been expected to notice.

Except I had.

Clearly they hadn't bargained on him having a friend here. A person who was never *meant* to be here in the first place. A replacement for another girl, a girl who'd already gone missing before she had the chance to disappear here.

But what was the *link* here?

I rubbed my eyes hard, my head heavy.

Was SeaMester the target here? First Will, then Raj. Who was next? Me?

Again, I thought of Thalia's scarf in Will's room, her picture with the magician's sister. It was something to do with the Sirens, I was sure of it, but nothing added up yet.

The things that masked person had whispered to me in the theater the other day. Did they have some bearing on what was going on? It was hard to remember what they'd said, I'd been so desperate to get away. Something about Orpheus and a ship of fools and pacts—and—

Seven is the bargain and seven have been promised—

Flashback to boarding the ship. A circle of seven at a round table; a laminated sign affixed to it. SeaMester. Will and me, Raj, Cintia, Con, Adora, and Justin.

Seven.

Coincidence? Were we all *promised*? What did that even mean? And if so, by whom?

I groaned aloud. I needed to focus my attention on finding Will. Getting sidetracked by conspiracies like *that* was undeniably entering the realm of crazy. People going missing on cruises was not.

I took another look at Apollo, still grinning out from the board, the CANCELED tape unnervingly present. Was he recovering, or worse?

"Pity, isn't it?"

Hilary stood directly behind me with a too-wide smile, nodding toward the board. Surely she wasn't talking about what had happened at the show—that had been much more than a *pity*.

"Oh well, I've never been a fan of magicians, so perhaps it's for the best."

She means the show being canceled, not whatever happened to him, I told myself before my brain dragged me down any more dark flights of fancy.

I nodded absently; something about her fixed grin and glittering gaze was putting me on edge. She looked different too. Her skin somehow plumper and dewier, her eyes brighter. As if noticing my stare, she patted her face with her hands.

"Just got back from the spa. Have you been? They've got some very unusual treatments down there." She smiled again, even wider, revealing almost every tooth in her head. "Anyway, must be off, my love."

I watched her walk away, her step almost sprightly, her walking stick absent, then sank, defeated, into a nearby armchair.

It felt like entire weeks now since the day we'd boarded, when Will had squeezed my hand tight in his. I missed him so much it was hard to think straight sometimes. Not in some cheesy-Hallmark-movie way but in the way his presence here had grounded me. Reminded me firmly of who I was, what I hoped to achieve. Without him I felt weightless. Just a balloon drifting aimlessly over the ocean, buffeting uselessly between winds.

I couldn't pinpoint exactly when things began to change for me. There wasn't that one pivotal moment like there is in movies. I only know that they did.

It started with a series of small kindnesses. Things he probably never even noticed he was doing and certainly never realized had the effect on me they did. That was Will. Yes, he could be loud and obnoxious, but there was a stability, a quiet decency at his core.

Loaning me his jacket when he noticed I was shivering in my thin raincoat during one winter walk home from college.

The box of Maltesers he'd left in my locker when I failed my quadratic equations assessment for the third time and Mrs. Williams had sarcastically asked me why I'd even bothered re-taking it.

That night in the kitchen at Keira Wylie's house party when he'd uncharacteristically shoved Caiden Ballard in the chest for drunkenly chanting "Shortney Kardashian" at me.

And the game we always played. Either/Or. Two random things we'd choose from and fire back at each other.

McDonald's or Burger King.

Monster or Red Bull.

Loki or Thor.

Netflix or Disney+.

Until it became people . . . Megan or Chloe. Jenson or Max. Mr. Owen or Mr. Keane. The criteria never specified—all part of the game.

And then that evening, the final pebble that caused the avalanche. The end-of-semester party when he picked me up from where I waited on the pavement outside, tipsy and tearstained, hugging my knees on the damp front lawn.

"Look at it this way, Liv. You had a lucky escape. You know, everyone reckoned he didn't deserve you," he'd said, his jaw clenched, as I'd sobbed and snotted into his shoulder while he'd tried to pour me into his car. My tears wasted over the latest guy I was *sure* I'd been in love with. Liam Sutton. A gamer like us, nice family, good hair. Perfect for me—until I caught him with one hand stuffed down Cara Radler's leggings in the downstairs bathroom.

I'd sat up at his words and stared at him as he drove along the coastal road that summer night, completely blindsided, my tears forgotten in an instant. It had all made sense suddenly. Every tiny action a small part of a giant pattern I hadn't seen until then.

But now I saw it differently.

Now I knew he'd only been going through the motions, made awkward by my drunken display, saying what he thought he ought to, terrified by my tears. But in my head—made fuzzy by cheap white wine, the cool salt air passing through the window, the silence, and the stars—it had meant something different, and I'd molded myself into his side until it became more silent still. Until he'd pulled over before the sea and I'd asked him the question I'd never dared—Lara Seaburg (impossibly beautiful, impossibly cool, wanted by everyone) or me. It didn't matter who I'd chosen. I'd crossed the final line. I'd included myself.

He'd chuckled, unbothered. "*You*, obviously. You know it's *always* you, Liv."

When I tried to recall the moment in the days following, I never quite could. Couldn't remember who had kissed who.

But lately, especially after his outburst, I had the ever-growing, sick certainty that it had been me. That all of it had been me. He'd been the sober one, after all. That I'd imagined some of his words and missed the meaning of the ones I hadn't. Still, he hadn't pulled away, hadn't wiped his mouth on the back of his hand and looked at me disgust. No, he *had* kissed me back. And I might have been tipsy, but I'd known even then that he'd returned every bit of my enthusiasm.

I hadn't been able to breathe as our lips met. It felt like we'd been building up to that one moment, that one evening in his car, our entire lives.

And when his mouth met mine, it had been obliterating.

A dark midwinter thunderstorm the sun couldn't get through. And within minutes we had tumbled into the back seat, this heavy desperation an enormous black wave, even more than I had felt with Con the other evening, any boundaries blurred by the intense familiarity of each other, those boundaries that we'd kept so carefully now crashing down, the word *finally* echoing around and around in my head, everything surprising me, but not surprising me at all.

We were a flailing mass of hands grasping and grabbing and half-discarded clothes, until someone—him, of course, I remembered *that*—had the wisdom to stop.

"Wait," he had said suddenly, sitting bolt upright as if disturbed from a dream, his lips kiss-swollen, his dark curls in disarray.

"Wait—*wait*. We can't do this. It's wrong. You're . . . you're like a sister to me. *And* you're wasted. Shit—*shit*. I'm sorry. I should have . . . I shouldn't have . . . This is a bad idea—it is . . . It's *wrong*."

I might not have remembered what came before, but I remembered every single word, every nuance of what he'd said after.

It's wrong.

Those words crushing, because to me, nothing had ever felt so *right*.

We'd never mentioned it since. Not really. Had texted each other cheerily at first, laughing off how drunk I'd been that night. But I felt the gradual pulling away. Initiated by me to begin with, out of sheer embarrassment, but eagerly picked up on by him. Plans apologetically canceled last minute. Always on the way out when I popped over.

I had thought that this would be our chance. I'd hoped when we were together, alone, he'd realize how much he had missed me.

But he hadn't.

And now—now *this*.

I wiped my eyes, burying my face in my hands.

My phone's insultingly cheerful message tone sliced through my thoughts.

I slid my eyes over to it, praying it wasn't Hilary again.

Will

Every single nerve in my body seemed to fire at once. It had been a whole day since his phone was switched off. Was it possible he'd heard me back there, in the infirmary? I grabbed my phone, my hands shaking so much I nearly dropped it, and fumbled to open the message.

[Image failed to download]

Image?

Cursing, I hurriedly logged in to the ship's archaic Wi-Fi again while heading toward the nearest deck, where the signal was generally better. I stood, the frigid wind cutting cruelly through my hoodie, and waited.

The photo was dark and blurred as if snapped in motion. Disappointment coursed through me. Hopes of a cheery selfie, Will in a hospital bed giving me the thumbs-up, immediately disintegrating. I squinted at the image, trying to make out what it was—clearly he'd sent it by mistake.

Half of the photo showed what appeared to be a girl, dressed in white. I could only make out the back of her head as she walked in front of the camera. Whoever it was had long, dark hair. Not one of the Sirens, then. Was it the same "nurse" I'd thought I'd seen Will with the other day? But surely they'd have to have their hair tied back for hygiene. Besides, she appeared to be barefoot. And where was this taken? The place was dark, the floor looked like metal sheeting rather than the polished wood and fluffy carpet of the decks, and despite the crappy quality of the picture, I got the feeling the space was cavernous.

I zoomed in closer. Could it be that same girl I thought I'd seen in the club—the girl Con kept insisting wasn't here? It was impossible to tell.

A wave of intense nausea washed over me. If it was Octavia, then what exactly did she—a girl who had gone missing in Con's *company*—have to do with all this? Was she in danger too? Did this implicate Con in some way?

But it *couldn't* be her. It made no sense. My mind was making enormous leaps trying to piece something together that didn't fit—at least not yet.

Whoever he was with, Will was trying to *tell* me something. This wasn't normal. He wasn't in the infirmary—clearly. He was in trouble and I was running out of time to find him.

I nearly screamed as the alarm of my phone jangled loudly in my hand. The next scheduled orientation activity was beginning. Justin had squeezed us all into the Sirens' sold-out show on the upper deck, of all things (*Find* Your *Inner Siren— featuring an exclusive performance!*).

There was no way *I* was going, but—

If my hunch was right, and the Sirens did have something to do with all this, then maybe I could use this time—a time when they were all occupied—to investigate a little more. Last night when I'd followed Leda, it had looked as if they all shared a suite of rooms on one of the fancier lower decks.

My heart pounded faster, the idea sending a rush of adrenaline through me. I'd just stop by the conference hall, make sure all three of them were there, and then, if the coast was clear, I would . . .

What? Break into their room? Rummage through their luggage? Even to myself, I sounded insane. And yet, I found my feet carrying me to the elevator, up to the deck where the show was being held.

An odd vibration stirred the air as I got closer to the auditorium. It took me a moment to realize what it was. At first I thought it was singing, maybe Thalia leading the audience in one of her depressing dirges, but as I got near the door, I hesitated.

It sounded like *chanting*.

Low and ominous; the same guttural syllables uttered again and again. Fear gripped me more tightly than before.

It's still probably just a song. All you need to do is check to make sure they're all in there.

My hand closed on the auditorium door and instantly the chanting seemed to stop, as if someone had hit pause on a recording.

"Liv!" shouted Cintia from directly behind me, causing me to jump eight feet in the air. "Didn't think you were planning on coming."

Behind her were Adora and Con. Interesting how he was so reluctant to take part in most of the scheduled orientation activities, but where the Sirens were concerned, he could apparently make an exception.

"I'm not, I just—just—wanted to let Justin know—"

Cintia shrugged. "You know, he seems off lately. Doubt he'll even notice. Catch you after, though?"

She opened the door.

The auditorium was packed. All three of the Sirens stood

on the stage. They were each scene-stealing in their own way—Leda with her obvious and voluptuous beauty; Lexie, lithe and breathy, midway between amusing and sinister—but it was Thalia who truly commanded the stage. Imperious and statuesque; regal and unsmiling. Today she wore an intricately embroidered black cotton caftan that had an almost ceremonial aspect to it.

She stood before the microphone, and the audience all inhaled in anticipation. Then she opened her mouth and began to sing.

Behind her, Leda and Lexie stepped out of the darkness and joined her. They didn't dance, didn't even do so much as sway, only filled the small auditorium with a sound that was half low chanting, half witchcraft.

> *The sea is my lover,*
> *Half drowns me with salt.*
> *He tells me the missing*
> *Were never my fault.*
> *The sea is my lover,*
> *Half chokes me with brine.*
> *Wraps me in his freezing grip,*
> *Takes what is mine.*
> *The sea is my lover,*
> *Adorns me with pearls.*
> *Drowns me in his whirlpool,*
> *One of seven girls.*

I blinked, wrenching my attention away from Thalia and re-calling our very first night aboard the ship, when she had sung to Will. No wonder he had been so entranced by her. Curiously, I looked over at Constantine, who had now taken his seat. He was gripping the armrest of the chair so tightly his knuckles were white, his breathing fast and shallow. As Thalia's voice flew about the small auditorium, a bright-winged bird soaring through the space, growing larger as the song grew in intensity, he shifted uncomfortably in his seat.

The effect of her singing wasn't entirely lost on me either.

Drawn like flames to darker songs—

It was like sinking deeply into a luxurious bubble-filled bath; the water steaming hot on a freezing night, palpably feel-ing the knots in your muscles, the kinks in your brain, ease out.

They hit the rocks and then are gone.

Who *were* these girls really? The innocuous influencers they claimed to be or something more sinister? The last part sounded like the tagline of a cheesy B movie and I wanted des-perately to laugh at myself, but a quick scan of the auditorium dispelled any humor.

Everyone was silent.

Every pair of eyes staring at Thalia, her arms raised as if mid-incantation, her own eyes staring dead ahead into noth-ingness. The atmosphere was heavy and sensual. No one ab-sently flicking through their phone or rustling bags of crisps. It was as if her voice had cast a spell on everyone who was sitting down.

Perhaps the Sirens were aptly named after all.

I recalled her leaning over Will like a snake entrancing its prey, and suddenly a sense of pure revulsion shuddered through me.

I couldn't listen anymore. My conviction those girls were somehow linked to all this now stronger than ever. Quietly, I exited the auditorium, rapturous cheers breaking out like waves behind me.

23

THE ELEVATOR OPENED ONTO THE DIMLY LIT LOWER DECK
and the same darkly ornate corridor I'd watched Leda disappear down last night. Unlike before, there was now a maid's
trolley directly outside the room. One of the double doors was
being held open while another maid came out with a bunch of
towels.

A sudden wild idea hit me.

Could I do it? Could I go through with it?

Damn right I could. I mean, I had to start doing *something*.

Taking a furtive look around and seeing the corridor was
completely deserted, I blustered up to the maids, plastering a
huge fake smile on my face.

"Oh, wow! Thank you so much for cleaning my room! I
hope it wasn't too much of a mess for you. *Super* appreciate it."

Without giving them time to reply, I bustled past the maid

holding the door and then, keeping the smile on my face, began to gently shut it, slipping my debit card into the light switch, causing all the lights to immediately blink back on. Just as I'd hoped, this seemed to reassure them and they nodded politely, leaving me to it.

I stood in the middle of the cabin, my heart racing. I knew I needed to be quick. If I was caught, there was no way I was going to be able to explain *this* away.

Unsurprisingly, the room was over three times the size of mine—a suite rather than a cabin—with three doors leading off into entirely separate bedrooms. Like Con's room, it was fastidiously tidy. Copies of high-end fashion magazines were fanned artfully across a glass table, while empty bottles of water were discarded on various surfaces. Above the desk was a large printout of our route across the Atlantic—similar to the one I'd seen in the captain's cabin—with seven neat circles evenly spaced out along the way. A little strange perhaps, but that wasn't what made me uneasy. No, *that* would be the neat red *X*s that had been drawn over the first three circles.

Three Xs for three missing? First Will, then the magician, and now Raj . . .

Rubbing a hand over my eyes, a headache already building, I took another—slightly frenzied—look around the room. And there, balancing on the arm of a dainty little sofa, was a laptop, the lid helpfully open. Pressing a random key, I felt a bolt of excitement as I realized the screen had been left unlocked. The browser was open, displaying Thalia's email account: *Thalia@ sirens.com.* Most of the messages seemed to be from high-end makeup brands or disposable fashion companies. Impatiently, I scrolled down until a familiar name caught my eye.

My breath stalled in my throat.

Bill.Rexham@McHaleWealthManagement

Rexham? That was Will's surname.

My heart thudded painfully at the sight of it. But the first name was wrong—*Bill,* one letter off.

No—not Will, Will's *dad.*

I doubled-clicked to open the message, my hand shaking on the touchpad.

> I trust you are still considering my offering?
>
> Time is of the essence, so I would appreciate your swift response.
>
> To sweeten the deal, I have a replacement in mind for the one you lost. Timid and compliant, she won't present a problem.

That was all there was. Four vague sentences. But it was enough to send a terrible shudder through me. Beneath was a signature complete with the name and address of the bank Will's dad worked for. It was unmistakably him.

Offering?

There was no way he could be talking about Will? *Surely?*

And as for the replacement? "Timid and compliant"?

Oh, Will. What has *your dad done?*

Well, if he was referring to me, then he'd badly underestimated, hadn't he? I clicked Thalia's sent items to see if she'd replied, and gasped.

She'd sent two words.

We accept.

What did that mean? What was accepted? What was going *on* here, and where was Will?

Scrolling up the chain to Thalia's first email, I noticed an attachment she'd sent earlier. My hand hovered over the touchpad as I took a hasty glance at the door, listening intently. The room and corridor beyond were utterly silent besides the ever-present hum of the engines.

Dry mouthed, I double-clicked on the attachment; a PDF simply titled *Nepenthe.*

The screen immediately filled with color.

It was a brochure or leaflet by the looks of it, the words *Welcome to Nepenthe!* typed in dazzlingly bold Art Deco style, glittering gold upon a black background. Glamorous photos of the *Eos* surrounded the text, the people in them adorned with diamonds as they sipped elegant cocktails and danced at masquerade balls.

The text swam before my eyes, the tone superior and smug.

Welcome to the world's most exclusive and exquisite club—Nepenthe.

Strictly members only—every applicant is carefully vetted.

And your reward for the utmost secrecy? Utmost luxury.

Scrolling down the brochure, I saw a familiar face.

Justin? It was the same earnest portrait he'd used on the

SeaMester website. Beneath his name was the title "Acquisitions Manager."

Something about the term froze my blood.

As I scanned the brochure again—the information was all frustratingly vague—one sentence toward the bottom caught my eye:

All our members agree it is a small price to pay for your dreams coming true.

Price?

The word filled me with such a heavy, final dread, I clicked out of the brochure with shaking hands.

Gathering myself, I opened the door to the nearest bedroom.

My eye was immediately drawn to the bedside table. On it stood another bottle of water, some discarded jewelry, and a book splayed facedown, its spine cracked. Well, of course they treated books like that, the monsters. It was a well-thumbed copy of the *Iliad*. Flicking through, it looked as if several passages had been highlighted. On impulse, I shoved it into my pocket.

My eyes widened.

Beneath where the book had been was something instantly familiar to me.

I recognized the cover: some characters from a random anime that Will had become obsessed with. I recognized it because *I* had bought it from Etsy last year.

Will's iPad.

What were *they* doing with it? Had he been here recently? Left it here?

With shaking hands, I thrust it down my leggings, grateful for the oversized hoodie I'd thrown over the top.

Other than that same briny, musty smell that pervaded the captain's room (What was it? His *aftershave*? Was he in on this too?), there didn't seem to be anything else of note in here.

An angry buzz from close by made me jump.

One of them must have forgotten their phone. It was lying on the desk by the door. On impulse, I picked it up. A message had arrived. Unlike me, the Sirens must have had chill parents, because the entire thing was visible on the lock screen. I read it, then dropped the phone as if it were alive.

Tavi Liddle: She's in your room

Tavi—*Octavia?*

What? Did she mean me? How could anyone know that? There was no one in here with me—

Was there?

I looked around wildly, half expecting to see a pair of silver eyes flash at me from under the bed, suddenly back in my cabin that night with the drowned Will-thing looking at me. A hungry look—

She's in your room

Whatever was going on—some weird joke, some cruel trick—I needed to get out of here. Now.

The phone flashed again.

She is IN YOUR ROOM.

Racing out of the bedroom, I fumbled for the main cabin door, wrenching it open, and walked directly into a soft, yielding body. I jumped back, already apologizing, my face blazing with shame, my mind racing for an excuse that could possibly explain my presence here.

But it wasn't Thalia, or any of the Sirens. It was Con.

He, too, jumped back, as if burned by the contact, staring down at me, incredulous. I immediately squeezed past him, desperate to get out of the room, slamming the door behind me and scanning the corridor in both directions.

It was empty.

"Liv? This isn't your cabin—what are you doing here?"

I took the easy tactic. Leaping to the offensive.

"What the hell, Constantine? I could ask *you* the same question. Are you following me?"

He gave a hard, unamused laugh, crossing his arms and peering at me with a teeth-itching look of superiority.

"Asks the person who's been caught red-handed breaking into someone's cabin."

I gasped in mock outrage. "Breaking in? I didn't *break* in anywhere. Do you see signs of a break-in? Forced entry? Splintered wood?"

"I saw you come out of a room that isn't yours. But no, you're right. I'm *sure* those girls gave you permission to be in there.

If I mention it to them, they'll nod and say, yes, of *course* we allowed Liv to go into our cabin and snoop about while we weren't there—"

"Fine. I did *not* have permission. *Clearly,* I did not have permission."

Constantine gave a lofty sigh. "I'd ask what you were doing . . . but I have a feeling I already know. Surprised you didn't wear your tinfoil hat to dinner the other night. I *meant it* when I warned you earlier. Justin is properly on your case. I think that manager has had a word with him again."

"Oh? And was that the only thing you meant earlier?"

I was pleased to see his face turn slightly pink and he looked away, his voice gruff.

"I was *worried . . . ,*" he said, fumbling. "About you. About what you were saying. You were . . . raving. I didn't mean to imply you were taking anything—medication or whatever— I don't even know why I said that—like I said, I was worried." And finally. "I'm really sorry."

I relented, offering him an olive branch.

"Fine. I'm sorry too. Look. Can we talk?"

He looked up, hopeful, eyes bright, and again I felt that flare of heat between us, flickering and fierce.

"Of course. Do you want to come to my cabin?"

No, no, *no.* I did not want to do that. Not right now.

"Let's head to the deck. I could really use some air."

We took the elevator up and emerged into the chilly gloom of the late afternoon, although there were still too many people milling around for what I wanted to say.

"Let's go over here." I pointed around the corner where the wind was brisker, remembering the weird shit Laila had said—about people watching from tanks. "It's quieter."

We perched uneasily on adjacent sun beds. The wind was frigid and cutting. I pulled the sleeves of my hoodie down over my hands, remembering I still had Will's iPad tucked precariously down my leggings. Constantine was looking at me in an enjoyably predatory manner that made me think he was going to be pretty disappointed when I started talking.

"So, I hope . . . I hope I can trust you," I began.

If he was disappointed, he didn't show it.

"You *know* you can. Has—has something else happened?"

I took a deep breath. Time to dive in.

"There is genuinely something terrible going on aboard this ship, Con. And now I think . . . I think we *all* might be in danger. All of SeaMester—I mean."

He hid it well, but I saw it all the same. That fatigue—the wariness—in his eyes that said, *Oh no, not this again.*

"Liv—"

"I *know,* I know. You don't believe me, think I'm *unhinged,* whatever—but . . . but just hear me out. I think I can prove it. And since your dad owns this boat, it's probably in your interests to know exactly what's going on with his *employees.*" I took a deep breath and did a quick scan of the deck. We were still entirely alone.

"First of all, Thalia *lied* about Will. She said she wasn't with him the night he disappeared; said she never went back to his cabin. But Cintia saw them leave together. Not only that, her scarf was in his room and Will's iPad was in hers—so *something* definitely went down before he went missing."

"Okay," said Constantine slowly, as if talking to a small child. "So, she didn't want to talk about whatever happened between them with you. I mean, fair enough. It's their business, after all."

"Totally agree—*if* my friend hadn't disappeared off the face of the earth the same night. You don't understand—you don't know him like I do. He hasn't once messaged me anything even remotely normal for him. Let's not forget he literally asked me for *help* and—an hour or so ago—he sent me this."

I showed him the image on my phone. Con frowned. I noticed he immediately zoomed in on the girl in the photo. After a moment or two, he shrugged and passed it back.

"Okay . . . What's it meant to be?"

"I have no idea—but does it look like he's calmly resting in an infirmary to you? Not to mention the fact we're all forbidden to see him for some reason. And—and I found something weird on Thalia's laptop—"

At this, his louche act dropped like a veil. "You went through her laptop? *Jesus,* Liv—"

"She'd sent this—this brochure to Will's *dad* about some kind of members' club. I mean—why the hell would she be emailing him about anything?"

Con frowned, looking genuinely perplexed. "To Will's *dad*? You're sure, now?"

He was silent while I floundered for a moment, treading

water. There was nothing else I could tell him without him completely doubting my sanity because none of it made any sense—not yet.

"*Yes,* I swear. It was the weirdest thing—talking about *offerings*—and—and replacements and—"

And Nepenthe. Wasn't that the company owned by Con's *dad*?

I stopped, dead, but far from looking like he'd been busted or caught out in some way, Con still looked utterly confused, fiddling with the hem of his coat, his brow furrowed.

"Okay—so hold on—Will's dad emailing Thalia does seem strange. What *exactly* did the email say?"

Was it my imagination or was he staring at me more intently now, a curious light in his eyes? I hesitated.

"I can't remember—not exactly. But it was weird—and really vague. Purposely vague—as if he couldn't say exactly what she wanted to, if that makes sense."

Then something else occurred to me.

"Con, what were you doing there? Outside Thalia's room?"

His gaze slid from mine. Was he about to lie?

"I, uh—was looking for you. When I saw you go into her room, naturally I wondered what you were up to."

A definite lie. When I'd gone into the Siren's suite, I'd been careful to check there'd been no one around who could deny the cabin was mine. But *why* was he lying? Was I putting my trust in entirely the wrong person?

On shaky ground, I decided not to press the issue now, instead digging into the pockets of my hoodie and holding up the copy of the *Iliad* I'd found in Thalia's room. "Then I found *this* in Thalia's room. Check out the highlighted parts. It's all about sacrificing some girl."

He plucked the book from my hand, flicked through it, then passed it back. "C'mon, Liv, this was written hundreds of years ago. Look, I'm trying to be open-minded, but I *don't* believe a group of influencers are running amok on this ship, pushing people overboard with impunity, do you? Do you *really*? I mean—*why*?"

I buried my head in my hands and groaned.

"I don't know yet. But I think the crew are in on it. Or at least a lot of them. Why did they lie about that doctor? You were there, you *heard* them. You know they lied. People *are* disappearing. And it's *sly*, the way it's happening. We're not meant to believe it. . . . I think we're meant to look crazy, but—but I do. I do believe it."

We sat for a while in silence as the light gradually faded around us, bathing the deck in shadows, the sun a liquid magenta strip on the horizon. Wordlessly, I turned to him. What was left to say? He didn't believe me and, honestly, I couldn't even bring myself to blame him. Awkwardly, he cleared his throat. Here it came, the rationalizing.

"Look, Liv. I know it's been difficult for you—without Will. More difficult than I think anyone realizes. Fact is, though, we hit New York in a couple of days, and all this worrying will be for nothing once he's wheeled off the ship and we all spend the day avoiding pigeons and eating all the terrible pizza the city has to offer."

I smiled wanly at the thought of it. At the sheer, desperate *hope* of it. Barely able to allow myself to imagine it.

"Will it change once he's back?" he asked suddenly. I looked up at him, surprised.

"Will what change?"

With astonishing ease, he leaned over me, nudging me back on the precarious sun bed, cupping my face in his hands and lifting it closer to his. I watched him shut his eyes, lashes long on his cheeks, that glorious aftershave filling my senses.

"This," he murmured against my mouth before kissing me, hard but sweet, leaving me immediately lost. Flung far out to sea. Every thought in my head sailing smoothly away from harbor. His weight settled over me, gloriously heavy, causing the sun bed to give an alarming creak.

And what, I needed to ask, was *this*? Because I already knew Constantine posed far more danger to me than he would ever admit. Beautiful, elegant, and monied—*titled*, no less—there wasn't much chance of him hanging around Liv from St. Leonard's Comp in the real world.

I willed myself to stop thinking, Con helping with that as his hand slipped easily beneath my hoodie and curved around my breast. Desire fizzled through me like a flare, and I pulled him closer, arching up to meet him.

"The hell is that?" He winced, drawing back and staring at my waist.

Dammit, I'd forgotten about the iPad.

Embarrassed, mainly at myself for getting so easily sidetracked, I sat up.

"It's Will's," I muttered by way of explanation. Constantine retreated entirely, sitting back and wiping his mouth with the back of his hand as if I were some bad taste he wanted rid of. "Like I said, it was in Thalia's room."

"She wouldn't have stolen it, Liv," he said offhandedly. Immediately distant again. "It's not as if she needs to. . . ."

He trailed off, but I knew what he meant. Girls like Thalia never needed to take anything. Not when everything was already handed to them on a silver platter. No, taking what wasn't theirs—whether it was an iPad or a place on a cruise—that was left to girls like me.

"That's not all," I said, feeling bolder now. "Con, don't you know a Tavi Liddle?"

The haunted look that flashed across his face told me all I needed to know—along with something else—could it be fear—or was it guilt?

After all, he was the last person to have seen her alive.

"Yes," he murmured. "You *know* I do. Why would you ask that?"

"Because someone with that exact name sent a message to one of the Sirens while I was in there—"

"Impossible," he snapped, cutting me off yet again with brutal precision. "Whatever else you saw, that's impossible. I don't know how many times I need to tell you—she's been missing for a while now. You must be mistaken."

But I was becoming more and more convinced I wasn't.

That passport—a girl's, the name violently scratched out—in the captain's cabin, of all places.

"I'm not mistaken," I said carefully. "I *know* what I saw." I thought hard. "The captain. We need to search his cabin. He has to have something to do with all this. When Cintia and I were in there that first day . . . I found Octavia's passport in there—"

Con shook his head.

"You never met her. You can't be sure it's—"

I cut him off, tired of his denials.

"You might not believe me, but Con, people *don't* just disappear. It's there, I can prove it to you."

He considered for a moment.

"All right. Say I go along with this . . . *plan*—how do you intend on getting *in* there? If the captain is heading up some nefarious plot, I hardly think he's going to leave his cabin wide open for investigation, is he now?"

I paused, annoyed at Con for pointing out that obvious flaw. I'd gotten lucky with the Sirens' cabin, but he was right; this wasn't a movie. I couldn't jiggle the lock a bit with a spare bobby pin and instantly gain access.

"Well . . . I don't know yet," I admitted grudgingly.

Con was quiet for a moment, staring thoughtfully into the distance, then turned back to me with a resigned sigh.

"I, too, am clearly insane, but . . . you know . . . I understand what it's like for someone you care about to go missing," he said. "You say you know exactly where his cabin is, yes?"

I nodded eagerly.

"Okay—well, turns out, I might have an idea."

24

WHILE CON WENT OFF TO PUT WHATEVER PLAN HE'D COME up with into action, which was probably just asking the captain nicely, I passed the next few hours in my cabin eating the stale muffins I'd swiped from the buffet dessert trolley and trying to unlock Will's iPad. Eventually, anxiety got the better of me and, unable to sit still any longer, I wandered down the corridor to Cintia's cabin. I needed to talk to her about Raj. Proving he and Will *had* vanished was the key to getting the others to believe me. Better yet—maybe he'd even be there with her.

She answered the door quickly, pleased to see me.

"Liv! Come in, everything good? You seemed a little distant earlier."

She waved offhandedly at a space on the bed. I grinned. And I thought Will was untidy. Every single surface in the room was taken up with clothes, cosmetics, and piles of books.

Where to start, Cintia?

"Yeah, sorry. I'm just so tired. And still worried about Will."

"Con seemed quiet too. You guys burning the midnight oil together? Please spill, I am desperate for some tea."

I looked away. "It's really not like that between us."

She gave a loud snort. "Who are you trying to kid? Adora saw you guys earlier, mid-sesh on the deck. Couldn't wait to tell me. Apparently, you nearly gave some onlookers a stroke."

I groaned and flopped back onto her bed, glad to finally have someone to vent to.

"It's disgusting. He's ridiculous. I can't stop thinking about him, however much I don't want to. It's everything, Cintia. That voice of his. He's smart, well-read. That way he pushes his hair back when he's thinking . . . His *eyes.* Shame he's such a—an entitled . . . overprivileged snob. Then there's the fact he thinks I'm *crazy*—"

"Alrighty. TMI about half a minute ago. And Will?"

Cintia, asking *all* the questions.

"We're friends, like I told you. We've only ever been friends."

Besides, he's gone now—

I shivered, forcing the thought away.

Cintia smoothed out the duvet with her hands and raised her dark eyes to mine.

"Well, I say good for you. Get it. And you know I'm no fan of Will."

"He's not always like that," I muttered. "You don't know him; not like I do."

Cintia arched a delicate eyebrow.

"I know he screamed at you—humiliated you—in front of an entire room full of people you'd just met," she said evenly. "At one point we thought he might even . . . you know . . . *hit* you."

I raised my eyebrows. "*What?* Seriously, Cintia, we had an argument, that was it."

"It didn't look like that from where we were sitting."

"Who's *we*?"

"The whole group," said Cintia, her face suddenly hard. "Looked abusive as all hell to me, and if you guys did have some kind of thing, you're better off out of it."

"He would never have touched me—it wasn't even that bad of a fight—"

She shrugged. "You don't need to make excuses for him. Anyway, he's out of the picture at the moment and I'm not mad about it."

The night of our public screaming match was still pretty hazy, thanks to my endlessly filled glass, but I remembered the argument pretty clearly—had been unable to forget it. Cintia remembered it wrong, but it wasn't a debate I really wanted to get into right now. What would it change?

"So, you're coming to this Murder Mystery tomorrow night, yeah?" she continued breezily. "I'll come to your cabin first?" She winked at me. "Raj and I grabbed a few bottles of vodka from an unattended drinks trolley."

"You know I can't wait," I lied. I had enough to worry about without adding *pretend* murders to the list. "Hey, maybe we could pop down and see Raj for a bit now? Keep him company or whatever."

Cintia shot me a wounded look. "I'm just back from his room, actually. He said he was tired."

"Hey—look, Cintia, I think you've got the wrong idea," I explained awkwardly. "It's just ever since I saw him backflip off the deck overboard—"

Cintia interrupted me with a fit of raucous laughter. "Seriously, Liv. I can tell you're good at writing stories."

I braved another look at her. Her eyes twinkled with humor, her smile so wide I could see all her teeth. I was wrong. Not about everything—but I was wrong about Raj—Cintia wouldn't lie. I was almost sure of it now.

"All right, all right," I conceded, reassured. "Think that's definitely a sign I need an early night. Hey, do you mind if I use your bathroom?" I added as I got up. "I drank a record-breaking number of coffees today."

Cintia grinned as I ducked into her small bathroom, identical to mine except for the clutter. It was while I was washing my hands that I noticed something oddly familiar poking out of the white linen basket that housed the clean towels, similar to the one in my own bathroom. Curious, I pulled out the black piece of cloth and then dropped it on the floor.

It was the mask I had seen backstage. The tragic grimace of the Greek chorus attached to a black hood.

What was Cintia doing with it?
Unless—

"Hey, Liv, you drowned in there?"

At the sound of her voice, as cool and calm as ever, I hurriedly shoved it back into the basket and left the bathroom. Cintia stood directly outside, making me jump.

"Well, I'll catch you later," I babbled, already half out the door.

There was some explanation, I rationalized, as I headed back to my cabin. Why would Cintia, of all people, be following me around the ship, trying to scare me? I needed to avoid these unwelcome flights of imagination, especially since there were only two days left on this bloody boat.

But still, it left me uneasy.

Back in my cabin, I spent another fruitless hour trying to unlock Will's iPad before admitting defeat and climbing onto my bed with a book.

A sharp knock made me start, and I watched as a piece of paper was slid beneath my door.

It was an official invitation to the *Eos* Murder Mystery evening. Something Will and I had initially been excited about, both being huge fans of *Sherlock*. Placed in the fold was a slip telling me I was to come dressed as Pandora from Greek mythology and helpfully informing me that I was *not* the murderer.

Pandora?

I remembered the story from school. Pandora, whose curiosity had almost doomed everyone.

Ironic, given the circumstances. Could it be deliberate? Worse than that, was it a warning?

Unable to relax, I returned to the problem at hand. I picked up my phone and looked again for the image that Will had sent. There must be some clue here, something that would help.

There wasn't.

Or if there was, I wasn't getting it. Not long after I threw my phone down in frustration, Con messaged me, telling me to meet him by the elevators. Should I tell him about the mask in Cintia's room? No. There was no way that creep in the auditorium had been her—it was probably part of her costume for the Murder Mystery tomorrow evening.

"Ready?"

Con loomed up behind me, dressed in black sweatpants, a black hoodie pulled over his head.

"Wow—all you're missing is a sack with a dollar sign over your shoulder."

He smirked. "I always like to dress the part. Right—lead on, then."

As we got into the elevator and pressed the button for the lowest floor, I began to notice a lightness about him that made me wonder if this was all some kind of a game to him.

"Okay, the captain's cabin is on the floor below this," I explained, gesturing to the panel as the elevator began to descend, "but we need a key card to access it."

Con rummaged in his pocket and brought out a slim white

object, inserted it into the slot in the elevator panel, and pressed the button as I'd watched Orlaigh do a few days ago.

"How—?"

He shrugged. "One of the very few perks of your dad owning a cruise line."

I was too grateful to even roll my eyes.

We exited the elevator into the softly lit corridor, our feet sinking into the luxurious crimson pile of the carpet. It was deserted, thankfully, the incessant roar of the engines much louder here.

"Can't believe I'm missing the gourmet delights of the buffet for this," hissed Con as we padded toward the ornate double doors at the end. "This it?"

An elegantly scrolled sign above it, which I'd missed the first time, denoted it as the *Charybdis Suite.*

You sail upon a ship of fools, drifting blindly into Charybdis—

"What *is* that?" I murmured.

"A cabin name." Con smirked. Yep, he was acting way too relaxed about all this. "It's also the name of a sea monster in Greek mythology."

"Your dad sure loves a theme."

I watched in horror as Con rapped loudly on the door, debating whether or not to leg it back down the corridor.

"Jesus, Con—what are you *doing*?"

"What kind of idiot tries breaking into an occupied house?" he muttered, inserting the key card when we heard nothing. The red light above the handle switched to green, and a satisfying click came from the lock.

The door swung open.

I gagged as we entered. That obnoxious briny smell of rotting seaweed was stronger than ever.

"Dare I ask what exactly you're expecting to find?" mused Con, watching me from the doorway.

"Something that ties all this together," I murmured distractedly. "If only so I can stop feeling like I'm going insane."

Truthfully, though, I had no idea. A handwritten manifesto from the captain explaining exactly what had happened to the missing passengers would be great, but that seemed somewhat unlikely.

"Some kind of logbook maybe? Or a list of passengers and cabins?"

Proving that Octavia Liddle had been booked into a cabin on this cruise would be one way to show Con that I was right.

Con only snorted. "It's not the 1800s, Liv. All that stuff is electronic now."

Ignoring him, I rummaged intently through the cupboards in the living space, finding only generic ship-issue crockery and teabags. The place was as sparse as an empty guest cabin. Exasperated, I went through to the bedroom. Hopefully the passport would still be there and Con would finally accept—

I jumped as he suddenly emerged behind me, in the bedroom doorway, white-faced. "Hey—I just heard the elevator open," he murmured. "We should probably come back later—"

"God—yes—"

Whether my suspicions were correct or not, rifling through the captain's cabin—of all people—was not a good look. Getting up, I followed Con over to the door that led back into the corridor, then gasped as his hand closed around my arm, yanking me back in the direction of the bedroom.

"What the—?"

"Look!" he hissed. "The door—*it's opening.*"

25

THRUSTING OPEN THE DOORS OF THE BUILT-IN WARDROBE, we toppled in, closing the doors behind us as softly as we could. Voices immediately drifted in from the other room.

"She's been *in* there—I'm telling you. The place stunk of her. It's a problem."

Unmistakably Thalia, her voice quiet but insistent. Beside me, Con was breathing fast, the warm bulk of his thigh pressed tight against mine. A sudden surge of gratitude rose within me as I imagined how impossible it would be to do this all alone.

"What would you have me do?" The captain's voice—there was no mistaking his gravelly tone—sounded oddly pleading. A strange dynamic, considering he was meant to be the one in charge of this ship. "Perhaps I should contact the captain now—make him aware of the situation. He might be able to—"

The *captain*? But wasn't *he* the captain?

"No," said Thalia, her voice smoother, more confident. "No. The four of us can easily handle this."

The four of us?

"Of course," soothed the captain. "I did not doubt it. And she has been promised, has she not?"

"Yes, but by *his* father, not her own. It's a shame—there's a chance she might—" Thalia mumbled something unintelligible.

A feverish heat flushed through me. Could Thalia be talking about *me*?

I remembered the message I'd seen on her phone. If she knew for a fact I'd been snooping through her room, then she might also have guessed I'd looked at her emails.

—a replacement in mind for the one you lost—

The idea was so terrible I couldn't even bear to finish the thought. Okay, so Mr. Rexham had always been a bit of an ass to Will—the stereotypical overbearing, overly competitive dad—but I never would have imagined he'd sink to this. To do *that* to his only son. It seemed unbelievable.

And did that mean Will was really, truly . . . gone?

"There's something else as well," snarled Thalia over the captain's apologetic burbling. "A problem with someone on your staff. I've been told they've tried to make a few calls off the ship. If the captain found out—"

Thalia once again lowered her voice, her hushed words almost hissed out.

Suddenly, the murky darkness of the wardrobe became flooded with a bright, white light. Beside me, Con had switched on the flashlight on his phone and was busily digging through some kind of expensive-looking leather document wallet.

"What are you *doing*?" I hissed. "Do you *want* to get us killed?"

Con gave a quiet snort as he nodded at the wallet he was holding. "*Killed?* No one could ever accuse you of being boring, Liv. This—this looks like my dad's—it's . . . weird."

From outside came a low, unpleasant chuckling that chilled me more than anything I'd heard so far, causing Con to pause his rustling. The hushed murmur of conversation continued for a few more moments and then immediately stopped. I leaned forward, straining to hear. Had Thalia and the captain left the cabin?

Con clicked off the flashlight, and his warm hand gripped mine at the soft sound of padding footsteps, growing louder by the second. An insidious sound, the sound of someone trying not to be heard.

I angled my head, tucking my hair behind my ear, and tried to align my vision with the crack in the wardrobe doors. The bedroom was darker than I remembered—as if something were blocking the weak light from the cabin window. Glancing over in that direction, I caught my breath, clamping my hands over my mouth. Someone, or some*thing*, unnaturally tall was standing before the fish tank, silhouetted gently in its aqua light. Something with eyes that glimmered like gold-green mirrors. There was a sharp sound—a sudden inhale or—or—someone sniffing the air? I clutched Con's hand tightly in mine, my entire body numb. Then came an odd beating sound—like the flapping of giant wings—and after that: silence.

Moments later, we heard the cabin door clicking firmly shut. Con shook his head in the dim light, motioning to me to stay a little while longer, but I couldn't bear the fetid seaweed odor of the wardrobe anymore. Kicking the doors open, I gulped in a deep lungful of air.

The room was empty.

"What the—*hell*—what were they talking about—did you hear? I mean, who did they mean by the captain—? That *was* the captain. Did that all sound normal to you?"

But Con wasn't listening. He was sitting—half-in, half-out of the wardrobe—his face milk-white as he stared down at something in his hand. It looked like a crumpled old piece of yellowed paper, stored in a plastic sleeve.

"What *is* that?"

"It's—it's a map," he replied, his voice cracking, still staring down at the crumbling paper as if he could hardly believe it was real. "It's—I think it's my dad's—I've seen it before—but why is it *here*?" he murmured, more to himself than to me. "What *is* going on—?"

Crouching down beside him, I gently took the paper from him. On closer inspection, the paper looked ancient, discolored and cracked with age. It depicted what appeared to be a roughly sketched system of caves beneath an island. But it wasn't the map that caught my attention; it was the crude sketch in the corner. A woman with the body of an enormous bird. Around me the world became quiet for a moment, the only noise the blood pounding in my ears.

"Con," I said slowly, although I already knew the answer. "What's that—that picture? What's it supposed to be?"

He stared at me, gray eyes wide with disbelief.

"I think—I think it's a siren, Liv."

In silence, we left the room and traveled back up to the livelier decks, where we were already overdue for dinner. I'd tried asking Con several times where he'd seen that map before—what it meant to him—but he'd been distracted—telling me he needed to think about things first—to get them straight in his head.

Well, he wasn't the only one.

I slowed as we passed La Mer, the à la carte restaurant, on the way to the buffet. There was a maître d' standing outside the front behind a lectern, no doubt stationed there to prevent commoners like me from loitering. Like most spaces on the ship, the restaurant was open-plan and, to be honest, the food didn't smell too different from what was being catered en masse down in the good old Neptune Lounge. Still, the setting was certainly fancier, all dark wood and crisp white tablecloths.

Con strode ahead, and I was about to follow him when I had the strong sensation that someone was staring at me. Scanning the room, I saw a couple seated at a table directly behind the maître d'. Both were scrutinizing me with oddly blank expressions on their faces. I did a double take. Their faces were eerily similar and somehow familiar to me. Both were fish pale with dull dark eyes and oily black hair, thin lips set into a bland line.

Then I remembered where I'd seen them before. They were Laila's parents. Perhaps they'd been trying to place me too. Laila wasn't with them tonight. No doubt they were making good use of the ship's babysitting facilities. The mother gave me a reluctant wave. Caught, I took a few hesitant steps toward them.

"Are you dining here tonight? We recommend the seafood," said the woman, her accent the same soft American burr as her daughter's.

"Smells great," I agreed. "Great prices to match, though, right?"

She gave me a wan smile. "It's a well-kept secret. The sea provides."

I squinted at her. That damn stupid phrase again. A weird thing to say, not to mention a complete non sequitur. Not sure what else to say, I brought up the only thing we had in common.

"So, uh, where's Laila tonight?"

The woman's smile faltered; her dark eyes grew flat.

"I'm sorry—who now?"

"Laila!" I said, feeling momentarily stupid. Was I wrong? Was that not her name? "I mean, she's a great kid. We've, uh, chatted a few times."

Beside her, her husband frowned. "We don't know who you mean."

I plowed on, my voice wavering. "But . . . I . . . No, I did. I saw her with you both. Aren't you her parents?"

"*Laila*? I've never heard of anyone with that name," snapped the woman. She was making a half-hearted attempt at appearing confused, but there was something weary and hard about her eyes that made me positive she was *lying*. Well, that and the fact I'd seen Laila sitting with them every morning for breakfast.

"Look, if you're not her parents, then I'm sorry. It's just I saw you guys together and *assumed* . . . Maybe I misheard her name. You know, she's the one with—"

"We're not parents at *all*," said the woman coldly. "We were never *blessed*."

Her husband placed a proprietary arm around her, his frown deepening into a glower.

"I'm sorry, kid, but you're mistaken," he said, his voice dark with menace. "We don't know who you're talking about. I don't know if you think you're being funny, but this isn't something we'd like to discuss right now. So if you're done—"

I shook my head, my anxiety about talking to strangers vanishing in the face of this outrageous lie.

"But I *saw* you with her. What are *you* taking about? Where is she?"

"Leave us *alone*," hissed the woman.

The man looked over his shoulder, apparently gesturing to the server, at the same time I remembered Constantine loitering ahead in the corridor, pretending to look at his phone.

"You best be careful who you talk to, young lady," the man continued, his voice raised now. "The next person might not respond as kindly." He turned to the approaching waiter. "Hey, excuse me, sir—"

Time to *leave*. My cheeks glowed hot as I walked swiftly away in Con's direction.

"What was going on there?" he muttered, following my gaze. "Drama seems to follow you everywhere."

"I don't know," I said, hurrying away from the restaurant, my stomach churning. "Mistaken identity, maybe. Pair of touchy bastards."

My mind occupied, I trailed Con silently downstairs to our usual table in the lounge, where Adora, Cintia, and Justin waited. Could I have been mistaken about Laila? Maybe. But at this point, however much I might have wanted to bury my head in the sand, I simply couldn't be mistaken about *everything*. It wasn't possible. I was going to need to act—and soon.

My mind wandered back to the conversation we'd overheard in the captain's room, the crumbling old map. It felt as if I was holding all the puzzle pieces in my hand—but I had no idea how to fit them together, make them into something whole.

"So no Raj, yet again?" I noted pointedly, with a slow-growing anger after I'd sat through two boring conversations about the weather. The table's mood seemed damper than before—even Adora seemed less thorny than usual, picking morosely at her food. Directly, I challenged Cintia. "How are his . . . muscles?"

"Great," she said, not even looking up from her plate. "Whole thing's wounded his pride more than anything. But I'll be sure to send him your regards."

Justin was also quiet, robotically spooning pasta into his mouth.

"Wonder who'll be next to mysteriously vanish from the table—hey, Justin? Should we start taking *bets*?"

I knew I was starting to create a scene, but by now I was past caring. Across from me, Constantine gave an incredulous shake of his head.

"Uh, no one's mysteriously vanished that I'm aware of. We have one person sick and another resting from a muscle strain. Everything *is* all right, isn't it, Liv?"

There was a clear warning in Justin's eyes.

NO! I wanted to scream at him. *Clearly,* NOTHING IS ALL RIGHT. *I haven't seen my best friend since he got KO-ed on the first night by some creepy influencer. All the staff on this ship seem to be pathological liars. I'm half seeing the most insane things, and yesterday I could have sworn I watched one of our group tumble off a deck in broad daylight and no one batted a damn eyelid! And, I think we are ALL in danger—*

"Oh, so you remember Will?" I snapped back. "Good to know. Have you even bothered to check on him these last couple of days?"

Justin put down his fork and gave me a cold stare.

"Yes, actually. He's not making the quick recovery we'd hoped he would. But the doc thinks there might be some better news tomorrow."

I refrained from sarcastically asking *which* imaginary doctor he was talking about, the news now only raising the vaguest hope. The others might have been fooled, but I knew the excuses would soon follow.

A peal of laughter erupted behind me, and I watched as the Sirens headed to the table behind us, all dressed in various different styles of sequins. Thalia in a structured white blazer dress, the shoulder pads dramatically pointed. Lexie in a short, spangly gold number revealing long tanned legs, and Leda in a chic black jumpsuit.

"I actually *need* to see Raj," I said, boldly looking across at Justin. "He's—uh—got something of mine and when I've knocked the last few times, he hasn't answered. If you could come with me, that would be great?"

"Oh? What's he got?" asked Cintia sharply, her eyes now meeting mine, challenging me.

Not *everyone* is out to get you, I reminded myself sternly. And certainly not Cintia.

"My, um, purse. I forgot my bag yesterday, so he was looking after it while I—I went for a swim."

Across the table, Constantine raised an eyebrow.

"Maybe Cintia could go with you, then," muttered Justin distractedly, barely listening anymore. "I'm afraid I have a meeting directly after dinner."

We finished the rest of the meal in an uncomfortable silence, the air thick with my unasked questions. As we got up to leave, I heard my phone vibrate. Without even thinking, I unzipped my backpack hurriedly, refusing to let go of the pathetic hope it might be Will. It wasn't. Only Mum telling me how excited she was for me and hoping I had taken lots of pictures. I'd tried to message her a few times, only for my words to remain obstinately unsent, a hateful red exclamation point next to all my veiled worries, thanks to the lack of signal out here. The sight of her words brought hot, instant tears to my eyes, blurring the room before me so much that I didn't notice Cintia whisk my purse out from the innards of my backpack.

"Guess we'll let Raj decide when he's ready for company, shall we?" she spat with uncharacteristic venom, dropping the purse onto the table. I stared at her as she stalked out of the lounge. The idea that she thought I might be some kind of rival for his affections was almost funny.

Con got up immediately afterward, muttering something about a headache, followed by Justin. Adora, who'd been unusually quiet all through dinner, began packing her bag to leave as well; no doubt the thought of being left alone to make conversation with the likes of me was a fate worse than death. I was about to get up to follow Con—we *still* hadn't talked about what had gone down in the captain's cabin—when Adora exhaled as if with annoyance and slumped back down again, looking directly at me.

I looked back at her, warily.

"Liv—I just wanted to ask . . . Are you all right?" She cleared her throat. The idea of Adora being tongue-tied was unnerving. "You've gone from looking like a deer in the headlights to—well, exhausted—*haunted* almost."

I gave her a weak smile. "Let's just say this trip isn't exactly going how I thought it would."

She nodded thoughtfully. "You and Con seem to be getting on well?"

I grimaced. I didn't trust her, and it did feel like a betrayal—but here was someone who knew the mythical Octavia, possibly one of the last people to see Will.

"I guess . . . Adora, how much do you know about Octavia? Con's ex—the one who went missing? He—he won't talk about her."

Adora blinked, then gave a dramatic look around the room, as if half expecting to see Con hiding beneath the table.

"For good reason," she said, her voice low. "He was besotted with her. Look, honestly, I didn't know Tavi all that well—we were acquaintances, not friends. But I *do* know—maybe Con's told you this already, although knowing him, I doubt it—that it wasn't just her that disappeared. Her little sister went missing at the same time—Flick. She was just gorgeous, a lovely girl—and only fourteen years old."

No, Con had not mentioned this. In fact, he'd repeatedly changed the subject every time I tried to talk about it.

"Thing is, Octavia had her problems. . . . Everyone knew that. She'd been struggling with her mental health for a while—convinced someone was out to get her—was on medication for it, I think. But I wish I'd listened to her more, y'know?"

"Adora," I asked, keeping my voice light. "I know this is a weird question—but is there any way that Tavi could be here—on this boat?"

Adora gave a firm shake of her head.

"No. No, there's no way. No one's heard from her or Flick since the day they went missing. And as for Con"—she took another swift look behind her—"well, just be careful there, okay? I don't think he's dangerous, or that he did anything to Flick or Tavi—but that doesn't change the fact he was the last person to see them both."

* * *

The light in the bathroom was on again.

I got up grudgingly. So exhausted, I could barely muster up the energy to be afraid.

Throwing on my bathrobe, I stumbled, half-asleep, to the bathroom door.

As my hand gripped the handle, ready to throw open the door, I paused.

The silence was all wrong. Too still. Pregnant with some unsettling event. It was as if someone was holding their breath on the other side of the door, desperate not to be heard, not until it was too late.

The steel handle seemed freezing.

I pushed open the bathroom door and screamed, the sound ripped out of me, wild and unconstrained.

Standing against the far wall, in a line, were three of them; all in white. White skin, white feathers, white hair—except their eyes, which were black—unblinking and entirely round like a fish's. They were smiling, but something was terribly wrong with the expression. Their mouths weren't mouths but deep bloodied holes revealing circles upon circles of teeth within. The gaping maws of lampreys. Their arms were raised above their heads, their hands wickedly taloned claws. They took a single long, synchronized stride toward me.

I slammed the door.

There's nothing there. There's nothing there. Of course there's nothing there.

I could barely hear anything above the shuddering gasp of my breath.

"There's *nothing* there!"

And when I wrenched open the door again, poised to scream, to bolt out of the room, there wasn't.

26

UNSURPRISINGLY, I HAD A RESTLESS NIGHT, DRIFTING BE-
tween nightmares. Next morning, not knowing what else to do
with myself and needing to get out of the suffocating confines
of my cabin, I headed to breakfast early. As I entered the cavernous Neptune Lounge, it seemed unnervingly quiet.

"Excuse me, miss—*cabin number*?"

I stopped, staring blankly at the steward for a few moments,
still half-asleep. They were always there, haunting the entry to
every mealtime, hawkishly recording who we were.

And then, a flashbulb moment. I summoned a sweet smile.

"I, uh . . . can't remember. Two hundred and . . . something,
I think."

The steward, a bored-looking guy only a year or so older
than me, raised a sardonic eyebrow.

"You can't remember?"

I cleared my throat, already feeling ridiculous. "Nope—sorry. It's completely gone. Is there any way—um—can you search by name?"

He gave a dramatic sigh. Con's dad definitely needed to increase whatever he was spending on staff training, that was for sure.

"Go on, then?"

"Uh, name's Octavia. Octavia Liddle."

My heart sped up to double time as I watched him laboriously key in the name. Disappointment flooded through me as he shook his head moments later, squinting at me suspiciously.

"How interesting. Apparently, you don't exist. Now, do you want to tell me your cabin number or do you want to go hungry?"

Defeated, I gave it to him. Turning to get a much-needed coffee, I gasped. Con was standing directly behind me, a disgusted scowl on his face.

"Good morning, Liv. Or is that not actually your name?"

He looked, unusually, like crap. Dressed in a hoodie and wearing blue Ray-Bans, his golden hair escaping from the hood in wild tufts. I bit my lip, not knowing what to say, but he only sighed. It didn't look as if he'd had much sleep either. Wordlessly, we slumped down at our designated table, which was of course empty.

"Look, you can't blame me for wanting to find out what's going on—"

"You're looking in the wrong places," he said sharply. "She's gone."

My mouth dried up. I'd known all along it was a painful memory for him, and here I was, pretending to *be* her.

"But," he continued, his voice low. "There has been something bothering me."

I leaned closer. "Go on?"

Con removed his sunglasses and focused his chilly gray gaze on me.

"That night in your cabin. Octopus night. The paperwork relating to your scholarship—it was organized by my dad's finance company. I recognized the name."

Hardly the groundbreaking revelation I was hoping for.

"Well, *duh*. How's that surprising? He owns the ship."

Con shook his head impatiently.

"You're missing the point. Why would my dad *pay* for you to come aboard his own ship?"

I shrugged. "Because it's a nice thing to do? Giving back and all that?"

"You don't know my dad. It's not like him to be charitable, and he's never mentioned a scholarship program before. . . . Why would he be so keen as to want to *pay* for you to be here? It's just . . . odd, that's all."

I thought back to Will's dad's email.

I have a replacement in mind.

No. Con had mentioned hundreds of times how estranged he was from his father. It was hardly surprising he didn't know the ins and outs of his business. But I kept quiet, as the perplexed look Con was giving me suggested he might say more.

But he didn't. Only raised a hand to give a laconic wave at someone behind me.

"Not interrupting, am I?"

Cintia collapsed beside me with a plate stacked full of eggs and bacon. Behind her, I could see Justin and Adora deep in conversation at the omelet station.

The talk at breakfast was dominated by the upcoming evening's entertainment.

"Well, I'm Aphrodite," preened Adora as she sat down, smoothing the front of her designer corset. I couldn't deny it was an inspired choice as I watched her toss that silken red hair about. "What about you, Liv?"

"Pandora," I said nonchalantly.

Cintia raised a perfectly shaped brow. "Curiosity got the better of her too."

I blinked. Had I misheard? The world dwindling away around me for a second as I took in what she had said. The *implication* of it. I recalled that mask discarded carelessly in her bathroom.

"And what exactly do you mean by that, Cintia?"

Immediately, she laughed it off. "Justin was telling us all how you had a go at the manager, trying to say Will being in quarantine was part of a global conspiracy or something." She smiled again. That too-large, sunny smile. "Just a joke, babe."

Justin said nothing, only stared down at his plate with a smug little smile.

After Cintia and Justin left, I shot a look at Adora, who

caught it. For once she took the hint and got up with a dramatic flourish.

"Is anything else wrong?" I asked Con the moment she left. "You look like shit."

He peered at me over his sunglasses, pushing down his hood, blond curls springing free.

"Uh, weird dreams, couldn't sleep," he replied, batting away my concern. He nodded at the book I'd stolen—borrowed—from Thalia's room. "So you're actually reading that, huh?" He pried it gently from my hands, opening it at the bent-down page. Scanning the passages highlighted by Thalia, he nodded thoughtfully.

"The death of Iphigenia. Pretty grim stuff, hmm?"

I looked at him.

"Death of *who*, now? I mean, I know the *Iliad*, but not well. They don't offer the classics at my school."

He smiled.

"Iphigenia is the daughter of Agamemnon, the leader of the Greeks during the Trojan War. You know—the wooden horse, Achilles, and Patroclus and all that. Well, he sacrifices her, to appease Artemis, so the goddess will allow his ships to sail to Troy."

"Wait, what? He sacrifices his own *daughter*?"

Constantine nodded thoughtfully. "Well, yes. Sacrifices must be difficult, mustn't they? They have to matter. That's the very nature of them. Sometimes your best sheep or whatever just won't do."

"So wait—he sacrificed her—he killed his own kid?"

"Indeed, he did. Bloody Greeks. Worked, though."

I paused for a moment, reminded once again of the acnient map he'd discovered in the captain's room.

"Hey—and weren't sirens originally Greek too?"

Constantine raised his gaze to mine and smiled again. It was an inscrutable smile, thin and flat.

"Yes, monstrous things. Birds with the heads of women who lured ships to wreck with their unearthly singing."

"Strange choice of name for a bunch of shallow influencers, isn't it?"

"Shallow?" Constantine laughed. "Well, I suppose that's not inaccurate. There's a glamour that goes along with the word now, isn't there? It tends to mean something tempting or seductive but inherently dangerous."

He removed his sunglasses. "The name of this ship is Greek—Eos, goddess of the dawn. *Nepenthe*—my father's shipping group—is a Greek word. The captain—Elytis—is Greek." He ran a hand through his short golden curls. "Believe it or not, I'm of Greek heritage. Leda is Greek." He paused, point made. "Lots of things are Greek. Particularly in shipping. It's not a coincidence. Greece was a thalassocracy; still is, to some extent."

I don't know if he was trying to impress me with his vocabulary, but I managed to refrain from rolling my eyes.

"Uh-huh. And what does *Nepenthe* actually mean?"

Constantine smirked slightly, as if pleased I'd asked. "It means *that which chases away sorrow*. Coincidentally, from the *Odyssey*. It's the name of a potion given to Helen of Troy. Pretty fitting for a company that owns cruise ships—or at least that's what my dad thought."

I nodded.

"So your dad . . . he sent you on this cruise?"

He nodded blithely as if it were nothing. "I thought I told you already. I get hauled onto his bastard ships at least once a year when he wants me out of the way. At least this time he can pretend there's a vague educational reason behind it."

Despite the weak rays of autumn sunshine glinting through the wide lounge window, I shivered. Was it even possible that Con had no idea what was going on aboard the *Eos*? And that photo I'd seen the other morning—the handsome CEO of Nepenthe, Christos Konstallis. Well, no wonder he'd looked familiar.

"He's self-made, y'know?" Con added with unexpected pride. "That's where the whole *sea provides* bullshit comes from. It's linked to some ancient Greek custom or whatever—apparently, he made some kind of bargain when he was younger, and a few years later made a fortune in shipping—"

"Bargain?"

I don't know why, but the word sent another shiver down my spine.

Seven is the bargain and seven have been promised—

Con shrugged. "Threw a few coins at the Acropolis and made a wish, I don't know. He can be pretty superstitious. Into old traditions, all that ancient stuff."

The sea provides but only if you feed it—

Ancient traditions like *sacrifice*?

"So, uh, how long has he been working with the Sirens?"

I tried to keep my voice casual. Not for the first time, my trust in Con balanced on a knife-edge.

"A little while now, I think. That's how I first met Leda and the others—they were the only other people under seventy the last time I was forced onto one of these bloody cruises."

"Is that right? And you didn't notice anything unusual on *that* trip? No unexplained disappearances, vanishing dancers . . ."

He looked at me, curious and half smiling, as if unsure whether I was joking or not.

"*No.*"

"So, uh, about that old map you found yesterday," I asked, trying not to sound as if I were relaying the series of questions currently jotted down in my phone's notes app. "In the captain's cabin. You looked pretty shaken up by it."

Now he looked away, a flash of uncertainty in his gray eyes. "Yeah, that was pretty weird, actually. It looked exactly like something my dad has framed in his office. But then again, y'know, I haven't been sleeping well lately either."

"And those things Thalia was saying in the captain's cabin—about being promised by someone's father—doesn't that fit with that email I read? The one from Will's dad? I'm worried she means me, that I'm in some kind of trouble."

He was silent for a long while, staring out at the sea before answering.

"C'mon, Liv. . . . Do you honestly think Thalia—an *influencer*, of all things—is planning something dark and nefarious?"

In the plain light of the morning, it *did* sound utterly ridiculous. There was no denying it.

"She was probably just talking about some business shit," continued Con. "An online promotion, or a deal. Look, I've been thinking, why don't you have a chat with her, Liv? Clear the air. Maybe then you'll see she's a regular person—"

Nothing about Thalia was regular, and I was convinced Con knew that.

Why are you so keen to act like nothing's wrong?

Is it your dad? Are you trying to protect him?

How much do you really know?

I bit my lip so hard with frustration at his stonewalling, I drew blood. I had to change the subject before I screamed.

"So, who are you dressing up as this evening?"

He shrugged. "I forget. I hate enforced entertainment."

I had to admit, I was disappointed. "So you're not coming, then?"

He stood. Definitely frosty Constantine this morning.

"I didn't say that, did I? Look, I'll see you tonight."

After Con left, I poured myself another coffee. I needed to be awake and fully focused today. As I sipped it, I absently flicked through the photos on my phone. It was hard seeing the photos of Will and me grinning away on the bus down, powered purely by energy drinks and optimism. Not quite used to the iPhone my parents had brought me as a present for getting the scholarship, I realized I'd yet again managed to take several seconds of video instead of a photo as I'd intended. Still, I smiled at the sound of Will's voice as he babbled on about some gaming meme he'd made that morning.

I paused the clip for a second, my heart speeding up.

In it, Will had unlocked his iPad and was holding it up to show me. If I replayed the clip and stopped it at the right moments, I should be able to figure out the code he was typing in. And, after several frustrating minutes of stopping and starting the clip, Will's voice no longer endearing and amusing, but now downright irritating, I got it.

Bursting through my cabin door, I scrabbled around my unmade bed until I found the iPad. Powering it up, I typed in the passcode, feeling ridiculously pleased with myself when it let me in.

First, I went directly to his photo gallery. The hot sense of guilt began immediately as I flicked through the most recent pictures. There were a couple of cheesy shots of us on the way down on the bus, a few of the group of us in varying states of inebriation on that unpleasantly messy first night. I'd hoped maybe his phone had synced with it and there'd be some shots from the infirmary—if only to confirm he was actually there—but there was nothing hospital-like at all.

Suddenly, I stopped scrolling as a familiar face caught my eye. I opened the picture for a closer look.

She was as strikingly beautiful as ever, a warm smile on her tan face, long dark hair falling over her shoulders like silk.

Will's arm was draped around her. I'd never seen the expression on his face before. A mixture of awe and affection.

Octavia?

A sickening mix of jealousy and fear curdled thickly in my stomach.

The photo was dated only a few days ago—the day *after* the night he disappeared. In it, Will was wearing a casual tee, and the two of them appeared to be sitting in a generic cabin. How was this even *possible*? He was supposed to have been laid up in a hospital bed, quarantined from others? And was *she* a nurse? She certainly didn't *look* like one, dressed in a simple black shift that contrasted beautifully against her golden skin. And Will looked even less like a patient.

I double-checked the date.

There wasn't much else. The only image he'd taken since then was the strange, blurred shot he sent me the other evening.

A strong feeling of guilt swam over me as I opened his WhatsApp, mixed with dread at what I might be about to see. I knew what I was doing was wrong, but how else could I help him?

Immediately I was faced with my own string of increasingly desperate messages. Somehow, they seemed ever needier, more pathetic than I'd imagined while sending them. This was chased by a feeling of anger as I imagined Thalia reading them, smirking. A flush of sweat broke out over me as I continued to scroll down through the rest of his texts.

The sight of her name hit me again like a frigid wave to the face.

Tavi Liddle.

Octavia Liddle.

There was no doubting it this time. Her pretty face staring out at me from Will's contacts; from a scratched-out passport in a bag swinging from a hook in the captain's bathroom.

Can't wait to see you on board, babe X

The very same girl I'd seen posing confidently beside Constantine on numerous sunny beaches on Adora's Insta.

The same Octavia Liddle who had gone missing before coming on this trip.

The same Octavia *I'd* replaced.

The same Octavia I'd seen slipping among the crowds in the club that night, who'd messaged Thalia, warning her I was in her room.

I thought back to Con's face that time we'd followed Leda.

That voice on the other side of the door—I thought . . . I thought I recognized it—

Only, Octavia wasn't missing; she was here on the ship—*hiding*.

Deep down, I'd suspected it all along. But *why? What was she doing here, and why was she hiding?*

Could it be because Con and Adora knew her? Both would surely recognize her if they saw her. Was she here to get some kind of revenge on Con? Or was she in as much trouble as Will?

I scrolled down through the rest of the messages between her and Will, shaking my head.

The screen flickered briefly.

I squinted, confused.

The rest of the messages—even the one I'd just read—were all now illegible, written in symbols I'd never seen before—giving them the look of some kind of file corruption. Had his iPad been damaged? As I flicked back, all his other messages (which I scrupulously tried to avoid reading—there were far more between him and other girls than I'd ever expected) seemed normal enough. Had he and Octavia been writing in some kind of code? Was that even possible on WhatsApp—but, more importantly, *why* would they do that? My thumb hovered over the home button. The temptation to open everything, every app, every photo, every message, to see *all* of him flayed open before me on the bed, was alarmingly strong.

I shook the idea out of my head. I'd hate it if Will did that to me. I didn't believe he ever would.

Only because he doesn't care, Liv.

Ignoring that poisonous thought, I stared again at the messages, as if I could turn the odd symbols to words through sheer force of will.

There was no way this could be a coincidence.

The illegible messages were dated from the day before we got on the ship up until yesterday.

Out of interest, I navigated to Instagram and clicked the Sirens' page again: 2.1 million followers and counting. Predictably, they were followed by both Adora and Raj. I scrolled down, surprised to see another face I recognized.

Kayleigh Warren.

Will's dad's fiancée.

Thinking about it, I shouldn't have been surprised. Kayleigh wasn't much older than Will and me and seemed all about that influencer life, forever posting pictures of herself in yoga pants while hawking protein shakes and diet supplements. It didn't seem off-brand for her to follow successful influencers.

Was *she* the connection between Will's dad and the Sirens? Was that how he'd met them? Heard about them?

I put the iPad down with shaking hands.

If what I suspected was even half-true, the actual best thing to do would be to barricade myself inside my cabin until the ship docked. But I knew I couldn't. If only for Will's sake.

For the seventy-ninth time, I called his phone. It was, as usual, unavailable, so I sent my seventy-ninth WhatsApp message down the usual black hole, flinching as it immediately pinged through on his iPad.

Thrusting the device aside, I headed directly to the ship's atrium, the need to do *something* a driving force within me.

Orlaigh was behind the desk, greeting me with a tight smile. Other than us two, the atrium was unusually empty. It seemed even darker than usual today, the tanks swarming with fish and other sea creatures.

Those black things . . . I think they're multiplying . . .

"Hello, Miss Larkin. And how may I help you this morning?"

I called up the image of Will's face, smiling out from his iPad, the photo taken only days ago.

I *had* to know.

I cleared my throat.

"Look, I *know* you know something. *All* of you do. What happened to my friend Will? Where is he, really?"

Orlaigh looked so convincingly confused that for a second, I was afraid I'd gotten it all completely wrong.

"I'm so sorry, miss—I'm not sure what you're talking about."

"Yes, you *are*. Will. The boy who was quarantined. I was told I could see him, and then you guys did a one eighty and denied you'd ever said that. I know you're lying. And it's not just him—where's Apollo, the magician? Someone knows something on this ship, and I'm not going anywhere until I get answers."

She nodded, as if suddenly understanding. I had to give it to her, she was a good actress.

"Apollo is still recovering from a tragic accident that occurred during his show. And, yes—the boy who is in quarantine—I remember now. I'm not sure of his condition, but I can call the infirmary and ask for an update, if you'd like?"

There was no point. They'd only lie. Or say I could visit him tomorrow and lie again while the sand left in Will's timer continued to slip away. Deliberately, I looked over her shoulder at the office, where I could see shadowy shapes moving behind the internal window.

"Okay, cool, so you *really* don't know, no worries," I said. "Do you mind grabbing someone else back there for me to talk to? Someone knows something. I'm sure of it."

Her mouth straightened into a worried line and her voice lowered.

"Don't."

A wave of exhilaration burst within me. *Finally,* vindication. "Don't what?"

"You can't talk to anyone else on the staff about it. They'll *know* it's me. I think Eduardo is onto me already, and he's not to be trusted at all. . . ."

She trailed off and I stood stock-still.

So, it was true.

Okay, so it didn't necessarily mean the ship, or all its staff, were evil, or even that people were being tossed off the deck, but it *did* mean I wasn't going completely mad. There was *something* wrong. The relief of it all almost made me keel over. I gave a deep, shaky sigh, clinging to the counter.

"Oh my . . . my God, *Orlaigh*. What's—what's going on here? Do you know what's really happened to Will? Is he *okay*? And the others? Raj—and Laila. Where *are* they?"

She looked around furtively. We were still completely alone.

"I'm not sure—and that's the problem. If I was, I would have acted some other way, but yes, I suspect they might be in some trouble. I was drafted in by an agency to work here last minute, and believe me when I say it's unlike *any* other ship I've ever worked on."

She cast her eyes behind me, at the large fish tanks, the strange pulsating creatures within.

"Look, it's important you understand nothing can be done until we're off this ship and safely docked. No one can suspect we know anything until we're on dry land—no one. It's far too dangerous. All I ask is that you keep a low profile until then. It's a little over a day until we reach the first port. Then, the moment we dock, I'll find you and—"

Keep a low profile?

"Orlaigh, what the *hell*? My best friend has been missing for days, and you're telling me something might have happened to him? How the *fuck* am I meant to keep a low profile? What, you want me to act like nothing's happened?"

Her words hardened to ice.

"If you want to *live*, yes."

The world slowed around me. Orlaigh was still looking at me with her steady blue gaze, stern and sober.

"If I . . . if I want to . . . live?"

She nodded, beginning to stack papers on the desk before her, not meeting my eyes.

"There's so many of them. And I know it started with those three girls. It happens a lot on cruises—you only need to look at the news. People go missing and nothing is said, nothing is ever said. There's always excuses. Always. On every ship. Oh, they got drunk and were sloppy on deck. They were on medication and shouldn't have been out there unaccompanied. They had mental health problems and it all got to be too much. Sometimes there's no evidence of them ever boarding. I've heard their families are paid off in some way. Astronomical sums, you know—"

But I didn't care. Couldn't hear any of it. It was as if I were sinking below the ocean, her words floating far above me.

"Are you saying . . . Are you saying Will is . . . *gone*?"

Orlaigh gave a resolute shake of her head. "No. No, I'm not saying that—I don't know. For all I know, he *might* be somewhere in quarantine. I'm not permitted on that deck, but I need you to know—I need someone to know—I think everyone in your program might be—" She shook her head again. "Like I said, we can't talk here."

I gave the atrium another quick scan. It was empty.

"No one's here; we're completely alone. Just *tell* me."

She nodded knowingly in the direction of the tanks, looming over us, the water almost black in the gloom.

"You need to stop now. They're always watching, Olivia. All of them, always. They have . . . ways."

I recalled one of the last things Laila had said.

They just stand in the tank, half-hidden at the back—in the shadows behind the weeds—and all they do is watch.

"Fine. So when can we talk? Will you come to my cabin? Now? Please?"

She gave me a decisive nod, then reached beneath the counter, bringing out an intricately carved wooden box.

"I can't right now; I need to help prepare for tonight. Here—we're supposed to hand out these props at the start of the evening, but since you're here, this is part of your costume. You're Pandora, right?" When I nodded, her face sagged in relief. "After this bloody Murder Mystery—if you can, wait up for me? I'll knock around midnight and tell you everything I know. Like I say—don't do anything stupid. And don't panic. I think it'll be all right, Liv. Just don't, whatever you do, draw any more attention to yourself."

27

I SAT IN MY CABIN FOR HOURS AFTER THAT, OPENING THE notes app on my phone and drafting a list of every single unusual thing I'd seen or heard since I'd been aboard, ready to share with Orlaigh. The relief that someone actually believed me was almost more of a weight off my mind than the idea of Will walking into my cabin. Still, more questions began to gnaw at me as I halfheartedly changed into my costume—a plain white bedsheet—for the upcoming Murder Mystery party. If the entire SeaMester group *was* in danger, didn't I owe it to the rest of the group to warn them? And if it was only us, then how did that explain what had happened to the magician—Apollo— and to Laila?

A loud knock at the door startled me out of my thoughts. I couldn't help but hope it was Constantine. Finally I could tell him I wasn't going mad—that someone else believed me—

someone on the staff, no less. And I could show him that the girl in Will's photo and the girl he'd been on vacation with were one and the same.

But as I got up to answer it, an unwelcome warning flashed into my head.

Con's father *owned* this ship. Con's father *employed* the Sirens.

I thought about what Adora had told me. That Octavia—and her sister—had gone missing while Con was in a relationship with her.

Could I *truly* trust him? Or was he playing some sick game with me?

Then I thought of what Laila had said as she stood in line for the buffet behind her oblivious parents.

They don't want to be old. That's why they're here.

And that phrase I kept hearing: *The sea provides but only if you feed it—*

Nepenthe. Meaning to drive away sorrow through forgetting. Would anyone, other than me, remember Will—or even care—if he *was* truly gone?

I opened the door.

To my relief, Cintia stood behind it.

I ushered her in, glancing in alarm at the enormous bottle of vodka she'd stashed under her arm. What had happened to her earlier insistence on soft drinks? Perhaps she was feeling the strain too. Maybe she suspected more than she let on. I also noted, a small sliver of warning running down my spine, that she was not wearing the mask I'd found in her bathroom.

"Ah, so you got your box, then, Pandy."

I rolled my eyes. "Yep, looking forward to schlepping this around all evening. Who are you meant to be?"

"Persephone: queen of the underworld, obvs." She was wearing the exact same white sheet as I was; the only difference was a string of plastic pomegranates tied about her neck.

We stared at each for a few moments, then collapsed into undignified laughter.

"This is *ridiculous*. When they said *Murder Mystery*, I was imagining *Downton Abbey*," I said. "You know, like sequined flapper dresses or . . . I dunno . . . gangsters or something—not a bloody toga party. Clearly this has been planned by a man. I mean, all these costumes consist of is a cheap bedsheet and some gold-sprayed rope."

"I hear ya. Here." She handed me a small bathroom glass filled with neat vodka. "Sorry, no mixers."

I sipped it and winced. "*Sweet Jesus*, Cintia."

I made a mental note to not have any more. This was *not* the night to be sloppy drunk.

"I need some liquid courage. Raj is gonna be there. You know how much I've been missing him."

I'd believe it when I saw it.

"So, are you guys a thing, then?"

Cintia winked at me. "Not *yet*, if you catch my meaning."

While she adjusted her dress before the mirror, I slipped into the bathroom and tossed the rest of my drink down the bathroom sink.

*   *   *

The Neptune Lounge had been decked out with huge Doric columns cut from Styrofoam and giant plaster amphoras, while staff in silver plastic breastplates handed out bite-size spanakopita and shots of retsina. Plinky harp music trilled over the speakers, and plastic vine leaves were draped over every available surface.

Only the dregs of SeaMester—Justin, Con, and Adora—were lingering by the bar.

Constantine smiled when he caught sight of me. Disappointingly, he was dressed in black dress trousers and a half-buttoned white shirt over a blue tee. Truthfully, I'd harbored a secret hope of seeing him in one of the short Greek-soldier outfits the waiters were braving.

"And what the hell are you supposed to be?"

"Odysseus, obviously," he replied. "The wiliest of the Trojan heroes and far too intelligent to do anything so trivial as dressing up."

"I'm pretty sure Odysseus disguised himself as a *sheep* at one point. Now who doesn't know their classics?" remarked Cintia with a grin.

Adora turned to us, passing a drink to Con. She looked astonishingly, eye-blisteringly beautiful in a diaphanous robe of translucent gold, her pale red hair falling in loose waves, adorned with a simple circlet of golden leaves. I had never felt more like a peasant, in what was basically a creased bedsheet tied at my middle with fraying rope. Con sipped his drink, which was definitely not his first, and cleared his throat.

"You must bind me with tight chafing ropes so I cannot move a muscle, bound to the spot, erect at the mast-block, lashed by ropes to the mast. And if I plead, commanding you to set me free, then lash me faster, rope on pressing rope."

"Uh, kinky," I remarked, a little lost for words.

"It's from the *Odyssey*—it's how Odysseus prevents himself from being lured by the Sirens. Think of it as the sequel to the book you're reading."

I rolled my eyes. Condescension wasn't as appealing as he clearly thought it was.

"Well, Con, if the rumors back home are to be believed, you're the one into ropes," said Adora.

I looked at her wide-eyed, my face beginning to feel uncomfortably warm. She had an unerring way of always making me feel like a sheltered little child. Grinning, she put a hand to her mouth and gave me an apologetic look. "My bad. It's the shots. Come on, Cintia, let's leave them to it."

I glowered, ready to turn away from him too, but he placed a hand on my shoulder.

"Wait—*wait*." He paused and I waited. "So, can you dance, Liv?"

I huffed a laugh.

"Are you serious? I didn't grow up with a governess teaching me how to waltz in the ballroom of my manor house. *No.* I think I'll go sit down with the others."

"No—here. I'll teach you. It's easy, honestly."

I looked up at him cautiously and he gave me an almost shy smile. How did he always manage to do this—make my suspicions about him disappear whenever he grinned at me? Relenting, I allowed him to clasp one of my hands in his, his grip cool and firm, and lead me out onto the dance floor, which was already packed with toga-clad couples swaying about. I couldn't imagine it was really Con's thing, but I was happy to play along. He lowered his head to mine, his warm breath tickling my ear.

"It's all a case of counting to three, which I imagine they *do* teach at your school? Just keep that in your head and follow my lead."

I looked up at him, remembering Adora's comment. "You like to be in charge, hmm?"

He smiled back in a wolfish way that left me clumsy and sweaty. "Yes, actually. Adora and I aren't a thing, you know, and never have been. Put it this way, she's far more likely to be into you than me."

"What's that supposed to mean?" I said, half pulling away.

"Exactly what it sounds like."

"Why didn't you tell me that earlier?"

"Why would I? It's her business, not mine. She enjoys winding you up, that's all. There's nothing in it."

"And Leda?"

He led me in a gentle square about the dance floor, picking up many appreciative glances from older ladies. "A *definite* mistake. Like I told you, she was only ever interested in me because of my father's connections."

It didn't entirely ring true. I remembered Leda's warning in the club bathroom.

"And—and Octavia?"

I was barely aware of the words leaving my mouth, but the instant they did, I felt his limbs stiffen, his grip on my waist momentarily tighten.

Do you know she's here? Do you suspect it?

Have you seen her?

"I'd—I'd—rather not talk about her right now."

He gritted the words out. But we *needed* to talk about her. About why the same girl I'd seen him on vacation with was in a recently taken picture of Will. About why her passport had been in the captain's cabin. Had he lied about her disappearance? And if so, why? I sighed, distracted now, the music beginning to give me a needling headache. Besides, he was right. Now wasn't the right time, not with so many people around.

He leaned closer, his hair brushing my face, the soft, clean smell of him filling my senses, his expression sincere. "Look, Liv. I know you've got a lot on your mind—and things have been tough for you, but they'll get better, I promise. I think what you need is a distraction."

He stepped closer, causing my entire body to dissolve into ribbons of fire.

Could I trust him? I certainly wanted to. But even now, I knew that wasn't the same thing.

At that moment, I was about to suggest we leave and forget the party, forget about Orlaigh, forget about Will, forget about every damn thing, when a gong sounded for dinner.

Sitting down, my mind slowly returning to earth, I realized Raj *still* hadn't shown up, which was irking me spectacularly, as was the way Justin was continuing to act like nothing had happened. He sat across the table from me, scrolling through his phone, entirely oblivious, and I wanted to SCREAM at him.

Acquisitions manager. What, exactly, was he managing? He was negligent, *that* was certain. And as soon as I stepped foot onto dry land, I would be making sure everybody knew it.

The gong sounded once more, and I followed everyone's turned heads to see the Sirens walk in, trying to make some big entrance and, admittedly, succeeding, with the captain leading everyone in a clap. Obviously they were all dressed as goddesses, in flowing white silk gowns, circlets of golden laurel leaves upon glossy hair.

"The ship's beautiful Sirens," simpered the captain in a way that made me want to heave. I imagined them dressed as *actual* sirens, like the etching on that old map, the things I'd dreamed were in my bathroom—half women, half monstrous birds—and a lunatic giggle bubbled to my throat. Until I remembered that harsh flapping sound in the captain's cabin, and then it wasn't at all funny anymore.

Following behind them, her not-inconsiderable beauty dulled a little by their light, was Orlaigh, wearing, in grim contrast to the rest of the guests, a black—rather than white—bedsheet tied into a toga. A black bandanna was tied tightly around her eyes. I shuddered a little at the sight. The captain raised his hand and an ominous drumbeat began. "And here we have Cassandra, Princess of Troy, cursed by the gift of prophecy."

He rambled on, introducing more of the staff, including the delightful Mr. Eduardo—apparently Agamemnon, the daughter killer himself, wearing a bedsheet that was far too short and revealed more than I'd ever wanted to see of his long, scrawny legs. Clearly he was a fan of murder mysteries, judging by the energetic way he was dancing around the guests tonight. I had to admit, for a guy his age, he had some moves.

The Greek cuisine was delicious, and we ate our way through piles of gyros and pita bread, Greek salad piled high with salty feta and juicy tomatoes. Looking around, I caught the eye of someone sitting at the next table. It was the nurse who manned the infirmary reception desk. She looked a little different in her crumpled toga, but there was no doubt it was her. Instinctively, I looked away, but then an idea hit me.

It was a risk, but there was a chance it could pay off, so I needed to take that chance.

I kicked Constantine under the table.

"Hey—hey—I need your help."

He gave me a wary look, but didn't say no.

"I'm going to pretend to choke—nothing drastic, but you're going to ask in the loud, entitled voice of yours if there's any medical staff around," I whispered, low enough that no one else could hear. "That blond woman at the next table should come over—she's a nurse. When she does, you need to bump into her or something, then grab her key card. Look—it's clipped to her belt."

Constantine blinked slowly at me.

"You want me to *what*? Did you spend your entire day drinking cocktails with the retirees? We're not in a *heist* movie."

I huffed. "I am well aware of that, but I *need* to get into the infirmary later and this is the only way I can think of. Please."

He stared at me for a few more moments, then pushed away his plate.

"You can't be serious?"

"You know I am," I hissed. "You *said* you wanted to help me—so prove it."

He rolled his eyes. "The things I do for girls dressed in bed-sheets. Fine, I'll give it a go, but I'm not promising anything."

Taking a deep breath, I launched into an impressive fit of gagging, coughing, and wheezing for breath. Con did nothing for at least five long seconds, regarding me soberly with a disdainful raised eyebrow. Then, once people started to look over and Justin roused himself, Con gave a low sigh and sprang into action, wrapping his arm around my shoulders and patting my back, his voice low in my ear, his closeness so intoxicating I almost began choking for real.

"This is probably the most ridiculous thing I've ever done. You *owe* me, Olivia Larkin," he hissed, before raising his voice.

"Hey—do we have any doctors in here? My friend's choking!"

To her credit, the nurse at the next table immediately kicked her chair back and came rushing over. I slightly lost track of events as she wrapped her arms around my torso from behind and performed the Heimlich. Before I lost my dinner, I made a strangled sound and took a shuddering breath, turning to my savior, full of gratitude.

"Thank you so much," I breathed, my eyes genuinely watering after the force of her thrusts. "I think—I think you saved my life."

During the spontaneous smatter of applause from the other diners, I tried to catch Con's eye—hoping for some sign that my plan had been successful. But he wouldn't look at me.

"Never a dull moment with you around—is there, Liv?" said Cintia, her dark eyes glittering.

Once the excitement at our table had died down, the captain rapped on a glass and Orlaigh stood—still wearing the bandanna across her eyes. I hoped she'd gotten to take it off to eat at least. Her voice was high and fluting as she addressed the diners.

"Ah, a bastardized reading of some of Cassandra's prophecies by Aeschylus, I think. What a treat," said Con, rolling his eyes. It took everything in me not to press him about the key card, but after my stunt, I could feel Justin watching me more closely. I'd speak to Con later, when we were away from the table.

"*—this is the lioness, who goes to bed with the wolf when her proud lion ranges far away,*" Orlaigh called over the crowd.

Con droned on beside me while I tried to listen.

"Of course, Cassandra's true curse wasn't the prophecies themselves, but the fact that no one believed her," he continued in the patronizing tone of an unpopular schoolteacher. Still, I had to admit his words seemed unusually prescient in the scheme of things.

At that exact moment, the doors to the Neptune Lounge flew open, violently rebounding off the walls, while high-pitched string music began to wail over the speakers. The room immediately dimmed, now lit only by the pale glow of the candles placed at every table. I clutched Con's thigh and he chuckled into my hair.

"Jesus *Christ*. They could have waited until after we'd eaten," I muttered, regretfully looking down at my half-full plate. Cintia shushed me as we witnessed a figure run in, draped in a voluminous black robe and that unwelcomely familiar eerie mask of the Greek chorus, mouth downturned in a chilling rictus. I felt myself grow cold. It was the very same mask that had been worn by the weirdo backstage in the auditorium—I was sure of it. The same one I had seen in Cintia's bathroom. And in their raised hand, the figure wielded a wicked-looking knife.

To my horror, the robed figure ran directly over to Orlaigh's thin figure, her words so much faster now, hurried and running together, and stabbed her several times in the chest with a wet, thunking sound. I shrieked and stood, my chair clattering to the floor behind me. Orlaigh's voice became high and strained, becoming a thin, breathy series of screams, then eventually stopped as she slumped slowly to the ground. Around me I could hear unsettled movement and uncertain murmurs. A strong hand pulled me back into my seat.

"It's not *real*," said Constantine disparagingly, but even he sounded less confident that usual. I half stood again, trying to see what was going on. But several members of the staff had gathered around her fallen body and were busy wrapping her in a black sheet, similar to the one the "killer" had worn.

"Hey, do you think she's all right?" I breathed, adrenaline pulsing through me.

"It's a game, Liv," snapped Adora tersely. "They do this same routine every time the damn ship sails."

Moments later the lights snapped back on again.

"The killer strikes!" said the captain into the mic with all the cheesy drama of a cabaret presenter, and after a slight pause, the room relaxed into relieved laughs and enthusiastic applause.

But as I watched the still form being carried out on a stretcher by four other black-clad members of the faceless chorus, a dark tide of uncertainty swelled within me. The sound of the knife hitting her chest echoed in my ears—a fleshy wet, tearing noise. A noise I never wanted to hear again; it had seemed so . . . real.

Events after dinner proved tedious. Now that the murder had been committed, we were meant to move about the crowded lounge, interrogating fellow guests while repeatedly reading our own info from the invite that I'd left back in my cabin.

Constantine sidled up to me, handing me an unasked-for glass of prosecco. "You look tense. Here, have a drink. And, if you need to be distracted, I have a few ideas."

I mean, I should have been delighted. Here I was, on a luxury cruise liner, apparently being seduced by a ridiculously hot rich guy, and yet all I could think about was Orlaigh's face. The way her mouth opened wide and soundless as the knife was driven into her chest. Those tight, strangled screams.

I accepted the glass from Con, smiling at him weakly. "Thanks. Hey, did you manage to grab the nurse's card earlier?" I asked, dropping my voice. "The stunt with Orlaigh—it just looked so real, you know? I'd feel better knowing we could check in on Will—"

"Liv, can you just . . . *not* right now?" Con cut me off, his expression tight. "I'm trying to have a pleasant evening with you, despite your frankly ridiculous scheme earlier. Can we please just . . . be *normal* for an hour?"

I took a deep breath, then a sip of my drink, washing away my fears. I could only push Con so far before he reached his limit—and as far as my worries about Orlaigh were concerned, I'd see her later tonight. Why couldn't I just relax, like Con suggested?

But still, her face.

I leaned into Con, grateful for the comfort his presence provided, and was surprised (and pleased) when he casually wrapped an arm around my shoulders. Impulsively, I turned my face to his and kissed him softly.

"Let's go back to mine?" he murmured into my hair. "I genuinely don't give a shit whodunnit. I mean, do you?"

His words were low and private as he smiled down at me, that blissful, genuine smile he so rarely used, and that dizzying heat I'd felt earlier returned.

It was tempting; besides everything else, we did actually

need to talk. But tonight was not the night. I recalled my earlier promise to Orlaigh. I *had* to wait for her. I had to *know*. And if I went back with Con, I was fairly sure I wouldn't be leaving until the following morning at the earliest.

I owed it to Will.

I gave him a regretful look. "I'd love to—you have no idea— but I *can't* right now." I paused, desperately searching for an excuse, but I couldn't find one. I watched the disappointment cross his face like a cloud across the sun and turn into a shadow of cold indifference.

"Look. Is this about Will again? I thought we'd talked about that. Truth is, the guy's a dick and—"

It took immense strength not to roll my eyes, but I managed to let him rattle on, retreating into my thoughts.

Should I just come clean and tell him I was meeting Orlaigh? But then I remembered her words from earlier.

No one can suspect we know anything—

Had she meant Con? She'd certainly seen me with him before.

His hand slid away from mine.

—no one—

Cintia swayed over, dragging me onto the now-raucous dance floor, and after knocking back my drink, I gladly followed.

"So where's Raj, then?" I shouted at her above the music. "I thought he was coming tonight?"

"Having trouble with his toga," she shouted back. "It was

looking pretty indecent last time I saw him. He'll be here in a bit."

I couldn't help raising an eyebrow. Another excuse? But if Cintia noticed, she didn't say anything.

An hour or so later, I was exhausted, overly aware of how late it was and ready to go back to my cabin. The fact that Raj still hadn't shown his face made me more determined than ever to get the truth from Orlaigh. She'd know what to do. She could start whatever procedure we needed. Call maritime law and insist they send someone to help us.

I scanned the bustling crowd for Constantine, preparing to say goodbye.

A familiar face drew my eye. Hilary. She looked like she was having a whale of a time, waltzing around the crowded dance floor with impressive speed. Where was her walking stick? She gave me a little smile, the secretive nature of it somehow sinister.

Finally I caught sight of Con, lounging on an area of cushioned seating at the very back of the room, pale curls askew, his shirt loose. Leda was leaning over him, practically *astride* him, mussing his hair. They looked well suited—a beautiful couple. A piercing spike of jealousy lacerated my heart, and I gasped at the sharpness of it. Definitely *drunk,* he caught my eye, his gaze languid but immediately sharpening. A second later, deliberately, he turned his attention away from me and back to her.

A flare of rage fired through me. I debated storming over there and chucking the contents of my glass (admittedly water) into his face. But I wasn't here to play childish games, not when there were far more important things at stake. With a brief shake of my head, I turned to leave.

"So many of them are like that, you know."

I started. Standing silently behind me was Thalia, holding a sparkling green cocktail between golden claws. She looked ethereal tonight. The flowing silk of her costume; the gold glitter on her eyelids catching the lights and making her glow.

"And Leda is *weak*. He hurt her before, but she would still give up everything to be in your position. She doesn't listen, refuses to hear me when I remind her what he did."

She looked me up and down, an inscrutable smirk upon her perfect features.

"Pandora, you really have let it all fly, haven't you? It would almost be admirable if it hadn't been for such a disappointing boy."

Somehow, I knew she was talking about Will, not Con. I turned to face her, all other thoughts entirely forgotten.

"What's happened to Will? What did you do to him? I know you were with him that night."

She gave a beatific smile.

"You should have heard how quickly he disassociated himself from you. How readily he chucked you under the bus. All it took was about sixty seconds of our attention, barely even half a smile." She reached out and a traced a feather-soft finger under each of my eyes where my dark circles lay. I shuddered at her touch. "Do you honestly think he would go through all this, through everything you have, if the situation were reversed?"

Her voice was low and singsong, almost a chant.

I had to hope he would. After all, wasn't that the point of friends? Friends like *us* anyway.

"Yes," I murmured. "I think he would. Where *is* he?"

Thalia smiled brightly, revealing large white teeth, the spell immediately broken. "Ha! Why are you asking me? Enjoy your evening. I'll point Con in your direction once Leda's had her fun."

Without dignifying her comment with a response, I headed back to my room.

Unfortunately, it didn't stop the damn image of the two of them swirling around and around in my head as I sat on my bed, desperately trying to focus on my book as I watched the minutes tick by. I stared at my useless phone, which remained obstinately free of messages just as it had most of the trip.

Eventually, I fell into an unhappy doze, snapping wide-awake to the buzzing of my phone's alarm around midnight, the time the party was due to end.

The ship was so silent, its engines humming rhythmically away beneath me. Time ticked steadily on, and I almost drifted back to sleep again. I was so tired; it was a struggle to stay awake. Especially since Orlaigh was already nearly an hour late.

I saw her again; the sound the knife had made, the way her face had paled.

No, there was no way that could have really happened. Not in front of pretty much all the guests. I was letting my imagination run down dark corridors again.

Would it hurt to get a little more sleep? After all, we'd be docking tomorrow evening. I could almost put it all behind me. Orlaigh had probably been working some punishing twelve-hour shift and had passed out on her bed. And as for what she'd said earlier, she was nervy, that's all. Long shifts and lack of sleep must get to you after a while. And Raj being pushed off the deck in front of everyone? *Ridiculous.* So I'd gotten Laila's parents mixed up with another couple, big deal. And as for me—well, it was my first trip abroad without my parents with a bunch of strangers; no wonder I was finding it hard.

Yep, I could explain it all away if I really had to.

Except for one thing: Will.

I struggled to sit up, wiping my eyes.

Will wasn't someone I'd just met, whose background I didn't know. Will had been my friend for years. Will, who had been there for every difficult time I'd had in the past few years; who had defended me, lied for me, cheered for me. Who always made me laugh with his endless supply of crappy gifs and rubbish impressions of our tyrannical French teacher.

And there was no way I was leaving this ship without him.

28

A SUDDEN SHARP KNOCKING INTERRUPTED MY DRIFTING thoughts, sending a flood of relief through me. I checked my phone. It was two a.m., but at least she was finally here.

"Okay, yes, one sec—"

But the knock was immediately followed up by a low and currently unwelcome voice.

"Liv? It's Con. Are you awake?"

I said nothing. A bewildered mixture of half terror, half relief coursed through me. Had *he* done something to Orlaigh? Why was he here instead of her—or—

"Hey? I'm—I'm sorry about before . . . I . . . um . . . I . . ." I heard him give a deep sigh. *"Liv?"*

"Oh, fuck off, Constantine," I whispered dully from my bed, as I conjured the earlier scene of Leda draped all over him, her silken hair dangling in his face. He knocked again, more insistently, and I got up, placing my hand on the door handle, debating whether or not to open it. Then there was a moment's pause as he slipped something under the door, followed by the soft sound of his retreating footsteps.

I looked down. Lying on the floor was a white key card adorned with a red cross. The infirmary key.

Did I really want to go there now? In the dark? And alone?

Well, at least Con could prove useful in that respect, though my heart sank slightly at the fact that Orlaigh still hadn't shown. Hurriedly, I pulled on a chunky-knit cardigan, stumbled into my sneakers, and wrenched open my cabin door just in time to see Con about to disappear back into his cabin. We'd need to be careful. Of all the places on the ship, the infirmary was the one place where staff were likely to be awake, checking in on any patients.

"Hey!" I hissed. "Hey—I'm awake."

He turned, a pleased smirk upon his lips. I took one more glance down the corridor, praying to see Orlaigh heading to my room, but it was deserted.

The image of her being carried from the party under a black sheet flashed into my mind and I blinked back hot tears.

Surely they wouldn't be so brazen—she *must* have been held up or lost her nerve or—

Con headed back toward me.

"Oh, good, I thought you were asleep." He looked down at the card in my hand, then back at me. Was he nervous? "So, we doing this, or what?"

* * *

Apart from a few harried-looking staff, the long ship corridors were mostly empty at this time of the morning. After an uncomfortably silent elevator journey, we finally stood outside the white door of the infirmary, the key in my sweaty hand.

There was nobody around.

I slipped the card into the slot. There was a satisfying clunk as the lock released. My heart juddered in my chest. So far, so easy. Now all we had to do was find Will. He would be here. If everything was okay, if I was just paranoid, if Con and Justin were right and I was wrong, then he *had* to be.

The waiting room beyond was lit only by a small desk lamp, the reception thankfully unmanned. Carefully, I closed the door behind us and waited, listening.

Abruptly, Con pulled me out of sight of the main corridor, pressing his finger to his lips. I glared at him, then fell silent when I heard the soft, hushed voices that were drifting down toward us. I followed him as he edged through the room, weaving between the two rows of chairs, and crouching behind them as the voices stopped and soft footsteps padded along the floor toward me. It was the nurse who'd "saved" me earlier. I held my breath as she approached the reception desk, praying she wasn't about to sit down and begin a twelve-hour shift. Instead, she noisily deposited something into a drawer and then left.

Beside me, Con exhaled softly with relief. He was scared, I realized, or at least on edge. If there was nothing to fear on his dad's immensely safe ships, then why could I hear his heart pounding over mine?

I crept over to the narrow corridor that led down to the individual sickrooms. All their doors were shut, weak light spilling from their circular windows.

Far up ahead, where the corridor turned around a blind bend, I could hear the clinking sound of metal upon metal—someone organizing a tray of medical equipment, perhaps. We'd need to be fast. I slipped around the corner and glanced into the window of the room where Will was supposed to be.

A dark curtain had been drawn across it. I tried the handle in vain. The door was firmly locked. Should I shout for him? Hammer on the door? That hadn't exactly worked out well for me last time.

"*Hey*—hey—look."

Con gestured to an identical door on the opposite side of the corridor, its window uncovered. I peered through.

Inside was a hospital bed. Steel trays and wheeled medical units stood beside it, their drawers spilling open, revealing gleaming silver instruments and packs of bandages. A professional-looking setup. What chilled me, though, was the sight on the bed. Someone lay upon it, unmoving. An adult, or young adult, by the size of things—roughly Will's size, I suppose, but it was hard to tell, as a black sheet was drawn completely over their head.

I stared, unblinking, for a few moments. Had they moved him? Was he *dead*? I continued to stare, desperate to see the subtle rise and fall of the sheet that would signal breathing, but the light was too dim to really tell.

"Didn't you notice how many old people are on this ship?" murmured Con in way of explanation. "Sometimes . . . it happens."

Nudging him out of the way, I took another look, desperate for some sign of life, then realized that the quiet sounds of someone working up ahead had now stopped. A horrible sense of dread washed over me like a fever. Con met my gaze, panicked, mouthing *Shit*. In desperation, I tried the handle to the room and nearly fell into it as the door swung easily open.

Footsteps echoed in our direction as we stumbled in, Con motioning furiously for me to get down as he softly closed the door behind us. Moments later, a dark figure strode past the circular window. I caught only a glimpse of them, but they appeared to be wearing an odd costume that covered not only their body but also their head; black and shiny—almost gelatinous-looking in the lights—like PVC. Someone who'd not had a chance to change after the Murder Mystery, perhaps.

From behind me came a muffled gasp. Con was paler than I'd ever seen him—almost green.

"What?" I said, turning to look at what he'd seen.

A hand had slipped out from beneath the black bedsheet, bloated and pale, the nails dark with what looked like dregs of seaweed, bringing that nightmarish image of drowned Will back into my head.

Shaking violently, I stood, barely able to grasp the corner of the sheet.

"Liv—what the hell are you *doing*?"

I ignored him. I *had* to know. I had to—

From outside, voices traveled down the corridor, louder now, agitated, and hostile. I couldn't make out exactly what they were saying, but I recognized one of them as the hotel manager, Eduardo.

"We need to go," said Con urgently. "Whoever that is—we can't help them—"

I tugged back the sheet a little, as far as my courage would allow, revealing damp golden hair instead of Will's dark curls.

Orlaigh?

I gasped. A heady mixture of relief and despair coursed through me, hot bile rushing into my mouth, and I staggered back, my foot catching on a steel medical trolley, causing it to crash noisily to the ground.

"*Shit*," said Con, grabbing my hand and wrenching open the door in one smooth movement. "Come *on*." And I had no choice but to stumble after him, back down the corridor and toward the door.

29

BACK IN CON'S CABIN, WE SAT ON HIS BED, BREATHING hard, both of us staring fixedly at the door, half expecting it to burst open any minute and for unknown assailants to drag us both to a watery grave. Neither of us had said much of anything since we'd gotten back, my lungs still burning with the exertion of sprinting halfway across the ship.

"She was *dead*," I finally managed.

Con looked at me dully. "What—who? All *I* saw was you being comically clumsy."

I stared at him, blank-faced. *No.* I wasn't going to let him laugh his way around the truth this time. "Orlaigh," I repeated. "She was under the sheet, dead."

He rubbed his hands over his face, looking as tired as I felt.

"How can you be sure? You didn't see her face. It was probably just an old person, like I said. Unfortunate, but not—"

"I saw her hair! And she wasn't *breathing*, Con! Her hand was all . . . bloated. How much surer do you want me to be? Besides, if everything was so bloody normal, why did you run out of there like you were being chased by a pack of wolves—"

"Because we're not meant to be snooping around areas out-of-bounds to passengers. Why else?"

I stared at him, my mouth dropping open in disbelief. I got up and headed to the door. There was no way I could continue to sit here pretending everything was normal, moments after witnessing my first dead body.

"Who bloody cares!" I hissed as I went. "Your dad *owns* the damn ship! Don't you think he might be interested in the fact that one of his staff got stabbed? *What* is it going to *take*, Con? How many people need to disappear before you finally admit something's wrong?"

"Liv—Liv, wait—"

Utterly sick of his constant denials, I stormed out, slamming the door hard behind me. Yes, we needed to talk more, but I was *furious*. There was being sensibly rational and there was being deliberately obtuse. If a dead body hadn't convinced him, maybe he was a lost cause.

Back in my cabin, I tried to rest, but it was impossible. All I could do was watch the minutes on my phone's clock tick by into hours as diffuse gray daylight began to spread beneath my cabin door, until *finally* it was six a.m.

It took five entire minutes of hammering at his cabin door to rouse Justin from his bed.

He looked *terrible*. I could smell the stale alcohol on his breath from where I stood several feet away; his eyes were yellow-crusted and bloodshot.

"Shit, you look . . . tired," I murmured.

He frowned at the sight of me.

"What's up, Liv? It's, uh, pretty early."

I scoped out the corridor. It was empty, but even so, I didn't feel comfortable discussing what I had to say in public. I nodded behind him.

"Can I come in?"

Justin's cabin was a musty-smelling pit strewn with dirty clothes, half-eaten plates of long-congealed food, and numerous empty mini bottles of spirits. I looked at him worriedly. Where was our squeaky-clean bespectacled leader from day one?

"Is . . . is everything okay, Justin?"

I mean, clearly it wasn't.

"Yeah, just a . . ." He gave an entirely humorless laugh that turned into a phlegmy cough. "Just had a good night, you know?"

"Look, I need to talk to you. I mean, seriously. About Will and . . . and Raj." I took a deep breath, steeling myself. "I've tried telling you before—but we all need to get off this ship, Justin—and right now. I thought I was crazy for ages—but I'm not. I know I'm not."

I hesitated for a moment, then plowed on.

"I think we're all in danger—all of SeaMester, I mean—including you. There's seven of us, right? And all of us are a lot younger than most of the other people on this ship. Remember

I told you about that creep in the auditorium the other morning? Well, I think they were trying to warn me. They said seven were needed for this bargain that's been made—and—and—"

I stopped, partly because I was aware of how ridiculous it sounded when I tried to explain it aloud, but mostly because Justin was—was *smirking*. He continued to stare at me in silence for a few moments, studying me intently with dark, mocking eyes. I'd once thought them a warm brown, but they were black in the dim cabin. The silence stretched out thinly, soon becoming uncomfortable.

I thought again of his picture in the brochure Thalia had sent to Will's dad, and a thin worm of fear burrowed deep.

Acquisitions manager. And what exactly did Justin acquire?

Eventually he spoke, slowly nodding as he did so.

"Is that right? We're *all* in danger? We're all gonna die in some weird bargain?" He gave a humorless chuckle, shaking his head. "How about that, huh?"

My voice less sure now, I carried on.

"Think about it, Justin. Will's been gone since the very first day of this trip and no one's seen him—"

Justin held up a hand with sharp abruptness, silencing me.

"See—that's where you're *wrong*, Olivia. I have visited Will every single day since he got sick. I saw him yesterday, in fact. In his bed, in the infirmary, where he's been in safe hands all this time."

"That's *not* true!" I said, raising my voice in indignation. "Every time I ask about him, all you do is brush me off—"

He exhaled lengthily, peering at me over the top of his gold-rimmed glasses. "Look, Liv. None of us wanted to be the one to tell you this, but the simple truth is, Will hasn't *wanted* to see you."

"*What?*"

The world seemed to recede around me, its color leeching away.

"Not even once. I was trying to be kind to you by brushing it off when you asked. We all know you have a little crush on him, but I'm sorry to say the feeling is not mutual. Not at the moment. At this point, I think you need to know . . . he specifically asked me *not* to let you visit."

It was as if Justin had punched me directly in the gut, my breath taken clean away. I watched his dark eyes lose their flat intensity, watched them round and soften into sympathy, and I *hated* him.

"I'm sorry, Liv. It can't be easy to hear, but I think, at this stage, you're better off knowing the truth. Some of the others have said you've become, well, paranoid. Convinced yourself that there's some grand conspiracy on board this ship. Fact is, everything's fine. Everything's always *been* fine. Raj has been resting with muscle strain, just as I said. Truth be told, he's a bit fed up with everyone being drunk around him since he's sober."

He broke off into an embarrassed laugh and gestured around the room. "Guess you can't blame him for *that*. And yes, Will is still sick but feeling much better. His exact words were that you were being 'a bit intense.' Calling him at all hours, messaging him nonstop, making him feel guilty when he was feeling too sick to answer. Dragging stuff up from your past—"

"He asked me for *help*, Justin!"

"Yeah, he told me about that too. Looked a little sheepish. Apparently, he'd been on some strong painkillers. You weren't the only one getting weird messages that day." Justin chuckled. "He told me . . . what was it now? That you'd gotten the wrong idea about your relationship and wouldn't take no for an answer. He said that in his state . . . he just didn't need the hassle."

Lies, it had to be lies.

All right, so we hadn't been on the best of terms lately, but Will was my friend. He'd always been my friend. He wouldn't sell me out to a bunch of total strangers.

Would he?

But that first night flashed before my eyes again. The anger—worse—the distaste in his eyes. That was what had upset me. I'd never seen that look in his eyes before that night. It had been as if he'd held a mirror up to me, revealing everything I disliked about myself. Every single insecurity, every late-night worry.

The guy's a dick . . . everyone reckoned he didn't deserve you.

"I mean, he showed me some of the messages—your messages, I mean. Please don't feel too bad. We can all get that way—you know—a little melodramatic or whatever—especially after a drink or two."

I miss you.

I don't regret it.

Please, Will. Please.

Justin rattled on. He sounded underwater, his voice muted and indistinct.

"He's been fine, though. I was torn about whether to tell you. . . . I know how you've been struggling, but I didn't realize how bad things had gotten for you until the others filled me in last night."

"So—so he's feeling better . . . Will? Not in a coma, under sedation, not in pain, or—" I shook my head, unable to process what Justin was saying. "You're telling me he just didn't want to see me? Did—did everyone know? The staff too? They were told not to let me see him?"

I said the words slowly. I sounded like an idiot, but I didn't care. I needed things clear in my mind. Justin continued to drone on, but I was past listening.

"Yeah, I mean, sure he's under the weather. Some viral infection they think, possibly contagious, but nothing major. He's been chilling, you know, glued to Netflix on his iPad—thank God for those, right? There's a little outside deck in the infirmary, so he's been getting some sea air and—"

I stopped listening. Every muscle in my body seemed to tense.

iPad?

Wait. Wait, *wait.*

The same iPad—indisputably Will's—that I'd squirreled away down my leggings on my way out of Thalia's room?

He'd never had his iPad, hadn't had it for days.

Justin was lying. Blatantly lying. Will didn't have his iPad. And, if Justin had lied about that, what else was he lying about?

I'd suspected all of SeaMester was in danger, but no, Justin wasn't in danger—of course he wasn't—he was *involved* in all this somehow—

Acquisitions manager.

I tried to breathe.

"Liv . . . ? Is everything okay? You look a little . . . off."

Get a grip, Liv. Get a grip. He can't know that you know.

I couldn't help it. I automatically looked over to the closed door of Justin's cabin. Catching this, Justin took a single step closer. It was so quiet in here. The only sound the ever-present throbbing of the ship's engines. No one would ever know if—

I wiped an imaginary tear from my eye—I was far too wired to actually cry—and gave a shaky sigh.

"Yeah, yeah, of course. It's just . . . a lot to take in, that's all. We've been friends for so long. . . ."

Justin nodded sympathetically, like he'd been expecting my reaction. There was a bleak static roaring in my ears and my whole body felt disconnected, as if shaken about for too long, unmoored.

"I'm sorry. It must hurt to hear it. You know, it's a shame you missed the after-party here last night. Will might have his issues, but the rest of us enjoy your company, Liv, so don't feel bad." He gestured at his disheveled state with a wan smile. "That's the reason for my devastatingly handsome visage this morning. You were invited, of course, but Con said you'd already gone to bed."

I was struggling for words. There was too much to think

about. Too much to examine. Justin cleared his throat, his voice becoming softer.

"Look, about Will. I did try to talk to him. I told him how genuinely concerned you were about him, but he was *adamant,* Liv. Maybe when we dock, you two can get some space together, clear your heads—"

I nodded meekly. Now the tears came to my eyes, spilling hotly down my face. Because we wouldn't get together when the ship docked. Somehow I just knew it. Something had happened to Will, and Justin knew exactly what. But I couldn't confront him. Not alone in the quiet confines of his cabin.

"Yeah, you're right. Maybe some space is—is what we need."

He gave me a sad vicar look and God, I *had* to leave. The oniony stench of BO and stale alcohol in combination with the steady rocking of the ship was making me nauseous. I headed toward the door, desperately needing to get out, get up onto the deck, and clear my head. And, to my relief, Justin didn't try to stop me.

I staggered blindly out of the cabin, searching desperately for any door that would lead me outside, the sour taste of bile filling my mouth. I needed to get away from the false joviality of the ever-present steel-drum music, the piped-in sticky lemon scent of the hallways, the endless cheery messages over the speakers.

Laughter seemed to echo in my ears, shrill and mocking. My skin was hot and clammy.

Wrenching open the door to the deck, I clattered forward and heaved my body against the railings, clutching against the rigid iron of the balcony, taking deep, regular breaths until eventually my nausea subsided.

Then, once the sickness and the disbelief cleared up, the tears began again. Heavy, choking sobs, my tears falling into the ocean below. Swallowed by it, its pitiless waters miles deep.

Could there be any truth in what Justin had said? That Will was okay and just hadn't wanted to see me. So what if he was watching stuff on an iPad? Maybe he'd just been using one the ship had loaned him?

And if there wasn't any truth in it, then why did it seem like such an obvious, rational explanation?

I'm sorry, Liv, this is wrong—

Why are you LIKE this—why can't you be fun Liv anymore?

Out of sheer frustration, I tried Will's number again, but it went straight to voicemail. For a brief dark moment, I considered hurling my phone into the sea.

Should I message him again, telling him I knew the truth?

No, there was no point. I knew my messages would only ping onto his iPad back in my cabin, unread and unheeded.

With a juicy sniff, I staggered away, slumping into a nearby rattan armchair. The sky above was white and featureless, throwing everything I'd learned into stark relief.

We'd fucked up that night in his car. I knew that now.

I think I knew it even then, from the exact moment his lips met mine. I'd thought—been convinced—that it had always been the both of us that felt this way. That every smile, every

encouraging word, *meant* something. And there was no denying the fierce heat of his body against mine, familiar but all at
once so different. Maybe that had been part of the excitement
of it all.

But I'd been drunk and he'd been sober, and the longer I
thought about it, the worse I felt. He'd told me, earnestly and
kindly, that it wasn't what he wanted, that he didn't feel that
way, not now. He told me I was drunk, and I'd definitely regret
it if we carried on. But I wasn't prepared to hear it. I'd lashed out
at him; even worse, I'd begged him. Didn't he *want* me? Wasn't
he attracted to me? Didn't he like me? *Love* me, even? Weren't
we friends, but *more* than friends? And he'd turned away, his
face so sad, telling me I was all of those things, I was more
besides, and that was why I shouldn't be wasting my time over
shithead boys like Liam Sutton. That yes, obviously he was attracted to me, telling me I *knew* that, hadn't he proved it only a
minute ago, but it didn't matter, it wasn't everything, there were
things that were more important and that—

A dark shadow blotted out the insipid morning sun.

"Ah, *here* you are. I've been looking for you everywhere."

I didn't look up.

I didn't want to see Constantine. Not now, maybe not ever.

He sank down beside me on the adjacent chair with a sigh.

Did *he* know about Will too? Had he been involved in last
night's pity party before he knocked at my cabin door? Poor
crazy paranoid Liv. I'd certainly confided in him more than
the others. I imagined Justin, his calm teacher voice explaining softly to everyone how Will didn't want to see me and to

be considerate of that and of my feelings. Had Con piled on, smirking in that cocky way of his as he related all my wild theories—the things I'd believed I'd told him in confidence?

Perhaps he had only felt sorry for me all along.

Constantine tapped his lighter on the glass-topped table, turning it over and over in his fingers. "Look, Liv, can we talk? Properly? It's—it's important, actually. I know the whole Will thing hasn't been easy on you, but—"

I cut him off with a loud groan, rubbing my face with my hands.

"Can you just *stop*? I don't want to talk about it. And I definitely don't want to talk about Will with you. You don't understand anything, you never have, so just leave it. Leave it and leave me alone."

His silence suggested pity.

Poor. Little. Liv.

Why can't she get over him?

He isn't even interested in her.

"Justin said Will didn't want to see me. That he specifically asked *not* to see me. Did you know that? Did he tell you guys?"

I forced myself to look at him as I said it. But if Constantine were an actor, he was a pretty good one. He looked and sounded entirely surprised.

"What? No? Is he okay, then? Have you seen him?"

"No. Never mind," I muttered darkly.

And there was something that still didn't make sense.

An appealingly pretty face, ink-dark eyes staring out of a battered passport. Will's arm around her as she grinned into the camera. Those strange messages. And had it to have been *her* with him, that time in the corridor, leading him down to the darkness at the bottom of the ship?

And how—*how* had I forgotten—how could I ever forget that ghost of a message?

HELP ME LIV

If there was ever a time to ask, it was now.

"All right, fine—I agree. We *do* need to talk. But I'm going to need to ask you something—something you're not going to like."

He looked at me warily, then nodded resignedly, as if knowing exactly what was coming.

"Okay. Go on."

"I need to know what happened to that girl who was meant to be here? The one whose place I took—Octavia—Tavi Liddle. I wouldn't ask if I didn't think it was important. What really happened to her, Con? How exactly did she disappear?"

30

HE DIDN'T SAY ANYTHING AT FIRST AND I WAITED FOR HIM to get up, to ram the chair sulkily under the table, shutter his face with an exasperated sigh, or something equally Con-like. But he didn't. Instead, he stared out to sea for the longest time, his sharp features etched in pale relief against the gray sky.

"I think I can trust you," he said eventually, his voice considered and thoughtful. Catching my expression, he gave me a sad half smile. "Okay, okay, I *do* trust you. So yes, I'll tell you if you want to hear it. But not here."

We made our way to Con's cabin, which was as obsessively tidy as I remembered. The bed neatly made; chargers regimentally organized on the desk. He sprawled across the bed while I perched primly in the chair. And without any preliminaries, he began to talk.

"From the outside, you'd think Octavia had everything—

after all, she was ridiculously wealthy—the daughter of an heiress, no less—beautiful, intelligent. But when I met her, she was running away."

He chewed his lip, as if playing the memories over in his head. "We'd met properly at a party, although of course I'd seen her around before—the Belgravia set runs in small circles, and she was the type of girl everyone noticed. Miles out of my league, or so I thought, but we got . . . talking that night and were soon . . . inseparable."

He paused at this, giving me a brief apologetic look. I leaned forward, gesturing impatiently for him to go on.

"Anyway," he said, obliging, "it wasn't long before she opened up and told me that her dad had gotten himself into some financial trouble; a few dodgy deals and investments had all come back to bite him, and they were at risk of losing her mother's ancestral home. A beautiful Georgian estate in the country that had been in the family for centuries. He was always a little rough around the edges, her dad. New money—a flash wheeler-dealer type—the kind of guy who could always talk the talk.

"Tavi never got along with him," Con went on, "but after we started dating, their relationship worsened. You see, she went from thinking he wanted her out of the way, to thinking he wanted to kill her."

Con's voice was soft now, as if he were almost talking to himself.

"*You don't understand,* she'd tell me, her eyes large and fearful. *I really think he wants to hurt me. Wants me out of the way—*

permanently. And like I said, she was clever, Tavi, smarter than anyone else I knew, which is why I didn't immediately dismiss her out of hand."

Unlike me. The thought was insidious, unwelcome, but it remained just the same.

He gave a shaky sigh and cleared his throat.

"Only a month or so after we'd gotten together, she turned up at my house late one night, suitcase in hand, banging on the door, hysterical, with her younger sister, Felicity—Flick—in tow. They'd always been close. Tavi was clearly agitated—babbling on and on about finally finding the evidence her dad was plotting to get rid of her. She kept ranting about some program—SeaMester, if you can believe it."

He offered me a wan smile, which I didn't return. Dread settled heavy in my gut, weighing me down as he continued. "They both needed a break—whether from Tavi's paranoia or from a genuinely bad home situation—that much was clear," Con said. "It was Tavi who insisted on Greece, so I suggested we take a trip to Ithaca. I mean, it made sense. My family is from that area, and Dad owns a villa on the island that's empty most of the year. As luck would have it, he was over there at the time, but the place was big enough that we wouldn't have to see each other if we didn't want to. That was where she found the map."

His words brought me out of my semidaze. "The map—the same old thing you found in the captain's room?" I asked. Con nodded, his expression solemn.

"My dad has one just like it, in his study. Tavi and I were

messing around in there one day, and when she caught sight of it, she paled—almost doubled over—her breath short and harsh, demanding to know why Dad had it. I couldn't understand why it had riled her so much. It was unremarkable—an old piece of parchment, yellowed and faded—just some tattered old sketch of the caves beneath the island that he'd picked up from one of the junk shops on the island. But she snatched it away from me and immediately shut herself in her room."

Con paused for a moment, as if struggling to go on, pushing a handful of golden curls out of his eyes while staring resolutely at the coverlet beneath him.

My thoughts drifted. Had Octavia somehow known what the map was when she found it—what it meant? Had she worked it all out? Had she gone to Greece to try to avoid the bargain her father had struck?

All those times I saw her with Will—was she trying to help him?

"I know I should have tried to get her to talk that night, but the next day, it was as if everything was perfectly fine," Con said. "I admit, this is when I began to question if she wasn't *truly* paranoid. I'd heard some stories about her through mutual friends—mental health stuff she suffered from, you know. Still, the next morning she woke up, bright and breezy, suggesting the three of us charter a boat to some local caves, suggesting we have a go at following the old map for a laugh."

I narrowed my eyes. Seemed like Con had a worrying habit of not believing the people he professed to care about.

"Anyways, we ended up going. Honestly, I didn't expect the

map to lead anywhere—we wandered for ages through these damp, dark caves until it felt like we must have reached the center of the island."

His voice caught, fear blooming in his eyes. "Then we found it. This . . . temple. Far more impressive than I'd thought it would be. The entrance was flanked by two enormous columns of what looked like black marble, and it was *vast* inside. Y'know, the kind of place you expect to be a World Heritage site with a permanent queue of tourists outside. It seemed odd to me that such an impressive place was so hidden away, so little known."

Fear slinked down my spine like a drop of ice water.

A *temple*? This was far from the story I'd been expecting.

"At the very back of the cave was an immense plinth of roughly hewn stone that must have once been an altar. It was crowded with things—trinkets and tchotchkes—little clay urns filled with what might have once been wine or olive oil. Shallow dishes full of coins that looked as though they belonged in a museum. Even a plastic wallet full of euros. Offerings, we thought, to some ancient god or goddess.

"Tavi joked we should leave something too—she wanted to leave the necklace I'd bought her a few days ago, joking it would be a good incentive for me to get her another. It was only some cheap souvenir—a silver coin depicting Aphrodite—but I sulked a bit and didn't let her. I can't help wondering if I had . . ."

He stopped again for a moment, staring intently at the floor.

"Anyway, she was thrilled to have found the temple, taking photos of everything, like a kid at Christmas. While she and Flick explored, I admit, I dozed off. Greece in August is crazy hot, and I'd had rather a lot of wine at lunch." He winced. "While asleep, I had the most vivid dreams. . . . I've never forgotten them. It was like I was drowning—in a warm black sea—and all the while I could hear the furious beating of wings and this strange, unearthly singing. And when I woke up, the temple was in absolute darkness and I was alone."

Constantine paused, his eyes over-bright.

"I called out for Tavi—for Flick. Neither answered, and I swear—*swear*—at the back of the cave, I saw these eyes glinting in the darkness like a cat's. It might have been Tavi, but—" Con swallowed and finally looked at me, a bewildered expression on his sharp features. "But—I can't explain why—I mean, we're talking about a girl I was in—incredibly fond of—but . . . I was afraid."

My voice was rough. "Afraid? Of her?"

He nodded, breaking his gaze. "Yeah. I know I should have gone after her; everyone asks why I didn't. But it was like all my senses were screaming at me not to—telling me it wasn't her. And when I finally found the flashlight and shone it at the back wall, where I thought I'd seen her . . . there was no one there."

He shuddered. "I spent hours wandering around in the dark cave, calling for them, but eventually I found my way back to the boat, just as the sun was going down. I hoped it had all been a terrible mistake, that they'd both be back at the villa waiting for me, but they weren't."

When he spoke again, his voice was smaller, quieter than I'd ever heard it.

"My father asked me, again and again, why I didn't go back in—why I didn't keep looking for them. Flick was so young—only fourteen—and the truth of it is . . . I was too scared."

I said nothing for a while, taking it all in.

"I wanted to raise the alarm immediately, file missing person reports and everything, but Tavi's father said no. He insisted she'd just run off—that it wasn't out of character for her to do something like this. And I wanted to believe him, so I . . . I just let it go."

He raked a shaking a hand through his hair, staring fixedly at the bedsheets.

"Con," I said quietly. While I wasn't exactly sure this was the best time to broach it, it felt wrong not to come clean when he obviously felt so terrible about the whole thing. I mean, if Con truly believed in cursed temples and glinty-eyed things that hid in the dark, surely it wasn't much of a leap to finally agree that events aboard this ship were far from normal. "Con, I don't think Tavi is dead. I think she's *here*. I'm sure of it—I mean, I've seen her. Aboard the *Eos*. And—and I think she might be in danger."

He blinked. *"Wh-what?"*

"I've been trying to tell you—I think she's here. Why else would her passport be in the captain's room? And I think she was with Will. She could be in trouble too—both of them—"

"No," said Constantine, cutting me off, his tone coldly decisive. "She's *gone*, Liv. And so is her sister. A cave-in, dehydration, drowning. I hate to think about it—it haunts me every single night—but her disappearance has nothing to do with whatever batshit conspiracy theory you think is going on with Will."

I exhaled in frustration. I had the feeling that Thalia could throw me over her shoulder in front of Con and lob me off the side of the ship before he would bat a laconic eyelid and finally admit something might be wrong.

"But I can *prove* it, Con. I have a bloody picture of her with Will dated a few days back. And that morning I was attacked—in the theater—whoever it was said the sea needed seven—seven were promised—or something. Humor me for one moment and imagine they did mean *sacrifices*—like in that book." I ticked the names off on my fingers. "Will—offered by his own dad if you read between the lines of that email to Thalia—then Raj . . . then the rest of us! Don't you think it's a bit of a coincidence that there are six of us on SeaMester? What if Octavia is alive and still hiding from her dad? What if she was right all along? What if she always knew she was meant to be the seventh? We need to *do* something, Con! Can you—can you raise the alarm with the captain—"

I stopped in surprise as Con gave a long, shuddering sigh and buried his face in both hands.

The realization hit me like a high-speed train. I gasped.

"Oh God. You already know, don't you . . . ? You *know* she's here."

He gave a sudden, sharp sob in response, his shoulders heaving.

"You *heard* her, that day we followed Leda to Thalia's cabin. You heard her voice, didn't you? That was why you were so freaked out. *That's* why you were lurking outside Thalia's room the other day."

I hovered, half out of the chair. Was he *crying*? Seeing his icy facade fracture like this was almost as shocking as what he'd just given away. My instinct was to go to him, comfort him. His breath hitched as he struggled to rein his emotions safely back in. But what *else* did he already know? What else had he not admitted to me?

Could I trust him at all?

But I wasn't made of stone. I couldn't just sit there and watch him like that. I sank down beside him on the bed and pried one of his hands away from his face, clasping it in mine.

"Hey," I said gently, tilting his face to meet mine. "I'm—I'm sorry—I know what it feels like."

"I don't know what to believe . . . ," he said softly, once his breathing had evened. "It's all such a mess. I mean, yes, you're right—I *did* think I heard her that night, but at the same time, I know it's impossible—"

"It's not impossible at all," I reassured him. "You said yourself she just disappeared. You never saw a body or anything—"

"But why would she be *here*?" he said, his voice breaking. "Why would she come here after everything she said? It makes no sense. So it can't be her—it *can't*."

He had a point. If she *did* believe she was the seventh, sent here by her opportunist dad, then why on earth would she come aboard? Unless, of course, she was being held against her will. I sighed. I needed Con to start joining some dots himself.

"Con—can't you see now that all of this is linked somehow? The Sirens, Octavia's disappearance in the cave. What's happening to SeaMester . . . If you know anything that could help—anything at all . . ."

Like what exactly is your dad involved in?

"I wish I did. I still can't believe some of the things you're saying—" He caught my arm as I began to pull away. "Not— not because I think you're crazy—I don't—I never did. But because—because it's my *dad,* Liv. I know I've said myself he can be a cold bastard, but *this*—what you're suggesting—*God.*"

Wiping an arm roughly across his face, he pulled me closer, crushing me against him, his breathing gradually slowing. It was intoxicating, being so near to him, like drowning.

"It's impossible, Olivia—it's impossible. He just *wouldn't*— and as for Octavia—you must be mistaken. We both are."

I moved back slightly, becoming snagged on his gaze, the sorrow in his eyes, the same shade as the iron-dark waters beneath us. Things would all be so much easier if I could just believe him.

Con wants what he wants—until he inevitably gets it.

Whatever it was, was still there, directly between us, an impending storm about to break.

"Liv," I corrected distantly, not knowing where to look anymore.

"Don't go—please," he said, although nothing in his posture suggested pleading. "I—I don't want to be alone." His eyes were hooded and hungry, like a wolf's. "I can't be alone right now."

He said nothing else, only bent his head, murmuring something into my hair. I turned my face and looked up, and he kissed me lazily, his mouth hot and wet against mine, the delicious smell of him circling around me, and, for a moment, I let go of all my doubts, all my worries, and allowed myself to relax into kissing him back, sliding easily into his lap. It was so easy and so, *so* good.

"Maybe it's you, Liv. Maybe *you're* the siren. You're so ridiculously lovely," he said, half sitting, one hand sliding under my top, his eyes now calm seas, his breathing so steady I wondered if I was affecting him at all, especially while I sat here, struggling to breathe. "And you can't even see it. You're *wasted* on him."

I shoved my hands into the softness of his hair as he pushed me down onto the bed, his heavy weight falling over me, my skirt hitched up about my waist.

"Is this all right?" he said, his words warm against my skin, his breathing faster now, catching up with mine.

"Y-yes," I stuttered against his mouth, his sure hands now beginning to explore places that left me squirming beneath him.

"You're sure?" he said again, one hand slipping away to rummage in the dresser drawer beside him.

But I didn't have time to answer, my voice silenced by a loud knock at the door.

"Fuck *sake*," muttered Constantine, staring darkly at the door. "Just ignore them—they'll soon get the hint."

He leaned back down and kissed me again, harder this time, but the knocking came again, sharp and insistent, followed by an unwelcome voice.

"Con, I *know* you're in there. Open up. It's important."
Adora.

I groaned, sitting up and hastily readjusting my clothes, the moment now entirely dissolved.

"I'll get it."

Adora stood outside, as glamorous as ever in an unseasonably thin dress of lace-edged lilac velvet and a chunky cream cardigan. If she was surprised to see me, she didn't show it. Instead, her bright gaze flickered from my face, barely even registering it, over to Con.

"Ah, you're both here—good. It's Cintia."

I was fully alert now. This was no time to mess about with Con—what had I been *thinking*?

"What? What about Cintia?"

"She's missing. Justin's looking for her now. She's not in her room, her bed doesn't look like it's been slept in, she's not even got her phone on her—"

Adora shook her head. Were those tears in her eyes genuine?

"Look," she said. "We've *got* to find her."

31

I HURRIED BACK TO MY CABIN TO GRAB MY JACKET. THE wind was fierce today, howling wildly about the ship and causing it to list alarmingly from side to side. As I crashed through the door, I kicked the stupid box-prop that Orlaigh had given me last night. I'd had to carry it around with me half the evening while dressed as Pandora, enduring endless jokes about "opening my box" and "my lid being tightly shut."

Something rattled within it as it skittered along the floor.

Weird. It had been empty last night. Hadn't it? I'd been pretty distracted after Orlaigh's "murder," but the box had remained under the table where I'd been sitting, untouched for the rest of the evening.

Curious, I unlatched it, revealing a note, an object concealed beneath it.

Don't let them take any more.
End it.

Beneath the note was a gun.

At first, I thought it was a toy. Some kind of joke. It was strange-looking; stubby and orange and made of plastic. Nothing like the sleek metal revolvers I'd seen on TV. Rolling around the box were some cartridges with "flare" printed on the side.

"The actual *fuck,* Orlaigh," I muttered, gingerly turning the gun over in my hands as if one false move would set it off. "You crazy bitch. Maybe you *were* insane."

Unsurprisingly, I didn't know a huge amount about flare guns other than that they looked like fireworks and were for signaling. Not knowing what else to do, I wedged it into the pocket of my jacket, along with several of the cartridges. Granted, I had no idea how to fire it, but it might come in handy.

Rummaging on the bed, I found the infirmary key card.

Before I began looking for Cintia, there was something else I needed to do.

I'd readied myself for confrontation, my hands shaking with nerves, but when I opened the door to the infirmary, the place was deserted, the desk unmanned. There was no time to dwell on why. All I knew was that it worked in my favor.

I headed directly over to the receptionist's desk and opened the drawers at random.

Bingo. As I'd hoped, a keycard.

On closer inspection, there was no yellow tape stuck over Will's door, no laminated warnings, no instructions to wash hands or information about quarantine, only a black clipboard in a plastic holder, the name *Will Rexham* scrawled untidily at the top in blue pen.

My heart was pounding so hard I was worried I was about to slip into cardiac arrest, so I peered through the window first, some ancient lizard part of my brain warning me not to barge directly into the room.

Someone lay in the bed, flat on their back—almost identical to how we'd found Orlaigh last night in the room opposite—the covers pulled over their head. My heart stuttered.

Could it be Will?

Had he been here all along? Was he dead? Or only sleeping?

The thought of coming face to face with a dead Will was far too much bear. I stared until my eyes watered—then I saw it. The subtle rise and fall of the sheet that told me whoever was under there was still alive.

I didn't care how I looked to everyone else; I'd happily accept being called unhinged, crazy, paranoid, mad. I'd take failing this stupid scholarship, being sent back on the first flight home. I'd take it *all*—I'd take *anything*—for Will to be all right and for all of this insanity to *end*.

Please. Please. *Please.*

With fumbling fingers, I dug out the key from where I'd dropped it in my pocket and unlocked the door, barely daring to hope.

"Will?" I called softly from the open door, almost afraid now. My heart thumped when I saw the sheet twitch slightly, as if the figure beneath it was moving.

"*Will*, thank God, you're still here. I thought—I thought—"

You'd been sacrificed by your own dad. That he'd lumped me into the bargain too.

I smothered a hysterical laugh.

"Are you okay? Are you awake?"

The figure beneath the sheets still didn't move.

"Will? *Hey*, Will. It's Liv."

The first note of alarm tinkled in warning. That unconscious feeling that something was wrong here. Not wanting to drag out my dwindling hope any longer, I took hold of the bottom of the covers and tugged them down.

A long, wavering scream escaped me.

Beneath them lay Thalia.

She flicked open her clever black eyes immediately, her lips curving into a cruel red smile.

Behind me, I heard the muted clunk of the door closing; of a key turning in the lock.

I backed away from her.

"So sorry to disappoint." She smiled, sitting up swiftly, the movement somehow unnatural, like a vampire in its coffin.

"Why—why are you in here?" I managed. "This is Will's room. Where is he? What have you done with him?"

There was no time for pretense now. My hand reflexively patted my pocket that contained the gun.

"Will, Will, *Will*," she mused. "Do you ever talk about

anything else? How long will it take you to realize that Will isn't the kind of friend you *need*? Look at you, Liv. Look at how you've grown without him around, without him holding you back."

"Where is he?" I said, raising my voice. "What did you do to him? Tell me."

She gave me a sunny smile, her golden hair floating around her face, suddenly beautiful again. "It's baffling to me—why do you even *care*? He humiliated you, in front of everyone on the ship, that very first night. Do you think someone who truly cares about you would do that? He tossed away your feelings like they were nothing, treated you like you were an *annoyance*. Is that why you didn't read *all* those messages on his phone, Liv? Were you afraid of what you might see? The truth about who Will really is? A *user*. Someone who led you on and on and then pushed you away when you finally worked up the courage to do something about it."

What *had* Will told her?

I swallowed hard. "Did you kill him?"

It was odd. Voicing the question aloud almost felt like a relief.

The smile disappeared from Thalia's face immediately.

"You know, you've been wonderful. You've proved again and again how brave you can be, how determined. You are loyal to a *fault*."

"Was it you?" My voice rose, insistent. "Did you three do something to him? Please—just tell me—"

I was begging her; I needed to hear it.

She stood—I say *stood*, but it was more like she rose, growing taller than before, towering over me—her effortless beauty now terrible, her eyes glittering like onyx in the dim light.

"You already *know*. Deep down, you've known for days now. There was no escaping his fate; it had been sealed before he set foot on this boat. Even if Will had been everything you wanted him to be, there was no escape for him. He was an unwanted child given up to the sea in exchange for something more . . . rewarding. Perhaps it's better he was such a terrible disappointment."

She paused, the smile reappearing on her strong features.

"You could join us, Olivia. You *are* smart—observant. You have proven your sense of loyalty—however misguided it might be—ten times over."

I gasped as I backed away, a half laugh escaping me. "*Join* you? What the hell are you *talking* about—"

I hit the counter behind me unexpectedly hard, the pain jarring up my spine, shaking me out of Thalia's eyeline.

Was she *hypnotizing* me in some way?

"Thalia—listen to yourself. You sound out of your mind—"

She gave a sharp shake of her head. "No, I don't. You know it all makes sense. Be honest—it's all right to admit it—you're relieved, Olivia. You're *not* mad. No, you're *smart*. You knew it all along. The sea is hungry and needs to be fed. So we feed it. It's a profitable business." She smirked at me. "Just ask Constantine. The whole ethos of Nepenthe is that the *sea will provide* to those who are brave enough, daring enough, to pay its price—a price we make it easy to forget. *Nepenthe,* a spell that banishes grief and strife."

My mind raced. *Could* it be true? It sounded like madness.

"The rewards are generous," Thalia continued. "Money, success, youth and all the confidence they bring. It's a fabulous lifestyle. You'll travel the world. I *saw* you the first day you boarded; cowed and scared, apologetic for just existing. You'll never feel *less* than anyone else again. Look at yourself, you're powerful now—determined. We *want* you, Liv."

I stared at her and glorious images filled my head. Images of another life, a different Liv. A Liv with gleaming skin, perfectly manicured nails, and long, glossy hair. A Liv with a social media page full of foreign climates, arms full of designer shopping bags, lounging by a pool, and surrounded by all the pretty things I could never dream of owning.

Was Thalia right? *Had* Will deserved it? I'd spent so long moping about all the positives I'd lost from our relationship, I'd ignored all the bad. He *had* cut me off almost immediately after that night, and despite my jokes, my self-deprecation, he'd had to have known how hurt I was.

"Of course he knew he hurt you." Lying back on the bed, arms crossed over her chest, Thalia smirked as if she'd read my mind, her eyes bright silver in the gloom. "But he didn't want to deal with it—with you. It was too messy. Too real. You weren't *enough* for him. Not enough for his ego. Not popular enough. Not beautiful enough. Yes, he wanted you—but he didn't want the reality of all of you. He was a *coward.* God, you've no idea how long I've wanted to tell you this."

"Thalia, that's enough," I said harshly. "You need to tell me exactly what you've done with him. This isn't a joke. This is someone's *life* we're talking about—"

"You know what the price is, don't you? To become like us? You were right to be scared—after all, you knew you had been promised. Unlike the rest of them, you figured it out. Clever, clever girl. And luckily for you, another has gone in your stead."

"Wh-what? Who?"

Was she talking about Orlaigh? Thalia merely smiled.

"Tell me!" I snapped. "You're mad, this is all *mad*. Where *is* Will?"

When Thalia next sat up, she had changed.

Her eyes were no longer silver but entirely dark, the whites swallowed by huge onyx orbs that stared madly into mine, reflecting nothing but a deep and empty abyss. A whirlpool of grief.

Charybdis.

Her skin paled to the chalky pallor of corpses, and her lips thinned and rounded into a lamprey-like maw; crowded needle-thin teeth emerged from red, raw gums, their points pricking her lips, thin rivulets of blood trickling down her chin.

The air filled with a fetid stench, the musty, ripe smell of rotten algae and blistered seaweed. I choked on it, backing away from her and toward the door, my grip on reality faltering.

And through the air drifted a mournful melody. Somehow, despite that horror of a mouth, Thalia was *singing*.

Through sheer force of will, I ripped my eyes away from her, the feeling of loss palpable as I did so, my heart seeming to painfully splinter. Desperately, I searched for the nearest object to throw at her. Anything would do. Anything to disrupt that hypnotic melody that was beckoning me, daring me to stay, to embrace my fate.

The sound continued to rise like some dark phoenix; shriller, sharper—now impossibly loud.

A mug shattered on the floor, a ceramic plant pot burst into fragments, a silver medical tray crashed against the wall, but still the song kept up. I dragged my hands over my ears and ran to the door, rattling the handle as hard as I could. Somehow, it was locked—but dimly I recalled I had the key.

I dug a hand into my jacket pocket, desperately searching for the cool feel of the plastic keycard. My mind was full of nothing but Thalia's hateful song, dark and circling like black water down a drain. And I wanted nothing more than to drown—

My fingers closed over the handle of the flare gun.

I could only hope that firing it was as simple as pulling the damn trigger; I couldn't think any further, thanks to that *song*. Forcing myself to confront whatever was behind me, I turned and pulled out the gun.

Thalia was no longer whatever monstrous form I'd just imagined, only a slender girl perched on a bed, her eyes now huge with fright.

"Olivia—stop—what are you *doing*—"

No—Will's bed, and Will was gone.

"I'll ask you once more. Exactly what did you do to Will?"

Thalia seemed to turn again. She was like melting wax before me, flitting in and out of my vision. I rubbed my raw, burning eyes, my head throbbing with a brilliant silver pain.

"I went back to his room with him that night, as you suspected," she said, her voice low and sibilant. "He couldn't believe his luck, that cocky facade of his dropping as soon as we were alone, revealing the unsure little boy beneath."

My finger slipped around to the trigger, seemingly of its own volition.

"Then it was only fair for me to do the same. Your friend almost crapped his pants when I revealed what I *really* was, and his mind went somewhere small and dark and briny. We kept him for a while, to play with. Then, once it was time, we fed him to the sea. That's how it works, Liv; that's how it's always worked. And nobody would ever have noticed—if it weren't for you. You've no idea the trouble you've caused."

Tears streamed hotly down my face.

"And . . . did—did his dad *know*?"

Thalia grinned in delight. "*Yes*. Of course he did! Now it's finally sinking in. Right now, Mr. Rexham is a very happy man, I'd imagine. He's rich beyond his wildest dreams and feels about twenty years younger. And he will be richer still, once we deal with *you*."

Oh, *Will*.

I raised the gun, squeezed the trigger with my finger. It wasn't even on purpose, more of an instinctual spasm. Dimly, I heard myself already apologizing through the earsplitting bang.

But Thalia went up in flames.

32

I DON'T REMEMBER UNLOCKING THE DOOR, LEAVING THE conflagration behind me, and walking calmly back to my room, the flare gun shoved deep into my jacket pocket.

All I know was that I was sitting on my bed, still and quiet, my mind running over and over the events of the last hour, when Constantine found me.

"Shit, Liv, what's *happened*? Are you okay? You look terrible."

"I—I didn't mean—I didn't mean to—"

He knelt before me, tipping up my face, looking at me with concern. "What? Didn't mean to *what*?"

I swallowed hard, tears streaming down my face. Right at this moment, some things were better left unsaid. Besides, I didn't think I could voice it even if I tried.

"Did you find Cintia?"

He gave a shake of his head. "We can't find her anywhere. Justin's alerted the Coast Guard, but—"

"So she's gone, then," I said dully, wiping an arm across my face. "There's meant to be seven, after all. Will, Raj, Cintia—I thought Justin might be in trouble as well, but now I'm sure he's in on this. So, Con, who's up next?"

I gave a shaky laugh. Con said nothing but took an uncertain step back toward the door.

"Constantine, did you honestly not *know* about any of this? I mean, it's your dad's bloody company they work for. Is he behind it all? Are you part of this? Did you take Octavia and her sister to that temple deliberately? Did you *know* what would happen to her, what her parents would receive in return?"

Constantine stared at me. Never had his gray eyes reminded me more of the sea. Dark and cold and unforgiving.

"What the—? Look, I'm now willing to agree that some deeply weird shit has gone down on this ship in the past twenty-four hours, but seriously—you think *I* have something to do with all this?"

I got up, facing him. This had gone far enough.

"Well, let's look at the facts. Your dad owns this messed-up ship. Your girlfriend disappears when she's with you, then reappears here. Explain that."

Constantine shook his head. "Okay, fine, no problem—she *isn't* here and you're mistaken."

"I've *seen* her and you've *heard* her; that's good enough for me. Are you two working together? You and Octavia. Have you been drugging me or something? Is that why I've been seeing some properly weird shit? Is that why they thought Will was feverish? Is that why you have a small pharmacy stashed in your nightstand? Either that, or you're deeper in denial than anyone I've ever met."

The wary light in his eyes was all the confirmation I needed, but still he stood, forcing a harsh laugh.

"Look, you can babble on about conspiracies and plots all you want, but I'm going to continue to focus on the facts and look for Cintia," he said, frowning. "All being well, we'll get to celebrate our last day of this god-awful orientation at the Atlantis Party later, before we dock and finally get off this ship. Until then, I think you better lie down, Liv. Seriously."

I couldn't help it. I burst into laughter, wild and shrill. The idea of us all chummily gathered around a table for dinner later in our best outfits, as if everything was completely normal, seemed hilarious. As if half our group hadn't been sacrificed off the edge of the ship by some bizarre Greek death cult, apparently sponsored by their own parents.

I ran a hand over my face. I needed to focus.

"Hey—wait—give me your passkey to the elevator. I've got an idea where she might be."

He patted his pockets, then dutifully retrieved the key card, but hesitated before handing it to me.

"You're going alone?"

I rolled my eyes. "Well, of course, Con. This ship's perfectly safe—you told me yourself. And I can trust *you*—can't I?"

Constantine gave me an icy look, then left, slamming the cabin door behind him.

Truth was, I was glad to see the back of him. There was no way he wasn't involved in this somehow. The very fact that he was even on this stupid trip when the shadowy figure of his dad seemed to be behind everything proved it.

Nepenthe.

That which chases away sorrow. A potion given to Helen of Troy to help her forget. And forget what exactly? Her children?

The familiar logo of the *Eos,* of Nepenthe, the sun sinking into a fathomless black sea, was everywhere I looked. It was like tumbling down a dark, dank rabbit hole, ancient roots crumbling cruelly in my hands as I tried to grab onto something solid, something to stop me from falling—

Will, Raj, and now Cintia.

But what about Apollo—and Laila? And could I be safe now, after what happened to Orlaigh? Then there was Adora. . . . And Con? Surely nothing would happen to him. So if he wasn't with us—then was he against us?

I rubbed my hands roughly over my face. My head felt thick and woolly. It was so difficult to think straight when nothing at all made sense.

I stood, the cabin wobbling unsteadily around me as I did so, my feet sinking too deep into the marshmallow-like carpet beneath me.

The important thing was, I needed to try to find Cintia. I couldn't just forget about her; from the moment I met her, she'd been a good friend. Will might be gone, but there was a chance she was alive.

I thought of the last message Will had sent me. The darkness and the strange riveted, metallic look of the flooring.

The hull.

I inserted the passkey and hit the very last button on the panel. Moments later, the elevator began to haul its way downward, my stomach free-falling with it.

As it reached the service levels, a few of the maids cast me uneasy looks as they got on and off. I stared directly back at them in defiance, daring them to challenge me. I was ready. This wasn't about me anymore; this was about stopping all this madness.

I wasn't sure what I was expecting once I reached the hull—some kind of vast, dark expanse—but instead the elevator opened into a brightly lit corridor, the overhead strip lights illuminating every corner of the space.

The noise of the engines was deafening here, so much so that you wouldn't be able to hear yourself below a shout. The glamour and polish of the upper decks was entirely absent. Here everything was about machinery and efficiency. Metal safety rails, humming dials, and steel plates covered every available surface.

Realizing how incredibly incongruous I looked in my skirt and sneakers, I shuffled into the nearest alcove and scanned the passage. It was so ear-splittingly loud here; I'd never know someone was behind me until they were literally on top of me.

I had no way of knowing where Cintia was being kept, so I took off down a passageway at random. It ended at a heavy iron door, the handle rigid metal. I yanked it down, the squeal of rust hidden by the furious churning and thumping sounds behind me, and stepped into cool, quiet darkness.

A long, empty corridor stretched before me, lit only by the safety lights set into the floor at regular intervals. The metal flooring clanged beneath my sneakers, and I looked down to see the same riveted iron panels that had been in the photo Will had sent me.

So, he had been down here. Was this where he—

Movement at the far end of the passage caught my eye; a figure quickly slipped out of view around the corner.

"C-Cintia?" I called hesitantly.

I hurried on. Around the corner was another door, heavy and half-rusted with a small glass window. There was no handle, only a large wheel at its middle. Beyond the glass, shadows seeped; a deep blue-gray, dancing and rippling on the walls of the room beyond like waves. Standing on tiptoes, I peered through the window.

Anything recognizable about the person was completely obscured, hidden by a shimmering iridescent bodysuit of the type I'd found in the captain's room. Behind them, a series of small rectangular metal doors had been set evenly into the back wall of the space—reminding me a little of the morgue lockers from the crime shows that Mum loved—bodies neatly stored away in drawers.

The figure had disappeared just out of sight of the window, but I could see their shadow against the wall, thrown large by the low lighting. They appeared to be removing the suit now. I needed to calm the hell down. They were probably a diver of some kind, changing after their shift—

—in the *hull*? And what was with those suits? Were they some kind of wet suit? Or *reverse* wet suit, they seemed so slick and shiny on the outside—

My breath cut off. In the shadows, the person was removing what must have been the hood of the wet suit, but beneath—beneath—

The shadows were alive with what looked like writhing tentacles, emerging Medusa-like from where the head should be—

I swallowed, swaying on my feet, all of a sudden much too hot but somehow shivering—

When I'd been looking for Will's suitcase the other day—those maids—those shadows I'd seen—

"A trick of the light," I whispered, my voice hoarse and unsteady. "Just a trick of the light."

There was a scraping sound as they opened one of the drawers, apparently climbing into it, from what I could make out, then silence.

I waited as long as I could bear; then, my hands shaking so much I could hardly even grip it at first, I slowly turned the wheel.

With a sharp grinding sound, the door inched open. I

slipped silently into the room, hurrying past the drawers—not wanting to look at them for any longer than I had to—and paused on the threshold of the room beyond. It, too, was barely lit, but even in the darkness, I could tell it was cavernous. I might not have been able to see it, but I certainly felt it. It was like standing in the belly of a whale. I stood in the doorway, the thrumming of the engines now hushed behind me, and waited for my eyes to adjust to the darkness beyond.

This, then—*this* was the space of my nightmares.

"Hey—hey, Cintia?"

My voice ricocheted violently against the high steel walls, darkness stretching away from me in all directions. The great vaulted ceiling disappeared high overhead, melding with the darkness, its walls lit in a soft, aqueous blue; a giant aquatic cathedral. I must have been deep within the bowels of the ship. The space was entirely windowless and had an odd feeling of pressure about it. My eardrums felt full, my head dull and heavy. The only light came from small green emergency lights, along the floor—a different kind of light altogether glowed softly from the walls.

As my eyes grew accustomed to the light, I saw that the walls were several hundred meters away on both sides and were not, in fact, walls at all, but enormous glass tanks, similar to the ones in the atrium each at least twenty feet high. My breath hitched as I caught glimpses of what floated within. Immense black shapes—some the size of whales—but with rippling tentacles and snapping beaks. Circling and diving in soft arabesques, their movements horribly hypnotic. What *were* they?

With a shudder, I looked away, remembering the figure clambering into that strange metal drawer—were the staff here—

No. Focus, Liv.

But there was nothing else in the space—not that I could see. Only the yawning black emptiness and those gargantuan tanks.

That picture Will had sent me; blurred and incoherent in his desperation. He must have been here—but *why*—

As I edged back toward the door, not wanting to stay a second longer, from somewhere far ahead came a soft sound. Someone was whispering, again and again. Something that sounded like a plea or a prayer. I followed the line of emergency lights—like cats' eyes or the lights lining an airfield— If it was Cintia, I couldn't just leave her here alone with—with those *things*. I considered using the flashlight of my phone, but that would instantly reveal me to anyone hostile lying in wait as well—not to mention the fact that it would illuminate the space around me, something I wasn't sure I wanted to see. The whole place had an eerie sense of reverence about it. Like a church or other holy place gone bad. Desecrated.

I continued creeping forward, the lights revealing nothing more to me than the floor, but the whispering increased.

The voice *was* Cintia's. I was sure of it.

What was she playing at?

"*The sea provides, the sea provides, the sea provides, the sea provides*—"

She was whispering those words over and over until they sounded meaningless. A bunch of unconnected sounds.

"C-Cintia? Are—are you okay?"

My foot collided with something soft in front of me. I stopped, kneeling to take a closer look. There was a bundle lying on the floor, directly before one of the lights. Something large wrapped in a black sheet. Gingerly, I prodded it with my toe. It gave way a little. A sickening feeling lurched through me. I bent down, the floor now seeming to shift and sway alarmingly beneath my feet, as if I were losing my grip on the world. With shaking hands, I pulled the cloth away. I gasped at what was revealed in the soft glow of a nearby emergency light, tripping back and landing on the steel floor, pain juddering up my spine.

Adora's beautiful face stared sightlessly out at me. Her once-sharp gaze now blank and clouded over. With a trembling hand, I reached out and brushed her cheek, her skin oddly hard and waxy to the touch. I couldn't help it. The cry was wrenched out of me, gasping and strangled. I had entered a nightmare. My body wouldn't listen to me, my hands wouldn't do as I asked, I could barely even breathe—

"A-Adora?"

And up ahead, in the darkness, the whispering had stopped.

Somehow, I managed to stand again.

The hull was eerily silent. I stared ahead, hallucinating, my brain unhelpfully imagining things that shouldn't be there in the darkness up ahead. All of the dead: Will, Laila, Raj,

Orlaigh, Apollo, standing there, in a deadly crescent, dressed in the black robes of the Greek chorus, their blank faces staring blindly, holes for eyes, mouths downturned in tragedy.

And now Adora. Beautiful, prickly Adora.

A light snapped on. A strong beam of white light—a flashlight—breaking up the darkness, illuminating Cintia ahead of me, small in the vastness of the space around us.

I let out a rush of breath.

"Cintia—it *is* you. Thank *God*. Who brought you down here? Was it the Sirens? We need to go—and now. Adora's—Adora's—"

I stopped, breathless again, unable to go on. I shuffled back from the body beneath my feet, wishing I hadn't found it. Could there be an innocent explanation? Perhaps she'd fallen or—

Cintia interrupted.

"All along, I've been trying to tell you, Liv. The sea *provides*."

In her white caftan, her black curls cascading down her back, and illuminated by the bright, white light of her phone, Cintia looked stunningly beautiful—unearthly, even.

A siren indeed.

"Cintia, come on now, what does that even *mean*?"

"None of this is by accident," she said, her soft drawl weaving around the words. "A bargain has been struck. We would never take that which wasn't ours to take."

A horrible clarity began to rise within me.

I thought of Will's dad. The car door slamming with indecent violence. The way he had roared out of the parking lot as if even dropping Will off was a huge inconvenience.

Dad can't wait for me to be out of the way. Think he's worried Kayleigh's got more of an eye on me—can't say I blame her, though.

I thought of what Raj had said, that first day aboard the ship.

My folks are predictably mad that I'm not planning a career in medicine. . . .

I thought of what Con had said—about Adora's parents never being around. Even Laila's parents, steadfastly ignoring her in the buffet queue. Leaving her to drift aimlessly around the ship like an unloved ghost. A sob came to my throat.

I had tried to push Thalia's words from my mind, but now they came rushing back. Could it be true? Could someone be that disappointed, that desperate for money or youth—whatever it is that they offered—that they'd—

Iphigenia. Sacrificed by her own father.

Orlaigh had tried to warn me, and look where that had gotten her. I shuddered, the severity of the shit I was in suddenly hitting me full in the face.

"I see it coming together for you," said Cintia with a grin. She had advanced on me quickly without me realizing. I staggered back, shocked. "And if you're not with us—well, we can't have that, can we? I know Thalia offered you the same choice as me. You were pretty stupid not to take her up on it, especially since the hard work of finding a replacement had already been done for you, what with that meddling bitch Orlaigh. The rest of the Sirens will be looking for you. We can't let you leave, I'm afraid. Not now. Not after what you did."

"Who?" I murmured. "Who'd you . . . not *Raj*?"

"No," she laughed. "His parents saw to that. It was that talentless hack of a magician. Thalia suspected he knew too much anyway. He was a last-minute addition to the staff, along with that airhead steward. In other words, a *liability*. No one's going to miss them."

If the others were on their way, all of them would easily overpower me and then I'd join Adora, wrapped up in a dirty cloth, ready to be bundled over the side of the ship like nothing but trash. I was no fighter. And who *were* the others? *Everyone* on this damn ship? Besides, nothing in this world could persuade me to run deeper into the hull, where it was pitch-black and God only knew what lurked back there—

"Cintia, what's *down* here?" I gestured to the strange tanks; the circling creatures unmoving now, as if watching us. Their tentacles undulating, drifting like smoke in the water. Their eyes black and all too knowing.

Cintia shrugged. "Some people always take it too far. Wanting too much, too quickly, can *change* you. Literally. There's always consequences for being greedy. So they serve us now."

I cast a reluctant glance at the tanks again. There was no sane reason for this strange underground aquarium to be here. And I was no marine biologist, but I'd never seen anything like these things before. Similar to squids, but far larger than those in the tanks above; their eyes too watchful and too intelligent, their beaks cruel. Now, no longer circling, their tentacles stroking the front of the tanks, as if listening somehow. Each sucker barbed and serrated. Onyx beaks snapping; curved and cruel.

Those strange rubber suits—had those people been these

monsters underneath? No—no, none of this could be real. Impossible—it was literally impossible—

I backed away.

"Cintia, Thalia said—she told me that Will was . . . that he's . . ."

I couldn't even say the words. Couldn't make it real.

"You already know he's dead," she said, a smirk on her face. "The bargain was kept. We fed him to the sea."

Fury, hot and spiteful, reared up in me, my body reacting beyond my control as I gave Cintia a violent, impulsive push. Startled, she stepped backward, tripping over the dark mound of Adora's body, stumbling to the ground.

"You total *bitch*!" I hissed at her, a wild fury possessing me. I aimed a wild kick at her ribs, knocking her phone out of her hand and sending it skittering away, shutting off its flashlight and leaving us both momentarily blind. "Will didn't deserve this. None of them did—Laila was a *kid*! You're insane—absolutely insane, the lot of you."

Cintia hit back. I screamed wildly, then gasped, the world blinking away in pain as her fist immediately connected with my stomach. Winded, I fell to the ground, narrowly avoiding landing on Cintia, fighting for air, my eyes not yet readjusted to the thick, unnatural gloom.

From somewhere far ahead, deep within the hull, came the sound of doors creaking slowly open; heavy and long rusted. Waves rippled on the walls, water now cascading from them in dark torrents, briny and fetid. The sound of wet, slimy flesh slapping against the floor; the sight of monstrous writhing shadows.

Something wet and cold curled around my ankle, snake-like and muscular. Sinking close to my skin and causing a sharp burning pain. With a wild scream, I clambered up and I stomped on it in a frenzy, loosening it enough to kick it away and run; suddenly grateful for the lack of light.

And somewhere close by, in the darkness—too close—I heard the beating of huge wings.

Cintia's voice was different now—breathless and sly.

"Are you ready to meet your destiny, Liv? There's no way to escape it."

Part of my brain was screaming at me not to look, that if I looked, I'd never leave, I'd never recover, so I turned and lurched back the way I'd come, away from the darkness.

33

THE LIFEBOATS.

They were my only chance. I was terrified of the sea, but if I stayed on this bloody ship, I was going to find myself either fed to those things in the tanks or flying through the air down to whatever they believed was lurking in the depths. And honestly, the latter scared me more. Those dreams of drowning had never left me.

I'd sprinted out of the hull, my footsteps clanging noisily, and up the stairs—there was no way I was risking the elevator—constantly expecting to be chased down by something monstrous, or at the very least, Cintia—but somehow I'd managed to make it back to the relative sanctuary of my cabin.

Why had she let me go?

But the answer was obvious. I was on a ship—I was trapped here, and they were toying with me.

Since I'd gotten back here, I'd sat on my bed for the best part of an hour, staring at my phone in horror, frantically googling how to activate the lifeboats--the only choice, the only hope I had left.

We were only a few hours away from docking, but before that I'd need to survive the ship's Atlantis party. A knock at my cabin door invaded my thoughts. I took a sharp breath, staring at the closed door in wild panic. There was nowhere to hide in here. If most of the staff were in on it, they'd easily gain access to my room and—

"Hey . . . Liv?"

Constantine.

My brief feeling of relief was immediately stymied.

Yes, Constantine, whose father owned this ship. A whole fleet of them. All under the name Nepenthe. A drug to forget grief. A family who'd struck some unholy bargain with these monsters. The sea provides but only if you feed it, after all.

God . . . I was such an *idiot*.

I ran my hand over the flare gun in my pocket, my finger gently brushing the trigger.

"Liv? I . . ." He trailed off. "Look, I know you're in there, and I'm not going anywhere until you come out. You promised you'd come to this stupid party—I mean, what even *is* an Atlantis Party?—and if you don't, then . . . then I'm going to sit in the corridor outside your room until you do."

Was that a *threat*?

Either he was wallowing so deep in denial that he was a liability, or he was part of this whole thing.

I stared at the door. I couldn't just hide in here while he sat outside like a jailer.

Maybe acting normal was the best course of action. Kinda like the orchestra playing as the *Titanic* sank. At least that way I could find a way to slip away from him and—

"Er, yes—yep," I said, rubbing my eyes. "I'm—I'm here. Just, uh . . . just give me five minutes."

I got up, splashed my face, and slapped on some concealer and blush to disguise my current death-like pallor, making the best of a bad job with a slash of pink lipstick. From the sliver of wardrobe, I yanked out my navy dress—a cute cap-sleeved lace number I'd spent ages picking out with my mum for this exact event. But right now I could be wearing rags, for all I cared.

Finally, I loaded the flare gun once more and slipped it along with the last remaining cartridge into the pocket of my dress.

I opened the door.

Constantine looked at me, first with appraisal, which dissolved very quickly once he'd taken a closer look at my face. He was predictably elegant in an expensive-looking suit of midnight blue, too well-fitting not to have been tailored. I swallowed down my brief disappointment at how this had turned out. In another world, another life, was a different Liv, a Liv who'd have made much more effort with her makeup, who would have spent ages fussing with her hair and who would have been walking on air at the thought of Constantine waiting out in the corridor for her. A Liv whose evening would have ended very differently.

If I thought about it for too long, I'd go even more mad than I currently felt. Con lowered his voice.

"How are you doing, Liv? You look . . . a bit off. Y'know, Cintia's turned up now. She's, uh, fine."

Yes, but Adora wasn't and Adora never would be. Leaving her parents free to trot around the globe, forever polishing their chakras.

I tossed back my hair and gave him a wide smile that probably looked unhinged. Was he one of the lunatics trying to kill me, or was I now the lunatic? When I entered the lounge, would the Sirens lunge at my head with a knife while everyone laughed, similar to Orlaigh's fate, following it with a smattering of applause?

I gave a sharp yelp of a laugh.

"Yep, doing a-mazing. I mean, how could I *not* be? Let's get this over with, shall we?"

I was an utter mess.

My legs shook, my hands shook. I felt dizzy, weightless. As if I needn't worry about anyone throwing me overboard, I was halfway there myself, floating untethered, drifting away into the inky night sky.

I clung to Constantine as he led me wordlessly down endless corridors until we reached the elevator to the upper decks. He paused before hitting the button.

"Liv. Don't take this the wrong way, but you *don't* look well. Are you sick? Did you eat something . . . bad? It's—it's not to do with earlier . . . ?"

He trailed off and looked so genuinely apologetic, I almost felt sorry for him. And I remembered what he'd said about *his* parents.

Maybe I *should* feel sorry for him. Maybe he'd been promised, too, just like the rest of us.

"No, nope. It's not you. We're great—earlier was great." I mean, in many ways that wasn't a lie. "I think—I think maybe it's something I ate. Bad buffet . . . I guess you warned me! I feel a bit faint . . . woozy, even. I . . . I'll see how it goes. It is the last night, after all."

He punched the button that called the elevator, then pulled me into him as we waited, kissing the top of my head with an affection that almost seemed real.

The elevator slowly arrived. Doors opening and spilling out the usual bland jazz. Inside, once we were alone, Constantine reached for me again, pulling me close.

The chanting was audible as soon as we stepped out of the elevator, drifting down the corridor like an unpleasant mist, a low, rhythmic rumble. I stopped. My legs unwilling to go any farther. Sensing this, Constantine turned to me.

"Hey, look. You're clearly upset—you don't need to come with me. Let's get you back to your room."

I stared at him as if he were stupid. This, I knew, was where I should leave him—turn and run for the lifeboats and let him face whatever waited here. But at the sound of the chanting, a grim resignation had washed over me, leaving me cold. Empty.

Did I really think they'd let me leave?

"It's impossible, Constantine," I said. "They're waiting. They're waiting for me—or for both of *us*. Can't you hear them?"

He gave me a quizzical stare. "What, do you mean the music? Yes, of course. It *is* a party, after all."

"It's not music, it's fucking *chanting*. I've been trying to tell you—this ship . . . the people on it . . . They're all part of a— a *cult*. They give people what they want, in return for a sacrifice. And Thalia, Lexie, Leda—they *are* sirens. But realer than you know. They're in on it, and if you're not—if you're not lying—if you're not part of it, then—" I sucked in a deep breath. "Then I think you're in as much trouble as I am."

Constantine rubbed both hands over his face, then took my hand, pulling me into him. He was pale and drawn, a bright spark of alarm present in his eyes. It was as if a curtain had dropped from his expression—finally, *finally,* I saw fear. Understanding.

"Listen, Liv," he started, "if any part of what you're saying is true, then I need to see it for myself. It's—it's my dad's ship. I have to know what's going on. I have to know exactly what he's involved in. Yes, my dad can be distant, brusque even— but this—the things you're suggesting—it's a whole other level. Like I said, if you want to go back . . ."

Yes—yes, of *course* I wanted to go back. Wanted to sit on my bed, stick the TV on, and call Will like old times, discussing all the amazing things we were going to do for the remainder of this trip. But that was impossible. Because Will was gone. And besides, what was hiding in my room going to achieve? If my worst suspicions were correct, they'd come for me next, and I'd be cornered there like a rat in a trap.

And on top of that, I couldn't let Con face this alone.

I sighed, dropping my head against his chest.

"No—I'm with you—but as soon as you know—as soon as you've seen—we're going to need to get out of here. And fast."

Constantine gave me a wary look but, with a firm nod, led me onward.

As we neared the doors, the chanting stopped. It was immediate. As if someone had clicked a radio off. I gave him a sideways look to see if he'd react, but he hadn't seemed to notice. It crossed my mind again that I might truly be going insane. Could anxiety do that to a person? Snap them in half? Wear them out until they splintered into sharp pieces?

I hesitated, ready to tell him to wait.

But Con had dropped my hand and was already pushing open the doors.

34

AT FIRST GLANCE, THE SIGHT THAT MET US IN THE LOUNGE was wonderfully welcoming. A part of me almost relaxed. It was a vision of hedonistic old-fashioned glamour. The walls had been draped with swathes of dark blue silk, cushioning the conversation and the clink of glasses. Trestle tables were laid out in a vast arc, groaning with silver platters piled high with seafood—much of it alarmingly raw. Candelabras provided a soft, intimate glow and, in the corner, a string quartet played a familiar, haunting song—one of Thalia's, no doubt.

But instead of the required blue evening wear, most of the guests were wearing odd outfits, similar to the one I had seen in the captain's room that very first day. Dark blue and purple robes or cloaks of what looked like an odd thin rubbery material, the colors of an oil spill, iridescent purple and blue, shiny and slick.

With a throb of burning panic, I noticed Thalia was absent from the center table that faced us, but the remaining Sirens were all present. Dressed in blinding-white shifts, their eyes heavily kohled, golden circlets around their necks.

Beside me, Con's hand had grown moist and limp in mine. It wasn't difficult to see why.

"Constantine," said Octavia, smiling and sitting comfortably amidst the remaining Sirens, silky dark hair spilling over her shoulders. "It's been a while. I've missed you."

I gripped his hand tighter.

"Oct-Octavia . . ." He gave a half laugh, half gasp of disbelief. "I didn't believe it—but—but *how?*"

Octavia gave a delighted laugh, clapping her hands together. "So sorry to disappoint. You must be feeling a little shocked? I mean, it's not every day someone you left for dead in a cave—along with their darling little sister—returns to surprise you."

I dropped his hand. He turned to me, then back to her, gray eyes wide with shock.

"*What?* You know that's not true—it's *not*—you—you disappeared. I fell asleep and when I woke up, you'd *gone*. I searched for you—I— Look, Tavi, we all need to get out of here—"

"Wait, *wait*, Con—darling. What's the hurry? You've only just gotten here. You can't leave without us having a little chat. I've always wondered how much you knew. Did you know exactly what happened back there—in that temple? On the island, in Greece? What was in there? Do you *know* what I had to do to get here?" said Octavia, her voice even and pleasant, as if she were chatting to an old friend. "Can you *guess*? Because once the bargain has been made, they have to take *somebody*. I wasn't about to let my own father send me away on some death cruise. Did you *know* she was only fourteen? Daddy always preferred her—it's hilarious how much his ridiculous plan backfired. Honestly, it's my only consolation—"

"What—what are you *talking* about?" Con stammered. "And where have you been all this time—"

Octavia's eyes hardened and her lips thinned.

"Stop pretending, Con—it's so tedious," she snapped, her voice no longer honey but cold as her eyes. "That map was in your dad's study; you must have known *something*. Daddy was going to offer me up on one of these stupid trips, and I couldn't let that happen. So, instead I made my own deal before Daddy could send me away." She shrugged. "Of course, I was always planning on asking them to take you. Then silly little Flick had to invite herself along. . . ."

Octavia stopped, frowning for a moment, as if recalling something unpleasant. "And when the time came, *you'd* already run away like the scared little boy you always were."

She turned her attention to me, looking me up and down and lowering her voice.

"He moves on *so* easily. It's about time someone taught him a lesson. You'll be thanking me in a few months' time—just ask Leda." Her voice was assured and confident as she strode into the center of the room.

"I am grateful the Sirens accepted my bargain. Because now, Con, I can do what I always meant to. How I've waited for this, for the tables to finally turn. The spoiled middle child of the head of Nepenthe himself. The worthless middle heir; beautiful and golden; heartless and clever. And ultimately *unwanted.* The sea, Constantine, it *starves* for you."

Con cleared his throat. I could feel him shaking. Either he was the best actor in the world or he really was as clueless about all this as I'd been.

"Look, Tavi, what in all manner of *fuck* is going on here . . . ? Someone needs to explain. Is this some kind of joke? I mean—Leda?"

He gave me a wild-eyed look.

"*Liv?* Is this real?"

"She's been trying to tell you since she got here," laughed Leda from the table. "But of course, you never listen—we were banking on that, and you did not disappoint. You were all offered up as sacrifice, just as Daddy would have offered me up if I hadn't made my own bargain first. Seven perfect sacrifices in exchange for youth . . . power—whatever they wanted." She turned, fixing her solemn dark eyes on me. "And it would have been perfect had you not come along and messed things up."

I reached into the pocket of my dress for the flare gun. Fitted my finger snugly against the firm plastic trigger. Christ, this wasn't some bad Agatha Christie television movie. We didn't have to *stand* here, listening to their mad speeches. These people were utterly insane—involved in something I couldn't even think about without going insane myself—clearly willing to kill, and we needed to get to the lifeboats.

I grabbed at Con's wrist.

"Hey—*hey!* Come on, we don't need to listen to this, we need to go—"

But Con wasn't listening. He was staring fixedly at the back of the hall, his face an unsettling shade of gray and visibly shaken.

"Con!"

I followed his gaze.

Somebody was pushing themselves through the crowd of revelers. As I looked, I caught someone's eye in the midst of the crowd—Hilary's—and did a double take. Now she was nearly unrecognizable, no longer in her seventies but at least two decades younger, her once-lined skin plumper and smooth, her hair a sleek ash-blond instead of white—

"D-Dad?"

I swallowed back a mouthful of bile as a tall figure stood before us. Darkness seemed to trail behind him, its shadowed tentacles making the candles flicker. He already looked *far* younger than in the gilt-framed photo where I'd first seen him, and now I'd place him at only ten years older than his son. Unlike Con, his hair was black, slicked back, the curls glossy and vital. But his eyes, the glittering gray of sea shale, were the same as his son's.

"Dad—thank *God.* What's—what's happening? What's going on here—"

I squeezed Con's hand tightly. If for some reason he thought his dad was going to be our savior, I had the distinct feeling he was about to be proved dead wrong.

"Son. I am disappointed we had to meet under these circumstances. Disappointed you put your trust in this girl who has caused us nothing but trouble; especially after how long it took to fix the last mess you made."

His voice was rich and commanding. Around us, the hall had silenced.

"What—what do you mean—? *Dad?*"

He was dressed similarly to Captain Elytis, right down to the hat—but instead of the usual impeccable captain's whites, he wore black. Black suit, black silken shirt, black cravat. Around him swung a vast robe of the same rubbery material most of the guests were wearing.

"Your little escapade back in Greece has cast a long shadow over Nepenthe. One that I am keen to vanquish. And now I have been called here, away from other pressing business, to the *Eos* and find that yet again you are involved in . . . in all *this*? I cannot keep cleaning up after your scandals, my son. I cannot keep having you spoil everything I have worked so hard for, child, everything I have built from nothing."

He shook his head, his expression darkening. Around him, the crowd smiled toothily, seeming to hold their breath in dreadful anticipation.

"The fact is, you—the most worthless of my children—you are *priceless* to Nepenthe, Constantine." His father smiled, cold and hard. "And now, it is time for you to pay for your mistakes."

Con sagged beside me, his hand clammy and limp in mine. And when he spoke, it wasn't the laconic, bored tone I was used to; it was the voice of a lost little boy.

"Dad—what's going on—? What do you mean? The stuff in Greece—you know it wasn't my fault and—and—what *is* happening here?"

He already knew. I was sure of it. I tugged on his wrist again.

"God's sake, Con. We *need* to go—now."

"No, no, no. We can't let you leave," said Lexie, her singsong tone almost blasé. "Especially not when that *bitch* has killed one of our own."

Con whirled around to look at me, his expression almost comically shocked. Before he could say anything, two figures loomed behind us, clad in those weird rubber robes, the hoods—ending in long rubber tentacles—pulled fully over their faces. Panic kicked in. An image of cold gray waters churning beneath me. Miles from any hope of land.

Con's dad strode determinedly toward us.

But I wouldn't be tossed off the side of the ship. Or forced down into the hull with those things. I *wouldn't*.

I aimed the gun directly at Octavia, my hand shaking so much that there was no way I would hit her, even if I wanted to. She whirled to face me, the movement oddly jerky.

Her face immediately changed then, like running wax, solidifying into something from my nightmares. Huge black eyes and that terrible needle-filled maw with row upon row of teeth.

Screaming, my hand shaking in huge clumsy spasms, I raised the gun in both hands and shot behind her head.

There was a deafening bang, and all sound whined away for a few moments.

I stared, fascinated, as the silks that draped the room caught fire like a rocket, flames racing around the room.

"Dad—!"

The captain—the *real* captain all along—surged forward.

"Fuck's sake, Con," I yelled, my voice breaking, grabbing at his arm. "Get it together! Your dad wants us *dead*—we have to *go!*"

The desperation in my voice seemed to kickstart something inside him, and my arm was wrenched almost out of its socket as Constantine yanked me toward the exit. I allowed myself to follow, lurching forward, almost tripping face-first as the world around me began to return and the screaming started.

"Do you know how to reload it? Do you have any more cartridges?" he asked as we skidded out through the doors and began barreling down the corridor.

"I think so . . . and yes! There's one left." I shouted. He spun around immediately and slammed shut the double doors to the lounge, wedging a chair beneath the handles.

"Will it hold them in?" I asked, my breathing shaky and fast.

"I think so—but wait—what if some of them are inno-cent . . . ? I mean, some could just be regular passengers. That's *murder.* Liv—we need to—we need to just *go*—"

I whirled around; it was time. "You're right, you're right. Come on."

He looked at me, confused for a moment. "Great—but where?"

"The *lifeboats,* Con, for God's sake! Where else?"

He gave a breathless laugh. Behind us, the door handles

began to rattle. I stared at them for a moment, then took off after him down the corridor.

"We'll need to take the stairs," he said as he ran. "Don't we need to radio an SOS or something first? How will anyone know to find us?"

I stared at him, shaking my head. "I don't fucking *know,* Con. This isn't the last boss in a bloody game. I have absolutely no idea what to do." All of a sudden, every shred of confidence I'd had in my plan collapsed, lost in a sweep of anxiety. *Were* the lifeboats the best idea? What if they expected that—what if they were waiting there . . .

I slowed. "Should we wait it out? There's probably sprinklers in there to put out the fire or something. . . . We could hold out maybe until we dock. We could hide—"

He grabbed me by the wrist and yanked me down the corridor at his long-legged pace, his strength surprising; his voice low and cracked.

"After all that, do you actually think we're going to dock tonight? Did you see what—what *I* saw back there? In the lounge. Did you see . . . what some of them *were? Did* you? I . . . I . . . Do you seriously think this ship is going to continue on course and we'll be allowed to skip off to shore? We can't stay here. We *can't.* We won't make it another hour."

His words filled me with abject horror. Hadn't I, all along, been able to rationalize everything because it had been only me and me alone who had seen these things? Only I had seen those monsters half-hidden in the shadows. Those creatures in my dreams or half dreams. And everyone telling me I was tired or anxious or mistaken. But now Constantine had seen them too.

I slowed, looking behind me at the deserted corridor.

Yes, cults were real, psychopaths who pushed people off ships were real, but the other things . . . huge, dark, deep underwater things, beautiful girls who were truly *monsters* with hideous wings—

They *couldn't* be—could they?

"Con—your dad—*did* you know?"

Around me, the world faded quickly, receding into blurred light and sound as I lost my footing. The carpet too soft, my feet sinking into it.

"Do I fucking *look* as if I knew? But what I do know is, if we don't leave," hissed Con in my ear, "if we don't leave *now*, we're both dead."

That last word shocked me into action.

Minutes later, we stood shivering at the muster station on Deck 5. It was silent here, no other passengers to be seen as the wind whipped mercilessly around us. I desperately wished I'd paid more attention at the drill on the first day, but I'd been bored, flicking aimlessly through my phone as the staff droned on. Cruise ships never sank these days and if they did, I'd cheerily assumed we'd all die. It was like the safety talk they gave you on airplanes—as if an airplane had ever in the entirety of the world's history landed smoothly on top of the ocean. Just a procedure designed to tick a health and safety box.

"What do we *do*?" I shouted to Con above the relentless

battering of the wind. He looked terrified, shivering in his overly smart clothes. Striding over to a locker on the wall, he returned with two life jackets. I stared at them, the reality of our situation now plain, leaving me sick to my stomach, adrenaline pumping through me, now making my thoughts overly clear.

"We're—we're not just going to jump, are we?"

The silence was giving the ship the air of dangerous normality. Getting into the ocean, even in the enormous lifeboat, seemed utterly ridiculous. I stared down at the gray churning waters, waves breaking with foaming white caps, and gagged in fear.

"Of course not. Put it on—quickly," he shouted, staring down at the lifeboat.

I pulled it over my head and attached the straps.

"Wait—*wait*," I called out. "We can't leave the ship—it's suicide. We don't know what we're *doing*. We need to tell the staff—get someone to help us—there must be someone. I mean, Orlaigh tried to help, didn't she? I know it was a bit weird back there, but there must be someone else—"

Constantine strode over to me, his eyes wild, and grasped me by the shoulders hard, his voice harsh and strained.

"Orlaigh, who is now *dead*, do you mean? A bit *weird* . . . ? You're right, Liv! They're all dead! You have been right all along and I finally believe you and *now* you decide things have gotten a *little weird*?"

I swallowed back a mouthful of hot bitter vile. Funny how being proved right and Constantine believing me was now the absolute last thing I wanted.

"We need to leave. Everything you said, Liv—you weren't insane—you were right! I can barely believe I'm saying this, but . . . fuck—*fuck*!"

He looked at me for another second, then impatiently headed back over to the lifeboat station.

I sank to my knees with a groan.

Then the singing started.

The sound drifting on the evening breeze, low and hypnotic, making us both pause. Forcing us to stop and listen. The words promised oblivion beneath the waves; a warm, sinking feeling; a sweet hopelessness. Nepenthe: that which drives out sorrow. We couldn't survive out there anyway, on the vast expanse of the Atlantic Ocean. There was no hope anymore. Better to succumb than to fight. And we were both so tired of fighting.

I turned in the direction of the melody.

"No—" Con had his hands jammed over his ears. "Don't listen—you *can't* listen. I think I've figured it out—we'll need to get in first—and deploy it from the inside—I think. The sea's pretty rough tonight. . . . Are—are you ready?"

Tears spilled down my cheeks, whipped away by the merciless wind. Below, the black sea roiled, its waves heaving.

"I can't—I can't leave. . . . I'm . . . I'm afraid."

Constantine turned back, a look of annoyed fury plainly visible on his face. "And here I was thinking it's a vacation. We *can't* stay here, Liv. At least this way . . . we have a chance."

He held out a hand.

"Come on—*please*, Liv. Please."

I stared at Constantine. Could I trust him? Or was this part of some horrible revenge, a final trap, leaving me alone with the son of the apparent architect of all this?

The drapes had been pulled across the windows of the viewing gallery that looked onto this deck. The lights bright yellow behind them. There were shapes silhouetted against them now; dark and strange and amorphous.

What choice did I have left?

I took his hand.

35

WE SIT SHIVERING IN THE LIFEBOAT.

Constantine has passed me his jacket. It's a small kindness, but in this gray purgatory, it feels monumental. Despite the chivalry of the gesture, it barely offers any warmth. He hasn't said much this past hour, only stares out at the buffeting waves, his knuckles white upon the rail. Every now and then, a tear drips from his nose.

I think he'd be embarrassed if I drew attention to it, so I pretend not to notice.

I can see lights in the far distance—a ship, I think—or maybe even New York. The waves move so much, the lights flit in and out of view. In some moments, they seem maddeningly near. In others, they're still a galaxy away.

"They're meant to die, you know—if their prey slips past them—if they fail."

His voice is soft and cracked. It's the first time he's spoken in an age. I stare at him, my voice distorted through the chattering of my teeth.

"Wh-what?"

"The Sirens. Do you think that's what they really were? I still can't believe it—what we saw—I can't—"

He shudders violently and then goes quiet.

Truly, I don't know. I can't speak of them. Or any of it. Not yet. Not until we're clear.

And anyway, why ask me? Wouldn't he know best? He was there, at the start, at the temple. His own father certainly knows it all. *The sea provides,* oh yes, it does, but the cost is terrific.

Am I even safe now? I look at Con for reassurance, but all I see is someone broken, someone trying to piece together the long-held parts of a jigsaw puzzle and horrified at the final picture.

I turn back to look at the ship behind me, its bright glow illuminating the night sky. I can't tell if it's simply the ship's lighting or the coming dawn or if the fire has spread. And if it isn't the latter, will this all happen again? To others? Will they come after us? Will we *ever* be clear of it?

On top of that, I don't know much about the mechanics of it all, but I have this rumbling, unpleasant feeling in my gut that if the ship does sink, if we do succeed in that way, then our penance will be being dragged down with it.

A fitting ending.

I think of all that is beneath us. The indifferent dark depths full of life alien to us. Those terrible, tentacled things in the hull. I think of the many miles we are away from shore. I relive my dream of drowning again and again, can barely think of anything other than that desperate, gasping, burning urge to breathe.

I think of the six of them: Will, Apollo, Raj, Orlaigh, Laila, Adora.

And the intended seventh? Me? Or Con?

Leaving the lifeboat would be an instant death sentence. There is no land in sight and I'm no swimmer. There's no real way to even tell what direction we are heading in.

Con fiddles with the equipment at the front of the lifeboat, but it is immensely complicated. I take one look and feel my hopes sink heavily to the bottom of the ocean.

So I sit, clutching the flare gun tightly to my chest. There's just one cartridge left, representing our last and only hope.

And all that's left to do is wait for the ocean to decide our fate.

It's impossible to guess at it.

The ocean is dark and deep and keeps its secrets.

ACKNOWLEDGMENTS

First of all, endless thanks to my exceptionally excellent agent, Claire Friedman, for championing *Those We Drown*. Without your keen editorial vision and expert guidance, I'm pretty sure this book would not exist. I am forever grateful to have you in my corner.

A million thanks to my ridiculously talented editor, Lydia Gregovic, who saw something in this book from the very start and whose enthusiasm and insightful suggestions made *Those We Drown* the book it is today. On top of that, a big thank-you to everyone at Delacorte Press who helped bring this book to life: Angela Carlino, Cathy Bobak, Colleen Fellingham, and Tamar Schwartz, as well as Beverly Horowitz and Barbara Marcus.

A heartfelt thanks to early reader Skyla Arndt for her kind words back when I was still an incredibly nervous writer, anxious about sharing my stories with others—it make me weirdly happy this book is now one of your comfort reads! Huge thanks to the effervescent Kat Delacorte, who has taught me so much about the publishing industry. Thanks also to Lyndall Clipstone for her support and generosity toward a debut author, as well as for being the first to offer a blurb!

More thanks go to talented writers, Ann Fraistat, Erica

Waters, Kara Thomas, Tara Goedjen, Amanda Linsmeier, and Lyndall Clipstone for taking time out of their busy schedules to read a debut novel and for sharing their wonderful blurbs. I am so grateful for your kind words.

Thanks also to Allison Saft and Ava Reid for reading one of my earlier manuscripts during Pitchwars. Reading your generous feedback was the first time I thought I might have a genuine shot at this.

Thank you to the fabulous Emma Spalding and the lovely Lydia Youngman for the cheesy chips and wine nights. You both are truly the best and I'm grateful for all your support. I never would have made it through that year without you both!

6(and 5)GS at Heron Park, thank you for your enthusiasm when I told you all I was publishing a book—I hope at least some of you read it and see this!

Thank you of course to my parents for all those Saturday-morning library trips and for teaching me the importance of reading. Dad in particular, thanks for letting me pore over your ghost story anthologies and and Stephen King novels at far too young an age.

And of course, I am forever thankful to Neil for your endless love, patience, and support—there is no way I would have the freedom to focus on writing without you! Plus I'm forever thankful to the absolute lights of my life, my gorgeous Ciara and Rory.

Finally, thanks to you, lovely reader, for taking a chance on a debut author!

ABOUT THE AUTHOR

AMY GOLDSMITH grew up on the south coast of England, obsessed with obscure '70s horror movies and old ghost stories. She studied psychology at the University of Sussex and, after gaining her postgraduate certificate in education, moved to inner London to teach. Now she lives back on the south coast, where she still teaches English and spends her weekends trawling antiques shops for haunted mirrors.